Under Different Moons

Kelly Pierce

ISBN: 9798366223478

To my family who has supported me
and my friends who think I'm awesome
and can't argue with that because this is my book.

Many thanks to Niki for walking me through
all the techno mumbo jumbo.

1

Frank wished he wasn't still on duty, because he really needed a stiff drink after the night he just had.

It was a normal enough night when Frank pulled his squad car up to the entrance of Dalton Park for the last two hours of his shift. Like every night, he turned his car off, poured himself a cup of coffee from his thermos, and settled in for a long night. It was a prime spot for picking up dealers and other low-lives that liked to prowl the park after dark.

He'd been sitting there almost an hour and a half, thinking that a short nap wouldn't hurt anything when he caught movement in front of the car. Someone wearing an old-fashioned cape with the hood up walked past the bushes concealing his car. He wondered if there was some kind of nerd convention with Lord of the Rings fans nearby and someone either got lost on the way or thought the park would be a good place to take cosplay pictures. They certainly went all out for their costume. It even looked like there were fake jewels set in the brooch holding the sides of the cape together.

The person carried two bundles, one in each arm. Suddenly one arm was empty, and one of the bundles rested on the park bench sitting almost a foot away. He never even saw the perp move. He shifted to get a better look, causing the seat to creak.

That small sound made the person's head snap around, causing the hood to fall and reveal the person's face. Frank's mouth had to have been hanging open for at least a minute at the sight. She could have been a supermodel—she was that beautiful. Her hair was white-blonde and seemed to glow where the moonlight hit it. It was pulled back from her face by a silver tiara with some kind of gems set in the swirling filigree. Her eyes were a dazzling blue he could see even in the darkness that glistened with unshed tears. Unlike most models he'd seen in magazines though, she didn't have a hint of a tan on her alabaster skin. With a swirl of her cape, she was gone.

Frank snapped out of the daze her beauty caused, craning his neck, unable to figure out where she had gone. Abandoning caution, he leaped out of his squad car and went over to the park bench and its mysterious bundle. Frank stopped short and almost pulled his gun when he saw it move. He supposed seeing women disappear into thin air was sure to make anyone jumpy. He moved forward, more cautious now that he knew the bundle was alive. For all he knew, the woman had decided to get rid of her rabid dog by leaving it in the park. But a sinking feeling in his gut told him that wasn't the case.

Frank reached the bundle and carefully moved the blanket around to reveal the pale pink face of a baby. He cursed that his suspicion proved correct. That pretty woman abandoned her child in a park known to be dangerous to anything daring to enter it after sundown.

This wasn't the first abandoned baby he'd ever found, but it was the first one that caused him disbelief. He couldn't believe that someone so obviously well off would just leave her baby in such a dangerous place. There was also the problem of that other bundle. They were identical, he was sure of that. What if the sweet-looking kid on the bench had a twin somewhere being abandoned in the same heartless manner? He had to take care of this one first though.

He picked the baby up and headed back to his car, jostling the blanket in the process, exposing an amulet nestled against the baby's chest. It looked like an opal surrounded by eight other precious stones, all set in gold. More gold wire crossed the opal in an intricate pattern. Frank's brow furrowed in confusion at the sight. Did the woman intend to leave the jewelry as a way to pay for the baby's care? Frank knew too much about the system to believe that would happen and wondered at the woman's naivete.

He placed the sleeping infant in the passenger seat and shut the door as quietly as he could. He and his wife never wanted children and he never liked hearing his nieces and nephews crying. The last thing his night needed was the ear-piercing wails of a startled baby. The door shut louder than he intended but when his nervous glance darted to the baby, the kid never stirred.

"Huh, never seen a kid sleep so sound before." Frank's breath caught as he bent over the baby and gently put a hand on the child's chest. "Thank God," he sighed when he felt the baby's chest move with its soft breathing.

Feeling a little foolish, he focused on the feeling of the amulet poking against his palm. Revealing it again, Frank wondered how quickly the thing would disappear if it was tagged as evidence. He trusted most of his brethren, but even if it didn't go missing it might not make its way back into the baby's possession when they got older.

Decision made, Frank pulled the amulet away from the baby's chest. When he discovered the thick gold chain was draped around the baby's neck he frowned at the possible choking hazard and carefully lifted the child's head to remove the necklace. He almost dropped the poor kid's head when their shockingly green eyes popped open.

"Don't cry," Frank commanded with an edge of desperation in his voice.

The baby only blinked at him as if to ask what was going on.

"Your guess is as good as mine, kid. Let's get this thing off you and I'll call for backup with some formula and diapers. If I'm lucky, they'll take you to the orphanage and I can spend the last..." Frank checked the time and grimaced, "twenty minutes of my shift filling out paperwork about you and your mom."

Frank glared at the dash clock as he put the amulet in his pants pocket. "I'm definitely getting home late tonight thanks to her."

He coughed with discomfort when the baby's eerie eyes latched onto his with something like censure in their jeweled depths. As far as he remembered, his nieces and nephews never focused on people until they were four or five months old. This kid barely looked a month old and was meeting his eyes better than most adults. It made him shiver, which made him realize he never turned the car back on, allowing the February chill to seep in.

With a nervous laugh, he turned the engine over and tried to convince himself it was the weather that brought on that shiver instead of unease. He called for back-up then, not only for the formula and diapers he mentioned but also because he knew he couldn't hold the baby and drive to the orphanage at the same time.

It took more than the twenty minutes left of his shift for help to arrive. Officer Robinson made a fairly valid excuse about getting the supplies Frank asked for as well as stopping at the station for a car seat. Frank could tell Officer Garcia just didn't want to be there because she knew Frank was going to take off as soon as they arrived and Robinson was going to stick her with the kid. He felt bad it was true, but the baby's uncanny silence and judgemental green eyes overrode his sense of guilt.

"Jesus, Frank," Garcia grumbled when she pulled the squirming bundle out of the car, "the thing soaked through its blanket. Didn't you notice the smell?"

"What was I supposed to do about it? You brought the diapers, remember?"

Garcia glared over her shoulder as she opened the back seat of Frank's cruiser and laid the baby down. She would be damned if she was going to stink up her cruiser with whatever was in the kid's diaper. Quickly removing the blanket she stopped short when she realized the baby didn't even have a diaper to soak. Whoever abandoned the child hadn't even bothered with a cloth version and instead swaddled the kid in linens that reminded Garcia of a nativity play her parents made her participate in when she was a girl.

Garcia made quick work of the old linens and barked orders at Robinson for the diaper and set of clean clothes from the station Frank forgot to ask for. Normally Robison would drag his feet in the face of her commands, but not only did she outrank him now but he also knew if he pissed her off one step too far he would be put in charge of the baby.

"Well, we've got her now," Garcia sighed as she set the baby against her shoulder. She started to hand Robinson the sodden mess of blankets and linen when a thick piece of paper dropped from the folds. Robinson ignored the bundle in Garcia's hand and went for the paper. Garcia rolled her eyes and threw the bundle in the floorboards of Frank's back seat. If he complained she would say it was because he'd get to the precinct first.

"What's it say?" Frank asked.

Robinson broke open a weird wax seal and read the only bit of writing at the top of the paper, "Kaia."

Frank nodded and peered at the infant against Garcia's shoulder. Kaia's eyes met his and Frank felt another shiver run down his spine. He could have blamed it on the weather again but the last half hour with her barely making a peep as they waited for backup told him it was all her. He jumped when Robinson slapped him on the back.

"Get out of here," the younger man smiled, "I'm sure you're ready to head back. Garcia and I will take Kaia to St. Mary's. You get to the nice, warm station and fill out what happened up to now. I'll finish it off when I get back."

Frank nodded and tried not to run back to his cruiser, still feeling those green eyes following him as he drove away. Ten minutes later, he was sitting at his desk filling out his report, not knowing how to make Jane Doe's disappearing act sound anything other than delusional, still wishing for that stiff drink.

Sister Mary Catherine opened the door to the two officers standing on the stoop.

"Hello, Sister," the male officer greeted her. The female officer just nodded before holding out the baby in a gesture that screamed 'here, you take it!' The sister could tell that the officer only got the 'job' of caring for the baby because she was a woman.

Sister Mary took the baby gently in her arms and looked down. "Does she have a name?" she inquired softly. The two officers looked at her in surprise.

"How do you know she's a girl?" the female officer sputtered. Sister Mary chuckled lightly.

"After working at this orphanage for more years than I care to confess, you begin to pick up on such details."

"Ah, according to the letter we found with her, her name is Kaia. She was found in Dalton Park. The officer who found her said her mother just put her on the bench and vanished. It's a damn shame." The female officer colored slightly at the sister's raised eyebrow and mumbled, "Sorry, Sister."

The man held out an odd-looking letter with a broken wax seal.

She figured the officers must have read the letter to get a sense of the situation. Sister Mary shifted the baby to one arm and reached for it.

"That was found tucked in her blankets."

"Thank you, officers. God bless you both."

Both officers tipped their hats at the nun and left. Sister Mary closed the door gently and took Kaia to the nursery. After making sure Kaia was snug in her new home, Sister Mary went to her office to begin filing the paperwork for their newest resident. She sat down behind her desk and pulled a fresh file from one drawer and a brown paper bag from another.

The necklace was placed in the bag, and the note was placed in the folder after Sister Mary had finished reading it. She pulled a form from another drawer and began Kaia's paperwork. The first name was easy, KAIA. The surname was quite a bit more difficult. Like most orphans, Kaia didn't come with one already picked out for her. Sister Mary thought for a moment before writing, DALTON on the next line. She hoped this would be only a temporary name and that her newest charge would be adopted soon. The same hope she held for all of her little lambs.

She filled out the rest of the information and put the paper in Kaia's nice, new file. She then wrote DALTON, KAIA on the top of the file before placing it in the filing cabinet behind her chair. She next wrote Kaia's name on the paper bag and placed that in the wall safe behind the painting of the Last Supper.

Sister Mary turned off the lights in her office and started for her cell. She stopped by the nursery one last time to check on Kaia. The baby was sleeping the sleep of the innocent, unaware of the excitement she had caused.

"Yours will be a very interesting life, my child," the nun whispered, smoothing Kaia's thick, white-blonde curls from her forehead, "God and His angels will most certainly have an exciting time watching out for you."

The port master of Tern walked slowly along the wharf, surveying his domain. The king might rule all of Jamaria, but on this wharf in the capitol, the port master was the law. He decided which ships were allowed to dock, and which were sent to the next port.

Yes, he, Jebadiah Grendel, was master of all he surveyed.

As he looked down the alley between two abandoned warehouses, he caught movement out of the corner of his eye. He slid deeper into the shadows thrown from the full moon as a cloaked figure approached, looking furtively over its shoulder. The person carried a bundle, cradling it tenderly as if it were going to break if jostled the tiniest bit.

A strong gust of wind blew through the wharf, tossing the cloak's hood back, exposing the mysterious person's face to the moonlight. It was a woman so beautiful she could have been fey, except her hearing was decidedly human. Otherwise, she would have heard his slight gasp of surprise. Though he supposed the sound from the nearby pub would have masked the sound quite well. Her white-blonde hair looked almost silver in the moonlight. A tear rolled down one pale cheek as she placed the bundle in her arms into an empty barrel at the mouth of the alley in which Jeb hid.

She reached beneath her robe, about to place a package with the bundle, when a sharp crack echoed down the wharf from somewhere out of the port master's view. She waved her other hand over the package, making it disappear. The woman straightened quickly and took a few steps away from the barrel, as if afraid to be caught near it. Her bearing turned regal, where before her shoulders had been slumped in sadness. Another cloaked figure bore down on her, sweeping the hood back to reveal a man with dark black hair, piercing green eyes, and skin so pale it made him look like a vampire. He grabbed her arm ruthlessly with one hand while stroking her cheek gently with the other.

"Ah, my love," he murmured, "Why did you run from me? Did you think I would not look for you?" The woman shuddered and tried to pull away from his intractable grip.

"I am not going back with you, Marius, and I am not telling you where I have hidden them." Her bright blue eyes sparkled with defiance and then pain when Marius's grip on her arm tightened.

"You are wrong on both counts," he growled, "My power is much greater than yours, and I'll eventually break you and the barriers blocking your mind."

"Never."

Marius' eyes lit with a feral light, and his grip tightened a little more, causing her to cry out slightly in pain. "Where are they!" he roared. The woman just laughed in his face, refusing to answer. Marius' face became mottled with rage, while the grip on her arm turned fierce enough to break the bone. Jeb felt the air crackle with unnatural heat.

The woman's eyes widened in pain as an inhuman wail escaped her mouth. Her arm blistered and smoked beneath Marius' grip. Marius jumped back just as she was engulfed by aberrant flames.

But, she didn't burn.

Jeb watched in horrified amazement as she exploded into steam and mist. A woman made of water had evaporated before his very eyes. He'd seen plenty of water nymphs in his time as port master, but he'd never seen one killed before.

Marius cursed and spat on the ground where she had been standing. "Look what you made me do," he muttered darkly, "Now it will be most difficult to find them." He turned and made his way toward the alley to begin searching for whatever the woman had been trying to hide.

Jeb held his breath in abject terror at the thought that such a powerful sorcerer would find him. A witness to such a terrible deed could only have one fate, and he knew it wouldn't be an easy death. As Marius neared the mouth of the alleyway, a huge crash sounded nearby, closely followed by sounds of drunken revelry. A group was making its way out of the pub, causing an awful racket that was sure to bring any authorities nearby. Marius' lip curled in disgust and anger. He turned and disappeared with the same sharp crack that had heralded his arrival.

The port master breathed a sigh of relief and rattled off a quick thank you to whatever god had seen fit to send him salvation in the form of drunken sailors, who were now walking past the alley, singing a dirty song and laughing uproariously at their own antics. He approached the barrel where the nymph had hidden her bundle. He knew that whatever it was, it had to be very important for a nymph to give her life for it.

Nymphs were known to be extremely frivolous and almost empty-headed creatures by most men. Jeb, however, knew better. His mother had been a maid in an important household and had taught him all about the magical creatures of their world. Nymphs were extremely intelligent but liked having fun more than anything else.

They were fiercely protective of whatever element they were born to and worked in harmony with nature and magic.

Jeb bent his tired back to the task of retrieving the bundle, and almost dropped it when it started squirming. His hands trembled as he shifted the bundle to cradle it in one arm, while the other moved to lift a loose flap of the soft, brown wool. He was in true danger of dropping the bundle when the pink, round face of a sleeping baby was revealed.

Jeb suddenly felt awkward holding such a precious bundle. He and his late wife had never been blessed with children. This was a new and slightly uncomfortable sensation for him. He gently tucked the blanket over the baby's face to protect it from the wind and made his way to the middle of the city. Jeb felt an urgent need to get to the castle as quickly as his old legs could carry him. He needed to talk to his old friend Herrod, the Master of the Guard. Jeb was forced to wait at the gate for what seemed like hours--but was in fact only ten minutes--until the sentry could rouse Herrod.

"What's the problem, Jeb," Herrod grumbled, holding his pants at his waist with one hand, scratching sleepily at his bare chest with the other, "It's the middle of the damn night." Jeb shifted uneasily, looking at the sentries with unease.

"I haven't seen you this nervous since you tried to stare down that unicorn trying to eat the same cabbage you wanted. Come on into my room."

Herrod waved him in and started walking knowing Jeb would follow. As soon as they were alone, Jeb whispered loudly, "You've got to get me in to see the king and queen right away."

Herrod looked at his friend appraisingly. He'd never known Jeb to make rash decisions, and he'd never known him to be a liar. However, the fact remained that he couldn't just let his old friend see the monarchs without good reason.

"What's going on?"

Jeb revealed the baby in his arms and described the events quickly. Herrod shook his head in disbelief.

"If I didn't know you so well, I'd accuse you of being drunk," he whispered trying not to wake the sleeping baby.

Herrod had dressed during Jeb's unbelievable story, so the two men headed toward the king and queen's bedchamber in extreme haste. Though it was after midnight, Herrod knew the king and queen would be awake. There had been a council meeting earlier, and it had just recently ended. Herrod nodded at the two sentries at the door. One of the men leaned slightly to knock on the door and then moved back to his rigid position.

The queen's maid opened the door, saw the master-at-arms, and closed the door again. The maid turned from the door and walked to the queen's bed. The queen gave her a questioning look.

"Herrod, Master of the Guard, and another man to see you, Your Majesty," she announced with a curtsy.

From behind the queen, the king ordered, "Let them in."

The maid ushered the two men in and then left the room discretely.

"What can we do for you, Herrod?" King Jonathan asked. The two men bowed to their monarchs, standing side-by-side next to the man-sized hearth. Queen Delia sat in a nearby chair and waited for the men's explanation for their unexpected arrival.

Jeb bowed again, holding his bundle carefully, and recited his story once again. Queen Delia's eyes flicked briefly to the bundle in his arms when he mentioned finding the baby but otherwise remained expressionless. When the port master finished his story, the king and queen exchanged an indecipherable look.

The queen stood and held out her arms in a silent command for the child. Jeb's hands trembled as he handed the infant over, still unsure of how to handle such a fragile being. The queen moved back to her chair and rocked the child gently.

The baby opened its eyes for the first time that night, revealing piercing blue eyes that took in all of its surroundings. When it caught Delia looking down, the baby smiled and gurgled merrily, causing Delia to smile in return.

"Thank you, gentlemen, for bringing this situation to our attention. I would like to speak with you in a moment. The guards outside will take you to the appropriate room." The king gestured toward the door, and the two men left, relieved that someone else was taking care of the situation now. The queen waited until the men left before discussing what to do with her husband.

"Jonathan, we can't just leave him out on the streets now that he's found his way here," Delia insisted before Jonathan had a chance to say anything.

"I was never going to let that happen, Delia, but we have three sons already."

"Had I borne this child myself, we would have gladly accepted him," she argued.

Suddenly, the baby started to fuss, and Delia felt a growing wetness against her chest. A wry smile crossed her face, and she left her chair once again and crossed to their bed to change the infant's wet cloth.

"He certainly acts like one of ours," she quipped.

Jonathan chuckled as Delia unwrapped the blanket covering the baby. She made two startling discoveries in the process. The first was a leather-bound book that rested beneath the child and was now slightly damp as a result of its location. The second was the fact that the baby she had assumed was a bouncing baby boy was in fact a girl.

Jonathan smiled as he sighed in resignation. After nine years of marriage, he knew when he was beaten. Especially as he spent five of those nine years hearing his wife's wish for a daughter. While he knew Delia would never go against him if he had decided to send the child to be cared for by someone else, he also knew that his wife wanted a little girl and he would never hear the end of it if he didn't go along with her unspoken wishes.

Jonathan paused a long moment before asking, "What should we name her?" He had been looking at the baby when he asked his question, and therefore hadn't noticed his wife's sudden pallor.

"Her name is Marina," she whispered, holding the open book out to her husband, "and I think it's best for the world we keep her."

2

17 years later...

The staff came at Marina's head faster than she could react.

WHAP!

She would be seeing stars for hours, if not days, from that one. Not to mention a very large lump under her thick black hair. Curtis laughed as he offered her a hand up from the ground he himself had knocked her on just moments before. "I told you to be quicker, brat."

Marina growled at her brother as she dusted the dirt from her backside. "You just have an unfair advantage. All that dancing in Dura has made you quicker."

"Sure, brat, whatever you say." Curtis brushed her accusation aside, and Marina pretended to pout for a moment. Curtis studied dancing in Dura and tended to become taciturn when anyone brought it up. Marina assumed it was because the only time his siblings brought it up was to trash him.

A light breeze from the Yolanza Sea tossed Curtis' golden curls, forcing him to bat them away from his laughing blue eyes. Marina's own blue eyes looked at his golden mane with only slightly feigned disgust.

"'Tis a pity the gods gave such beautiful features to a man," she commented, ruffling his curls back into disarray. Curtis scowled at the old jest.

"'Tis a pity the gods gave such a masculine form to a girl," he tossed back, commenting on Marina's distinct musculature from all their sparring and lack of curves. Marina growled again, which was Curtis' only warning before she launched herself at him.

For a few moments, they were lost in a cloud of dirt and flailing limbs that soon left them dirtier, more bruised, and gasping for breath. They lay on the ground a few minutes after they were finished wrestling just to look at the canopy of leaves above them and try to breathe normally again.

They had gone just outside the castle grounds in the Rejos Forest to keep away from prying eyes. The Princess of Jamaria was not supposed to be wearing pants. And a Prince of Jamaria certainly was not supposed to be teaching his sister how to spar.

The gods only knew what would happen if people found out she was engaged in something as unfeminine as sparring with her brother. A princess was supposed to be a pale, delicate flower who would not be allowed anywhere near something so dangerous. She was meant to be seen and admired from afar and only heard through the dulcet tones of song when she was permitted to lift her voice at all.

Marina was pale--and even glad to sing on occasion--but she was no delicate flower. She had a mind, and she was damned tired of hiding it to placate society. Of course, even her mind betrayed her at times. The last time she allowed herself free reign, Duke Avery's son thought it would be a good time to press his suit.

She remembered she was riding her horse, Oasis, when Reginald Avery pulled his stallion up alongside her mare. Marina was never able to tolerate him before, and his posturing had not endeared him to her any further.

He waxed enthusiastic about his many land holdings he would inherit and how many unicorns grazed on his land. As if he owned the majestic creatures! Everyone knew they had the right to travel wherever and whenever they pleased.

When she challenged him to a race with a kiss as the prize if he won, he lost.

It was only natural.

Oasis was one-quarter unicorn herself and only allowed Marina to ride her out of a sense of loyalty because Marina saved her from a couple of ogres when she was just a foal.

Reginald became red-faced in outrage, claiming he was tricked most vilely. Queen Delia, of course, punished Marina by taking away her riding privileges for a month.

Marina shook herself from her reverie and turned on her side toward Curtis. She punched him soundly in the arm to signal that it was time to head back to the castle. He rubbed his arm ruefully before lifting himself with a harsh groan. It was meant to garner sympathy, but Marina only laughed and picked herself off the ground for the second time that day.

As was their custom, they raced back to the castle. The foliage around them kept them hidden from everyone else. Whoever lost would have to come up with the excuse for the night if anyone, especially Queen Delia, asked. Curtis reached the wall first, inspiring some rather creative curses from Marina. Curtis just tsked silently as he opened the trap door hidden in the wall.

They discovered the door and its adjoining tunnels and passages almost twelve years ago. Back then, they kept it all a secret because they feared punishment from their parents. It did not take them long to realize that there was a better reason to keep their secret. The tunnel allowed them both to escape the constraints of castle life and find a small scrap of sanity and freedom from time to time.

The tunnels led to many places, such as all of the bedrooms, the throne room, and the Council Chamber, where the Lords and Ladies of Jamaria met with their monarchs to debate, create laws, bring grievances, and converse about the welfare of Jamaria.

They memorized most of the tunnel system years ago and could find their way around in complete darkness, which came in handy quite often.

Curtis and Marina parted at one of the many forks. Marina reached the door to her room and looked through the peephole. She saw the fire on the hearth, despite the heat of the spring day. She moved slightly to take in more of the room and saw her maid, Hilde setting out the evening's clothes. Marina shifted again to look at the hearth and saw a tub. She almost groaned in pleasure at the thought of the waiting bath. She silently encouraged Hilde to leave quickly.

"Where is that girl?" she heard Hilde murmur. "I sent someone to get her almost an hour ago. Now I'll have to get another bucket of hot water and find her myself." Hilde left the room, muttering to herself the whole time.

As soon as the door closed, Marina slid the panel open and stepped into her room. After making sure it was closed securely, she ran toward her bath, stripping as she went. She slid into the water with a sign of mingled relief and pleasure. She allowed her head to go completely under to try to remove at least some of the dirt from her hair. She sifted her fingers through her hair, scratching her scalp in the same movement.

Staying under, she tried to hold her breath as long as she possibly could. She could not be completely sure, but she thought that she could do so for almost ten minutes. She had to be careful practicing this particular habit. Not because she ever ran out of breath so far, but because she never knew when Hilde would walk in.

For a rotund gnome, Hilde was extremely light on her feet. Only once in the month since she discovered she could do this had Hilde walked in on Marina in the bath and almost drowned her in the attempt to 'save' her. That was one time too many, however, so Marina tried not to tempt fate.

Marina sat back up, rubbing her face to clean it and wipe away some of the water. She sighed, remembering that her parents had planned another boring ball where she could meet potential husbands among the landed and other privileged. That meant another night of fake smiles and pretending to enjoy insipid conversations and having her toes stepped on.

She grimaced in distaste at these thoughts. She would never get out of it. Her mother would hound her the rest of the night--if not her life--if she tried to avoid it altogether. Her only hope was to stay in plain sight for the first hour and hope to be able to slip away unnoticed as soon as possible. It usually worked. Her mother had not seemed to catch on so far.

At that moment, Hilde came back to her room with a steaming bucket of water to heat the tepid water in her bath. She backed into the door to open it, so she did not see Marina until she shut the door.

"Milady," she gasped in surprise and not a little disapproval, "where have you been?"

"Nowhere important," Marina replied with an innocent smile.

Hilde just cocked a disbelieving eyebrow and dumped the hot water over Marina's head. This left her sputtering in surprise.

"What was that for?"

"I'm sure you know better than I do," Hilde answered wryly.

Marina just grinned and reached her hand out for the bar of lavender soap next to Hilde. After she washed, she stood up and retrieved the towel Hilde handed her.

Marina rubbed the water from her skin and hair until both shone. She stepped over to her bed where her clothes waited.

Hilde chose the dark blue overdress and embroidered sky blue underskirt. The overdress split at the waist, allowing ample view of the underskirt. Even though Marina loved the outfit, she sighed in defeat and began to dress for the evening with Hilde's help.

She looked at the mirror when they were done and assessed her looks. Her brother was correct when he said her form was more suited for a boy than a woman grown. She was willowy where she wished to be curvy, flat where she wished to be round. Her hair, now piled on top of her head in a fashionable coif, was waist length and black as midnight. Hilde despaired of ever seeing it straight and always needed hours to tame the wild curls into some semblance of order. Her eyes were a dark, midnight blue that were complemented nicely by her dress, which fit her lanky frame snugly.

She smiled wryly at her reflection and wondered how she became so dark-headed when the rest of her family was so light. Her parents and three siblings were all blonde and slightly tanned. The only aspect of herself that was pale was her skin. The sun could not turn her brown no matter how much time she spent beneath it. She shrugged her narrow shoulders at her reflection and finished getting ready for whatever her mother had planned for the night.

Marina lifted her head proudly and descended the stairs. The ball tonight had no real significance. It was a chance for the people there to see and be seen. She was not even halfway down the stairs, and she was already tired of both. The idea that in three months there would be another ball for her eighteenth birthday made her grit her teeth in annoyance. She really did not want the bother of a ball and would have preferred a little adventure in her life.

When she made it to the bottom of the steps she was mobbed by men. They varied in age, size, and appearance, but not personality. The limited number of men Marina thought of as intelligent were either already spoken for or deemed unsuitable by her mother, either because of their bloodlines or their reputations. Sometimes, it was a combination of the two traits.

The man on Marina's left, Reginald Avery, the Earl of Wently, was tall, thin, and exceedingly handsome with dark blonde hair and arresting features. He was also exceedingly greedy and annoying. Unfortunately, he was also thought of as a good match by her parents and many of the other courtiers.

Wently had been pursuing her for almost three years for the land he could get in their marriage. He was seven years older, and not nearly as clever as he believed himself to be. She saw through his machinations like crystal on a sunny day.

On her seventh birthday, he treated her most cruelly and tortured her throughout the day. He had not changed much from that sickly-looking bully. Even Marina heard rumors of how horribly he treated his staff despite her sheltered upbringing.

With Wently trying to occupy all of her attention, the crowd surrounding her quickly dispersed. She thanked the gods that she had been able to keep more than half of her dance card empty. The Earl's steely gaze had frightened many of the men off. When the last suitor finally drifted away, Wently seized Marina's arm.

"Your highness, I hope you have saved a dance or two for me."

Marina removed her arm from his grasp and perused her card thoughtfully. She made sure he could not see the numerous empty spaces before moving her pencil to the card.

"I believe I have one or two free, but I must be sure to leave myself time to catch my breath. I do not think I can spare but the first reel, sir. Excuse me, but I think I see my first partner"

Marina wrote his name in for the dance she suggested and smiled innocently at the Earl's frozen expression. She turned to the man walking up to her and dismissed Wently from her thoughts. Gerard was the Alpha of the northern werewolf pack in Jamaria, so Wently did not protest at all when she took Gerard's arm. Though Gerard was the ambassador for the Rejos Pack, he was also one of those thought unsuitable by her mother even though he was both kind and brilliant. She always enjoyed dancing with Gerard. Tonight was especially gratifying because the dance after his was the reel.

Gerard moved into position for their waltz and Marina could not help but compare him to Wently. Where Wently was blonde, with chiseled good looks, pale skin, and cruel eyes, Gerard was darker but far kinder. His skin reminded her of rich mahogany and his hazel eyes were kind until they turned amber as his wolf rose to the surface.

Marina was struck by sudden curiosity.

"Gerard, were you born in Krax'mra? Or perhaps in Brookland?"

Gerard chuckled. He was used to this question from many mortals. They assumed he was younger than the Great Shift. It was difficult for someone to see him and consider he was nearer to 1500 years old than the 25 he appeared.

"Neither, your highness."

"But, then where were you born?"

"I am a son of Aksum. The kingdom where I was born is probably long lost to the sands by this point. I haven't seen it for centuries, and I will never see it again."

Marina was at a loss. She could not remember ever seeing Gerard look so sad while a smile touched his lips. Perhaps it was better to dance in silence for now.

It was too bad her mother thought werewolves were not considered good matches. Marina felt more friendship towards Gerard than romantic feelings, but he would make someone a good husband someday. Though perhaps, her mother was correct and Gerard would be happier with someone who could share his eternal lifespan rather than mating with a human like her who would leave him after only 60 or 70 years.

When Gerard was forced to relinquish her hand, he growled slightly at the Earl. She was sure Wently almost wet himself on the spot. Marina surreptitiously shared an amused grin with Gerard before moving into position with the Earl.

She was extremely grateful when the reel ended sooner than even she expected. For the next dance, she was without a partner, and ready for the reprieve. Wently tried to steer her toward a secluded alcove on their way off of the dance floor.

"You look tired, your highness. I have seen a lovely corner where you could rest your feet."

Marina didn't want to make a scene, but she didn't want to be alone with Wently anymore. "I do not think that is proper, my lord. I should get back to my family."

"Nonsense. Your mother would scold me if I let your delicate feet blister or pain you in any way."

"I promise I am well," Marina said through teeth ground together in a semblance of a smile. Marina was trying to pull her arm away from where it rested on Wently's, but his other hand was holding onto hers tightly. She was getting very close to forgetting all decorum and knocking the man out flat for his tenacity.

"But, Princess–"

Suddenly, Curtis appeared almost like magic at her side.

"Excuse me, sir. I must steal my sister from you. I promised to introduce her to an old friend of mine."

Curtis wedged himself between the two to take Marina's arm. Wently was forced to let her go, or risk making a scene himself. He bowed stiffly and watched them walk away with malice sparkling in his gray eyes.

"Thank you, Curt," Marina muttered when they were well away, "It looks as though I'll have to go easy on you during our next fight."

Curtis smiled briefly at her jest before turning serious.

"You be careful around that one, Rina. He's likely to cause you more trouble than you know how to handle on your own."

"Thank you again, Curt," Marina patted him on the arm to show her understanding, "I will be sure to keep an eye out for myself when he is around."

Curtis nodded and they continued walking around the ballroom, chatting with friends along the way.

3

The ballroom was large, even by Jamarian standards. And Jamarians were well known throughout the Kingdoms to throw the most elaborate parties, second only to the Durans.

The crystal chandelier hung suspended in a ceiling tall enough to accommodate even the tallest visiting giant. Ten-foot-tall windows lined the western side of the room. They were each around four feet wide and separated by ornate columns. Some of the windows were also cleverly disguised doors that led to balconies and the garden.

After dancing for almost an hour, Marina made the escape she wished for through one of the hidden doors. She breathed in the salty sea air greedily and walked across the balcony to the nearby stairs. She descended them slowly and made her way to the garden below. It was a maze of plant life and statuary. Some of the marble statues were depictions of gods, others of young amorous couples. There was one, however, that was different from all the others.

It was a young man with a sword raised above his head. He was very handsome with an athletic body and stern visage. His forehead and jaw were broad, and his supple mouth was twisted in the midst of a war cry. His eyes were captivating and hinted at a more dangerous wildness than what could be seen in the statue's stance. His nose was long, crooked, and looked as though it had been broken many times. He was also completely gold, whereas all the other statues were either white or gray marble

Marina's father told her the story many times of how this statue came to be. At one time, this statue was a living, breathing man. He was the Master of the Guard for the soldiers of Jamaria, the youngest man ever to have received that honor before or since. He reached his position when he served under King Banor, a king so full of greed he declared war on anyone and everyone with any kind of wealth.

At one point, the gods sought to punish Banor for his greed by cursing him with the golden touch. Everything he touched turned to gold, whether he wanted it to or not. The gods' idea backfired, however. Banor loved his gift and used it on everything in the palace.

The gods received vengeance in the end, as Banor refused to learn his lesson and give up his gift. He soon died from lack of food and drink, but not before he turned his Master of the Guard to gold. The young man angered his king in some unknown fashion and was sentenced to death. Before the guards present could take his sword from him, he tried to attack his treacherous king.

No one knew for sure exactly what happened, but the king obviously touched him just as he was raising his sword above his head. When the king died only two days later, the curse was still upon him. Everything the king turned to gold had stayed as it was, even the young Master. Many people pleaded with the gods to free the man, as he had been a good man.

With the king dead without ever naming an heir, Jamaria's enemies were quick to fall upon the defenseless country. The gods sent a message declaring that it was not yet time for the Master at Arms to rise from his golden sleep. He stayed as he was and had been that way for almost two hundred years now.

Luckily, another young man, Kurt DeGriffin stepped up from the soldier's ranks and led the army against Jamaria's enemies. He defeated them and was crowned king soon after. A stone statue of King Kurt and Queen Brenda DeGriffin stood nearby the golden warrior in honor of the man's memory and to remember how the current dynasty gained power. Marina stepped closer to the golden statue and ran her fingers over his cold face.

"I wonder when your time to live again will come?" she asked quietly.

Marina stood looking at the statue for some time, lost in thought.

The sound of footsteps broke her out of her thoughts and caused her to turn. Wently stood a few feet away, leaning against her ancestor's statue.

"What is bothering you, princess, that you would abandon your adoring followers?" Marina could see the malice in his eyes when he took a step forward. "A dance card as full as yours should not allow for such a long absence."

Marina took a wary step back. Soon, Wently forced her back until she was sandwiched between him and the statue. He brushed his hand over her face in a vile echo of her earlier caress of the statue. She pulled away in disgust, bumping her head against the statue in the process. It felt like hitting leather that had been left outside in bad weather and dried in the sun.

Wently's lip curled in a sneer.

"Perhaps I only prefer the improved conversation I can find out here among these statues to that of people such as yourself," Marina said softly in answer to his earlier question.

While Marina never thought of Wently as a smart man, even he could not miss the insult in her answer. Her lips curled in a satisfied smile when the jibe hit its mark. The expression was fleeting, however, as Wently reached his hand back to strike her across the face. She readied herself to block the blow as Curtis taught her. Before either of them could move, a terrible battle cry ripped through the night. Marina saw shock fly across Wently's face as a sword swung down from above.

Marina barely recognized the sword separating Wently's upraised right hand from its arm before the arm wielding the sword slammed into the side of her head. Blackness overwhelmed her, and the last thing she heard was Wently's screams of pain.

Kaia stood on the platform in the ready position: knees bent, toes at the edge, fingers pointed and just touching her toes, butt in the air. It always struck her as an undignified way to begin a sport that was poetry in motion. The starting gun sounded, and she and six other girls dove into the water.

She pulled into a perfect freestyle stroke, turning her head to take a breath on every other stroke of her right arm. When she reached the other side, she dove quickly, turned, and shot through the water with a powerful push off the wall. She counted to five and returned to the surface, seamlessly pulling back into her stroke with its steady rhythm.

The moment her hand touched the side, she knew she won. The girl two lanes to her right finished point-two seconds later, the other five girls following close behind. All seven girls were breathing hard from their exertion. Kaia knew she was the only one faking that breathlessness. Coaches came to the side of the pool and assisted their athletes out, towels waiting in their other hands.

"That was a close one, Griffin," Coach O'Connell cheered.

Kaia slowly became aware of the crowd cheering her win. She grinned broadly, finding her mother in the crowd who gave her two thumbs up and a grin of her own. The towel the coach gave her was warm and Kaia snuggled deeper savoring her win. She sat on the bench where her teammates waited and watched as the last heat of the day was getting set up. Amanda, her friend, was on the first platform preparing to swim.

"C'mon, Amanda!"

Kaia added her cheers to those of the rest of the crowd. The crowd quieted and resumed cheering wildly after the starting gun sent the remaining girls diving into the water. Kaia watched the water churn in the wake of the swimmers. Then a flicker at her feet caught her gaze.

Like any pool, there were puddles everywhere. The largest one was under the feet of the dripping swimmers. She looked down, and the noise around her was muffled instantly. Distantly, she could hear the roar of the crowd as someone won the heat, but she was distracted by what she was seeing in the puddle below her.

There was a huge, elaborately decorated room filled with people. There were hundreds of them, all dressed in beautiful clothes that looked as though they'd been modeled after the costumes in Robin Hood.

Some of those people didn't look human. One group had iridescent wings protruding from their backs, their clothes strategically making room. Another was made up of short, squat people with long, thick beards. One or two of these people wore dresses, hinting at female forms, but had beards just as impressive as the men.

In one corner of the room, there were men and women who towered over the crowd by at least five or six feet. Then there were women interspersed throughout the room wearing diaphanous dresses, with vegetation growing on their faces. These women captivated her the longest, for each one was different. Some were covered in the bright green leaves that can be seen in the middle of summer and thick, dark bark. Others sported delicate flowers in various hues and spindly twigs. And still others had something that looked like water lilies and reeds. For all of these women, this flora looked like beautiful and intricate jewelry that covered their arms, legs, and faces.

This motley collection of humans and creatures circulated around the edges of the room, making way for the large number of people dancing gracefully in the middle. Kaia was drawn in even further when she saw a young woman in the middle of the crowd. She was dancing with a darkly handsome man. He was tall and muscular, built like a quarterback. He had thick black hair and hazel eyes. His dark skin was complemented beautifully by the dark green jacket he was wearing over tan pants.

Then they turned in their dance, and Kaia saw something that shocked her out of her appreciation of his looks. He was dancing with her - or rather someone who looked very similar to her. The only differences between her and his partner were the girl's thick black-blue hair and bright blue eyes.

Granted, these were big differences when compared to Kaia's own shoulder-length white-blonde hair and emerald eyes, even more so when one considered that Kaia now had brilliant purple hair under her yellow swimmer's cap since she dyed it last night. Kaia heard the music come to an end, but barely, as the sound in this other world was muffled as if coming through a wall. When it ended, her other self curtsied to her super cute partner as she was claimed by another.

Kaia could almost feel the growl the dark-haired man directed at the pretty-boy intruder. His brown eyes flashed a brilliant yellow as he watched the couple line up for the dance. Kaia watched her dark counterpart dance. When the dance was over, she escaped from her newest partner with the help of a different charming young blond man.

The image blurred and shifted. Suddenly, the girl was outside and now Kaia watched the girl walk in a beautiful garden full of statues. She stopped in front of one statue, and Kaia heard the girl say something that was just as muffled as the music. Kaia saw the pretty boy her counterpart danced with coming up behind the girl. He didn't look like he was up to any good, and Kaia wanted to shout a warning.

The girl turned after a few moments and saw him. They exchanged some heated words, and then Kaia saw something strange happen. The statue that had been pure gold was slowly changing color. It started to look real. The clothing looked softer, and his skin became flesh-toned gold. Then, a scream broke through it all and she watched as his arm came swinging down. Kaia watched him hit the girl and felt as if her own head was split open. Blinding pain ricocheted through her head causing her to clutch it and pass out.

4

Queen Delia DeGriffin was looking for her daughter when her carefully planned party descended into chaos.

Every guest in the room went still when a battle cry ripped through the festivities. Moments later, a shrill scream sent an arrow of panic through Delia's heart. Something deep inside her knew her daughter was in danger.

"Oh gods, Marina," she moaned.

Gerard, standing a few yards away, heard the Queen's distress and broke through the crowd at a run. A cadre of guards followed behind him quickly. Despite his many years and many battles, Gerard found himself truly fearful for the first time in several hundred years. The princess was a tough bit of goods, but he didn't think he would handle someone harming her with anything approaching rationality.

He was the first to find her. Even he was pulled up short by the surprise of seeing Marina on the ground covered in blood. A quick sniff, though, told him the blood was Wently's and not Marina's.

The next problem was finding out who the stranger binding a sobbing Wently's bloody wrist with Wently's party jacket was. There was something familiar about the man, but what concerned Gerard was the fact that he dropped Wently's arm as soon as he heard them come running and was standing over the fallen princess with the sword he'd propped next to the injured earl.

"To the princess!"

Gerard glared at the idiotic guard who put forth that dumb idea. The last thing he needed was a dozen guards agitating the stranger with a sword who could just as easily stab the princess as any of them.

"Enough," he growled.

Most of the time, he tried to keep his werewolf side under wraps to keep the humans and weaker creatures of the Kingdoms happy. But he wasn't upset to learn these guardsmen were still wary enough around him to hesitate before rushing into battle.

That was when the queen arrived. Gerard cursed the fact he didn't have time to de-escalate the situation before he could assure the queen Marina was safe.

Delia thought her heart would fail her the moment she saw her daughter. She stumbled and Jonathan was forced to steady her. His voice was rough when he ordered his men to stand down. Delia looked at her husband in confusion, but relaxed when she saw the stranger standing over her daughter lower his sword when there was no longer a group of soldiers threatening him.

Gerard approached the man slowly, just like he would a newly turned wolf. From the magic he could smell dissipating from the man, he could prove just as dangerous. As he got closer, his nose told him some important information.

"The blood is not Marina's," he told the queen. He knew she was having the hardest time seeing Marina on the ground. By her relieved sob, he was glad he gave her the information.

"Who are you?" he asked the stranger.

Before the man could open his mouth, King Jonathan barked out an order. "Seize him. Someone get the royal physician to see to Earl Wently and my daughter."

The guards moved quickly to follow his orders. Gerard was surprised when the stranger dropped his sword completely when the guards approached them. The stranger was looking from the king to Marina as if he recognized them both.

Queen Delia rushed to her daughter's side as soon as the stranger dropped the sword. She wept and cooed over her unconscious daughter as the guards grabbed the stranger in rough hands.

Gerard chose to lead the dungeon. Partly because many of the younger guardsmen were unsure of the rarely used location. However, he also felt he needed to keep an eye on the guards to make sure they didn't become too rough with the man. They still needed answers.

As they walked away, the stranger looked back one last time at the unconscious princess. Gerard could swear he saw something like regret in the man's eyes.

Marina slowly became aware of her surroundings. Her head felt like a herd of centaurs were having a drunken revel inside. She felt her head gingerly where the worst of the pain claimed her attention. Her groan of pain seemed to reverberate inside her head when her questing fingers found the huge knot just above her left temple. Sinking further into her pillows, she wished the pain would end.

This caused her to realize she was in her own bedroom. A candle glowed faintly behind the bed curtain on her bedside table. The curtain on the opposite side was gently parted, revealing her mother's concerned face in the dim light. Marina tried to force her eyes to bring her mother into focus, but she only caused her head to hurt worse.

Queen Delia's cool hand on her brow felt like the best of healing balms to her pounding head. "How are you feeling darling?"

"I'm all right. What happened?" Her memory at the moment was even fuzzier than her vision.

"I was hoping you could answer that. At the moment, Wently is being attended to by the palace physician and we have his disturbingly silent assailant in the dungeon."

This surprised Marina more than hearing Wently was injured. The castle dungeon had not been used in more than one hundred years. Marina sat up with the queen's help and struggled to remember what happened.

"I remember leaving the ball to get some air," she began haltingly, "And stopping in front of the statue," Delia did not need to ask which one, as everyone in the palace knew of her fondness for the golden warrior, "And Wently cornered me..." Marina stopped as the rest of the night's events fell into place. She stared at her mother in horrified surprise. "The statue came to life. It attacked Wently."

She said this in the barest whisper, as if afraid that even in this magical world she would not be believed. Delia's eyes widened in shock. She did notice something wrong when she came upon the scene in the garden. Until Marina's revelation, she could not determine what it was.

"What happened after that, Mother?"

The queen gave her daughter a brief description of the events she saw in the garden. Though she was missing pieces of the puzzle before. Now the stranger's presence made a bit more sense, but there was still a mystery surrounding how he became disenchanted they would need to answer later.

Delia shook her head to clear her mind and continued. "The physician examined you and deemed you basically unharmed and ordered you to be taken to your rooms. He had the servants help carry Wently to his laboratory to heal him. They will not be able to save his hand, but they can at least keep it from becoming infected."

Marina took her mother's shaking hand trying to soothe her.

"I am fine, mother. I have inflicted worse injuries upon myself."

She tried to paste on her normal grin but could tell she failed in her effort when Delia's eyes filled with tears. Delia straightened her spine and hid her distress behind a formal mask. Marina and her brothers called it "the stately look."

"Well, in that case, we should get this man out of the dungeon. He was obviously not able to stop himself. It was just the end of an action that began more than two hundred years ago."

Delia's face softened again as she gently brushed a lock of hair from Marina's face.

"Rest, darling. Hilde will bring you some willow bark tea to soothe your head."

Marina's face twisted in disgust. She found willow bark tea vile, but she knew her mother was right. It would make her feel better.

Delia got up and let the bed curtain fall closed behind her. When Marina heard the door shut, she gingerly moved to the edge of the bed. When that did not send her into a faint, she got out of bed and wrapped herself in her bedrobe. She picked up her slippers but kept them off for the moment so Hilde would not hear her leave. Thinking of Hilde, she remembered her maid would be up soon with the tea.

"That blow to the head is making me forgetful," she muttered ruefully.

She slipped back under her covers and waited for Hilde, who came in just a few moments later. She was tsk-ing in disbelief as she made her way across the room, tea tray in hand.

"My poor darling," she murmured, "you just drink this up and get some sleep." She handed Marina the mug and fussed with the pillows as she waited for her mistress to drink the concoction. Marina took a sip and grimaced as if in pain. It was not hard to fake—the tea tasted horrible as usual.

"It is too hot for now, I will just set it aside for the moment and rest my eyes." Marina did just that and soon regulated her breathing to fake sleep. It took a considerable amount of effort to keep from slipping into true sleep.

Hilde stood there for a few minutes. She was suspicious of how meek her mistress was being. She glanced at the stunning bruise on Marina's temple and decided the man had hit the poor girl harder than she'd thought. Hilde applied a cool, wet rag to Marina's temple and left the room quietly. As she shut the door behind her, she pinned the guard at the door with a steely glance.

"Be sure my mistress gets the quiet she needs," she ordered sternly. The guard nodded, keeping his eyes forward.

In her room, Marina opened her eyes and got back out of bed, slippers in hand. She took a quick gulp of the tea to calm the worst of the pounding in her head. Closing the curtains around her bed, she went through the hidden door to the cool corridor beyond.

Gerard watched in amusement as the guards tried to make their prisoner talk. The Master of the Guards was young and had only been master for two years. He was getting more frustrated the longer they asked questions that yielded no answers. The stranger's expression never changed from its stony mask, but Gerard could smell his confusion and fear.

"What is your name?" The master's face was red from frustration. "Did someone send you here? Say something!"

Gerard could tell the master's anger was about to get the better of him and decided to step in.

"Master Mittman, may I offer a hypothesis?" Gerard could see the master's surprise and confusion. Few people expected an educated werewolf, even these days. "It could be that your prisoner is unable to speak rather than unwilling. Perhaps we should give him a piece of parchment and a pen. Do you know how to write?" He directed the last at the prisoner, who nodded.

A glimmer of relief passed over the man's face before settling back into its former wooden position. Gerard suspected he was glad someone finally understood without forcing him to make a fool of himself.

Mittman motioned to one of the guards standing by the door to follow Gerard's suggestion. A sudden scent made Gerard's body stiffen suddenly, but imperceptibly. Only the prisoner noticed and tensed as well. Gerard relaxed again when he recognized the scent.

"Master Mittman, could you leave me alone with the prisoner for a moment?" Mittman hesitated, making Gerard laugh and sigh at the same time. "Don't worry, I won't eat him."

Gerard knew his eyes had changed to their wolfish yellow and smiled thinly when Mittman flinched. Mittman nodded and left with the remaining guards following behind. The prisoner's confusion was plain to see, but Gerard ignored him. He turned to the right and looked into the deep shadows beyond.

"You can come out now, Princess."

He saw the prisoner stiffen. Marina laughed quietly and stepped out of the shadows.

"I would not have tried to sneak in if I had known you were in the room." Marina smiled and looked at the prisoner, "I almost thought you would turn into a statue again before I got to see you. But you are still here."

Her voice softened, as though she was speaking to a wild creature, and she took a few steps closer to the prisoner.

"What do you mean 'statue?'"

Marina took in her surroundings as she explained what happened in the garden. She had only been in the dungeon once when she first started exploring the secret passages throughout her home. It was dark then, and she never felt the need to go back. The room was small, but the torchlight could not light the room enough to clear it of its gloom. The shadows she had hidden in were formed by a small crag that looked like a natural formation of the walls.

The now living statue sat at the end of a square pine table, his wrists and ankles bound in heavy chains. The leg chains were attached to the floor by an iron ring so he could not escape from the room. Gerard looked at the prisoner when Marina finished her explanation.

"Well, that would explain why he can't talk at the moment. A spell that lasts that long can make it hard to return to normal quickly. It also explains why the man is so stiff."

Marina chuckled at his joke. Gerard was a lot more fun when he was not around people who feared his lycanthropy. Marina met his wolf only once. While she respected the strength and viciousness he was capable of as she would that of a wild animal, she did not fear him. She believed he had a tight hold on his wolfish instincts when around her and most people.

"How are you feeling?" she asked the man.

"He can't speak. I'll see if the guard brought that paper I asked for."

Gerard turned and left the room. Marina knew then that she was right in thinking the man before her was trustworthy. Gerard would never leave her alone with the stranger if there was even the smallest chance she could be in danger.

"I am sorry you have been dragged down here. It has not been used for almost as long as you have been...incapacitated."

The man smirked at her choice of words.

"Do you mind if I ask you a question?"

The prisoner lifted an eyebrow at the sudden blush that covered her face. He nodded and Marina took a deep breath.

"Do you...were you...aware of what was going on around you for all those years?"

The man leaned forward and looked at her more closely. Suddenly he broke into a wide grin. Marina blushed harder in horror. She remembered all of the tea parties she'd had when she was younger; the many times she played in the garden. The most horrifying memory of all was when she was thirteen. That was too humiliating to think about now.

She covered her face to hide her overwhelming embarrassment. "Oh no, you were!"

The man started coughing badly. Marina looked up and started forward, afraid that he was going to be sick. His coughing forced him to double over and he was clutching his stomach. She moved behind him and pounded him on the back, hoping he had not swallowed his tongue or something equally hazardous. Marina's hand halted in midair when the cough changed to a new sound entirely.

The man was roaring with laughter now. Marina slowly lowered her hand and moved so she was facing him. Tears of mirth rolled down his cheeks. His eyes were closed, so he had no warning when Marina's fist slammed into his jaw. His laughter stopped abruptly as his head snapped back from the force of the blow. The chair rocked back, teetering for a moment on two legs and Marina was grateful for the many muscles she had acquired over the years from sparring with her brother.

Marina would have been happier to see him fall over, but he balanced on the two legs and held it there. The look he gave her as he rubbed his jaw was filled with surprise, admiration, and a large amount of annoyance.

"I didn't know girls could hit that hard," he rasped. The coughing and laughter seemed to have cleared up almost two hundred years of disuse.

"Yes, well, a lot can change in a couple of hundred years," she snapped. "So do you have a name, or should I call you Goldie?"

His eyes narrowed, and he sat forward, causing the chair legs to hit the stone floor with a bang.

"My name is Fahad."

Marina nodded in acknowledgment.

"Marina," she replied curtly. Fahad's eyes flashed to the door suddenly.

"Someone's coming."

Marina looked at the door and quickly made her way back to the shadows. Gerard came in, annoyance written across his features. "Obviously your voice has returned. You've convinced your guards you've been driven mad, and they now fear the king's wrath." He shut the door behind him and threw the now useless piece of paper in a crumpled mess in front of Fahad.

"Why would they fear Father? We both know it is Mother we need to be afraid of." Marina emerged from the shadows again, a mischievous smile on her face.

Fahad shook his head in disbelief. "I still can't imagine why I'm alive when I struck a princess. In my day, harming royalty came with a quick end."

Gerard smiled thinly at Fahad, "Believe me, if I hadn't gotten to you first, you would be dead. Mittman is eager to prove himself to his king as well as his men. The death of the man who attacked the princess would have been a perfect opportunity."

Marina rolled her eyes at the mention of Master Mittman. "That man is slightly mad. He gained his position by being top of his class in strategy and battle theory. Too bad I could beat him in combat with my eyes closed."

Fahad looked at her in disbelief. Gerard smiled and answered the silent question.

"Don't let her slight frame fool you. Princess Marina could probably take on one of my new wolves and win. You should therefore not underestimate Master Mittman. He's one of the top fighters among the palace guards. He's also one of the most clever, hence his promotion."

"Thank you for your advice. I'll try to stay away from him, just as soon as he unlocks these chains."

A bell rang in the distance, muffled through the stone walls. Marina looked at the ceiling guiltily.

"I better get back in case Hilde comes in to check on me. Keep him safe, Gerard." She knew it was probably an insulting command. Gerard would have done it regardless.

"Yes, Princess," Gerard placed his hand over his heart and bowed. Marina nodded her thanks and left the same way she had come.

"She must trust you a great deal," Fahad commented carefully. In his day, werewolves were regarded with fear as bloodthirsty monsters with very little human intelligence. Yet this werewolf was nothing like what Fahad expected. Gerard smiled without humor.

"Much has changed since your time. Marina's great-great-grandfather started peace negotiations with the nearest pack when his sister was turned. He preferred the possible mistrust of his people over losing her forever. He was lucky she was so well-loved by the people as well. She was a member of my pack until she left more than one hundred years ago."

Gerard looked out through the grill in the top corner of the cell to the quarter moon above. He was still looking out in silence when

Mittman came in a few minutes later.

"The king wishes to see the prisoner," Mittman grunted.

Gerard helped Fahad to his feet and unshackled his ankles. They walked side by side to meet King Jonathan.

5

The wet cement floor made Kaia shiver, waking her from her odd dream. A dull ache pounded in her left temple with each beat of her heart. She could hear a low buzz of worry and speculation around her. As she opened her eyes, she saw a group of people crouched around her. Her mother's concerned face hovered over her own.

"What happened, Griffin?" Coach O'Connell barked.

"I don't know," Kaia muttered. She touched her head gently and felt the pain start to fade.

"She probably just over-exerted herself on that last heat," her mother interjected, "I'm going to take her home to rest. I'm sure she'll be fine once she has a bit of a nap and a good dinner."

Kaia smiled wryly at her mother's words. It was a wonder she was so skinny when her mother's answer for everything was a good meal. Meredith Griffin helped her daughter stand and walked with her to the locker room.

"I'm fine, mom," Kaia assured her in exasperation, "stop hovering."

"I know sweetheart, I know." She smoothed Kaia's slightly damp hair back. Someone had removed her cap while she was unconscious. Merry's eyes were worried, but her smile was reassuring. Kaia sighed and went to the shower to wash off the chlorine. The hot water helped to soothe away the last remnants of pain.

She remembered the first daydream only vaguely, but the second part in the dungeon she had, while she was unconscious, was slightly clearer. The dream was odd, but at least she got to see that guy again. He looked fierce, but when he smiled, she thought he looked kind of sweet.

She wanted to follow him when he left the dungeon cell, but she was stuck with her long-haired doppelganger and the reanimated statue.

Their voices were muffled, so she didn't hear a word they said. When the girl left again, Kaia tried to stay to watch her hottie but was once again stuck following the girl. The secret passageways were interesting, so Kaia paid attention to those as closely as possible as she was being dragged along. The girl drank some weird-smelling tea and went to sleep, sending Kaia back to the real world to face a pounding headache.

Kaia shook her head and got out of the shower to dress. The locker room was empty now. She assumed her mother probably went to get her purse so they could leave. She got dressed and found her mom waiting at the locker room door. Merry put her arm around her shoulder, and they walked to the van. Once Merry started it up, she just sat there for a moment, lost in thought.

Merry was the world's best mom, but Kaia almost never saw her this pensive. Usually, her mom was a bundle of energy. No matter what emotions she was feeling, Merry generally felt them deeply.

"Mom? You okay?" Her mother turned and smiled at her.

"Feel like a DQ run?"

"Umm, sure. Who would say no to a Blizzard?"

Kaia was completely confused. Usually, her mother went pale at the smallest injury. Even the slightest amount of blood sent her running from the room. They drove in silence for a few moments before Merry broke it.

"Do you want to tell me what happened?"

Kaia looked out the window, watching the town fly by. It was hard to put the whole experience into words without sounding like a complete lunatic.

"What did you see, Kaia?" Merry's voice was tight with anxiety. Kaia's head whipped around quickly. She could only look at her mother, even more confused than before. Merry was looking straight ahead

"What do you mean, 'see?'" she asked warily.

Merry closed her eyes briefly before focusing again on the road and replying, sounding tired. "Just tell me and I'll explain when you're done."

Kaia looked at her mother carefully before starting her story. She began slowly, sure her mom would turn the car around and head toward the doctor's office a few blocks from the pool and immediately put her in for psychiatric evaluation. She kept going and when her mom's expression didn't turn into one of horrified disbelief, her voice got stronger and the words poured out in a torrent.

By the end, the only thing she left out was just how hot she thought the man from her dream was. She felt too possessive of him to share him with anyone else, even her mother. Even if he was only a figment of her imagination.

Merry was quiet for a few minutes before they pulled up to the Dairy Queen.

"Mint Oreo?" she asked, looking at her for the first time since leaving the locker room.

"Sure, my fave," Kaia replied weakly.

Merry ordered Kaia's Mint Oreo and a cookie-dough Blizzard for herself. The van went quiet again while they waited for their turn at the drive-up and while Merry paid. They drove another two minutes before the silence became too unbearable for Kaia.

"Mom, what's going on?"

Merry sighed and smiled thinly at her daughter. "I've always known this day would come, yet I'm still having trouble finding the words." The smile was more of a grimace of pain at this point.

"Okay," Kaia's voice broke slightly, "now you're just starting to freak me out. Please tell me what's going on."

"All right," Merry's grip on the steering wheel tightened, making the faux leather groan, "Let me start by saying that you've been the best thing to happen to me my whole life." She reached over and squeezed Kaia's hand.

"Thanks, mom," Kaia whispered.

"I'm not...I'm not who . . . or what . . . you think I am, and neither are you. I know you're going to think I'm crazy at first...if you don't already. You see, I'm not from around here."

"I know, you told me you moved here from Washington when your mother died."

"Well, sweetheart, that wasn't altogether the truth."

Kaia looked at her mother in confusion. She never knew Merry to ever be anything but honest. Merry hadn't even hidden the fact that Kaia was adopted from her, just always said that she was a miracle child because Merry wasn't able to have any. Merry squeezed Kaia's hand again, tears beginning to form in her eyes.

"I came to this world more than one hundred years ago. I arrived in 1888. Not far from where you were found actually."

Merry looked at Kaia's face. She could tell her daughter was taking the information in, but not quite believing it. How could she blame her? If she grew up in the Kingdoms, the idea of magic would be an everyday thing. Here on Earth, however, it was the stuff of fiction. At least as far as most humans were aware. Merry continued.

"Things were easier back then. I invented everything about my life at that point and moved to Montana where I had plenty of space and no one could question who I said I was or where I came from.

"For the first three or four decades, it was easy to move around every five years or so to keep people from wondering why I didn't age. Then the damn government started to keep better track of its citizens through social security numbers and the like. That made it more difficult to change my identity and still be able to survive.

"I had to start faking birth certificates every twenty or thirty years and move around more. Meredith Griffin is actually the fifth name I've chosen for myself. I was able to keep names longer at first and only changed them when I got tired of them.

"I was born Merylyn DeGriffin, crown princess of Griffin House of Jamaria."

Merry pulled into the garage and looked at her daughter as the door slowly closed behind them. Kaia's face was frozen in shock as she stared straight ahead. She didn't even blink for several minutes. Merry pulled her hand from her daughter's frozen one and laid it gently on Kaia's cheek.

Kaia flinched, causing Merry to pull her hand back. Kaia felt bad for the movement when she saw the pain in her mother's eyes. Yet she also didn't feel like she could have helped her reaction. Her mother wasn't making any sense. She couldn't possibly be as old as she was claiming to be. For God's sake, she was only forty and people were always telling her she could pass for twenty in a heartbeat.

Merry sighed because she knew the hardest part of her tale was yet to come. And it would only make life harder for her daughter. That sigh made Kaia restless and sent her running from the car to the house, and eventually her room. She locked the door and rested her forehead against the cool wood.

All the information was spinning around and around in her brain making her dizzy. She turned and slid slowly down until she was sitting with the door supporting her back. When Merry started, Kaia thought she was going to tell her Kaia's birth parents were raving lunatics. So it was only a matter of time until their ticking time bomb of a daughter blew up as well.

Nothing could have prepared her for what came out of her mom's mouth. Kaia wrapped her arms around her legs and put her forehead on her knees. It was a lot of information to take in. She just needed time.

Just a few seconds.

Merry sat at the kitchen table, the Blizzard before her long since melted. The cookie dough chunks floating around looked less than appetizing. She heard Kaia's door unlock and open slowly. She had to force herself not to jump up from her chair. Her fingernails bit into her palms and she closed her eyes as she tried to control her eyes before her daughter could see that her normally brown irises were a deep gold.

Merry had been sitting there for almost six hours trying to figure out a way to break the rest of her story to Kaia in a way that wouldn't send her running screaming from the room. Kaia's footsteps were soft and hesitant, but she sat in the chair across from her with bravado and looked her in the eyes.

"I'm sure you have a lot of questions," Merry started softly.

"Oh, you think?" came her daughter's sarcastic reply.

Merry smiled wryly. "Good to know I haven't shocked the spirit out of you."

Kaia merely huffed impatiently and crossed her arms over her chest. Merry loved the fact that no matter how much Kaia claimed she was a grown woman who could fend for herself; she still acted like a child from time to time. Even though Kaia was leaning back in her chair acting as though none of it was bothering her, the redness around her eyes and the way her purple hair looked like it was almost standing on end from having a hand run through it too many times indicated otherwise.

"I guess it's hard to know where to start exactly," Kaia conceded with a nod of her head. She leaned forward and put her elbows on the table in agitation. "I suppose the first questions I have are: exactly how old are you? And how have you been able to stay alive for so long?"

Merry looked at Kaia for a few seconds and took a deep breath. "I'm one-hundred and ninety-two years old, as of May."

Kaia's eyes widened at the number. "I guess a book of poetry for your hundred-and-ninety-second birthday was a bit pathetic then. It seems like I should have gotten you a rare diamond or something like that to really celebrate the fact that you are exceedingly freaking old."

Merry smiled and a tear fell down her left cheek. "No, I love Byron, and it was a beautiful present."

Kaia took a deep breath and stared forcefully at her mom. "How is that possible, mom? You shouldn't be sitting here, looking the way you do, at sixty-two, let alone..." Kaia paused to do the math, "A hundred and thirty years more."

"The thing is, darling, werewolves don't age once they've been changed."

Kaia woke up to the sun streaming through her curtains. She couldn't remember coming up to bed, or much of the day before, at all. Then it all came rushing back at her all at once causing her to sit up quickly and eliciting a frightened squeak from her throat.

"No," she whispered to herself, "it was all just a horrible nightmare. It couldn't have been real. I'm just nervous about the meet today. Or was it yesterday? Did Amanda and I go out celebrating and party a little too hard?"

"I sure hope that wasn't the case. I'd hate to have to ground you over something that didn't happen."

Kaia yelped in surprise at her mother's voice from the doorway. Merry bit her lip and Kaia could see the pain flair in her eyes again.

"Sorry, mom, you scared the shit out of me."

"Watch your mouth, Kaia," Merry sighed.

"Sorry," Kaia mumbled looking down.

That was when she noticed that she was still wearing her clothes from the day before. Considering her last conscious thought of the previous night was thinking "That's not possible" before passing out at the kitchen table, she supposed this was just par for the course.

"Ummm, mom? How did I get to my room?"

"Well, my final admission was a bit too much for your system yesterday, and you passed out at the table."

Kaia winced at that particular show of weakness.

"Awesome," she bit out, "nothing like passing out twice in one day. But, that still doesn't explain how I got up here."

Kaia's room was in the attic of their three-story Victorian at her request. It had the best view and allowed her to listen to her music at a volume both she and her mother could agree upon.

The only downfall was that it required climbing three flights of stairs, one of which was extremely narrow and difficult to traverse. Especially with the detritus Kaia left on the steps when she came home.

"I carried you. My kind are incredibly strong and agile. Not to mention you're an extremely light girl. I keep telling you that you need more meat on your bones."

"Trying to fatten me up, huh?" Kaia returned shortly.

Merry winced at the thought that Kaia could even joke about such a thing.

"I didn't mean it, mom. I'm sorry."

Merry moved slowly toward Kaia. "It's okay, I understand this is all a lot to take in. I wish there had been a better way to break it all to you. Unfortunately, with what happened yesterday, I knew it was only a matter of time before you started questioning a lot of things. Not only about me, but about yourself as well."

Kaia's eyebrows came together in confusion. "Why? What's wrong with me? Am I a werewolf too?"

"You sound incredibly calm about that being a possibility."

Kaia laughed in surprise. She passed her hand in front of her, indicating the walls of her room. They were covered in posters of movies like Frankenstein, An American Werewolf in Paris, Night of the Living Dead. She was a horror movie and sci-fi fan. While she had never believed any of it was true, it hadn't kept her from imagining it all.

Merry snorted in disgust. "You know I hate that Hollywood stuff."

"I always used to think it was because you thought it was rotting my brain or something. I never would have believed in a million years it was because you were actually a part of it all yourself."

"Yes, well, that drivel is more likely to rot your brains than I am to turn you into something like me."

Merry's responses were so very like the woman Kaia had grown up with. Nothing like the drooling monsters portrayed in the movies she'd seen. Kaia looked at her mother before saying anything else. The truth was, even if Merry did turn into a hairy wolf every month, it didn't change the fact that this was the same woman who had raised her for seventeen years.

"Mom," Merry's eyes lit up at that, "I think you owe me another Blizzard after that revelation."

Merry grinned as she nodded.

"Not to mention a heck of a lot more information."

Merry's smile dimmed a bit at this, but she nodded once again. "Have a shower, get dressed and we'll head out for lunch. You slept the morning away."

6

Marina quietly stretched for what felt like the hundredth time as she waited for Fahad's trial to begin. She was alternating between hunching to look out of the peephole behind her parents' thrones and stretching to keep her back from paining her. This was one of the times when she cursed the fact that she was taller than most, as the hole had clearly been constructed for someone shorter.

Marina cut her musings short when she heard the constant buzz of conversation end abruptly. She crouched quickly and saw her mother and father sit while Curtis and their oldest brother, Antonio, stood behind them.

The crowd before them was smaller than that of most trials, as it only held the council members. The king and queen felt it would be better to keep the trial from the public because it was quite strange—even by the standards of the Kingdoms—and because it concerned the son of one of the council members. Wently's father, Duke Avery, looked grim at the situation before them all. Marina was sorry that such a kind and peaceful man had to bear witness to what could be his son's downfall.

"Guards, bring the men forward," her father commanded.

Wently and Fahad stepped into the hall with palace guards close at hand with unsheathed swords. Wently was looking haughty as ever, but there was a hint of pain to his snobbery. Even though the palace physician was one of the best in the Kingdoms, Wently's wound was too terrible to heal with herbs alone. For some unknown reason, his body would not respond to the healer's magic. Fahad's movements were encumbered by the chains around his wrists and ankles. Wently had no shackles in deference to his position in the court as well as to accommodate his wound.

King Jonathan waited until the men halted in front of him before he addressed them.

"Lord Wently, young man, you have both laid serious charges before one another. Each has claimed that the other was attempting to harm Lady Marina, crown princess of Jamaria, my daughter." An edge Marina rarely heard entered her father's voice when he said the last. "Wently, as you are a potential member of our council,-and a member of our court-we will allow you to speak first."

Wently bowed stiffly to the king before he began to speak.

"Your most royal majesty," Marina had to suppress a snort of disgust at his obsequious attitude, "I seek justice from this low-born ruffian. He assaulted the crown princess and crippled me for life. His crimes are egregious and should be met with the harshest punishment available in Jamarian law."

Marina wanted to shout her denial of Wently's charges but kept silent so she would not betray her presence. She felt anger toward her mother for keeping her from the trial so she could tell the court what really happened. The queen had taken one look at the still worsening bruise on the side of her face and declared her too badly injured to attend.

It was not fair and Marina quailed at being treated like a piece of glass, but she had stayed quiet to keep her mother from questioning how Marina was more than used to cuts and bruises. Even with everything going on, she still wanted to keep her sparring sessions with Curtis a secret. In fact, she was sure that the blow Curtis inflicted earlier the day of the ball only made Fahad's hit seem that much worse. It stood to reason that knowledge would make it ten times worse if her mother discovered the secret she and Curtis shared. That was why she was hidden in the secret passageway, despite the pounding in her head.

"Believe me when I say, the guilty party will be treated harshly for the events of last night, Lord Wently." Marina felt a chill at the anger suppressed beneath her father's authoritative voice. Marina did not know what the harshest punishment under Jamarian law would be, but she assumed it would be a painful death if the underlying threat in her father's tone was any indication.

"Young man, you will be next to speak. However, before you tell this court what occurred last night, you must present the information you refused to give my guards. We will not proceed until we are satisfied with how you came to be in our garden in the first place."

Marina was confused. She knew Fahad spoke to Gerard in the dungeon, so why was her father asking a question to which he should already know the answer?

Fahad bowed stiffly, causing his chains to clink heavily. The cumbersome weight did not help the fact that he looked incredibly uncomfortable with the courtly action.

"Majesty, my name is Fahad Pruitt of Hanson," Fahad paused when his declaration caused some gasps and quickly muttered conversations.

"Silence!" Jonathan bellowed. He did not seem surprised by Fahad's name. "Sir, you claim to be Fahad of Hanson, who has been trapped in a cocoon of gold these last two hundred years? How do you expect these men to believe such a wild claim?"

Fahad looked at Jonathan with annoyance and suspicion. Marina felt a smile begin to form on her lips as she realized what her father was doing. He could not ostensibly give Fahad his support, but he could lead him in the right direction. Gerard must have spoken to the king after talking to Fahad. Marina was not aware of Gerard and her father were friends or merely political allies.

"I suppose, majesty, I expect them to look at the empty space in your garden where a golden statue used to stand and hope they will be smart enough to figure out the truth on their own."

Jonathan grunted at Fahad's answer, but Marina knew from experience that this meant he was amused by the answer and trying to hide it. It was something she heard many times when her mother caught her doing something she should not be doing, and her father was amused despite himself. Delia gave her husband a quick look of annoyance to prod him on.

"Enough, Sir Fahad, give us your testimony."

Fahad looked to his right, where Wently fumed quietly as he

began to realize just who Fahad was. Marina knew Wently planned to play his word as a noble against Fahad's as a seemingly low-class peasant. Now he began to appreciate his tenuous position.

"I don't know exactly what happened. There have been moments these last two hundred years when I've been completely aware of everything that's occurred around me. But, there are others when my mind was a blank- as if I were asleep without dreaming.

"All that I can recall of last night is moving for the first time in all of those years. I don't know what-or who-awakened me. When I became fully aware of my surroundings, I saw your daughter on the ground before me and this man, Lord Wently, screaming. After that, my only thought was to stop this man's bleeding and protect your daughter."

Jonathan nodded gravely and Marina saw hope begin to spark behind Wently's malicious gaze. She could not let him get away with his lies, but she could not reveal herself now. The thought of having everyone in the court staring at her made her skin crawl. Not to mention only the gods knew what kind of trouble she would be in if her mother discovered Marina disobeyed her.

"I think, your majesties, that the only way you are going to discover what happened would be to ask your daughter. Though I'm not sure why you didn't do that in the first place."

Marina felt her pulse jump when Fahad said this. There were not many people who would believe she would be willing to stand up for herself. Truthfully, she was unused to speaking up for herself with anyone but those she knew well. With Fahad, she felt as though she knew him all her life because of the time she spent talking to him in the garden. And so she was far more forward with him the night before than she had ever been with any of the courtiers in the next room.

Delia motioned for Jonathan to lean in closer. They kept their voices low to keep from being heard by the rest of the court, but Marina's position behind the thrones allowed her to hear every word.

"I do not want Marina exposed to this. She is still in a great deal of pain."

"The lad is right, Delia. Marina will be able to clear up all of this in a moment. I only kept her from the trial until now because I wanted to give Fahad a chance to prove himself before the council. Now that he has, you and I both know that Marina is the only person who can tell us the truth."

Delia looked upset, but she nodded to acknowledge she knew her husband was correct. She began to motion for a guard to retrieve Marina, but Curtis stopped her.

"I will get her, mother. I have a feeling she is not far, and I know her favorite hideouts." He glanced quickly at the point in the wall where he knew Marina was hiding signaling her. Marina smiled at how well her brother knew her. Without ever saying a word to him, he knew she was disobeying their parents and watching. Marina left her hiding place and made her way to the panel hidden in the hall leading to the throne room. Curtis met her there moments later.

"Let us wait a moment before we go back in," Curtis looked behind him to be sure no one had followed. Then, he got his first real look at her since last night.

"By all the gods above and below," he breathed, almost reverently. He reached out a hand to touch the bruise but stopped before he made contact. "I think that is the most impressive one you have ever had, Brat."

Marina could sense the worry behind his joking tone. She knew her brother better than most, so she saw past his general merriment, which caused most people to believe he would never be a serious young man like Antonio.

"Yes, it is. Stop being such a worrywart and escort me to the throne room. As you told our parents, I could not have been far." She winked to show she was okay, but she could tell Curtis was not falling for her act.

He took her arm in his anyway and led her to the large oak doors. When he knocked twice, they opened silently to admit them into the council's still buzzing presence. Marina almost wished she had stayed in bed as her mother ordered when she saw the looks of shock and horror on the faces of the council members. At the very least, she wished she had thought to wear a veil or even a large farmer's hat to conceal her bruise.

"Thank you, Curtis," her father acknowledged. Curtis released her arm after giving her hand an encouraging squeeze and returned to his position behind their mother's seat.

Marina curtsied when she reached the step in front of her parents.

She was nervous and not sure she would say the right things that would convince the court to let Fahad go. She was not used to speaking in front of large crowds. That was usually left to her brothers.

Though she could be counted upon to stand before the people of Jamaria during festivals and holidays with her family, the speeches were presented by either her parents or Antonio. Curtis did not often speak to the public, but he had the innate ability to say whatever the crowd wished to hear. His jovial nature could always bring the people to raucous cheering. Their middle brother, Benedict, was so far removed from politics he was on a ship somewhere captaining a Jamarian naval vessel.

There was no joviality in anyone's face today, however, and Marina hated the way her stomach was tied into knots of fear. While she was normally somewhat shy, she did not enjoy showing her weakness. She gripped her hands tightly in front of her and stared straight ahead.

"Princess Marina," her father intoned, "you have been brought before this court and its council to inform us all of what happened last evening. I know I need not remind you of your duty to the kingdom and your family, and I am sure everyone in this room has the utmost faith in your honesty and honor."

Marina bowed her head in acceptance and began her tale. She told them, in increasingly confident words, of Wently's cruel attack and Fahad's miraculous awakening. There was not much to tell on her side, as she had been knocked unconscious for much of the excitement. But, she knew from the testimonies Wently and Fahad made before she entered, that she clearly took Fahad's side of the events.

Marina could not see Wently's face, but her previous experience with him caused her to imagine it was mottled in rage. So she was unprepared for the look of betrayal she saw upon his pale face. He looked as though his greatest friend had betrayed him.

"Majesties," his words came out as though he could not catch his breath, "I beg that you reconsider accepting this testimony. The princess could have been bewitched by some errant spell escaping during Sir Fahad's disenchantment. And let us not forget the horrible injury inflicted upon her by this same event. While I can now understand how Sir Fahad could have caused such havoc without his own knowledge, please know, my benevolent lord and lady, that I would never seek to harm your sweet daughter."

Wently bowed submissively and Marina could hear the sympathetic murmurs coming from his peers. Fahad could not hide his look of disgust at Wently's performance and Marina could feel her blood begin to boil. How dare this cretin try to throw himself upon the mercy of the court by implying Marina could not help but lie because she was either bewitched or had been damaged mentally from Fahad's blow? She stared at him, wishing from the depths of her soul that she could force Wently to tell the truth.

The sympathetic murmurs became cries of alarm when Wently suddenly jerked upright like a marionette whose strings had been pulled. His face became red and his mouth began to work itself open and close. Fahad looked worried, but whether it was for himself or the others around them, Marina could not tell. Then again, it was difficult to focus on anyone other than Wently at the moment. She felt as though her boiling blood was causing something to boil up within Wently as well.

"I would kill you right now if it were not for the guards standing so close." Wently's words were strangled as if each were being ripped from his throat. He was pointing directly at Marina with a murderous glint in his eye. "If not for this peasant with an overblown sense of importance, I would have gotten the pleasure of wiping that smug smile from your face last night with a blow you have had coming since we first met."

Several people screamed when Wently belied his own words and lunged for Marina's pale throat. He seemed beyond reason, not even noticing that he only had one hand with which to throttle the princess. Marina did not think but relied upon the training Curtis provided. She blocked Wently's arms with a sweep of her own that threw him slightly off-balance. Taking advantage of that, Marina grabbed her skirts to lift them over her knees and kicked the back of Wently's left knee. He fell, ironically looking as though he was ready to propose. Marina, her foot still in the air from the first kick, lashed out again, catching Wently's sneer of contempt with the ball of her foot.

As soon as Wently was knocked to the floor, Marina felt weak. Her blood was no longer boiling, but flowing sluggishly through her veins. She fell to her knees beside Wently, no longer feeling that strange connection to him that had lasted throughout his confession and attack.

Blood trickled from the corner of Wently's mouth. He stared at her with pure malice for a moment before reaching up for her neck again, a little slower than before. Marina knew she did not have the strength to defend herself again, so she fell backwards to avoid him.

She never saw Fahad move, but he was suddenly behind Wently. He slammed his fists onto the back of the earl's neck, finally knocking him unconscious.

The room was deathly still as the courtiers tried in vain to process all that just occurred. Most looked at the earl's prone form with shock and disgust. Others were more focused on Marina. Their reactions ranged from admiration to distrust, with a few noblewomen looking at her with more disgust than was being directed at Wently. After what felt like an eternity, the king's voice split the stunned silence.

"Guards, pick that man up and take him to the dungeon." The king stood to give his orders and pointed to the two guards flanking Wently's limp body. Then, he motioned to the guards standing by Fahad. "Remove Sir Fahad's shackles and escort him to Our audience chamber." The guards hurried to do as the king bade, trying to make up for their earlier inaction. Marina felt bad for them because no one could have anticipated such events. One guard was also enlisted to help prop up the queen so Curtis was finally able to help his sister instead of his mother.

Marina could feel her muscles begin to quiver as though she had gone through a full sparring session with her brother. She moved to a sitting position but did not yet trust her legs to support her. She was a little ashamed of how everything was affecting her. Yet she had never defended herself from someone who actually wished her harm before. She thanked the gods that Curtis taught her so much over the years.

Fahad came to her side once he was released, looking worried.

"Princess, are you well? You look as though you're going to be ill." Fahad looked like he wanted to put a comforting arm around her, but was afraid that the chains that had so recently been removed would once again be clamped around his wrists and ankles.

"I am quite all right. I merely need to sit for a moment to gather my wits. Thank you, Sir Fahad, your concern is appreciated, as was your assistance with Lord Wently."

Suddenly, Curtis was beside her and wrapping an arm around her shoulder. Marina sagged into him gratefully and caught an odd expression on Fahad's face before she shut her eyes in exhaustion and let her brother carry her away.

Fahad tried to shake off the small sense of jealousy he had felt when the princess was wrapped in the other man's arms. He wanted to do that himself, but she looked so fragile, he was afraid she would break. She didn't look anything like the strong, confident young woman who would brave a dungeon to chance a peek at him.

The guard who removed Fahad's chains beckoned to him and started to walk, assuming Fahad would follow. He had barely gone two steps when he felt someone come up behind him. His gaze snapped around and found Gerard walking next to him.

"That was quite a display back there," Gerard spoke quietly so the guard would not hear them.

"I have always reacted quickly, especially when there is danger."

"I wasn't speaking of your defense of the princess. I was speaking of your overt concern. You must be careful when addressing the princess, especially with so many nobles present. You may have won her father over last night, and you may have a certain legend attached to your name, but don't mistake her position in this court. Her parents have never courted offers from other nobles for her hand, and no one would take it well if she were to become involved with someone like yourself."

Fahad wanted to be angry at the wolf for interfering, but something struck him as odd and kept his anger at bay.

"What do you mean her parents have not courted offers for her? Most royalty see their princesses as a chance to solidify relations with other nobles. The Kingdoms cannot have changed that much since I was trapped."

Gerard gave Fahad a look that almost seemed to indicate he was proud of Fahad. "And they have not, pup. Such is the mystery of our fair princess."

With that, Gerard broke off their conversation and turned into a corridor to the right. The guard ahead of Fahad never stopped, so Fahad could not follow Gerard or he would never find the room he was being led to. Though he still wasn't certain of his position in this new court. Perhaps he should follow old instincts and leave before things got worse.

7

Kaia and Merry sat on a green park bench, admiring the way the light reflected off of the duck pond. They had gotten a couple of breakfast burritos, tater tots, and drinks from a local café and brought them out to the park. Partly because it was such a beautiful summer day, and partly because they didn't want anyone to eavesdrop on their conversation.

Kaia bit into her burrito and waited for her mom to begin her story. Kaia had bombarded her mom with so many questions that Merry hadn't been sure which one to answer first. They decided during the car ride to the café it would be easier if Merry told her story and Kaia asked questions afterward.

"My world doesn't really have a name like Earth does," Merry began, "We simply call our land the Kingdoms. There are eight—or at least there were eight when I left. The one thing you cannot change when dealing with mortals and immortals alike is the endless politics of life.

"I grew up in a country called Jamaria."

Kaia looked at her mother as if she was still expecting her to shout "JK" and laugh at Kaia's gullibility. When she didn't, Kaia carefully repeated the name back to her mother. "Ham-aria?'

"Yes. It was beautiful, full of people of different races and creeds who lived in relative harmony with one another. However, in my time, there were still fears ingrained in each of us by so many years of inexperience and hatred. Many of the creatures you know of in your fairy tales and supernatural movies were feared even in our land of magic and wonder."

Kaia looked at her mother and wondered if she knew that her voice had taken on a strange accent and her words were more formal than anything Kaia had ever heard from her before.

"Among those were the werewolves. Like your world, we believed that these creatures were bloodthirsty and evil. So, we tried to protect ourselves as best we could with silver weapons and wolf's bane. I was traveling to a nearby country, Kenter, when my party was attacked by a lone wolf, called Baorith."

"Why were you going to another country?" Kaia took a quick bite of her burrito and tried to appear innocent when her mother glared at her for interrupting again.

"I'm only answering this one question and then you'd better keep your mouth shut."

Kaia nodded, trying to keep the smirk off her face when Merry broke back into the speech patterns Kaia had grown up with instead of her more stuffy tone—which came back when she restarted her story.

"I was on my way to be married to the Prince of Kenter." Merry glared at Kaia again when it looked like she was going to ask another question. Kaia took a large bite of her burrito to cover the fact that her opening mouth had been about to do just that.

"It was a political arrangement put into action by my father and carried out by my brother after our father's death. Like most marriages of convenience, it was convenient for everyone but me." Merry smiled ruefully to herself before continuing. "Baorith savaged everyone in my party, including me. All but two of us were killed instantly. Baorith was busy killing the only other near survivor when three wolves broke through the tree line to attack him. I did not stay conscious long enough to see what happened, but I was told later that Baorith died slowly and in much pain. I think that helped me get through the next year.

"When I woke, it was a week later and I was in a cave with a man I never met before. I was frightened of him because he looked so fierce and unlike anyone I had ever met in my years at court. He told me what happened. I didn't want to believe what he said next—that I would turn into a wolf that night and every night until the cycle of the full moon ceased; and that this would be my curse until the day I died...if that day ever came. I kept trying to deny his words until the first change came upon me."

Kaia watched as a single tear cascaded down Merry's left cheek. She put an arm around her mother and leaned her head onto her shoulder, feeling the top of her head brush Merry's cheek. The tear soaked through her hair to her scalp.

Suddenly, Kaia was thrown into another vision. She saw her mother standing, arguing with some man who was hidden in the shadows. Then, Merry's body convulsed and she fell hard to the floor. She braced her shaking body on her hands and knees and convulsed again. Kaia was glad then she couldn't hear anything because Merry's mouth opened into what had to be the most horrific scream Kaia could ever imagine. Kaia watched in detached disbelief as her mother's body contorted violently and sprouted fur. She almost didn't notice the unknown man was also changing.

His change was smooth and flawless. He was a man one moment, crouched to all fours, and was now a beautiful white wolf, with long graceful legs, short fur, and golden-orange eyes that burned with a fierce intelligence. He sat on his haunches and waited for Merry to finish transforming.

When she was done, Kaia saw a wolf with a multi-colored brown and grey coat panting in pain and fear. Merry the wolf took one look at the male and immediately tried to bolt. The bigger wolf seemed to have seen this coming and blocked her escape. Merry cowered as the big wolf stood over her and waited.

Finally, Merry turned over and showed her belly. The male opened his jaws and Kaia gasped in dismay. Even though she knew her mom was fine and made it through this ordeal, she didn't want to see her get savaged. But, the male only put his open jaws around her throat and squeezed gently before letting her regain her feet.

He then led her out of the cave and into the woods. Kaia's vision faded when she could no longer see them bounding through the trees.

Merry's arm was gripped tightly around Kaia's shoulders when she finally came back to the now. Merry turned them both a little so she could look into Kaia's eyes. Her own were frantic with worry.

"What happened?"

"I think I saw your first change." Kaia's throat felt dry and thick. She needed a drink, so she gently shrugged off Merry's tight grip and reached by her feet to grab her Coke.

"Oh, baby." Merry's voice broke as she thought about what her daughter just witnessed. It was difficult watching someone go through their first change. The first was always the worst because it was so unexpected. It wasn't until Merry was taught to control her changes that they became smooth and almost painless. It would never be completely painless, but once she learned control, it mostly felt like she was popping her joints instead of breaking every bone in her body.

"How did you deal with it all?" Kaia spoke around the lump in her throat.

"I couldn't deal with any of it for a few months. But everyone in the pack worked to bring me back to who I once was; or as close to that girl as they could get with the curse upon me. It was not until I had full control over myself that I learned they had ulterior motives for helping me as they did.

"Once I was under control, the man who saved me and stayed with me those first few weeks took me to the palace to see the king, my brother. We had to sneak into the palace using a set of secret passage ways I hadn't even known existed."

Kaia didn't mention she knew those passageways from one of her visions. She was oddly reluctant to share all of her experiences just yet.

"We entered my brother's bedchamber very late that night. He and his new bride were surprised, to say the very least," Merry continued with a wry smile, "When we finally calmed them, my brother and I were left alone to reunite and speak of the pack's plan to form a treaty with the Jamarians."

"But, I don't understand. You don't seem like you're very happy about what you're telling me, so why did you go along with that dude's plan instead of telling him to go f—" Kaia cut herself off at Merry's glare and switched words midstream, "stuff himself?"

Merry's laugh was brittle as she thought of how to answer. "I am afraid, my dear, that my sheltered existence before my family sent me to my bridegroom caused me to believe I was in love. Just because he saved my life and helped me restore my sanity, I became enamored of him."

Kaia noticed that Merry had never said the guy's name. She wanted to ask, but she felt awkward trying to delve into her mother's love life. It didn't help that all of this happened a hundred or so years ago, which meant that Merry's feelings about this guy had been given more than a century to solidify.

"It was not until much later that I finally realized he would never return my feelings. I stayed for a few more years after that. Whether it was from stubbornness or some loyalty to my brother, I still don't know. But, after my brother died, I decided that I had done enough as the public's figurehead of a dignified werewolf and left. It may have been cowardly to have gone without leaving more than a note of farewell, but I could not risk having anyone—especially not him—convince me to stay.

"I stumbled upon the entrance to this world completely by accident. I won't go into everything that happened after that, just know that being a lone wolf was much harder than I ever anticipated. I suppose the best part of all this is that all my years alone here did help heal my wounded emotions from my unrequited love." Merry gave Kaia another self-deprecating smile and continued with a hint of irony in her voice.

"Now, I realize I could not have loved him as I thought I did or I never could have left him behind. The one thing Hollywood mostly gets right is the fact that my kind mate for life. It was just the remnants of my humanity that led me to think I actually loved him."

Merry sat in silence for a few minutes, and Kaia mulled this story over in her mind. She knew her mom was leaving a lot out, but for the most part, she was satisfied. She wished to know more about her mom's past, but prying didn't seem like the right thing to do at the moment. Even with all of the decades that had passed, the memories still seemed pretty fresh to Merry.

"I suppose I only have questions about the most important part of your story, which you seemed to have left out, by the way."

Merry just looked at Kaia and waited.

"The part where you got me, of course." Kaia grinned and took another sip of her Coke. Merry smiled, probably glad to be spared the questions about her past.

"Well, for that part of the story, we are going to go on a little road trip."

Kaia didn't know how to react to that declaration. It seemed like it would be just as easy to tell her what happened. It wasn't like she had to see anything to know the whole story. When she told Merry this, her mom merely smiled mysteriously and said,

"I wouldn't want to take all the fun out of this."

"Oh, yeah, because it's been so much fun getting so shocked by your many announcements that I've passed out."

Merry looked guilty at Kaia's obvious annoyance but felt better when Kaia continued.

"I better get some really good birthday presents out of all of this. I'm thinking of some serious butt-kissing gifts when this is all said and done."

"Now, you know I would never completely spoil you. I wouldn't want to turn you into one of those ungrateful types."

Kaia and Merry both laughed and finished the rest of their meal in silence, each thinking of how their lives were never going to be the same.

8

Marina woke suddenly to the pitch-blackness of her chambers. She couldn't remember for a moment why she was awake in the early hours. Usually, she fought Hilde for the better part of the morning about when exactly was the proper time to wake. Marina maintained that Hilde's proclivity for waking before the sun rose had to be unhealthy.

As she heard the cock crow for what must have been the second time, her memory returned and an excited grin covered her face. She dressed quickly in her favorite pair of breeches and threw a jerkin over the shirt she wore to bed. Her hair was shoved into a loose cap and some of the soot from the fireplace went onto her face. She knew her features were far too feminine to be confused for a boy, but her form was boyish enough to pass. As Curtis pointed out oh so helpfully the other day.

Marina checked her appearance in the mirror one last time, pausing when she caught a flicker of movement in the glass. Thinking Hilde had snuck in, she turned to survey the room. There was no one, but Marina could not shake the feeling that she saw a flicker of purple in her mirror.

Finally deciding it was a trick of the light, she looked into the mirror again and deemed herself suitably dressed to be mistaken for a stable boy. She slid into the secret passage behind her and hoped Hilde would leave her be until at least the noon hour. She should not need nearly that much time, but it would at least give her the opportunity to wander around the castle if she chose.

This was Fahad's first morning as part of the castle guard. After his trial, Marina and Curtis were both too curious about what the king would say to leave well enough alone. The audience chamber where Fahad was taken was littered with peepholes, and they were at various heights, so they could both find one that fit them.

The king gave Fahad an appraising look before speaking. Unlike most of the courtiers Marina grew up around, Fahad stood up well under her father's gaze. Most began to fidget, imagining the king was determining some terrible punishment for something they had done and thought he would never discover. More often than not, they would confess to something they had gotten away with until that moment. Marina was able to hold out longer than she used to, but even she confessed most of her secrets. She was beginning to suspect he possessed some magical quality that forced people to become completely honest around him, but she could not prove it—yet.

Fahad had simply waited politely for the king to say something. The silence between them stretched on so long that Marina almost yawned and gave away the one secret she and Curtis had both been able to keep thus far from their parents.

"The real question, Sir Fahad, becomes: what shall I do with you now?"

Marina jumped a bit when her father abruptly broke the silence, but she quickly pressed herself closer to the wall to hear the rest.

"I'm afraid, your highness, I don't really have any way to help you make that decision. Just know I will gladly serve your house however you see fit."

The king nodded his approval and sat in a nearby chair, inviting Fahad to do the same. Marina soon became bored with their light conversation and mentally checked out for a moment to admire Fahad's features. She had not really gotten a chance to do that since the dungeon, and she had been too mad at him for laughing at her to appreciate what she saw.

His features had not really changed since he was a statue. They were still as strong, but now she could see his skin was a dusky tan and his hair a brown so dark that it was almost black. His eyes were too far away to see, but she remembered them as a light brown, though they could have had a green cast to them as well.

"Yes, sire. Thank you for the chance to prove myself."

Marina snapped out of her reverie at the sound of Fahad's voice. His tone signaled the conversation reached its end.

"Do not be absurd, young man. You do not need any kind of chance to prove yourself to me. You have done quite well in the way you have comported yourself thus far."

"Thank you again, sire, but we both know I must do more than prove myself to you. Your people will wonder about me regardless of what may be said about this trial."

Marina silently cursed herself for not listening as she should have. Now she did not know what was going on. The king stood and acknowledged Fahad's formal bow.

"You are correct. So, let us both wish for the best tomorrow."

With that, her father left the room and signaled to someone outside the door. The guard who escorted Fahad there then led him from the room. Marina cursed out loud then and made her way to her brother.

"All right, I freely admit I stopped listening there for a while. What did father decide?"

Curtis gave Marina an extremely smug grin and walked away without a word. Marina had begged for nearly an hour before her monstrous brother finally told her that Fahad would be the newest guard member. What had really angered Marina was that Curtis had extorted her favorite quarter staff as his price for giving her the information.

"I will make him pay for that," she grumbled to herself as she waited to escape the passageway into the stables. She hated getting to the practice yard this way, but there was no direct passage. It was an open field and would therefore be impractical for a secret passage. The stable was always difficult because there was usually at least one person awake at all times, and even if they accidentally fell asleep, the horses would invariably wake up if she or Curtis walked in. It was the closest entrance to the field, however, so she bore up under her impatience and recited in her head the poem her dull teacher was forcing her to memorize.

She got to the part about the maiden riding the unicorn to the sacred pond when she saw her opportunity. The stable boy let himself out for a moment to relieve himself, and she stole out of the door. It was hidden behind a rack for the stable equipment, which made it that much more troublesome. If she did not shut it just right, it was given to sagging beneath the weight of the rakes and shovels.

The stable boy did not even notice when she snuck out the door behind him. She sent a silent thanks to the gods that he was probably so sleep-deprived he likely would not have noticed if the king walked by in full military regalia.

The Guard was just beginning to line up around the practice yard when she finally got to it. There was a weapons shed at the west end with a large tree next to it. The sun was beginning to rise, so she was able to take advantage of the tree's position against the light as well as the guardsmen's sleep-blurred vision to climb it without being noticed.

Marina was able to pick Fahad out of the crowd of men easily. She noticed that he had become friends with the guard who guided him around the castle the previous day. The ability to make friends so easily was a trait to be admired. For her, most people were too afraid of her position to strike up a conversation with her, and they did not know how to react on the rare occasions she tried to do so herself.

Fahad and the other guardsman jostled each other and made jokes as they waited for Mittman's orders. Mittman looked even more remote than usual. His eyes took on the frosty quality of the morning air as he addressed his men.

"Today, we welcome Sir Fahad Pruitt of Hanson to our ranks."

This announcement caused a few of the guardsmen to give Fahad new looks of respect. Many of them served the castle long enough to know of his legend, others heard of him through stories heard in tavern songs and poems. Others ignored him as they were doing since the morning began. A rare few looked at him as though he had personally offended them. Marina was a little confused by those men but paid them no heed as Mittman continued.

"I can see that many of you are familiar with his name. However, he comes to us as a new recruit. As such, we will teach him how our guard trains."

Many of the men laughed as they anticipated the fight that would soon begin. Mittman chose two of the men from the group and barked out an order to fight. They selected their wooden practice swords and moved to the center of a ring painted in the dirt.

Both men were at least half a foot taller than Fahad's six-foot frame and sporting powerful muscles. Despite their heavy frames, they moved with speed and agility as they sparred. Marina was impressed despite herself. She watched carefully and noticed a couple of holes in the defense of each man that she could exploit with her smaller and even more agile build. If there was one thing Curtis had taught her over the years, it was to take any advantage she could, because in a real fight no one would care she was a woman. Wently most definitely proved that true.

Finally, one bruiser landed what would have been a killing blow in a true fight on the other, and Mittman called a halt to the sparring session. The men ribbed each other good-naturedly as they returned to their places with the rest of the men. The master called the winner back into the ring and motioned to Fahad.

"Sir Fahad, I have been told that you were the best fighter of your time. You have seen two of this Guard's best, and I'm sure Tom would be happy to test your skills against his own."

Tom did not seem as certain as Mittman, but he offered no protest to what amounted to a direct order. He returned to his position in the center of the sparring field and watched Fahad make his way over.

Marina could see the various reactions this caused among the men. They all began to quietly exchange bets on how long Fahad would last before Tom flattened him. Marina wanted to believe Fahad would be able to hold his own, but she did not know if it would be possible given Tom's obvious physical advantage and Fahad's two centuries of inactivity.

The men circled each other for a few moments before Tom came at Fahad with a deadly swing of his wooden sword. Fahad parried quickly and the two exchanged blows for a time. Fahad proved to be a quick and efficient swordsman. Marina could see that he had also studied the holes in Tom's defenses during the previous sparring session.

Tom was tiring after sparring so soon again, and Fahad took advantage of a powerful, but wide swing Tom made in an attempt to finish the fight quickly. Fahad tucked and rolled beneath the wild swipe of the blade and came up behind Tom. When Tom felt the point of Fahad's practice blade against his lower back, he froze. Surprise and anger flashed across his face as he lowered his own blade in defeat.

Mittman's face was flushed with rage that Fahad bested Tom so quickly. His long stride brought him to Tom in a matter of seconds. Their noses almost touched as Mittman began to rain abuse upon his soldier.

"That was a pitiful display. How can you call yourself a soldier? A milkmaid is more like. Can't even best a man who's been mummified in gold for more than two hundred years. I may as well strip you of your uniform and find you a dress."

Tom looked ahead, trying to keep his anger from his face. Marina could see his fists balled at his sides and hoped for his sake he could contain himself.

Fahad came to stand next to Tom and stopped Mittman with a quiet, "Sir."

Mittman turned his malevolent glare upon Fahad and moved to stand in front of him. "You have not been given permission to address me, soldier."

"Forgive me, sir, but I believe that had Tom been fresh for the fight, we would have been more evenly matched."

"You may keep your opinions to yourself," he turned to Tom again, "And you may take your worthless self around the practice yard. Perhaps running ten laps around the yard will make a man of you."

Tom nodded and began to run. Before he could go more than a few steps, Mittman stopped him with a hand on Tom's sword arm.

"Give me that weapon," Tom handed the sword to his commander and continued running as soon as Mittman released him. Mittman turned to face the rest of the men, leaving Fahad where he was.

"Since I obviously can't count upon any of you to best a former statue, perhaps I shall test his mettle myself." Mittman smirked at his own pun and enjoyed the laughter from those men who looked at Fahad as though he crawled from a pigsty.

The combatants faced each other in the center of the field. There was no circling or testing of skill. The action was sudden and violent.

Mittman attacked as soon as they finished saluting each other.

Fahad barely had time to bring his sword up to meet the quick downward strike of Mittman's blade. Wooden or not, it could have broken Fahad's left collarbone if he was a hair slower.

Mittman's attacks were fluid and precise. Fahad was agile, but Mittman's movements had more force behind them. Fahad was quicker, and at times it was only this that kept him from feeling Mittman's quickening offense.

Fahad was beginning to tire, and Marina could see that Mittman would soon win this fight. She cursed the inevitable and pressed a hand against her stomach. A knot of tension was beginning to build there, making her insides churn.

Mittman, seeing Fahad begin to falter, became cocky and started to lose some of his earlier finesse. It did not seem to matter overmuch, however, because Fahad's swings never had much finesse to them, and the speed that served him so well at the beginning of the fight was quickly waning.

The whole company gasped in shock when Mittman slipped for no apparent reason. Fahad, not fully aware of what happened, used Mittman's momentum to deliver a blow that sent Mittman sprawling to the ground. The company was eerily quiet in the aftermath and Marina could hear the two combatants breathing heavily. Marina felt her tension immediately disappear, which struck her as ironic given how tense the guardsmen were now.

Mittman's face was red, both from exhaustion and humiliation. When Fahad offered him a hand up, Mittman knocked the offending appendage away with his sword and picked his way off the ground under his own power.

Fahad nodded a brief salute and turned to resume his place with the rest of the guard. His back was turned, so he could not see the hate-filled glare Mittman was leveling at him. Marina was not sure that he would have cared had he seen it anyway. Fahad paused for a moment to look at the ground. Marina could not see what caught his attention, and she was surprised when he turned to look around the practice yard as if to catch her spying upon them. He frowned, shook his head as if denying something, and continued back to the edge of the field.

Marina was so caught up in puzzling over his behavior, she forgot to pay any attention to what Mittman was doing. So, when she felt something pull on her left foot, she was not prepared for it and came tumbling from her perch with nothing more than a startled yelp.

9

Forty-five minutes into their drive, Merry turned off the highway onto a two-lane road. They passed a sign reading: "St. Mary's Home for Lost Lambs: Left in 5 miles."

"Is this where you got me?" Kaia asked, turning from the window.

Kaia hadn't said much up to this point. Instead of asking more questions, Kaia spent the car ride contemplating what her mom told her so far. It turned out she could handle only so much shock in one day and she decided to save her quota for whatever was coming next. The last thing she wanted to do was pass out again. That was just embarrassing...and annoying.

"You make it sound like I got a puppy instead of a daughter...but yes. This is where you were living when I found you," Merry answered quietly. "When your mother crossed over, it caused quite a stir within the community of Kingdom-beings."

Kaia raised a pale eyebrow at the term. "I'm sorry, did you just say there's a community of Kingdom-beings?"

Merry smiled, "Yes, yes I did. I am not the only creature who has crossed the barrier. It is extremely rare, however, so it is a minuscule community. There are only fifteen of us in the Western hemisphere, and probably around thirty or forty in the Eastern. That's not even counting those who have been there since the shift. I'm not sure they really even count."

Kaia looked out of the passenger window for a few seconds to consider this.

"Why were you the one to find me?" she wondered aloud. "Didn't any of the others want me? Or, at the very least, want to find out what was up with me being here?"

"There were several who wanted you for their own. However, the nun who ran the orphanage at the time was...let's say, selective when it came to who got you."

Kaia was about to ask Merry what that meant when the orphanage came into view. It was a three-story brick colonial, a common sight in upstate New York. There was ivy wrapped climbing the front of the house, giving the structure a whimsical charm. It didn't look as institutional as Kaia imagined. Instead, it looked more like someone's ancestral home. Kaia didn't know why she expected something from a horror movie, though she suspected it was because she watched so many. However, she figured admitting that would cause Merry to give her that smug mom look.

The house was well-maintained and it looked as though the black shutters recently received a fresh coat of paint. The sun shone down on a scene of children playing in the grass behind a chainlink fence with two women watching over them.

One was a nun who wore a simple blue dress and white wimple. Her wizened face was alight with laughter as she watched a boy and girl play tag. This destroyed another of Kaia's illusions of the angry nun wearing her black habit. The other woman was wearing a black pantsuit and looked miserable in the summer heat. She was carrying a clipboard and trying to capture the nun's attention.

Both women looked up when they saw Merry's blue SUV pulling into the circular drive. A look of extreme annoyance crossed pant-suit-lady's face when the nun brushed past her to greet Merry and Kaia.

There was a small parking area close to the orphanage's double doors, and Merry pulled in next to a grey Prius. Considering it was the only other car in the lot, Kaia felt it was safe to assume it belonged to pantsuit.

The nun moved faster than Kaia thought nuns ever could and was waiting for them before they'd even unbuckled their seat belts. She was on the driver's side, so she greeted Merry first.

"Good afternoon, I'm Sister Mary Catherine. What brings you

lovely ladies to our home on this beautiful day?"

Merry shook the hand Sister Mary offered, and replied, "Hello, I'm Meredith Griffin, and this is my daughter, Kaia. We actually came to speak with you, if you've a moment to spare."

Sister Mary's ice-blue eyes sharpened at their names. She turned her shrewd gaze to Kaia, who had come around the front of the van to stand next to Merry. The nun raised an eyebrow at Kaia's bright purple hair and Kaia could swear her eyes literally twinkled with amusement.

"Give me fifteen minutes to get the children settled and I will be happy to meet with you. Please, go inside, and Suzy will show you to my waiting room." Sister Mary gestured to the double doors and smiled when Merry thanked her and began to walk away. Kaia hesitated before following, wanting to look at the children playing a bit longer.

"Really, Sister," pantsuit lady said, exasperation clear in her voice, "we need to get going on this audit. You have put us off long enough, and I'm not leaving until this is done."

Sister Mary's smile didn't waver as she said, "Lucky we have such comfortable beds, is it not?" Kaia smiled when the official gritted her teeth at the sister's rebuttal. Sister gave Kaia a conspiratorial wink and moved toward her charges.

"Kaia," Merry called, "come on. Let Sister Mary get her work done."

Kaia gave the playing kids one last look before following her mother. She wondered what it would have been like to be one of those children, growing up a Lost Lamb instead of with Merry. She had noticed some of the older children looking at Merry with undisguised longing and felt a deep sadness that they didn't have anyone like Merry.

Sister Mary seemed like a kind and loving woman, but her attention was split so many ways, it had to be difficult to give every child individual care. Kaia caught up with her mom and impulsively grabbed her hand. It wasn't surprising when Merry gave her a startled smile. Kaia rarely held Merry's hand in public and hadn't initiated it herself in longer than she could remember. Merry squeezed her hand and led them through the front door.

As soon as Kaia stepped through the oak doors, the last remnants of any thoughts that this place looked like a horror movie setting were sufficiently quashed. It was bright and comfortable, with artwork from several children covering any spare space on the wall. The art ranged from the crude abstract prints of preschoolers to some truly wonderful oil paintings and other mixed media.

The walls were curved to accommodate the double staircase that ran up the two walls. Beneath both sets of stairs, there were cutouts with wall hooks for coats and hats. Kaia could imagine the noise of this foyer when the children were getting ready for the day.

The stairs were a deep brown, but the decades' worth of scuffs and scratches kept them from looking oppressive. Instead, they looked polished and well-loved, like much of the house. The walls were a cheery blue around the drawings and paintings, and two bay windows reaching almost to the ceiling gave the whole foyer a pleasant glow.

Between the two staircases, there was a second set of double doors. These were open wide to reveal a living room area. When they entered, Kaia saw two doors leading to the right, and two to the left. Directly in front of them, there was a fifth door.

This one was also open, giving Merry and Kaia a glimpse of a large old desk. They passed through the gauntlet of couches, chairs, and tables to find a young brunette with grey eyes hidden behind thick black-framed glasses tapping away at her computer. Her face was tense and serious, but she softened enough to give them a polite smile. Her nameplate declared that Suzanne Phillips was guarding Sister Mary's office, whose door was directly behind her.

"Hello, ma'am," she greeted Merry, "How may I help you?"

"Hi there, we're here to speak with Sister Mary. She asked us to wait here until she could get the children settled."

"Of course. Please have a seat in our den." Suzanne waved them back to the door they just walked through. "Can I get you anything to drink while you wait?"

Merry and Kaia exchanged a glance before shaking their heads. Suzanne's question was polite, but the flat way she delivered it told them she really couldn't be bothered to play waitress.

"Thank you, we're fine," Merry said with a polite smile.

Suzanne nodded and turned her attention back to the computer. They sat in silence, listening to Suzanne tap away for about ten minutes before they heard a stampede of children enter the house and thunder up the stairs.

Kaia saw a few of them cast a curious eye toward Merry and herself. Some of the others had the same raw longing in their eyes from before. Kaia shifted uncomfortably at how easily that could have been her. Finally, Sister Mary walked through the door. She shouted good-naturedly at a couple of the children to slow down and did a wonderful job of ignoring the bureaucrat trailing behind her.

"Bless my soul," she exclaimed, "I'll never get used to all that energy my little lambs have stored in them." She grinned, and Kaia saw those cunning eyes twinkle again. "Please, allow me to show you to my office." She waved at them to stand and bustled to her office.

"Sister Mary, I really must insist we get this done as soon as possible." The woman with the clipboard snapped. Kaia had to admire her for her tenacity, but she was glad when Sister Mary just ignored her and sailed through the door as if the woman never said a word.

As they passed Suzanne's desk, Kaia heard the receptionist sigh and ask the pantsuit woman if she wanted refreshments with as much enthusiasm as before. Kaia tried not to laugh when the woman took Suzanne up on her offer and got another loud sigh for her temerity at interrupting Suzanne's work.

Sister Mary closed the oak door with a practiced flick of her wrist once Merry and Kaia crossed the threshold. She nodded toward the chairs in front of her wide mahogany desk to indicate they could sit down. As Kaia perched on the rock-hard wooden seat, she took in the nun's office.

It was extremely sparse, and except for the battle-scarred desk and chairs, looked like any other office with several filing cabinets and a basic computer. There were scattered pieces of children's art on the walls, a statue of Mary crushing the snake beneath her foot in a corner, and a copy of DaVinci's Last Supper on a wall. There were no knick-knacks or plants to give this space the same homey touch enjoyed by the rest of the house.

"I'm so glad to see you again Ms. Griffin," Sister Mary began. "I'm always happy to see how my children have gotten along in the world. I've been especially eager to see you given the unusual circumstances surrounding our lovely Miss Kaia here."

Kaia looked at her mother in confusion. Merry didn't look at her, and instead gave the nun a half-smile.

"Yes, I wanted to come sooner, but our schedule didn't really allow for it. In fact, we're in a bit of a hurry now. I was wondering if you had those items for Kaia handy. I know we agreed to give them to her on her eighteenth birthday, but we may need them sooner rather than later."

Sister Mary frowned in thought for a moment. Kaia wasn't sure what was going on, but she was suddenly very excited to find out.

"The Lord surely works in mysterious ways," Sister Mary finally said, "I wasn't sure why I had the sudden urge to move her belongings to my private safe, but I see now it was for this moment."

The nun pushed herself from her chair with a muttered groan. She took a step away from her desk before stopping, apparently remembering something.

"Not that I don't trust you, but please face the Virgin for a moment."

Merry suppressed a smile and turned to the statue of Mary in the corner. She twirled her finger at Kaia to indicate she should do the same. Kaia rolled her eyes and turned in her chair. As she focused on Mary's serene expression as she smashed a pissed-off snake, Kaia was listening intently to what Sister Mary was doing.

She was making a lot of banging noises around the filing cabinet areas, but there was also a softer sound, more like wood than metal. Then, she could hear a noise that reminded her of spinning the combination on her locker. Finally, there was the soft wooden sound again followed by a filing cabinet being opened and then closed.

"All right, you may face forward again."

Kaia felt like one of the sister's charges and realized this room wasn't as comforting as the rest of the house because this was where the kids went when they were in trouble. It made sense, really. What kid could feel comfortable mentally when their butt was falling asleep from the hard chair and they were sitting beneath the Virgin's benevolent, snake-strangling stare?

Kaia's mind came back to the situation at hand when she saw the paper bag and weird-looking letter in the sister's hands. The bag had something written on the side, but it was a little faded and she couldn't quite make it out. The letter had a broken wax seal and strange writing.

Merry took the letter when Sister Mary held it out. Merry turned it over in her hands a couple of times and gave the nun a significant look when she fingered the broken seal.

"Don't look at me like that," Sister Mary chided, "the police made a copy of the letter before they brought it to me. I'm a little surprised I got the original instead of the copy, so I suppose we may all count ourselves lucky in that."

"What does it say?" Kaia asked quietly. She was both nervous and excited about the letter's contents. It was the first piece of her past before Merry, but she wasn't sure if she was ready to read what was inside.

Merry frowned as she read the letter and looked up at Sister Mary in confusion.

"What language is this?" her voice was a little strained, and Kaia's heart sank at the question.

"I've never found out," Sister Mary sighed, "I know a few people from the nearby university, but they've never been able to figure it out. The closest we got was a variation on Ancient Greek, but it didn't match anything they had ever seen before. I think that little letter could have become quite famous if I hadn't sworn them to secrecy." She looked a little sheepish when she said that. "I wasn't entirely within my legal right to share that with anyone, and I'm lucky enough that the people I know are good at holding their tongue when necessary."

Merry smiled a little before looking down at the letter in her hands once again.

"I was really hoping this would help us," she murmured.

"Maybe the other item will," Sister Mary handed over the paper bag to Merry, and Kaia could finally make out the faded words. They said Kaia Dalton.

"Was that my mother's last name?" she asked before she could stop herself. Merry's hand tightened on the bag and waited for the nun to answer.

"No, my dear," she answered softly, "You were found in Dalton Park in town, so with no other name, I gave you that one."

"But, where did my first name come from?"

Merry answered this time, handing Kaia the letter.

"It was written on the letter. That's the only part I can understand, and even that was a little hard to read given the way it was written."

Her name was a mess of swirls and swoops. It looked like something a little girl would have written if she were familiar with the ancient writing contained in the rest of the letter. She would have continued to study her birth mother's handwriting if not for Merry's sudden gasp.

Kaia and Sister Mary both looked at her in alarm when Merry sprang from her chair and dropped the bag's contents on the desk. Her face was bone white and her eyes were taking on a yellowish hue. Kaia wondered if that ever happened before, but she never noticed because she didn't know her mother was a werewolf.

She looked at the bag and saw a gold necklace intermingled with the crushed paper. She barely heard Merry's strangled "No" as she reached out to pick it up.

The chain was heavy and old, and it carried an equally heavy and old amulet. The gold of the design was like fine wire wrapping around nine stones. The center was an opal with a brilliant fire of blue, gold, green, red, white, and the barest sprinkling of black. It looked like a picture of a nebula her science teacher showed the class last year. Kaia wasn't exactly sure of the names of the eight other stones, but they were in an alternating pattern of white, red, yellow, green, and black. There were two reds, yellows, and greens, but only one white and black.

The white was definitely a pearl, and one of the greens was jade, but she wasn't certain about the rest. Each of the outside stones were roughly half the size of her pinky nail, while the opal was almost the size of a robin's egg.

Kaia held the chain aloft, letting the amulet dangle. It turned and danced too much after being picked up, so she grasped the amulet with her other hand.

As she felt the pull of another vision, her only thought was: *seriously*?

10

Marina was not used to being manhandled. Curtis may have tousled with her many times over the years, but he never handled her as cruelly as Mittman was now.

When the Master pulled her from the tree, he let her hit the cold, hard ground. Not waiting for her to catch her breath, he jerked her upright by the collar of her coat. His hand banded her arm like steel as he marched her toward the line of soldiers.

Marina was a little afraid at the moment. While most of the time she would boast to her brother how much better she could fight than Mittman, right now his anger was palpable and she felt like she was dealing with an angry badger. She did not want to fight him in this state, especially because that could risk exposing her identity. She knew that was safe for the time being because there was no way Mittman would jeopardize his career by treating the princess like a low-born peasant. But if he realized who she was and revealed her, her mother would be furious if she found out Marina was running about in public in Curtis's old clothing.

"I seem to have found us a new recruit," Mittman snarled, "Perhaps we can teach this urchin how to go from spying like a coward to fighting like a man."

Marina kept her eyes focused on the ground to keep from looking at any of the men. They were silent, and she wondered if they were also a little afraid of Mittman's anger. Mittman shook her violently before pushing her away.

"Go on, you snot-nosed snoop, why don't you pick up a sword and show us what you know?"

Marina kept her eyes down and mumbled, "Sorry, sir. Didn't mean no harm in't." She tried to affect a dockside accent and knew she was failing miserably.

"I'll make you a deal," Mittman's voice was suddenly smooth and oily, "If you can best just one of my men, I'll let you go on your merry way. However, if you lose, I will have you in the stockade for the rest of the day." A few of the men laughed at what they saw as a grossly unfair deal. Marina seethed for a moment at the sound of their laughter before she counted to ten and calmed herself.

She was not sure how to handle this. If she lost the fight, her mother would eventually come looking for her. If she won, the man she fought would be humiliated if he found out he was beaten by a girl. If she got one of the laughers, she figured that was fair, but she also did not want to expose her skill.

She fought down her smile as she considered the best solution. Still looking at the ground, she nodded her agreement to the deal and flinched when Mittman forced the practice sword into her hand. It was clumsy compared to her own and did not feel as comfortable as her quarterstaff. For her purposes, however, it was perfect.

Mittman called to the smallest of the soldiers. "To keep it fair," he said with an evil smile. Marina did not feel comforted in the least. The man may have been short of stature, but the slabs of muscle in his arms declared that he would be a fierce opponent in a fight. Luckily for Marina, she did not plan to fight.

Once Mittman cleared the sparring ring, Marina grasped the awkward sword in both hands and raised it over her head. The men laughed again when the point of the sword bumped against her buttocks. Their laughter stopped, however, when she hurled the weapon at the bulky man before her. She stayed just long enough to see him throw himself to the ground to dodge the sword before she took off like a shot.

Her arms and legs pumped vigorously as she headed back to the stable. Mittman yelled for three of the men to give chase and Marina put on another burst of speed. She had forgotten about Tom, who was turning for his tenth and final lap. They almost collided, but Marina was able to execute a quick pirouette that kept her from hitting his solid mass.

Tom was so surprised, he stopped in his tracks and promptly lost his balance. Marina figured his legs must feel like boiled noodles after his grueling punishment. She should have felt bad, but she was just glad he had not stopped her.

She was well ahead of the men when she reached the stable. This was good. Because this was where her plan got sticky. If the stable was its usual bustle of activity, she would have run herself into a trap. If she was lucky, there would have been a mad rush for horses at first light this morning after yesterday's events with Wently and the council.

The stable doors were open wide, and she could see they were readying a horse for travel. The rider had not arrived yet, so she did not know whose it was. The stable hands gave her some surprised looks as she bolted past them to the back of the stable. Her luck was holding so far, as there were no servants in front of her. She chanced a look behind her and saw the men who were tacking the horse were now looking at the approaching soldiers. They gave her a nervous glance, looked at each other, and unanimously decided that their job would be much easier if they took it outside.

Marina's face lit with a feral grin as she reached the tool rack and wrenched it open. One of the hay forks shifted, but otherwise, the tools stayed where they were. She quickly darted through the small opening she made and closed the door behind her. She tried to be careful about putting the door back and winced when the fork fell to the stable floor. Her best hope now was that the men who chased her weren't smart enough to put two and two together.

The men ran into the stable seconds after she secured the door. She had to stay to see if they would discover her secret. It would be awful if anyone else discovered the passages mostly because Curtis would never forgive her. Two of the men were part of the group that laughed at her and did not seem to like Fahad. The third was actually Fahad himself. She caught her bottom lip between her teeth, surprised and a little worried. This man could definitely add, and he already had some knowledge of the passages thanks to her late-night visit a couple of days before.

The first two men swore in frustration over her escape. They did a cursory check of the stalls surrounding them and one of the men actually discovered a hole at the back of one of them. They must have thought it big enough for her to get through because they went running from the stable to chase nothing.

Fahad stayed behind and surveyed his surroundings a little more closely. He picked up the hay fork, and Marina's stomach sank a little bit. She knew she was done for now, and waited with dread as he approached the tool rack. He replaced the fork and narrowed his eyes at the rack. After a few moments–during which Marina dared not to even breathe or blink–Fahad turned away and exited the stables. Marina sank against the nearest wall and finally breathed and closed her eyes.

"Well, that was too close for comfort," she whispered to herself. As she walked down the dark tunnels, she decided her curiosity about Fahad's sparring abilities was thoroughly satisfied. She sadly would not be sneaking out to see the men practice ever again now that her disguise was worthless.

The poorly sprung, open wagon swayed wildly from side to side, causing Wently to hit the wall hard. He cursed and tried to right himself, only to fall sideways when the wheels hit another deep rut. This jarred his injured arm and he held it against his chest tightly, moaning in pain.

He cursed the people who brought him this misery; first among them, Princess Marina. If the stupid bitch just came to heel as he expected, none of this would have happened. He had spent years of planning his ascent to the throne, and it had all been ruined in one night.

Wently had spent every waking hour since his youth planning his rule. His family was so far from the line of inheritance, the first plan had been to marry Marina. While the idea was distasteful when she was a knobby-kneed and ugly child, she had become beautiful seemingly overnight.

Of course, as the princess's husband, he would not have been much closer to the throne. She had three brothers to get out of the way first. Antonio, as the heir to the throne, was to have been the first casualty of Wently's success.

Wently traded with the Borderland mercenaries to kidnap and kill the prince during the upcoming fall festival. There was only one more meeting left to finalize the plans, and now Wently would not only miss his final payment, but the damnable mercenaries would keep the obscene amount of money he already paid.

Benedict would have been far easier to get rid of. As a captain in the Jamarian navy, a death at the hand of pirates would be easily accepted. In fact, Wently had not even made official plans to assassinate Benedict in the hopes that his dangerous lifestyle would save Wently the trouble—and the gold.

Curtis should have been either the easiest to kill. Wently never saw him do more than dance or flirt with the women of the court, so he was sure he could have easily hired a gang of miscreants to murder the boy. However, the idiot was never alone. He was either constantly surrounded by his friends or by women. Wently did not necessarily care about collateral damage, but he did think whomever he might have hired would charge more for Curtis's hangers-on.

Yet the thought of all of his plans crumbling brought him right back to the princess. Even if his plans had not been ruined, he would still want to murder the wench. The entire court saw him humiliated at the hands of that strip of a girl, and he would find a way to revenge himself upon her if it was the last thing he ever did.

The wagon lurched to the side again, breaking Wently's internal rant and bashing his head into the unforgiving wood. "Must you hit every damnable rut in this road?" he screamed.

One of the guards riding beside the wagon looked at Wently with repulsion. Wently fumed over the commoner's audacity to look at him with anything but the respect and deference due to someone of his station. He finally managed to work his way back to a sitting position when the driver veered slightly and they hit the worst rut yet. This nearly sent Wently tumbling over the side of the wagon. The guard who gave him that derisive look laughed along with the five other guards and driver at the former earl's discomfort.

Wently would have shouted at their insubordination, but a cry of warning from the lead guard made him hold his tongue.

"There's something ahead," the lead guard warned his men.

The men all drew their swords and the wagon stopped. Three guards stayed with the wagon while the others went ahead with great caution. Wently turned and propped himself up a little higher on the side of the wagon to see what was going on.

There appeared to be a young woman sitting in the middle of the road. She was filling a nearby basket with apples that had fallen around her. One of the guards approaching her sheathed his sword and pulled his horse to a stop. As he dismounted, Wently could hear him say, "Here, girl, let me help you with that."

Those were the last words he spoke. The woman stood abruptly when he was within an arm's length of her and stabbed him with a long knife previously hidden in the folds of her skirts. The other guards reacted quickly, charging forward on their steeds. Their leader made a swipe for her neck and was unprepared when she dove to the ground, rolled, and came up beside him. She drove her knife between his ribs and pulled it out again smoothly before throwing it between the eyes of the next rider.

The guards beside Wently rode to the aid of their comrades, while the driver quickly abandoned his seat and ran for the forest. The woman picked up one of the fallen guards' swords and was facing off with the three remaining men circling her.

"Put the sword down, woman, and face the King's justice," one of the men demanded. Wently fell back in disbelief when the woman lashed out with her sword and took the man's head from his shoulders. She was so fast, the man's expression never changed even as his head rolled on the ground.

The last two guards, seeing their friend beheaded, charged the woman together with matching battle cries. One man swung for her neck while the other swung for her middle. The woman dropped her sword and executed a neat backflip, leaving the men cutting at nothing but air before hitting each other. The man who swung for the woman's neck hit his comrade just under the helmet. There wasn't enough momentum behind the swing by the time it hit the other man's neck, so the blow was not clean enough to sever that man's head from his shoulders. Meanwhile, his comrade gave him a blow to the hip. With the light armor he was wearing, the hit was debilitating, but not deadly.

He looked on in horror as his friend died from the fatal neck wound he caused. The sword fell from his suddenly limp grasp, and he momentarily forgot about the woman. That brief inattention cost him his life. While he looked at his friend in disbelief, she retrieved her knife from between the eyes of the first guard and came up behind the last man. Even though she was easily half his weight, his distraction gave her the advantage she needed to grab his helmet, pull his head back, and slit his throat.

Wently let out a fearful whimper as the man's hot blood spurted into the air. He leaned his ear against one shoulder while holding the other with his only hand, trying to block out the horrifying gurgle coming from the dying man.

As the woman calmly wiped the blood from her knife, Wently began to move toward the back of the wagon. The guards had left it open this whole time, not worried he would try to escape from a moving vehicle. Now, however, was a perfect opportunity.

He slid toward the back, keeping his eyes on the woman. She was looking at the dead men as if making sure they would not rise unexpectedly. He dared to look away when he reached the edge to see what he was doing. When he turned back to look at the woman again, his heart almost stopped when he saw that she was gone.

He whipped his head around again and saw her standing directly in front of him. Nothing could have stopped the girlish scream that ripped from his throat. He cowered in fear and waited for her deadly blade to descend upon his unprotected flesh. Her kind smile left him gaping like a stunned fish.

Neither of them spoke for a few moments as Wently tried to get his bearings. Now that he was no longer in mortal peril, he could study the woman more carefully.

She was probably a head or two shorter than him and built like a voluptuous goddess. Her breasts were full and straining against the soft wool of her low-cut red dress. Her long, lustrous, dark brown hair was swept back from her face, setting her full lips and large dark brown eyes off to their best advantage. Her skin was the color of soft cream, and her lips stained a beguiling shade of red.

She was a woman made for passionate nights, and Wently could feel desire quickly replacing his fear. His pulse jumped in anticipation when she stepped closer and wrapped the red-tipped nails of one hand around his neck. Fear now mixed with desire as he vaguely wondered if she was going to choke him.

"Come," she purred, her lips deliciously close to his ear, "My master awaits your arrival."

Wently could only nod dumbly as she led him from the wagon and helped him mount one of the fallen guards' horses.

11

Kaia was in a cavern with eight other people. Some light streaming in from a couple of holes in the rock bounced off mirrors spaced around the structure to light the whole room. The mirrors were still insufficient to lift the gloom, so the rest of the illumination came from torches spaced at even intervals around the cave walls. The space was almost perfectly circular, and a short stone object stood in the center of the room. It looked like either an end table with a slight curve to it or a really shallow bird bath.

The eight people in the room moved to surround the table in a coordinated action. Kaia stepped back toward the wall before she remembered they weren't really there. Or she wasn't. She still wasn't quite clear on the semantics of her visions. The people stood around the tabletop and each placed something at the edge.

Kaia stepped closer, trying not to touch the burly man and thin woman on either side of her. She lost focus on the table for a minute when the woman caught her attention. She had pointed ears and yellow cat eyes. Like, they were literally the eyes of a cat. Her olive skin shone in the mirror light and her green eyes glowed. Her outfit was something out of Marc Anthony and Cleopatra. Though she had Elizabeth Taylor beat by a mile. Kaia shook her head in disbelief before looking down at the table again. She didn't really recognize what was on it before.

"Son of a..."

The table had a circle in the middle with eight lines shooting out to the edges. It looked like a child's drawing of the sun or a spider that met an untimely end from a book. Each wedge had intricate designs carved into them, and each also had a precious stone the size of a half-dollar in a groove made just for that stone.

The woman with cat eyes motioned to a doorway at one side of the cavern, and Kaia saw a man approach them. He had shoulder-length red hair with a silver crown nestled among the curls. His chest was bare and his lower half was covered only by a shimmery loin cloth that appeared to be made of fish scales. A silver band wrapped around the bicep on his right arm, and in his hand was the amulet that sent Kaia into this vision.

He handed Cat Lady the amulet and bowed to her before stepping back against the wall. Kaia was surprised to see the opal in the middle was a milky white without any of the fire she just saw. The woman placed the amulet in the middle of the circle and the other seven people with her all placed their hands upon the stone they had set on the table. Apparently, Fish Scales wasn't part of the sharing circle.

The other seven who were part of the group were evenly spaced around the altar. Six were men and there was only one woman other than the cat lady. Kaia felt like there was sexism happening here, but she didn't have time to dwell on it because she didn't know how long the vision would last. Kaia circled the table and gave everyone a good look.

The woman next to Cat Lady was dressed in something that looked like a Roman dress, her mane of curly auburn hair was done up in the most complicated French braid Kaia had ever seen. On her left was a larger Asian man whose style reminded her of the movie 47 Ronin. The original, not the Keanu Reeves version. She like that one too, but...Kaia shook her head and tried not to get distracted.

To Cat Lady's right was a tall, burly man wearing a blue tunic and tan pants covered with fur-covered boots. His white-blonde hair was covered with a metal helmet. He looked like a Viking and she wondered if the hammer at his feet was for the aesthetic or actually a weapon.

Beside him was a tall, Indigenous man with black hair down to his waist. His clothing looked like tanned hide with the most amazing beadwork on the top of the tunic. He was bouncing slightly on his toes like he was a kid hyped up on sugar. Everyone else was stoic, but he looked like he was one second away from either laughing or running around the room.

He was sandwiched between two Vikings. The guy on his other side was wearing an outfit similar to that of the blonde dude, but without the hammer or helmet and with thick black hair. He was next to a short, stocky man with curly black hair. What really stood out, though, was the prosthetic right leg he was rocking. Everyone was wearing outfits that looked centuries old, but this guy's leg was some kind of copper alloy that looked centuries ahead of what Kaia's world had to offer.

The final guy was another, shorter, Indigenous man. His outfit was absolutely the best out of the group. He had markings on his face that were either amazing makeup or the world's coolest tattoo. His hair was done up with bright feathers and his outfit was a long tunic with a plated collar. Polished stones were set into gold jewelry throughout the ensemble. Gold cuffs circled both wrists and went halfway to his elbow.

Kaia stopped admiring the guy's fit when the Egyptian-looking woman began to chant and the others joined in. Kaia strained to listen to the words. She was very proud of herself when, for once, the words were not muffled. However, she was disappointed when she realized they weren't speaking anything close to English.

"Crap, just when I was starting to get a handle on this whole vision thing, another wrench gets thrown into the works."

Kaia forgot her annoyance when she noticed that the carvings in the stone began to glow an eerie blue. The gems sparkled and shimmered from the reflected glow. When Kaia looked at the amulet, however, it seemed to be absorbing the light instead of reflecting it. In fact, the longer the chanting went on, the darker the amulet became. It was as if it was creating a black hole centered on the opal.

As the chanting began to grow louder, the carvings and stones glowed brighter. Finally, it became so blinding that Kaia had to look away. She was glad she did so when the room flashed with blue lightning and the chanting reached a deafening roar.

When she opened her eyes, she saw the gems on the table reflecting a blue glow that came from the amulet gems instead of the carvings. The light was transferred to the amulet and shone from the gems set into the gold webbing.

The cat-woman reached for the amulet and picked it up carefully. She looked as though she was prepared to be burned, but was pleasantly surprised when nothing happened. Now that the cavern was quiet, the glow was beginning to fade from the amulet. The opal, once that milky white, now sparkled with the colors she saw before the nun handed her the amulet.

"Do you think it has worked?" the burly man with the awesome leg asked the cat-woman.

"I think your metal works have proven your skill once more, Vulcan. Whether the spell works or not can only be tested. Coyote," she turned to the excitable Indigenous man across from her. His smile turned shifty--as if he was about to do something horribly funny, or possibly just plain horrible. "As you have many lives to give--even more than I--this council asks that you attempt the crossing.

Coyote blinked out of existence, and Kaia gasped in amazement. She wasn't any less amazed when he suddenly appeared again, but closer to the woman who seemed to be running the show.

"I can run through all the worlds, except Fourth World," he told them. When a couple of the people looked confused, he yipped with laughter and said, "There are too many names for the place for all the deities here. How about the place we're all trying to leave? Does that work for everyone?"

Apparently, it did, because the whole cavern breathed a sigh of relief. Coyote cocked his head to the side and studied the amulet.

"Are you sure this thing will stand the test of time, Kitty?"

The woman's nostrils flared and her pupils became vertical slits of annoyance. Though the woman never moved, Kaia felt an overwhelming sense of power as the woman's presence seemed to grow until Kaia thought it would break the walls of the cave.

"I am the Lady Bast, and you will address me as such. Just because you do not stay dead does not mean I will not enjoy snuffing out your insignificant life several times over."

Coyote grinned and clearly enjoyed getting Bast's back up. Bast shook her head, making her silky black hair undulate like an inky river as she release some of her power along with her anger.

"As to your question, Trickster, there are always holes in any spell that one may not foresee. I only know that what we have wrought here is a thing of permanence. If any god, human, or other creature should ever try to reverse this spell, it could doom both worlds."

Everyone shifted uncomfortably at the thought. Kaia wasn't sure what exactly Bast meant, but the woman's words sent chills up and down her spine.

Bast walked over to the man who handed her the amulet earlier. "Guard this with your life, Neptune. The fate of two worlds now depends upon its protection."

Neptune bowed and turned from the room without ever making a sound. Bast looked at the small assembly of people before she turned her gaze in an unlikely direction. Kaia felt her heart stutter when Lady Bast's yellow eyes met her own.

"Let us return home," Bast said softly.

Kaia's vision began to blacken around the edges, and she could feel herself returning to the present. Her eyes fluttered open and she became aware of a throbbing in her hand.

When she looked down, she realized she was gripping the necklace so tightly her knuckles were white. She opened her fingers slowly and allowed Merry to take the amulet away from her. Merry pinched the gold chain as if it were contagious, dropped the amulet back into the bag, and shoved the bag in her purse.

"Kaia, are you all right, my child?" Sister Mary asked softly. She gave Merry an odd look, but schooled her expression and focused on Kaia.

"Oh, yeah, sorry I'm fine," she shook her head and stared at her palm. The amulet was face down and her palm was now sporting red marks from the impression of the gold wire. She recognized the pattern from the stone table. The amulet was designed to look exactly like a miniature version of that table, and Kaia suddenly realized that the stones matched the positions of their larger counterparts.

"I've had children go spacey on me before, but never quite to that extreme," Sister Mary said with a slight chuckle. She still looked a little worried, but she knew better than to press the matter.

"Thank you, Sister," Merry said. She stood and held her hand out to the nun. Sister Mary looked a little surprised that their interview was over so quickly, but she took it all in stride.

"You are both quite welcome," she smiled at them both benignly, but Kaia caught another worried look in her eye. "Before you leave, might I have a chance to say goodbye to Kaia alone? I know you're in a hurry, but I'd like to catch up with her quickly before you leave."

Merry looked at Kaia and raised an eyebrow as if to say: Do you want to stop and chat with the nun? Kaia thought about it for a second before nodding to her mother.

"Of course," Merry finally replied, as if Sister Mary hadn't seen their silent exchange, "I'll just be out in the den. Please do hurry though, there's somewhere we need to be."

Sister Mary nodded and walked Merry out. When she closed the door, she motioned to Kaia to sit down again. Kaia did and waited for Sister Mary to sit as well. She was a little surprised when the nun sat beside her instead of returning to her seat behind the desk.

"Kaia, I'm so glad I was able to meet you," Sister Mary began. When Kaia began to return the compliment, the sister waved her hand to stop Kaia's words. "That being said, there is something I did not tell your mother."

Kaia looked at Sister Mary expectantly, but the older woman looked like she was working herself up to something big. Kaia wasn't exactly sure she was ready for more revelations.

"I am actually from the Kingdoms myself."

"God dammit."

Kaia was surprised when the nun laughed at her blasphemy instead of grabbing the nearest ruler. Sister Mary shrugged at Kaia's surprise.

"Yes, I'm sure you are shocked. Even your mother likely doesn't know. I can tell she's a werewolf, but even her nose is unlikely to guess what I once was."

"And...what were you?"

"A mermaid."

"What the actual f–"

"No more of that. I know. Another bit of fantasy added to your life. But, it's how I recognized where you are both from. It's also why I know that amulet is important."

"Yeah, I'm starting to get that."

"What I really wanted to talk to you about is your forthcoming journey."

"What–?"

"There is no doubt in my mind you will go to the Kingdoms. If not now, then in the near future. But I don't want you going without one warning."

Kaia leaned forward at Sister Mary's earnest look. The nun clasped Kaia's hands in her own before she continued.

"There are many wonderful things in my world. But so many dangers as well. Be very, very careful whom you trust."

Kaia nodded. She didn't have any words. Eventually, the nun stood and encouraged Kaia to do the same.

"I hope the things your mother left you help you."

"Wait, if you're from the Kingdoms, can't you translate the letter?"

"I'm sorry, Kaia. I don't know any of the written languages of the Kingdoms. I wasn't interested in things like that when I was younger. And by the time I made it to this world, it was all I could do to learn English."

"Oh, well that sucks."

Sister Mary chuckled and put her hand on Kaia's hair. She smiled kindly and led Kaia towards the door. "I'm sure your mother will do whatever is within her power to keep you safe. That's part of the reason I agreed to your adoption, despite my qualms about sending you to a werewolf's household. I could tell from our first meeting your mother would be a force to be reckoned with should anyone or anything seek to harm you. I can't tell you how glad I am to have been proven correct."

Kaia grinned at the nun's characterization of her mother. She figured at least part of that protective instinct came from Merry's werewolf side, the rest was all Merry.

"However, you have a difficult road ahead of you. I will be praying to the Blessed Mother and Saint Christopher that you remain safe in your travels."

"Thank you, Sister, I appreciate the good thoughts," Kaia replied.

The nun nodded and bid Kaia and Merry a fond farewell. As they left the orphanage, Kaia could see the woman with the clipboard once again bearing down on the wizened nun. Kaia smiled at the thought of how that small and weak-looking frame housed a fiery spirit and almost felt sorry for the uptight bureaucrat.

When they were buckled into their seats, Kaia turned to Merry. "Where are we going?"

"For now? Massachusetts. After that? I'm not entirely sure."

"Well isn't that just unhelpfully mysterious?"

Merry just smiled and started for Massachusetts.

They drove for six hours, only stopping once for lunch. Merry didn't want to waste any time, so they ate their McDonald's in the car. Kaia was unused to that kind of luxury, considering Merry hardly ever let anyone bring food into the car, let alone eat that food.

She was napping when the feeling of the car slowing to a stop woke her. They were only stopping at a stop sign, but Kaia stayed awake.

"Are we there yet?"

Merry glared at her, and Kaia smirked. Even though she knew her mother hated the battle cry of road-weary kids everywhere, she couldn't help throwing it out there whenever possible.

"We'll be there in about twenty minutes."

Kaia nodded and watched the trees fly past her window. The sun was low in the sky behind them. It wouldn't set for another couple of hours, but the trees were beginning to obscure its light.

"So, tell me again why this Lisa chick doesn't like you?"

Merry sighed in exasperation, "I've said this at least fifty times, we had a falling out and we haven't spoken since."

"Yeah, but what did you fall out over? Was it a guy?"

Merry stared straight ahead and didn't say a word.

"No way," Kaia gasped in shock, "you lost your friend because of some dude!?"

Merry's mouth tightened at the corners, "I never said she was my friend, I just said she helped me out a lot when I first got here."

"But you weren't friends? Then she must feel a big connection to other people from the Kingdoms to help you out with nothing in return."

"Who says she got nothing in return?" Merry asked, aiming a glare at Kaia, "I gave her all kinds of news about the Kingdoms. She hadn't set foot in our realm for almost four hundred years before that. I thought it was a fair trade for setting up my new identity and a little money to get me started."

"Really? You got a way to start a new life, and all she got was some news about how things were going back home. How is that a fair trade?"

"Well, as an advisor to the Jamarian court, I think you could say my information was a little more precious than that of your everyday Kingdom dweller."

Merry sounded unbearably haughty when she said that, so Kaia had to throw salt on the wounds.

"And then what? She stole your boyfriend?"

Merry began to blush a little with shame. "Actually, I think I stole hers."

Kaia's mouth gaped open like a hooked fish. Merry's blush intensified as she rushed to defend herself.

"I didn't know he was Lisa's beau. She always stuck to the East Coast, and I was living in Montana at the time. How was I supposed to know she had dibs on the druid? And anyway, who ever heard of a kelpie dating a druid? Those stupid men are strictly tied to the land!"

Merry was beginning to sound indignant, and Kaia was starting to wonder how long it might take to outgrow high school drama. This sounded just like when Amanda accidentally 'stole' Debbie Carter's secret boyfriend. No one knew she was dating Simon, but Debbie freaked out all the same when Amanda kissed him.

"Did it ever occur to Lisa to be mad at the druid, not you?"

"She was mad at both of us. I'm still not even sure how she found out. But one minute I was...um...talking to Liam, and the next a white horse was barging into the room and carrying him off into the night. It wasn't until the next day that Lisa came back and told me she never wanted to see either of us again. I thought she meant I needed to stay away from her, but when she tried to kill me, I figured later there was a reason Liam never contacted me again."

Kaia wasn't sure what to say to all of this. Especially when it sounded like Merry and Liam had been doing a lot more than talking when Lisa barged in on them. And that was just too gross to contemplate.

"Umm, mom?" Kaia finally said after a few minutes of silence, "How can you be sure we can trust this woman given your not-so-great history?"

They were driving through a town called River Brooke. The outskirts of the town gave off a quaint, country feel, while the street Merry was driving down looked like time and people forgot about it.

All the buildings were brick with chipped and crumbling mortar. Kaia had seen old brick buildings before that contained bright veins of white where someone swooped in and saved the decaying building from further disrepair by replacing the old mortar with new. None of these buildings had those startling shocks of white to show that someone, anyone, cared what happened to these crumbling structures.

They pulled up to one of the buildings just off the square. An old battered sign declared they were about to enter The Ruedan's Haven. As they got out of the car, Merry finally answered Kaia's question.

"I'm not exactly sure we can."

12

Marina thought she would be the first person to the breakfast table, given her early morning activities. She was not expecting to find Curtis there, nearly decimating the bacon tray.

"Hey, brat," he said around a mouthful of the meat.

"By the gods," she replied in revulsion, "did you not learn anything from our etiquette teacher?"

Curtis swallowed and grinned, "Only that if I'm to be improper, I should choose a time when I am mostly alone. Given that you don't really count as someone I wish to impress with my good manners, I feel that if you're offended, you may go lick a toad."

"I would," she shot back, "but I do not wish to lick any part of you. I've no idea where you have been."

Curtis stuck his tongue out at her, which she ignored in favor of putting food on her plate. Curtis left her alone for a few moments, though Marina suspected that was more so he could shovel more food into his mouth than any courtesy to her.

When he seemed satisfied, he leaned back in his chair—another breach in their etiquette training—and asked, "So, why are you up so early, Brat?"

Marina kept her eyes on her plate and tried to ignore him once again.

"If you don't tell me, I may be forced to ring for the palace physician. I've never seen you awake this close to the dawn for anything less than extreme illness or something incredibly exciting."

Marina moved her eggs around with her fork, trying to come up with something that did not sound as pathetic as watching Sir Fahad from a tree. She nibbled on a piece of bread to keep her mouth occupied.

"You know, I did hear some very interesting news from one of the palace guards," Marina choked on the bread, but Curtis kept going as if he did not notice. "It seems that some boy was caught spying on the training for the new recruits. They were going to punish him, but he ran away. Then, he just vanished...in the stables...near the back..." Curtis folded his arms over his chest, pretending an innocence Marina knew could not be trusted.

"Any idea who that could've been?" he asked playfully.

"I am afraid not, it could have been anyone." When Curtis just cocked a disbelieving eyebrow, Marina muttered, "Anyone with extensive knowledge of the secret passageways, that is."

She could not stand his teasing grin, which caused her to blurt out, "Not that it is any of your business. I may do as I please. If I wish to spy upon the Guard training, then that is my right. Besides, sometimes it is a welcome change to see some good fighting for once."

Curtis scowled at her biting remark and was prepared to snap out a rejoinder when the door to the dining room crashed open, hitting the wall.

A servant looked around the room wildly before gasping out, "Pardon me, Your Royal Highness. Where might I find the king?"

Marina looked at her brother in fear. Only a great emergency would cause a servant to burst in like a wild thing.

"I believe he is still in his private chambers," Curtis told the servant. "What is going on?"

The servant only said, "Urgent news," before dashing away. In unspoken accord, Marina and Curtis sprinted after the servant. The three of them ran through the castle, causing the servants and nobles they passed along the way to either cry out in alarm or quickly back against a wall to give them room.

The King's guards blocked the servant's path when he reached the wing designated for the royal family. The servant was winded and could not immediately speak when one of them asked, "What business have you?"

Marina wanted to shake the servant to get his answer out faster, but she restrained herself. After gulping air for a few seconds, the servant finally gasped out, "Urgent news...for the king...Lord Wently..."

He did not say anything else for a moment as he stopped to try and catch his breath. Marina's blood went cold at the mention of Wently. Her mind jumped to several conclusions about how the servant would end his sentence. She was both expecting and dreading what the man said next.

"He has escaped."

Marina was beginning to grow weary of hiding out in secret passageways. Though she loved that she was able to do so, she really wished that she did not have to use them with such frequency. It would have been greatly preferable to be sitting next to her parents and Antonio as they discussed what was going on.

"Move over," Curtis whispered, "I can't see anything."

"Why does that matter?" Marina hissed, "Just stay quiet so we can hear what they are saying."

They each made a gruesome face at one another and tried to stay as quiet as possible.

"He could not have done this on his own," the queen said. She repeated this phrase several times. Antonio and the king both nodded, as they did every time she said this.

"The question is not whether or not he was helped, the question is: who helped him?" the king asked, turning to Antonio.

Antonio had an extensive network of sources and spies. Marina was amazed that she and Curtis were able to get away with anything, but she supposed the youngest members of the Royal Family were not high on Antonio's list of priorities for intrigue.

"According to my sources, we may be dealing with the sorcerer known as Nightshade."

The king and queen both drew in sharp breaths at the name. Marina looked at her brother for an explanation but he stared straight ahead with a stony expression. Marina guessed he knew something, but she was not sure if he would be telling her later or not.

"Was it him, or one of his servants?" the king asked Antonio.

"It was one of the servants. Based upon the driver's description, we believe it was Snow White."

Marina was now completely confused. Snow White was the name of one of the legendary princesses in the Kingdom's histories. She shared her status with names like Cinderella, Aurora, and Ariel. However, all these great women died long ago. Marina wondered at the idea of an evil sorcerer giving his servants the names of women who stood for good.

"How many soldiers did she have with her?" the queen took her turn asking.

Antonio looked uncomfortable when he answered, "According to the driver, there was only the woman."

"One woman took out six armed guards?" Marina bristled at the tone of disbelief in her mother's voice.

"Perhaps she is a Duran Death Dancer," the king suggested. Marina felt Curtis stiffen next to her and flashed him another questioning glance.

"What?" he hissed.

"Nothing," Marina answered quickly, turning her attention back to the conversation.

"That is likely," the queen responded. "That is the only fighting force at the moment that employs female fighters."

Antonio looked uncomfortable again when he disagreed with their mother, "Actually, I have heard that the Kenterians have allowed several women into their ranks within the last couple of years. The newest president has taken a favorable stance upon women becoming equal to men."

Marina waited for her mother to show some sign of displeasure, and was pleasantly surprised when she heard, "Well, I always did think President Franklin was a forward-thinking man. I was quite surprised when he passed the law allowing all citizens to vote, including women and lower magical creatures."

The king looked at his wife in surprise but covered it quickly when she turned to look at him.

"Jonathan, what should we do about this situation? I do not know what Nightshade wants with that horrible young man," Marina swallowed a huff of laughter at Delia's opinion, which changed so drastically within two days, "but I can assume it is nothing good. Either for our kingdom or any of the rest."

The king nodded and clasped his hands behind his back. Marina thought of this as his classic thinking pose.

"Antonio," her brother stood a little straighter at the sound of his name. Marina was surprised his spine did not snap, as Antonio already had exceptional posture. "I believe we should make the most of your network of informants. Whomever you can get in Jamaria, as well as however many of your international spies you can induce to follow this trail. I will go through our more official channels to see if the other kingdoms will assist us in capturing this fugitive."

Antonio bowed slightly to show his agreement. "If I may, father, mother, I will leave immediately to attend to this."

When their father nodded, Antonio walked quickly from the room.

"My dear," Marina heard her father say quietly, "you must not worry about Marina." At the sound of her name, Marina gave an involuntary jerk "We cannot know if this is the work of Nightshade or not. Antonio's spies have been known to be wrong before."

The queen wrapped her arms around her middle as if to ward away a chill. The king wrapped her in a hug from behind her and rested his cheek upon her head.

"But never about the important information. When it is something this serious, Antonio is always sure to bring us the most accurate information."

The king turned his wife to face him and stared into her eyes. "Be that as it may, we must remember that Marius has not discovered the truth these seventeen years. Perhaps we can hope that Marina's mother was wrong. Perhaps he will not find his children. Perhaps the fate she described can be avoided."

Marina felt all the breath leave her body. Her father's words made no sense to her buzzing mind. Her mother was standing before him. Why would he speak about her as if she were not there?

"Do you think we were wrong to keep her true nature a secret? What if we could have prepared her better for what may come?"

Marina only dimly felt Curtis grip her arm and begin to pull her away. He was not fast enough to keep her from hearing what the man she had called 'father' all these years say, "We may not be her parents by birth, but she has always been the daughter of our hearts."

Curtis dragged her away without a whisper of protest from her lips. She could barely breathe, let alone beg him to stop. But he did. They were high above the other inhabitants of the castle, as they halted in an abandoned turret. The direct route was sealed off centuries ago, and could only be accessed by the secret passages. Marina and Curtis created their own haven away from their daily lives years ago. But it did not feel safe at the moment.

Marina dropped down onto one of the old cushions they purloined from a guest room long ago and hugged her knees to her chest. Her entire body felt numb except for the burning knot in her stomach as she tried to process what she overheard. For once, she wished she never found the tunnels throughout her home. She could never unlearn what she had just discovered.

Curtis was pacing back and forth in front of her, running his hand through his curls over and over again. It was as if he thought he could pull the answers from his head one tug at a time.

"I am sure we heard them incorrectly," he burst out, stopping in front of her. "Perhaps they were...speaking of another Marina."

Marina finally looked at him, raising an eyebrow in disbelief. "Another Marina? Why would another Marina be the daughter of their hearts? Curtis, they were speaking of me. We both know this to be true."

She stood abruptly, suddenly needing to move. The turret room was small and with both of them pacing it felt claustrophobic. She felt as though something was boiling inside of her, trying to get out. "Why does this have to be true?" she screamed.

Curtis looked stunned by her outburst. But neither of them was prepared when a dense fog began to form and swirl around them. Marina was too upset to really absorb what was happening, but Curtis' cry of alarm caused her to snap out of her fear and rage. She turned to take in the moisture surrounding them. It was so thick it was difficult to even see Curtis who stood mere inches away.

"What...what is going on?" Curtis shouted.

"I do not know," Marina sobbed. She was not sure when she began crying, but the tears were falling fast and hot. The fog was getting denser, and she did not know what to do other than stand there.

Finally, she heard the sound of glass breaking and felt the hot summer air blow through the turret. She tried to catch her breath and calm her thoughts. The fog was slowly moving out of the room, dissipating as it hit the sun.

Soon, the room was clear once more. Curtis was standing near the window staring at her. He looked a little scared, and Marina did not know how to react to that. She never knew Curtis to be scared of anything.

"Marina," he finally gasped out, "are you well?"

Marina could not help the hollow laugh that escaped. "No, I am most definitely not well. I may never be so again. My life is a lie, and I may never hear the truth. How can I look at them again, Curtis?"

He flinched, and Marina was not sure if it was a reaction to her question or the raw pain in her voice. He took a hesitant step toward her, and Marina could not stop herself from hurling her body into his open arms.

Though Curtis was away at school for much of her life, he was always the brother to whom she brought all of her troubles. How could she face the idea that he never was her brother at all?

Curtis seemed to read her mind, "No matter who your parents may be, you will always be my brat of a sister," he whispered hoarsely into her hair. "You will be my sister until all the kingdoms fall, and no one will ever hurt you as long as I am here."

Marina closed her eyes and let her tears soak his shirt. Her heart lifted somewhat at his words, but she knew that he could not stop her heart from breaking. No matter how many bones she had broken, or bruises she had received, nothing had ever hurt as much as her parents'--the king and queen's--words.

Or at least, that was her thought before a more terrible, physical pain than anything she ever imagined or experienced pulled at her middle. She felt as though she was being pulled, pushed, squeezed, and stretched all at the same time. Her whole body went rigid, and she could only watch without comment as the fear returned to Curtis' eyes. She could see his mouth forming her name over and over again, but she could not hear it over the roaring in her ears.

It felt like it lasted both a lifetime and half a second. Finally, it was over, and she could breathe again. Her body shivered in reaction, and she was glad that Curtis had been holding her up.

"Marina," his voice was a bare whisper, "are you all right?"

Marina would have smiled at the idiotic question that she was hearing for the second time only moments apart, but the residual pain was too great to think of ever smiling--or possibly ever moving--again.

Curtis lowered them both onto the nearest cushion and cradled her in his arms as he would a child. He stroked her hair with one hand and waited for her to answer him.

"Curtis," she rasped out, barely able to hear her own voice. He leaned closer to hear her say, "something's coming."

13

"Mom, are we going inside sometime this century? You may live forever, but I don't wanna spend my next few birthdays waiting for you."

Kaia hiked the backpack her mother insisted she carry with her when they left the car up a little higher, trying to relieve the tension it was causing. It mostly carried clothing and some of the survival gear Merry had shoved in there.

Merry pinned her with an annoyed look before taking a deep breath and opening the door. Kaia was hit instantly with the smell of old books. It smelled of aging paste and paper, and a little bit of earth. There was also something else mixed in with these comforting aromas that Kaia couldn't quite identify, but could tell Merry did by the way her nose crinkled in distaste.

Someone coughed heavily from somewhere in the back of the store, but Kaia couldn't see anyone. The room was dark and the bookshelves were positioned with only enough space for one person to walk through at a time. Kaia figured it required some intimate contact with the books if two people needed to pass by one another. She was all for reading, but the thought of getting that up close and personal with a bookshelf made her feel a little claustrophobic.

Kaia wondered how her mom was holding up in such a confined space. She figured werewolves needed open spaces to feel comfortable if the little Merry told her on the drive was any indication.

"I'll be with you in a second," a voice came from nowhere and everywhere at once. It was raspy and deep, like a woman who had been smoking since birth and didn't care how many surgeon generals told her she should probably stop. There was a slight lilt to her voice as well, telling Kaia that this woman once lived somewhere in the British Isles a long time ago. "What can I help you ladies look for today?"

Kaia looked at Merry in confusion. "How does she know we're chicks? Or that there's more than one of us?" She looked around the ceiling to see if there was a hidden security camera. She thought businesses had to tell patrons when they were on CCTV, but maybe this woman was too old to know better. Then again, maybe the kelpie who owned the place didn't care about laws in general.

"Don't worry," Merry said calmly, "Lisa has a sense of the dramatic in situations like this."

"There are situations like ours?" Kaia never claimed to be good at hiding her emotions, so she didn't even try to hide the disbelief underlying her sarcasm.

"Ah, I smell a wolf among us." Kaia jumped when the raspy voice came up behind her. She looked around quickly to see a bent and wrinkled old woman with iron grey hair and rheumy blue eyes. She looked like a clichéd old woman, not at all like someone who could have snuck up on two alert women. Especially when the only way she could have gotten behind them would have been to either come in through the door or jump one of the waist-high bookshelves on either side of Kaia and Merry.

"Good afternoon, Lisa. I see your bookshop is doing...well. And I must say your newest look is quite...stunning."

Kaia figured Merry meant it was 'stunning' to see that the old woman hadn't caused herself to go blind with all of the bright 60s-style prints she was wearing. She was one psychedelic old lady. She definitely didn't know how to dress her age if the hip-hugging bell bottoms were any indication. Then, Kaia realized she had her mom called the woman Lisa. She was twice as confused as before that some mythical creature would wear something that audacious. It also seemed a bit odd that the kelpie wasn't aging too well.

"Heh heh. My wee tame wolfie, I always said it was a good thing they turned someone with a hint of diplomacy." Lisa's nostrils flared as she leaned in closer to sniff Merry. "And still keeping to that odd non-human diet, are we? 'Tis a wonder you haven't wasted away to nothing after all this time."

She clicked her tongue disapprovingly at the fact that Merry wasn't eating humans, and Kaia had to suppress a horrified giggle. Bad enough the old lady was a horrible dresser, now she was sniffing Kaia's mom and subtly suggesting Merry start chowing down on the local population.

Kaia apparently hadn't suppressed the sound well enough, because Lisa's suddenly sharp eyes were now focused on her. Those eyes, which Kaia originally thought were blue, seemed to go straight through her soul. Their color constantly shifted between the hazy aqua of a tropical sea to the deep green-black of kelp. Kaia was captivated and couldn't have looked away if the books of this small shop tumbled and buried her alive.

Lisa broke contact first, looking somewhat contrite. She bowed her head and held out her hand for Kaia's. Kaia looked at Merry for approval, who nodded. Kaia extended her hand carefully into Lisa's surprisingly firm grip. The older woman's hands were warm and rough with hard use.

"I apologize, cousin. I didna know you were one of us, though I should have assumed as much what with that one bringing you to me." Lisa tossed her head in Merry's direction without looking up from the floor. "May I gather your scent? I wouldna take yours without permission, us being related and fair being fair." Kaia looked at her mother in confusion once again, but this time there was no nod. Merry shrugged as if to say the choice was Kaia's. Kaia was wishing she asked a little more about what a kelpie was before she answered.

"Uh, yeah. I guess that'd be fine." Kaia barely uttered these words before Lisa crowded into her personal space and took a huge whiff of her neck and hair. "Jeez, lady! Get out of my bubble!"

Lisa wasn't listening to her anymore, though. Her eyes were staring slightly above Kaia's head and had taken on a milky-white hue. "Child of Yara, inheritor of the sea. But your blood has been tainted, defiled by a human sorcerer. Conceived in hope and love by your mother; avarice, malice, and trickery by your father. Your path will be shared with another, thusly conceived and birthed under a dark moon as you were birthed under the full. You bear your mother's shame and your father's quest for power. Tread lightly young one, for the path is full of danger and you may be alone far longer than you anticipate. Do not fear the darkness within you, but let it be your strength in the dark."

Lisa finally released Kaia's hand, leaving Kaia feeling like a boat with nothing anchoring it to the dock. Merry put a firm hand on Kaia's shoulder, grounding her again to the present.

"That was creepy." Kaia was trying to joke about it, but it still didn't feel funny to her. She was trying really hard not to freak out, curl up in a ball on the floor and start crying like a baby. She hoped she didn't look that weird and frightening when she was in one of her visions.

Lisa looked a little ashamed of herself when she said, "Sorry, cousin. I never know when I'm going to get a flash of insight. I don't think I've had such a strong one as that since I tried to tell that nice boat captain to beware of what lies beneath the surface. The bad thing about insight like that is that it doesn't make much sense until you're in a lifeboat, watching an 'unsinkable' ship go down in freezing water." Lisa shook her head in remembered regret that she wasn't able to stop anything.

"Are you talking about...?"

"Stupid iceberg ruined 1912 for me."

"Wow, so you're, like, really old then."

Merry squeezed Kaia's shoulder, trying to get her to stay quiet. Lisa looked amused, however, and just nodded her head.

"Aye, my dear. After more than six centuries, you could indeed say I am 'really old.' Not that you'd believe it by how young I look."

Kaia couldn't help but raise an eyebrow at that. Lisa may not have looked her six hundred-plus years, but she didn't look like a hot young thing either.

Lisa frowned at Kaia's disbelieving look and turned to look at the door behind them. She gasped in surprise when she caught a look at her reflection.

"Well bollocks. I forgot I had this face on today." Lisa was engulfed in a sudden mist that caused Kaia to jump back in surprise. Within seconds, the mist completely cleared, leaving a woman in her mid-twenties staring at her reflection in the door's window. Her iron-gray hair was now a dirty blonde wave down her still psychedelic back. But at least now the clothing made a little more sense on this younger woman's 5'6" toned frame. Kaia saw that the ever-shifting eyes were still on display when the new Lisa turned around again. Lisa pouted newly plump lips on her otherwise plain, thin face, looking mildly upset.

"You said I looked stunning, Merry. I thought you were commenting on the new hair color I chose for myself."

Merry looked at Lisa's hair and shrugged. "I'm sorry, Lisa. I figured you knew what you looked like. That and I don't really see a difference in your hair color. It looks the same as it did a hundred years ago."

Lisa spun back to the window and rasped a curse under her breath. The mist was back again for a split second, leaving Lisa with dark brown hair when in dissipated just as quickly.

"How did you do that?" Kaia gasped.

Lisa laughed, "Dearie, I'm a kelpie. A distant cousin of your kind."

Kaia looked at her mother in confusion. "What kind am I?"

"I'm not sure, sweetheart. That's not actually why I brought you here. But we have time to get some answers. As far as I know, there's no hurry for getting you back to Jamaria."

"That's where you're wrong, old friend," Lisa interjected, "We need to get her moving as quickly as possible. There're people waitin' for this wee one. But dinna fash yourself, lass. I'll answer your questions while we work. It'll take at least three hours to get everything prepared for your journey through my gate."

"What gate? What are you both talking about?"

Lisa ushered them out of her way so she could lead them through the maze of shelves. Kaia found out she was correct about getting intimate with the shelves and it was just as uncomfortable as she dreaded. When Lisa finally squeezed past Kaia she answered while she strode ahead.

"The gate to our world, child. Or did you really think you were human through and through? You're the child of a Nereid, or what the mortals here call a sea nymph. You've got a bit of human in you, dinna get me wrong, but it's far overpowered by your Nereid roots."

Kaia was starting to feel dizzy from all of the information and the labyrinthine shelves. "I'm a sea nymph?"

"Only half. Just like one of those slutty gits to get pregnant by an evil sorcerer." Kaia frowned at Lisa's casual slut shaming but decided not to interrupt for now. "Humans here may think my kind are evil, but they never really give any thought to just how stupid sea nymphs can be. Always too caught up in romance to really think about the consequences. Your father may be a mite evil, but at least he gave you, and hopefully your sister, some brains."

Kaia stopped abruptly, causing her mother to almost run into her. She gave fleeting thanks for her mother's wolf reflexes before the shock caught up to her.

"What do you mean, sister? I don't have a sister."

Lisa turned around an annoyed look on her face. "Listen, if we're going to keep stopping every time I give you a startle, you're never going to make it to the Kingdoms in time." Lisa spun back around and continued her quick stride to their mysterious destination. Once again, she answered as she raced forward, never losing breath or pace.

"I may not always understand my visions, but I do get the major points. Your mother's name was Yara, and she's one of my cousins from the sea kingdom. I don't know who your father is, but my Sight gave me a pretty good sense that he's a bad man.

"When I said there were two of you conceived the same way, I figured you've got a sibling out there. I can still smell her a wee bit, which tells me you've a twin. I mostly assume she's a lass because it's the way my mind works."

"Just keep breathing, Kaia," Merry murmured. "I know it's a lot to take in, but you need to process it and keep moving. Lisa's our only hope for getting you to the Kingdoms, and Jamaria."

"But, you've already said you don't trust her. What if we end up dead or something?"

"She's the only reliable way to and from the kingdoms. She is mercurial, like most immortals, but she promised Liam that no one would come to harm from one of her gates, and I trust her promise to him. He was the one who created the gate and put her in charge of it."

"Keep up, lassies. Time is short and you've places to be." Lisa's voice seemed further away, and Kaia picked up her pace. She thought she lost Lisa for a moment before she saw the flash of color that was Lisa's wardrobe. "C'mon, lass. You can't be done with your questions."

Lisa stopped her near sprint in front of an old wooden door, carved with an intricate design. Kaia felt like the trip took way too long for what she imagined was the minuscule size of the bookstore. Then again, if Lisa was hundreds of years old, maybe this was less a bookstore and more a collection. For all Kaia knew, Lisa may have expanded into some of the other buildings on the street, causing some of the abandoned appearances. That was one question Kaia didn't really feel like asking, so she left that answer to her imagination.

"What, exactly, is a kelpie? I've heard of them before, but I've never really known what they were."

Lisa's eyes lit up at the prospect of talking about herself. "Well, humans only really know kelpies as fairy folk who can shape-shift into beautiful horses that drown and eat unsuspecting travelers. Some believe we can shift to human, but they only talk about the unbelievably gorgeous men who seduce pretty humans. They completely forget about the fact that there might be women too—mostly because we're never as pretty as the men." Lisa shook her head at the injustice. Whether that came from thoughtless humans or the fact that men were better looking than women in their species, Kaia didn't know and was afraid to ask after the 'drown and eat humans' part of the story.

"Why is there a gate to another world in the wilds of Massachusetts? Shouldn't we be going to Stonehenge or something like that? I would at least think we'd be going to the pyramids in Egypt"

Lisa scoffed at Kaia's questions. "Oh, lass, those structures have long since been abandoned as access points to the Kingdoms. Too many tourists have made it difficult to slip into the secret passages that lead to the actual gates. Nothing like having some stupid person snapping away with their camera to ruin a perfectly good secret."

Lisa finally reached for the old brass door knob and opened the door.

"This gate was constructed in the 12th century. That was long before Columbus sailed the ocean blue; back when this land held a bustling community of Naumkeag. The man who built this door came over with some Vikings and decided to stay once he found this passage to the Kingdoms. He only built a small cottage 'round the door to stake his claim upon it. The Native people were afraid of him, as anyone would be of a great druid. They called him the ageless one and held the land around us as sacred. When those stupid witches started creating problems in the 1690s, he kept to himself and became just another hermit in the woods.

"By the time I arrived here around 1790, a town had sprung up around him and he was established as a rich man who owned most of the town buildings. I recognized him at once for what he was. He left this collection of stores around us so I could keep the gate safe in his absence.

"Little did either of us know, his absence would last much longer than anticipated."

Lisa stroked the carvings on the door lovingly. Based on Merry's stories, Kaia was a little creeped out by Lisa's last declaration. But she couldn't help taking a step closer to see the design. When they first walked up to it, the carvings looked like some kind of floral design. Now, Kaia could see tiny scenes of people dancing, fighting, laughing, relaxing, kissing, eating, and basically going about their daily lives. The details of their faces, clothing, and body language were amazing.

"How did he do this?" Her awed question was barely a whisper. "And how are we supposed to travel anywhere?" The second question was more audible when Lisa opened the door and Kaia finally got a look at where the door was leading them. It looked like someone had dug into the side of a hill and only left enough room for two or three people to squeeze in.

"I've the same answer for both questions." Lisa's ever-changing eyes held amusement. "Magic, my love, makes my world go 'round."

Lisa laughed as she ushered Kaia and Merry into the hole. Kaia could see that someone had placed stones on the floor with more intricate carvings. These, however, looked like words in some language Kaia couldn't understand. They began at the left edge of the door frame and circled around in a tightening spiral to the middle. As Merry and Kaia turned to face Lisa, the words began to glow an eerie blue one letter at a time. Merry gripped Kaia's shoulders tightly and Kaia looked up at her mother to see why. Merry's face was a mask of anger as she stared back at Lisa. Kaia gasped when she saw Lisa gripping a gun aimed at Merry's chest.

"I promised Liam no one would ever come to harm in my gate. I never promised I would send you to the proper place. I do apologize, cousin, that I am delaying your journey, but I did leave you enough time to find your way if you've a mind to."

"I thought you said it would take three hours to prepare the gate," Merry spat as the glow from the stones spiraled closer to the center.

Lisa shrugged and waved the gun toward the stones. "Sure and it did, Merry m'love. But my Sight told me an old enemy was approaching two days ago and I knew I'd need to have the site prepared. Lucky for Lady Kaia there, the preparations stick for some time."

Kaia's jaw dropped in shock when Lisa smiled at her as if waiting for a thank you from her even with the gun pointed at her mother.

"But...but why are you doing this?" Kaia could barely get even that simple question out around the lump of fear in her throat. Even knowing the story Merry told her, Lisa had been nothing but kind to them so far.

"Because," Lisa's eyes were now a stormy blue-black as she stared at Merry, "your mother ruined everything for me. I loved Liam more than anyone I've ever known, and he gave up everything for her. He could never love me back because Merry got in the way. He made me promise I wouldn't kill her, but I won't have to lift a finger with where you'll be going."

With that declaration, Lisa threw the door closed and the words on the floor brightened. Merry hugged Kaia to her as the room went completely and blindingly white.

Kaia felt as though she was being pulled, pushed, squeezed, and stretched all at the same time. She heard her mother scream her name and felt the loss of Merry's arms around her. Kaia tried to scream back but felt like all the air in her lungs was being pulled out in a rush.

Eventually, there was a terrible loss of all sensation before it felt as though she finally came to a rest. Her senses were reeling, and she had no idea where she was other than someplace hot and dry.

14

Curtis helped Marina to her room after their odd experience in the turret. Neither of them said a word throughout their trek through the castle walls. When they finally made it through the tapestry in Marina's room, Curtis broke the silence.

"I think we should tell mother and father what happened."

Marina walked stiffly to her vanity and sat down. She did not want to acknowledge how much it hurt to hear him say mother and father and know that they weren't hers. Even though she knew Curtis still thought of them as theirs, they could never really be hers again.

"We do not have to tell them what you overheard if you wish, but we need to tell them what happened in the tower."

Marina looked at her reflection in the mirror, studying her pale and taught face. She looked as though she had missed a month's sleep instead of the few hours that morning.

Could that have only been a few hours ago? It was barely ten in the morning, but it felt like she had been awake for days. Her adventure this morning seemed pale and fruitless in light of everything that happened so recently.

"Marina," Curtis pleaded, "please answer me."

"No," Marina said, her voice hollow, "It was probably nothing. The king and queen need not hear of a hysterical child's excitement. They've much more pressing matters to attend to."

She looked at Curtis' reflection and saw that he badly wanted to argue with her. "Curtis," her voice was sharper than intended and she strove to modulate her tone, "cease your worry. It has been a trying morning for us both. Please, let me rest and gather my thoughts. I believe I shall keep to my rooms today."

Curtis still looked as though he wanted to disagree, but she turned and gave him a pointed look. He shook his head in distress, but finally acquiesced to her wishes. When he pulled the tapestry aside to walk through the door, he could not stop from making one last appeal. "Please, Marina, let me help you."

Marina gave him a sad smile. "There are some things that even you cannot fix, Curtis. Please, just go."

Curtis nodded in defeat and disappeared. Marina sat there for a long time, not really knowing how much time passed before Hilde came in to check on her.

"Ah, here you are, child. Your mother has been beside herself with worry. You didn't come down for luncheon, and we all know how you enjoy Cook's roast pheasant."

Hilde's broad and normally infectious grin began to fade as she took in Marina's wan expression. The kind gnome placed the back of her hand against Marina's forehead and frowned with worry when she felt the clammy skin.

"My poor wee one. Whatever is the matter with you?"

Marina tried to smile in reassurance, but could not muster the strength to move her face.

"I am fine," she said with absolutely no conviction, "I just do not feel much like eating at the moment."

Hilde's expression took on a whole new level of alarm, and Marina wondered if her heart was truly broken when even that didn't elicit the slightest smile from her. Usually, that kind of terror on Hilde's face gave her a mischievous sense of glee. However, it did not seem all that funny at the moment.

"Please, Hilde, I do not wish to be disturbed at the moment."

"But, milady—"

"In fact, I believe I would like to be alone for the rest of the day. Please tell my...mother not to worry, I am just over tired today. Perhaps it is a delayed reaction to the events of the last two days. I am sure I only need some rest to get me back to my old self."

Hilde did not seem convinced, and Marina wondered how she came to be surrounded by so many stubborn people. Before Hilde could form a suitable argument, Marina grabbed her hand and squeezed it tightly. "Really, Hilde, just leave me to my rest and I will be well by tomorrow."

Hilde's mouth compressed into a mutinous line, but she relented when Marina finally worked up the strength to give her a reassuring smile.

"As you say, milady. I will check up on you first thing in the morning. If you've not regained your former vigor, I know some wonderful gnomish recipes that will have your hair standing on end."

Hilde's grin was back, and Marina found herself giving her sweet but confrontational maid a shadow of her true smile. As Hilde was making her way toward the door, Marina was struck by a horrible and draining thirst.

"But first," she burst out, almost causing Hilde to fall over in surprise, "could you bring me a pitcher of water?"

Hilde nodded, giving Marina a strange look as she slowly closed the door. Marina walked to her study and poured some water from the pitcher that was already there and slaked the dryness in her throat. It did not completely help, but it did at least dull the feeling.

She closed her eyes and focused on the strange sensation in her stomach. A dull pulsing had taken up in her belly ever since the initial pain hit her. It was strange, but also oddly comforting and familiar.

The pulsing grew slightly stronger when she started walking to the east, and she wondered what would happen if she followed this pull. Her eyes snapped open at the thought.

It was such a simple yet complex question. Normally, she would never think of doing something as bold as following some odd sensation to whatever was beckoning her. But the morning's events caused something inside her to shift. She did not know if it was her sense of self or if there was a greater problem on the horizon. All she knew at the moment was that her parents' conversation had left her feeling stormtossed and a little reckless.

A knock at the door slowed her racing thoughts and she turned to see Hilde returning with the pitcher of water she had requested. The thirst had diminished to the point that she no longer felt a pressing need to down the entire thing, but she was grateful to have more.

"Here you are, milady. Will there be anything else?"

Marina thought for a moment before saying, "Actually, I believe I am already feeling a little better. Could you send someone up with a food tray for me? Please include enough for supper so I shall not be disturbed for the rest of the night."

Hilde looked happy to hear Marina's request and hurried to carry it out. Marina watched the woman scurry away and waited until she was safely out the door before moving to carry out the plan beginning to form in her mind.

The packing would not take much time, for there were only three outfits she would be taking with her. The first set was easy to choose, as she had a small stack of Curtis's cast-offs stored just inside the secret passage's entrance to her room. Luckily for her, Curtis was always an athletic boy who grew quickly, which meant there were several old outfits from his youth that were still in good repair. Marina was also lucky Curtis anticipated her need for men's clothing when she started begging for fight training when she was only five years old.

The second set was a bit harder. While she had many options when it came to Curtis's cast-offs, many of them were of too fine a quality. The last thing she wanted was to attract attention by looking like a nobleman's son. She felt confident in her fighting skills but did not wish to court thieves and kidnappers. It would take far too much time and effort and she did not feel like she had either to spare.

The clothing she wore at dawn was wrinkled from being thrown in her wardrobe when she dressed for breakfast. This might have caused her some pause at any other time, but she figured her clothing would be more convincing for a commoner at this point if it looked a little more lived-in.

She debated with herself for a few moments about whether or not she should take any female clothing before deciding it might come in handy. There were rare instances where being a woman alone could work to her advantage. She added a simple skirt and blouse the queen commissioned when Marina begged to learn how to garden a few years ago.

Marina ignored the pang that struck her heart when she thought about how delighted the queen had been when Marina presented her with the first rose from Marina's personal garden. They both laughed when Curtis stole the flower, caught it between his teeth, and began to dance with the queen. They laughed even harder when Curtis stabbed himself in the lip with one of the thorns.

Marina balled the skirt up and threw it into the oilcloth bag she was using, not caring it would end up just as wrinkled as the shirt and trousers from the morning. When she heard a knock at the door, she quickly stowed the bag under her bed to hide what she had been doing.

She tried to sit casually on the mattress as one of the kitchen maids placed the tray Hilde had sent up upon a table in Marina's sitting room and curtsied to excuse herself.

As soon as the maid was gone, Marina ran to the food and began to fill her hollow belly. She never even noticed her hunger before the smell of roast pheasant had reached her nose. Now she was glad she sent Hilde for the meal. As it was meant to last until supper, Hilde loaded the tray with far more food than Marina could eat. In fact, she probably would not even be able to finish the tray for supper either.

Marina smiled at her good fortune, for this meant she would not have to steal nearly as much from the larder as she had intended. She hoped that Cook would not notice the missing food in that case. Then again, she knew Cook watched her larder like a hawk, so it was still a slim chance.

Knowing her best opportunity would come around midnight or later, she lay down to sleep, hoping the building excitement and that feeling in her belly would not keep her awake for too long.

The castle was in an uproar the next morning, and Fahad could see that Mittman was close to pounding the next person who gave him a bad report. The princess's disappearance was discovered only ten minutes ago, and no trace could be found.

Her maid, Hilde was sobbing uncontrollably in the chair next to the girl's fireplace, and Mittman was not able to hide his displeasure at dealing with the woman's hysterics.

"Cease your noises, woman," he snarled, "and tell us what you know."

Fahad almost laughed at the fierce scowl the gnome fixed upon the Master of the guard. She looked as though she was ready to pound someone too, and if Fahad were a betting man, he'd put his money on the gnome.

"I've already told you," she snarled back, "I've no idea where the princess might be. She sent me away yesterday complaining of not feeling well, and I--stupid woman that I am--listened to her." She finished this declaration with a keening sob that made everyone in the room wince.

Gerard felt especially pained, given his sharper hearing. He didn't understand how one woman could make such a terrible racket. The king and queen were standing near the window and he could smell their worry and fear. The king was trying to hide it, but the queen was wringing her hands as tears ran down her cheeks. Her legendary composure had abandoned her when she discovered Marina was missing.

Gerard wondered if his suspicions about the secret tunnels were correct and if there was an entrance here in the princess' room. He closed his eyes and inhaled deeply, trying to sift through all of the scents currently surrounding him to find the unique fragrance of Marina. She always smelled of the sea, despite almost never leaving the castle, and as he predicted her scent permeated the room.

However, he was able to pick up her most recent movements if he concentrated. She had made several movements between her wardrobe, her table where the empty food tray rested, and her bed. Focusing on the smell of the roasted pheasant, he began to move toward the tapestry beside her bed.

Before he had taken more than two steps, Curtis moved in front of him. Gerard's eyes opened slowly as he gave Curtis a curious look. The others in the room were ignoring them, save for Fahad, who was taking a keen interest in Gerard's movements. Only Gerard and Fahad noticed the subtle shake of Curtis' head. Gerard turned back to face the king and queen and cleared his throat to stop Mittman's futile interrogation of the sobbing maid. The monarchs gave Gerard an expectant look, and the king held out his hand to permit him to speak.

"Your Majesties, I believe I may be able to follow Marina's scent and find out where she has gone, but I need to be alone. I cannot currently distinguish between the many scents within the room."

The queen stopped crying immediately and regained her composure long enough to issue a command, "Everyone, leave this room at once. Leave Gerard to do what he does best."

Everyone began to file out under the queen's watchful gaze. Gerard put a hand on Curtis' shoulder when he tried to leave as well. The queen looked at them curiously and Gerard gave her a small smile.

"I believe he may be of some help, Majesty. I ask that he be allowed to stay."

The queen nodded solemnly and began to leave the room as well. She stopped before she crossed the threshold and walked back to Gerard. She took his hand in hers, startling him, and stared deeply into his eyes.

"Find her, Gerard. Whatever happens, you must find my daughter and bring her home safe."

Gerard bowed to the queen and murmured, "I will."

She nodded again, this time with great dignity, and finally left the room. Once she was safely gone, and he could no longer hear anyone loitering in the hall, he turned on the prince.

"Where has she gone, Prince?" He tried not to growl, but even royalty needed to be scared sometimes. He was not truly worried for the princess, because he knew Curtis was training her in combat. And if the boy was not a Death Dancer, Gerard would eat his own tail.

"I'm not sure, but I know how she got out of the castle."

Gerard did growl this time, his impatience with the prince growing. "I know she used one of the secret passageways, I just didn't know there was an entrance in her room." He ignored the prince's surprised look and went on. "I don't care about how she got out, I just want to know which exit she left from."

Curtis looked down at the floor, somewhat ashamed that he had been so worried about protecting the secret he and Marina had been keeping for so long. It was not that he cared more for the tunnels than his sister, he just knew that when he found her, she would tear his throat out if she discovered he told anyone.

"I cannot be certain. I would have thought the stables, but Oasis is still in her stall, so she probably would not have bothered exiting from there. It is normally the busiest location in the system." Curtis looked excited as he realized where she would have gone. "She must have taken the forest exit. It leads directly to the west entrance of the Rejos Forest. That site has the least amount of traffic."

Gerard nodded abruptly and started for the door. He stopped

without warning when he sensed a movement to his left. Spinning, he found Fahad stepping out from behind a window curtain. Gerard let loose a stream of expletives that had Fahad grinning and Curtis suppressing his own smile, knowing it would not be a good idea to further antagonize the wolf.

Gerard wasn't sure if he should be impressed with Fahad's spying skills, or angry at his own lack of vigilance. He settled for both and decided to direct his anger at Fahad. "Well, aren't you impressive? Who decided you were exempt from the queen's orders and invited to join this conversation?"

Fahad leaned against the window sill and gave Gerard an even look.

"I knew something was going on, and I decided to discover what you two were up to. Don't take it as a sign of mistrust, but I didn't figure you were necessarily willing to keep me in the loop. We've only known each other for a few days, and while I think we may someday be friends, I could not wait for you to learn to trust me."

Gerard settled for merely growling at the man instead of conceding the point. His estimation of Fahad rose when the man chuckled at the sound instead of cowering or even flinching as most would. He then marched from the room, going to see if he could pick up Marina's scent in the forest. The other two men followed behind him at a somewhat more sedate pace.

"Do not worry," Curtis assured Fahad, "I am sure that was a growl of affection."

Fahad raised an eyebrow at the man beside him.

"No, really," Curtis deadpanned, "an angry growl sounds completely different and causes a sudden and unpleasant moisture in your undergarments."

Fahad snorted in amusement at the thought and kept following their lupine guide.

15

The buzzing in Kaia's ears would drive her crazy if it didn't knock it off soon. She was lying on her back on something incredibly hot and gritty and her arm was being pulled at an odd angle by her heavy backpack. It had somehow been pulled from one of her arms and caught in the crook of her other elbow.

When she opened her eyes, the bright light of the sun dazzled her, worse than the blue light that had sent her here. Kaia hoped her brain hadn't been scrambled by that crazy lady's closet.

"Mom," she called out, still not completely able to see more than a blinding white all around her. When Merry failed to answer, Kaia began to get nervous. She slowly rose to a sitting position, disentangling herself from the backpack. Leaving it on the ground, she stood up and willed her eyes to adjust to the light. Her surroundings came into focus, but there wasn't much to see.

She was in a desert full of rolling white hills. The sand seemed to reflect the sun's light, making the sky such a light blue, it may as well have been white too. After turning in a circle, Kaia realized with dawning horror that she was completely alone.

"Great," she forced the tears burning behind her eyes to stay where they were. She couldn't waste the water and she didn't want to give in to her fear.

"Mom!" She hoped Merry was just over the next dune. "Mom,

where are you?" She waited in silence, barely daring to breathe as she yearned for a response. The only answering sound was the slight breeze kicking sand over the dunes.

Kaia could feel the panic welling up inside of her. She slowly lowered herself back to the ground and brought her knees up to her chin. The heat from the sun was becoming more uncomfortable by the second as it pounded down on her bare head. She pulled her bag to her and began to search through it, only stopping for a second to look at the torn strap on one side.

"Okay," Kaia always felt a little better when she talked to herself, "Obviously the heat and sun are my first problems. Thank God mom had me pack this bag, 'cause I've got a shirt in here that'll let me go Lawrence of Arabia on this mother."

Kaia pulled out the long-sleeved white T-shirt she packed in the event they were going somewhere kind of cold. She tried to wrap the thing around her head as best she could, using the sleeves to secure it in place. The lightweight cotton was stifling, and she wasn't sure why this was supposed to be a good idea. But if the people in desert movies used the technique, who was she to question desert survival tactics?

She felt like a brimmed hat would work better to protect her from the sun, but for one thing that had never been her style. For another, she didn't have one, so there was no use in wishing for it now.

Her mouth and skin were already beginning to feel dry and she began to worry about how quickly she was becoming dehydrated. The very air seemed to be drawing the moisture from her body each second. She searched her pack again and found a water bottle. It was empty, and she barely refrained from throwing it as far as she could in frustration.

"At this rate, the desert might kill me in an hour, and who knows how far it is to the closest water source. Not to mention I have 360 degrees of directions to choose from, and no idea which one won't kill me. Or which one will kill me the quickest."

Kaia could feel the burn of tears against her eyes again, so she gritted her teeth and squeezed her eyelids shut. As she sat there, becoming more despondent by the second, she felt something brush the edge of her awareness. She wasn't sure what it was, but it gave her a sense of peace, and cool refreshment, like an icy glass of water on a summer day.

She stood slowly, slinging the backpack over her shoulder by its only good strap. Keeping her eyes closed, she took a halting step in one direction. The sensation decreased, so she changed to another direction until she got a hold of where that sensation was coming from. When she got her bearings, she began to plod methodically onward. She knew if she stopped for any reason she wouldn't be able to work up the motivation to move again.

Her eyes stayed shut, not only because it helped her stay focused on that feeling of coolness–or even to save her eyes from the sun. She kept them closed so she wouldn't have to face the unending landscape. She figured if anything tripped her or smacked her in the face it would certainly force her to decide whether or not she was dreaming.

After what felt like hours, Kaia became aware of two things: first, that the quality of the air she was following had abruptly changed; and second, that there was a faint rumbling ahead of her. It was like an extremely quiet stampede, but when she opened her eyes she discovered it wasn't quiet because of distance. Kaia didn't know if what she was seeing was a mirage, a thirst-induced hallucination, or actually real. The creatures bearing down upon her were a hideous combination of men and spiders, and they were huge.

Even though Kaia wasn't necessarily afraid of spiders, that didn't mean these things didn't freak her out to no end. Their bodies were about the size of a smart car, with legs that looked like they could stretch to about seven feet apiece. Where most spiders had those segmented eyes, these creatures had the upper body of men. Kaia wasn't sure which sight she found creepier.

They stopped almost ten feet in front of her, and she noticed that several of the spider men had bows and arrows drawn and aimed at her. Four of them were threatening her with deadly weapons, while the other three just gave her steely looks. Her mouth was feeling especially dry at this point, and she couldn't even work up a squeak of fear.

The creature in the middle crept forward until he was standing a few feet from her. He lowered his body until it was a few inches from the ground, so his head was only a foot taller than her instead of five.

"Who are you, and why are you on Krax'mran land?"

Kaia opened her mouth, but no sound came out. The movement irritated her dry throat, and she began to cough uncontrollably. She fell to her knees, trying to catch her breath.

Suddenly, something leathery was shoved into her hands, and she vaguely heard the man command her to drink. The liquid was slightly warm and tasted a little meaty from the skin, but to her, it was the sweetest thing in the world at that moment. She was all set to drain the skin dry, but it was pulled roughly from her hands.

Kaia was gasping after her coughing fit coupled with drinking so much water that quickly. She gave the man a pleading look, and croaked, "More...please."

If she hadn't been dying of thirst, she probably would have found it strange that she lost her fear of these men so fast. All it took was a little water, and she was willing to let them shoot her with as many arrows as they wished once she was done. Thankfully, they only sneered at her request.

"There will be no more water until you answer our questions," the spider-man who gave her water said. Kaia assessed the creatures around her and tried to focus on their human halves more than the spider bits.

All the men wore nothing but crossed leather straps that held their various weapons. They all carried bows and arrows, but only the one she answered was the leader and one other carried a full sword. The other five all had various short knives in sheathes draped around their waists.

The leader had ebony skin and eyes so dark they appeared to swallow up his pupils. His head was completely shaved and the desert sun bounced off of the smooth skin. Kaia couldn't stop a small smile from forming on her lips when she thought that it made him look slightly angelic.

The men around her shifted uncomfortably at her smile, and Kaia wondered what that was all about. The younger man next to the leader drew his sword, and Kaia was amazed to realize that these fearsome creatures were afraid of her.

"I don't know what I'm doing here," she finally answered. She moved to stand up again but stopped when one of the archers drew his string back a little further. An arrow to the chest didn't seem like a good plan, so she sank back down, letting her butt rest on her heels.

"Liar," the leader spat, "you are here to spy on us and tell your master of our campsite."

"No," Kaia shook her head, "I swear I'm not spying on you. I don't even know what—I mean, who—you are. And, seriously, I tend not to listen to anyone, let alone someone who called themselves my master."

The younger man began to lower his sword. Without the imminent threat, Kaia realized he was a younger version of the leader. He had fewer lines on his face and a head full of box braids that fell to his waist.

He looked slightly confused at Kaia's words. "Where are you from, woman? You do not speak like any human we have encountered."

"I'm from upstate New York."

The men all looked at each other in confusion. Kaia realized New York wouldn't ring any bells around here, so she switched tactics.

"I'm from Earth?" She hoped that one would make more sense. But who knew what the people of this world called her home?

This changed the looks of confusion to looks of mingled wonder and fear. The archers, who had also relaxed their stances, snapped back to attention. Kaia sighed over the renewed threat and eyed the leader's water hopefully.

"Listen, I swear I'm not here to spy on you or hurt you. Could we please reconsider the 'no water' thing?"

The leader looked like he was reconsidering his earlier position. But Kaia was not surprised when he said no again.

"You will be taken to our village. We will interrogate you there."

"Whatever," Kaia sighed.

Kaia couldn't see a thing. The men used her makeshift turban as a blindfold, and it was surprisingly effective. She would have listened to their conversation to alleviate her boredom, but they switched to some kind of language that sounded like a mixture of an African tribal diFahadt and the low whine of cicadas.

She still wasn't sure how she felt about their offer to let her sit on one of their backs. From the intense discussion that arose from that offer, Kaia could tell that was not something they normally did.

"Enough," their leader had finally shouted, "She will go with Waitimu."

The younger man glared at Kaia when their leader made that declaration. She figured Waitimu was not too thrilled about the idea.

"But, father—"

The leader sliced his hand through the air for silence. "It is either this, or our journey takes four times longer. You know the human cannot keep pace with us."

Waitimu scowled at his father but didn't utter a word of protest when Kaia was placed upon his hairy back. The spider hair was prickly, and Kaia tried to touch it as little as possible, but her capris made that very difficult. Her hands were tied in front of her so she could hold onto his weapon strap and at least try not to fall off.

It didn't help that the intense sun was causing her to sweat uncontrollably. She felt bad poor Waitimu was not only being forced to carry her, but he was basically taking a bath in the process.

They traveled for almost half an hour when she felt Waitimu slow down. She wasn't sure how fast they had been going, because the ride was gentle, with almost no jarring movements beneath her.

She barely restrained herself from saying "Are we there yet." Even she knew it wouldn't be a good idea to tick off the monsters with bows. She strained to hear what was going on beyond the chattering conversation that she had no chance of understanding.

That was when she became aware of an insistent pulling sensation in her stomach. She hadn't noticed it before, but perhaps that was because it was pulling her forward, in the same direction they were traveling.

With her sight blocked off, it was easier to focus on that pull. As she focused on that feeling of damp coolness, she felt her mind almost drifting away from her body. She no longer felt the sun beating down on her covered face or Waitimu's prickly spider hair against her calves. Instead, she felt surrounded by crisp air and smelled the unique scent of the dirt the day after a heavy rain.

It felt similar to the visions she experienced before, but also a little different. Her eyes snapped open when she realized she no longer felt the weight of her blindfold.

She was surrounded by trees in an unknown forest. It looked like any other forest in upstate New York, but there was something strange about her surroundings—other than the weird way she had shown up there. Someone was walking toward her, but they were looking at the ground, so she couldn't get a good look at their face. It looked like a boy with light brown pants that were tucked into dark leather boots at the knee. The boy had on a light shirt that was pushed up to his elbows and was covered by what looked like a long vest.

He had a pack slung over one shoulder, much like she carried her backpack for a while. His head was covered by a page-boy cap. She could see a large purple bruise on one side of his face. When his gaze snapped up to meet hers, she realized she had been wrong to assume this was a boy.

She supposed the clothing and the way the girl walked threw her off. But the moment Kaia looked into those blue eyes set in a face so similar to her own, she knew it was the girl from those first visions. Lisa's words came back to her, and she realized that she wasn't dreaming. The girl was real, and apparently her sister.

Kaia didn't know what to do, so she just raised her hand slowly and said, "What's up?"

The girl looked at her in confusion before scanning the canopy above her. "It is a forest, so the obvious answer is: leaves. What is not obvious is: who are you?"

Kaia smiled a little, "Well, that's a bit complicated. My name is Kaia, and I'm—"

The world shifted under her, and Kaia suddenly felt like she was falling. It wasn't very gratifying to discover that the feeling was correct when she hit the sandy ground. The forest disappeared and she was once again looking at the fabric of her shirt. She was upset at losing her connection with her sister and stood up in a temper.

"What the hell, Waitimu?" She couldn't see where he was, so she settled on yelling at the air. "I know I'm your captive and whatever, but there's no need to dump me on my butt like baggage. Seriously, dude, that was just uncool!"

She was seething and didn't notice the silence until she stopped yelling. The air was cooler than she expected, and she moved carefully to remove her blindfold. What she saw made her quickly forget her anger. Kaia's mouth gaped open as she turned to take in her surroundings. She was in an oasis, and the trees were filled with intricately designed webs. There were web bridges between branches and what looked like funnels going into the hearts of the tree's palms.

When the Krax'mran began to emerge from these funnels, Kaia guessed that these were their homes. The creatures spread around the treetops, to watch what was happening on the ground.

Kaia turned back to the leader and saw that he was sitting on a stone dais that rested next to the largest tree Kaia had ever seen. It even made Waitimu's father look small, and his body alone was the size of a MINI Cooper.

"My people," he began, raising himself as high as the stone and his legs would take him, "our scouting party has discovered a spy in our desert. She claims to be of Earth," he had to stop for a moment when this declaration caused a lot of hushed conversations above, "We know this to be impossible, and we are prepared to do whatever it takes to make this woman speak the truth."

Kaia did not like the sound of that. She was still feeling weak from lack of water, though the air did have a tinge of moisture that was slowly reviving her.

"I, Reth, your Headman, call upon our Anansini. The speaker of our Father will reveal the truth."

This brought forth a weird sort of cheer. It was like the roar of a crowd and the chirping of crickets all rolled into one. Kaia caught sight of Waitimu standing beside his father and followed his gaze to a point directly above her.

There, she saw something that would stay with her forever. As much as she thought she was getting used to the sight of these people with spider bodies, nothing could make her okay with the idea of a huge spider slowly descending from a branch directly above her. It didn't help that the woman attached to the string of webbing that looked far too weak to hold her massive frame was wearing a costume of webbing and feathers.

The costume made even her human half look strange and frightening. Now, instead of looking like a human merging into a spider, she looked like a bird demon merging into a spider. In Kaia's opinion, this wasn't an improvement. She would've moved as far away from the woman as possible, but a ring of warriors surrounded her and blocked off any escape. The best she could do was to move just far enough so she didn't get squished like...well, a spider.

The chirping roar had gotten louder the closer the woman got to the ground, but as soon as her front two feet touched the ground, the trees went eerily quiet. The feathers swayed with the woman's slightest movements, making it look like she was constantly trying to take flight.

Her features were obscured by a beaded half-mask, leaving only her full mouth and firm chin exposed to the crowd. Her skin was lighter than Reth's, looking a little like burnt caramel. Her eyes were a golden brown that captivated Kaia.

"This child has traveled far," the Anansini said. Her voice was deep and musical, and Kaia could tell that even though the woman spoke softly, the whole crowd heard her.

The woman raised her arms to the sky and looked up. She began to sway back and forth, like a reed in the wind.

"Our Father, Anansi, show me the weavings of her line. Unwind her Fate before me so I may see the dangers in the path of your People. Open the eyes of your servant, Adebomi, so that I may see."

Kaia was fascinated by Adebomi's movements and was thus unprepared when Waitimu grabbed her from behind and held her still. Her fascination turned to fear when Adebomi unsheathed a knife that had been hidden amongst the feathers, and advanced.

"Stop!" Kaia screamed. "What do you think you're doing? I'm serious, stop it!"

No matter how hard she struggled against Waitimu's hold, she could not break free. Her gaze shifted frantically between Adebomi's intense eyes and the obsidian blade of the knife.

Waitimu's hold on Kaia's arms shifted so that he was holding her left hand out. Kaia didn't imagine anyone was going to shake that hand, and she struggled harder to break free. As the knife descended upon her, she squeezed her eyes tightly shut, and screamed like a banshee.

There was a pinprick of pain, and then Waitimu released his hold. Kaia fell to the ground as she lost the support he had been providing. She looked at her hand to see a small slash in her palm. It was bleeding, but it wasn't as bad as what she thought was coming. Waitimu threw a cloth into her lap and watched with thinly veiled amusement as Kaia wrapped it around her hand.

Kaia looked up just in time to see Adebomi lick the blade, which had collected a small portion of blood. Kaia's face screwed up in disgust, but she tried to hide it. Who knew what they would do if they disapproved of her reaction to their ceremony?

Adebomi's eyes rolled back into her head, leaving nothing but the whites of her eyes showing behind the mask. Her eyes snapped back in place after a moment, and she regarded Kaia with awe. She opened her mouth to speak but was interrupted by a harsh shriek.

Reth sprang from the stone dais and picked Kaia from the ground by the back of her shirt. "That is our alarm. Your traitorous comrades must have come for their spy. You will die before any of our people spill their first drop of blood."

Reth used his other hand to reach for his blade but was stopped by Adebomi.

"Husband, you must not do this," she stated calmly, "I have seen her weavings, and she is not what you think. Go to your battle, the girl shall stay by my side."

Reth's face contorted in confusion, but Kaia was grateful when he released her. Even though she ended up falling from a height of five feet, it was still better than slowly strangling because of her own stupid shirt.

As she gasped for breath, Adebomi reached a hand down to her. "Come, child, we must get you to safety."

Kaia was about to put her hand into Adebomi's when a phalanx of soldiers on horseback broke through the tree line. This caused pandemonium, and Kaia knew there was no time for safety.

16

On her third day of travel, Marina felt eyes on her. She looked around quickly, wondering if it was the girl from before. That was an unusual experience as she was starting her day this morning but she was looking forward to seeing the strangely familiar girl with purple hair again.

This was not to be, however, as there did not seem to be anyone around when she turned to take in the forest around her. She was still in the Rejos, but it was beginning to thin out. There were sounds of a village somewhere to the west of her and she was avoiding it.

She had been in Kenter for almost a day and a half, keeping to the less traveled sections of the forest. Even though she knew her disguise might keep her from being recognized as a girl—and the princess—she did not quite trust that this would keep her out of trouble.

Though it was rare, one still heard of people foolish enough to attempt robbing their fellow travelers. Gerard's pack kept a close eye on those traveling through their territory, however, and those fools were quickly dispatched. Sometimes the pack did this on their own, and sometimes they turned the criminal over to the local authorities.

Marina was not sure if the eyes she could still feel upon her were the presence of a pack member, or a highwayman. Either way, her hand moved to the dagger hanging at her belt. She was almost relieved when a large wolf materialized out of the woods and sat down in front of her. Her relief quickly turned to consternation when she recognized Gerard.

"What are you doing here?" she demanded. The look he gave her told her to stay where she was as he moved to go back into the forest.

"Do not look at me in that manner. I have done nothing for which I am ashamed, and I will act as I see fit."

Gerard huffed in exasperation and disappeared into the forest. Marina debated whether or not she should stay where she was and decided he could simply find her again. So she strode forward, trying to control her anger at being followed like a naughty child. Her temper kept her from being as circumspect as she normally was, however. He found her within moments, and he did not look happy about her leading him on a merry chase.

Now that he was back in his human form, he took the opportunity to chastise her. "Princess, what were you thinking? You have the entire palace in an uproar, and your mother is beside herself with worry,"

Marina could not stop the stab of guilt this caused. Her solitude these last few days gave her time to think. She was no longer angry at her parents for keeping the nature of her birth from her, but the hurt was still there. This, and that still insistent pulling, had kept her going when the guilt would have made her turn back.

"I am sorry to have pained...my mother. But certain circumstances have set me on this course, and I will not be swayed."

Gerard raised his eyebrow at her hesitation but was not given a chance to question her. Curtis and Fahad appeared at his sides, both moving with far more stealth than Gerard would normally credit humans. Curtis advanced on his sister in anger. Fahad moved to stop him, but Gerard held him back.

"Your concern is wasted," he muttered as Curtis enveloped Marina in a fierce hug.

Fahad quirked a smile as the siblings began to yell at each other. He heard Gerard's conversation with the princess, and this seemed to be a much louder version of the same.

"Are you an idiot?" Curtis started as soon as he let Marina go.

"Of course not," Marina shouted back, hands on her hips. "That title has always been yours, and I would never dare try to take it from you."

"Mother was crying like a babe when we made our farewells. How could you be so immature and inconsiderate? Did you completely take leave of your senses?"

Marina went pale and still. Curtis backed away from his position only inches from her face.

"Marina," he said in a far calmer voice, "I am sorry. I know that what we heard that day was difficult, but it was no reason to run away. I spoke to mother and father," he paused at her sharp intake of breath, "I told them that we heard their conversation."

Marina turned away and wrapped her arms around herself. She suddenly felt chilled, and she wanted to run to warm herself again.

"They were upset that you found out that way, but they understood your anger. All we ask is that you come back home so they can speak to you."

Marina shook her head and finally broke her silence.

"I did not run away because of...that," she looked to Gerard and Fahad, uncertain of whether or not she wanted them to know. When she saw Curtis' look of disbelief she continued.

"Well, that was perhaps part of the reason. Mostly, however, I wished to follow this feeling I have been having. Ever since that moment in the tower, I have felt an urgent need to find someone--or something."

Curtis looked worried now, and Marina was not sure how she could reassure him.

"Princess," Gerard interrupted them, "Let us travel to the village to discuss this. We have not eaten today, and I can smell rabbit stew."

Marina's mouth kicked up at one corner in a rueful smile. "Trust you to follow your stomach before anything else."

"Nothing is more important than rabbit stew, milady," Gerard said with a serious tone and a twinkle in his eye. Marina looked to the sky as if asking the gods for guidance before turning toward the village.

Gerard insisted they finish their meal before they did anything else, much to Marina's amusement. Curtis and Fahad looked as though they would rather be on their way back to the castle, but Marina was glad they were quietly eating their own stew instead of insisting they return. Once the barmaid cleared the table, Curtis immediately moved to stand up.

"I am not going with you," Marina stated forcefully.

Curtis fell back into his chair and surveyed her with mingled anger and disbelief.

"You cannot think to keep to this ridiculous journey, trying to find something that is mostly likely extremely dangerous? You forget, I saw the pain it caused you. What if you are heading toward certain death?"

Marina gripped the cup of ale in her hands and looked into the foaming liquid. She debated for a moment whether or not to tell them of her encounter with the purple-haired girl who called herself Kaia. It was not that she thought they would not believe her. These were the Kingdoms after all, and entities appearing or disappearing were known to happen upon occasion. Her problem with revealing what she saw stemmed from a selfish desire to keep the experience to herself.

Something seemed so familiar about that girl, and she did not want someone else to analyze what happened. After a moment's silence, however, she decided that this would be the best way to reassure Curtis.

"I saw something this morning that makes me think I am being led to someone important." She looked up to see all three men staring at her expectantly. If it were not so unnerving, she would have laughed.

"This morning, as I was walking, I saw a girl. She said her name was Kaia, and I think I am supposed to find her."

The men exchanged confused glances.

"But, I thought you said you saw her. Why would you need to find someone you have already found?" Curtis asked. Marina had to grit her teeth because he asked the question as though he was speaking to a small child.

"She was not actually there," Marina snapped, "I think she was an apparition. Or, at least, it did not feel like she was there. Something was off about her presence."

Marina was still a little confused by her experience. The girl had been solid enough, but Marina had sensed some otherness about the girl that told her not to trust her eyes.

"What did she look like?" Gerard asked.

Marina thought for a moment before answering.

"She looked a bit like me, but as though something had shifted the colors of my features."

The men looked confused again, and this time Marina could not help her amusement. "I know it sounds odd, but the girl—Kaia—had green eyes and purple hair."

Curtis snorted at the description. "Are you telling me there is a purple-haired version of my sister somewhere in the Kingdoms?" he scoffed.

"Do not act as though I am mad. I am only telling you what I saw. I think that feeling I had the day I left was her calling to me."

Curtis began to look worried again, causing Marina to sigh in exasperation.

"Look," she snapped again, "I am telling you this so you will know why I left, and why I will not be going back with you. You can believe me or not about Kaia, but I ask—no, I demand—that you trust my instincts enough to believe me when I say she means me no harm."

Marina loved her brother dearly, but she wished he would stop treating her like a child. One would think Antonio or Benedict would be the worst in this situation, but they had concerns other than worrying about their sheltered sister.

Only Curtis still tried to protect her from almost everything. He only started teaching her to fight because he was away at school too much to be there to physically protect her himself. Now that he was home more often, he tended to treat her like a child unless they were sparring.

"So be it," Curtis finally said. Marina stared at him in surprise. "Marina, I know you well enough to see that you will continue on this path no matter what I say. So, I will not force you to return home. However," the smile that had broken across her face dimmed a little at this, "I will be joining you."

"Curtis, you do not need to—"

"Do you really think I would leave you to journey alone?" he broke in incredulously. "Not only would mother skin me alive if I returned without you, but I also would never forgive myself if something happened to you and I could have prevented it by being there."

Marina thought about this for a moment before nodding reluctantly. "Fine," she sighed, "we will go together."

She turned to Fahad and Gerard. "Thank you both for helping Curtis to find me. You may return to the castle, as I am sure you both have more important matters to attend to than finding a princess who did not truly want to be found in the first place."

Fahad regarded her with a sardonic smile and said, "Actually, the king has assigned me as your personal guard,"

"About which Mittman was thrilled," Gerard muttered under his breath.

Fahad continued without acknowledging this statement, "And he has explicitly ordered that I am not to return without your royal self. So, I'm afraid you are stuck with me as well."

He crossed his arms and leaned back with a self-satisfied smirk, and regarded Marina's annoyance with apparent humor.

She looked to Gerard, who regarded her evenly. "Oh, I'm coming too. My pack has been keeping an eye on you for me. They'll want to know how this journey turns out."

Gerard watched the princess pout in annoyance and smiled at the childish behavior when she was trying to convince all three men present she should be treated as an adult. However, inside, there was something else pushing him to join Princess Marina. Like her, he couldn't explain why her mission felt important to him either. For now, he would claim the authority due to him as the Rejos pack ambassador to follow her and claim curiosity to his fellow travelers. Hopefully, by the time he got the princess, prince, and young statue home he would lose the restless feeling in his gut.

Marina huffed in frustration and crossed her arms as well. She knew it was not very becoming of a princess to pout, but she was well away from the castle and in disguise. Pouting seemed the appropriate response, and who would tell her mother? "Fine, but we are burning daylight, so let us go."

Curtis paid their tab before they sat down, so they all downed the rest of their drinks and left the tavern. Their horses were tied up outside, and Marina moved to greet Oasis. Curtis and Fahad left the horses in the tavern's stable and circled back to confront her with Gerard. She supposed she should at least forgive them for intruding upon her quest because they brought her mount.

"Thank you," she said to Curtis as she swung into the saddle, "I missed Oasis these last few days."

Curtis acknowledged her subtle attempt at making amends with a nod and a smile as he mounted his own steed. Fahad adjusted the bundle behind his saddle and looked up at Marina.

"Where to, Princess?"

Marina closed her eyes for a moment and concentrated on the feeling that had been leading her thus far. She gasped when she felt a sharp pang of fear. Her heart beat faster as she gripped the pommel in front of her, turning her knuckles white. As she concentrated on the whirling emotions, she caught a glimpse of a nightmarish scene of battle.

It was a blurred rush of images, but she could almost hear the battle cries and scraping of metal on metal. Through the maelstrom of what looked like Krax'mran and humans fighting, she saw Kaia like a beacon in the darkness. She was trying to escape the battle, but there were combatants all around her, cutting her off from any escape.

Marina winced every time Kaia had to duck or fully crash to the ground to avoid the swinging blades or fists around her. One time, she narrowly missed being hit by an errant arrow, and Marina let out a strangled scream of warning. Kaia looked at her with panic in her eyes, and Marina saw her mouth the word 'help.'

Suddenly, the vision was broken when Marina was pulled from her saddle. She was breathing heavily as if she had been running, and she could still feel the edges of fear pulling at her.

"Marina," Gerard said gruffly.

She turned her head to see that it was he who pulled her from the saddle and was now holding her upright. His eyes were edged with gold, and she could see the wolf was dangerously close to surfacing.

She gulped in a few more breaths and moved away from his grasp. Fahad and Curtis were on either side of Gerard, forming a tight circle around her with Oasis at her back.

"I am well. It was only a vision. I was not expecting it, I thought I was merely searching for that feeling again, but something is happening to Kaia. She is in danger, we must find her." Marina could feel her panic rising at the thought that they would likely be too late to save this girl who was becoming increasingly important to her.

"We will," Curtis assured her, "Just calm yourself and we will leave. I am certain that whatever you saw, she will be fine until we can reach her."

Marina allowed herself to be soothed by his words and quickly mounted Oasis. "Let us go. I want to be halfway across Kenter before night falls."

"Do you know where we are going?" Curtis asked as he put his mount next to Oasis.

"To Krax'mra."

Curtis frowned his disapproval and Marina shook his head.

"You can argue all you want, but I'm going."

Curtis sighed in reluctant agreement and mounted his horse. Fahad mounted without any protest and the three riders set off. Gerard ran beside them, and Marina realized a horse would not allow him a seat and their three steeds would not allow a wolf to run alongside them. She winced as she realized this meant Gerard would be forced to run afoot throughout their journey.

"Will you be able to keep up?" she called to him.

"We'll see who is falling behind at the end of the day, milady," Gerard challenged with a wicked grin.

With that, he picked up his pace and was soon in the lead.

17

Kaia dodged around Krax'mran and humans alike as the fighting started. There was no way she was getting in the middle of a bunch of warriors with swords and other weapons. She lost Adebomi almost immediately after the humans on horseback crashed into the oasis and now she was scrambling for cover.

She stopped for a second when she saw her backpack lying abandoned near the throne. Running to it, she put it on her back and finally felt halfway secure. During her run, the Krax'mran mostly ignored her. For some reason, every human she passed tried to grab her.

Kaia looked around for an escape route and found herself completely surrounded. She tried to make herself smaller when she saw the girl again in the middle of the battlefield. Her voice felt small and childlike when she called out for help only to see the terrified girl immediately wink out of existence.

It was the most confusing and terrifying experience of her life. Without even her possible sister to rescue her, Kaia shrank back against the throne when the battle closed in on her. She jumped when a human sprang up in front of her.

He was a classically handsome man with smiling eyes. Kaia didn't know how to respond when he gave her a courtly bow as if they weren't in the middle of an epic battle. Taking her hand, he kissed the back and gave her a winning smile.

"Good day, milady. I am Sir Robin and I am here to save you from these monsters."

"Uh, okay."

Robin took her stunned answer as agreement. Using his bent position to his advantage, Robin put his shoulder into Kaia's middle and picked her up in a fireman's carry. Kaia's shriek of surprise was cut off when the momentum from being thrown over Robin's shoulder shifted her backpack directly over her head.

Her face was forced into the small of Robin's back and she had to turn her face to keep her nose from getting smashed as he started to run. The backpack bounced on her head, giving her a hell of a headache. Eventually, the running stopped and she was flipped back to her feet.

She had to hold onto Robin's arm to keep from falling. She either had a mild concussion or all the blood was rushing to its proper place. Whatever it was, it was making her dizzy. It didn't help when Robin all but threw her on top of a horse before swinging up in front of her.

Gripping Robin's waist to keep her balance, she winced when Robin shouted something. As quickly as the fighting began, it was over. Almost as one, the two dozen humans ran away from their opponents and mounted their own horses. With another shout from Robin, the band of men crashed out of the oasis the same way they came in.

Kaia turned her head and barely saw Adebomi's pitying frown before the trees got in the way. Kaia turned back and wondered if this could be considered a rescue or if she was going from something bad to worse.

Kaia gripped the rider in front of her tighter. She wasn't used to riding a horse, and she felt like she could fall off at any moment. Robin placed his hand over hers in reassurance and kept going. For almost an hour they rode at a break-neck pace and were only now slowing to a gentle gallop.

Kaia still wasn't sure what happened in the Krax'mran camp, but she did know Robin and his band of merry men were acting as her rescuers. This day was, by far, the weirdest of her life. She still wasn't sure if she needed rescuing from the Krax'mran, but she was on

Robin's horse now, so she supposed her only option was to see how much odder this day could get.

Kaia wondered if someday she might find Robin's heroics terribly romantic. All she could think about at the moment was how much her head and left hand hurt. She also wondered if she cracked any of Robin's ribs because she spent that entire first hour holding onto him like a python.

She didn't mind hanging on to such a good-looking guy. His wavy black hair, gray eyes, and strong features made him look like a Disney prince. He was muscular, but not in an overly pumped-up way. Overall, Kaia definitely preferred cuddling up to him over any of the Krax'mran, no matter how hot Waitimu's human half was.

"Look, milady," Robin pointed ahead of them, "we near my master's castle."

Kaia looked up and saw a fortress that looked like something out of a fairytale. It was beautiful but forbidding. The grey stones stood out incongruously against the creamy beige sand of the desert. She'd been expecting something more like the palace of Agrabah, not the castle in the Kevin Costner version of Robin Hood.

There was a thick wall surrounding the castle, and Kaia could see men walking around the top. As they got closer, she could see that each corner, which had a sort of guard tower, had an archer or two posted on that tower. There were no banners or flags anywhere, and Kaia wondered if that was something they only did in movies, or if Robin's master just didn't have a flag or coat of arms.

They rode toward the opening in the wall, and Kaia saw the threatening teeth of the portcullis above them as they passed through. There were also heavy wooden doors crossed with metal that could close behind the portcullis. It looked like the castle was meant to have a moat, but the desert climate couldn't support that particular method of defense.

"Wow," Kaia said under her breath, "We're not fooling around with safety here."

"This is the safest place in all of the Kingdoms, milady," Robin answered, "Our Lord must be careful to guard both his people and his possessions."

"You can call me Kaia. I'm not really a 'milady' kind of girl."

"Of course, Lady Kaia," Robin replied with a devastating smile that made Kaia blush. He dismounted first and held his arms up to Kaia. She slid down less than gracefully, but that didn't stop him from looking at her with a mingling of amusement and adoration. Kaia felt her heart falter at the twinkle in his eyes.

"Thank you," she giggled. She blushed again at how idiotic she sounded, which only caused Robin's smile to widen.

"Come," he offered her his arm, and she took it awkwardly, not certain how to behave in this kind of situation. "Lord Marius will wish to greet you."

"Is that the name of your master, or whatever?"

"Indeed. I believe you will find him to be a most gracious host. Far better than those vile Krax'mran."

"Um, sure. At the very least he won't do any creepy rituals involving knives and blood, right?" She laughed nervously when Robin only gave her a bland smile.

She turned her head to see a young man following them with her backpack in his arms. Kaia wasn't sure how she felt about Adebomi after the thing with the knife but she was glad she got away from the Anansini long enough to get her things back. Being without her supplies from home felt surprisingly vulnerable. That feeling was surprising because other than a small knife Merry gave her and Kaia's Zippo lighter, nothing in the backpack could be considered a threat.

The more she thought about it, the more grateful she became for Robin's good timing. While the Krax'mran didn't seem exactly evil, their intentions didn't seem all that kind either. At least Robin was proving to be incredibly helpful and appeared to have her best interests at heart.

They stopped just before they reached a set of stairs leading to the castle's door. Robin bowed deeply in deference to the man standing at the top of the stairs, and his hold on Kaia's arm forced her to do the same.

"My lord, Marius, I have brought a guest."

Kaia shivered when Marius' cool green eyes passed over her in silent appraisal. He was unnaturally pale, especially considering the hot desert sun beating down on them. She wasn't sure how he could stand the heat. He was wearing tight-fitting black pants, a black jacket, and a poofy, frilly, gray shirt. He looked like something out of a gothic romance novel.

His face lost some of its fierceness when he bestowed a benevolent smile upon them.

"As I see, Sir Robin. And how did you find such a delicate flower so close to our home?"

"My scouts were searching for Krax'mran camps and reported the abduction of a human woman. We immediately followed their path and rescued her."

Marius' sharp gaze was focused on Kaia's face, and she tried not to squirm under the intense scrutiny. His gaze flicked briefly to her hair, which caused a tightening at the corner of his mouth. Kaia couldn't tell if this was from amusement or reproach, but either way, it made her shrink in embarrassment. She was suddenly glad the purple was going to wash out within the week.

"How did you get to the middle of the Krax'mran desert, my dear? The border is several days away by horseback, and you do not appear to even have that advantage."

"Well, I sort of dropped in unexpectedly," she admitted. When Marius narrowed his eyes at this statement, she hastened to explain. "I was sent here by some kind of spell, but I'm not really sure what happened, or why I got sent to that particular location. I really wasn't sure where I was supposed to end up other than the Kingdoms in general."

Marius considered the child before him. Her garb was strange and her hair a violent shade of purple unseen in nature, even among the fae. So her words made an interesting kind of sense. He would not get too excited by her mention of travel. She did not seem particularly bright given her manner of speech and could mean a spell from anywhere in the Kingdoms. He would not let himself hope the gaps he believed existed in the ancient spell that split the worlds really existed without better proof.

"Ah, well, you are fortunate then that you arrived so near to my home and that Robin was able to save you from the plague that is the Krax'mran."

Marius gave her another dashing smile and made a gesture inviting her in. "You must be exhausted from your long journey. Robin will show you to a guest chamber where you may rest and refresh yourself. Please, feel welcome to stay as long as you wish, and do not hesitate to ask for whatever might make you more comfortable."

Kaia smiled demurely at Marius' solicitude and said, "Thank you, I really appreciate that."

Robin gave her a flirtatious wink and led her up the stairs to her room. The castle was elaborately decorated with several paintings, tapestries, urns, antique furniture, and other pieces of opulence. It was perhaps a little overdone, but Kaia was too impressed by what she saw to judge Marius too harshly.

As they walked, Kaia noticed that all the servants were incredibly beautiful. It was like walking through NYC during fashion week. She wondered if that was a prerequisite for working in Marius' castle, and hoped that wasn't true. Marius already vaguely creeped her out, and the thought that he might also be extremely shallow just made her like him a little less.

Then again, perhaps she was just being overly sensitive. After all, he had offered his hospitality when he could have just as easily turned her away. Not to mention the fact that he employed Robin, who was not only fantastically hot but also quite sweet.

When Robin showed her the guest room, she decided that she really jumped too quickly to presume Marius was a creeper.

Her room was amazing.

It was delicate, but not overly feminine. There was blue wallpaper with a fleur de lis design embedded into it that made it look like it was shimmering. The bed was made over in soft blue and green fabric with only the barest edging of lace. It was a four-poster bed, which Kaia always wanted, but Merry said was too impractical to get into her attic room.

The furniture was all a deep brown that might have looked overly masculine if it hadn't been for the graceful scrollwork etched into the legs and sides.

"Wow, Robin, this is mind-blowing! I think this is the most perfectly designed room I have ever seen. It's even got my favorite colors."

Robin gave her a seductive smile and took her hand.

"I am glad it meets with your approval, Lady Kaia," he murmured, kissing the back of her hand. Kaia silently cursed the pale skin that revealed yet another blush.

"You will find a set of clothing in the wardrobe, should you wish to change. I shall send for a tub and some warm water so you might bathe. Cossette will attend you."

"Oh, don't bother her. I can...um, attend to myself. I've been doing it for a while now after all," she joked.

Robin looked confused at her refusal.

"But, milady, nothing would make Cossette happier than to see that you are well taken care of."

"Listen, that's sweet and all, but I'm not into the whole someone-watching-me-take-a-bath thing. Tell Cossette she would make me really happy by just giving me some soap and a washcloth. Some water too if you don't mind. I'm still really thirsty."

Robin gave a small bow over the hand he still held, and kissed it again. "It is as my lady Kaia wishes," he acquiesced, "Please, send Cossette to me when you desire a tour of my master's home."

With that, Kaia was left to wait for her bath and Cossette. She used that time to explore her room. She placed a hand on the edge of the bed's mattress and pushed down. It was pleasantly soft and comfy. Nothing would have pleased her more than to plop down on it face first, but she was way too dirty for that.

Someone knocked on her door, and she quickly moved to answer it. A group of servants streamed in. Two large men carried a copper tub and placed it in front of the fireplace. Several more people came in carrying steaming buckets, which they quickly and efficiently dumped into the tub.

Kaia was extremely impressed when she noticed that not one drop fell upon the floor. Soon, she was left alone with only one girl, whom she could only assume was Cossette.

Cossette had a head of wild auburn curls that was swept back with a pretty blue ribbon to match her eyes. Her pale skin was dotted with a sprinkling of cinnamon-colored freckles. She had a wide, generous mouth, which was shaped into a warm and welcoming smile.

"Good evening," Cossette chirped as she gave Kaia a deep curtsy. Kaia was surprised to see that the sun was indeed going down.

"Robin has told me that you wish to bathe without my help. I will be nearby, however, should you change your mind."

Kaia had to give the girl points for persistence. Cossette curtsied again, much to Kaia's embarrassment, and let herself out.

Kaia noticed that someone placed a pitcher of water and a cup on the desk. She hurried over to it and swiftly poured herself a large portion. It was cool and sweet; far better than the musty stuff in animal skins both the Krax'mran and Robin gave her. She closed her eyes and took a deep breath at the relief of being at least slightly more hydrated. The cup was empty, so she poured some more. She sipped this a bit more slowly as she undressed and headed for the tub.

The warm water soaked into her dry skin, and she felt as though all of her energy was being restored. She no longer had the urge to plop down on the bed and sleep for a week.

She wanted to take her time, but she was also eager to go on that tour Robin promised. After soaking until the water cooled to room temperature, she quickly scrubbed the dirt and sand away. She found it odd that the water level somehow lowered while she had been in there, but gave up thinking about it as soon as she opened the wardrobe.

It was a medieval girl's dream. There were dozens of opulent dresses in soft materials that Kaia never saw before. She was relieved to see that none of them had an overabundance of ribbons and flounces. While Kaia liked their femininity, she knew from experience that too many embellishments made her feel like she was suffocating under the girlishness.

She put on a soft, emerald green number that complimented her eyes. It made her hair look even weirder, but nothing really could have helped the electric purple. Though it was fading, so now it was more light purple than electric. As she tried to lace up the back to keep the dress from gaping in the front, she was annoyed to realize that she was going to need Cossette's help after all.

She stuck her head out of the door, expecting that she would need to search for the girl. Much to her surprise, Cossette was waiting patiently next to the door jamb. Kaia was a little disturbed by that, but she decided to look past it. Who knew how long it had been since Cossette served a guest in this remote castle?

"Oh, milady," her mouth formed a delicate O of delight, "you look lovely." Kaia noticed that the delight did not seem to reach Cossette's eyes.

As Cossette laced her up, Kaia watched the girl's expressions in the mirror. While she kept up a lively stream of chatter, and that warm smile never left her face, her eyes seemed to stay impassive. They didn't light with passion or amusement, and Kaia wondered if they ever glowed with anger or resentment.

Cossette finally left after brushing Kaia's hair into a shiny blue halo. Barely five minutes passed before Robin was there for the tour. He was, as always, sweet and amusing, and Kaia generally enjoyed their time together.

The only awkward moment came when they neared the west side of the castle. As they passed a door, Kaia asked, "What's in there?"

"That is of no concern to anyone but the master." Robin's voice brooked no argument, and Kaia fought the urge to argue. It wasn't in her nature to let something like that go, but Marius was her host, and she figured he had a right to his privacy. It didn't stop her, however, from turning her head slightly to give the thick oak door a questioning look.

18

Marina was thirsty, again. The further away they got from Jamaria, the more rapidly she drained her water skin.

"By the gods," Curtis muttered ruefully as she grabbed for his. "I cannot understand how you do not need to piss every five minutes the way you've been going."

"Do not be crude," she sniped back after she took a swig.

"We will need to refill our skins, and none of us know where the next water source is," Curtis whined.

"One mile to the southwest," Marina and Gerard answered at the same time.

All three men gave Marina a questioning look. They expected Gerard to know these kinds of things, but as someone who never set foot out of Tern before, Marina's answer was odd.

"What?" she asked defensively.

"How do you know that?" Curtis demanded.

"I am unsure. Perhaps it is because I am still thirsty. In fact, I will ride ahead and fill both our water skins, as I am the one who drank the most from both."

With that, she spurred Oasis forward. She did not care that all three of her companions voiced their opinions that they thought this was a bad idea. As she knew they would, they followed her as soon as they realized she would not be turning around to argue.

Oasis leaped over a small bush and landed in the soft mud at the bank of a pond. It was still and mossy, with a stand of reeds on one side that looked like it should house a chorus of frogs, though it was currently quiet.

She dismounted and knelt in front of the water. Cupping her hands together, she brought some to her lips. It was slightly warm from the midday sun, but as it ran down her throat, she was surprised by how clean and refreshing it tasted.

"Princess!" Gerard pulled her up by one arm, causing her to choke slightly on the water.

"By the gods, Gerard, what are you doing!"

She was forced to get this out between coughing fits. Her face was red from the coughing as well as some anger.

"You need to throw up. Now." He moved her away from the water and put a hand on her neck to force her to bend at the middle.

She fought to stand back upright, but she was no match for the wolf's strength.

"I will do no such thing," she gasped out, "Why would you even suggest something so disgusting?"

"That water is poisonous," he shouted, "and you need to expel what you drank."

Marina looked at him in horror. She felt fine, but who knew how long it would take the poison in the water to affect her? She tried to vomit, but it would not work.

Curtis and Fahad looked panicked, and Gerard looked determined. Marina could not help but cry. This was completely unfair. Now she would never know who that mysterious girl was or what she meant to Marina.

She did not want

A villager found them this way a few moments later. Curtis and Fahad had resorted to yelling at Marina to retch the water out, while Gerard kept an iron grip on the back of her neck to keep her from standing up.

"Did he drink the water?" the man asked incredulously.

"Yes," Fahad replied, turning to him only briefly before focusing his attention back on Marina.

"Are you sure?" he still sounded like he did not believe them.

Gerard finally let go of the sobbing Marina to glare at the man.

"I saw it with my own eyes. I can smell the poison in this water. What is the antidote? How can we save her?" Marina stopped crying at the desperation in Gerard's voice. She looked at the man with hope shining in her eyes.

"There is no antidote," at their crestfallen expressions, he hurried to add, "but he might be okay. That water should have killed him as soon as it touched his lips. It was poisoned by a group of rebels, and they made sure to use the good stuff."

The four men looked at Marina with varying expressions. Curtis looked both relieved and furious, Fahad looked relieved but a bit confused, and Gerard was looking stoic. The villager was looking at her with a touch of awe.

"How did you survive, lad? That water has killed so many people and animals. I have to make a trip here twice a day to clear them out. I made up a sign, but the rebels must've taken it down."

"I do not know," she replied hoarsely. The combination of coughing and crying had made her throat feel raw. "I simply took a drink and it tasted fine."

"Huh," the villager scratched his balding head in confusion, "That don't make any sense a'tall. Nearly every account we've had where there was someone else 'round when the other person died, it was always the drinker saying, 'this water tastes like piss,' right before he croaked."

"I have never had that particular experience, so I cannot confirm that. I thought it tasted sweet and clean." Marina eyed the pond suspiciously, as though it was an animal that had unexpectedly bitten her.

Gerard inhaled deeply and turned back to the pond. His head cocked to the side in confusion. This normally made Marina smile, but it did not seem so funny at the moment.

"That's strange," he said to himself. He bent a knee and cupped a hand to capture some water. Everyone gave a horrified gasp as he licked the moisture from his palm.

"It's fine," he wiped the remaining liquid on his pants and brushed some of the mud from his knee. "Whatever poison I smelled, it's gone now."

The villager looked at Marina with awe once again.

"Milord," he bowed deeply to her, "my village could never repay the service you've done us."

Marina blushed at the compliment and rushed to deny it. "I did not do anything," she assured him, "I only drank of the water. Perhaps the poison had worn off?"

Gerard's incredulous look told her that was not likely, but she truly did not believe she could possibly be the cause of the pond's return to clean water. She looked around for Oasis, and found her standing some distance away munching on the grass.

"Or, it could have been Oasis," she pointed to the horse desperately, "she is a quarter unicorn. She could have stepped in the pond and purified it."

Marina was not certain why the idea that she could do magic terrified her, but it did. She suspected it was because the royal family did not have any sorcerers in the ancestry. If Marina really could perform magic, that took her one further step away from the family she thought was hers.

"Well, sir," Curtis said, jovial now that the crisis was over, "I think the proper repayment for a miracle would be a fine noon meal. We've only road rations, and some home cooking would be grand."

The villager grinned at them all and gestured for them to follow him. Fahad, Curtis and Marina all chose to walk instead of riding so they could converse with him. As they walked the man, who introduced himself as Fergus, told them about the rebel's many attacks on the village.

"They've been a menace for generations now. Ever since the first president was elected almost seventy years ago, they've been fighting to put the monarchy back in place. As you can imagine, it's naught more than a bunch of former nobles who miss their cushy estates and servants.

"No matter that their rebellion has gotten them all of nowhere. Lately, they've taken to poisoning water sources when villages like mine prefer to either stay out of the fight or choose to side with the president."

Marina chose not to take offense to Fergus' slight dig at the nobles. From what she was hearing, he had the right of them. These men and women cared so much for the power their parents or grandparents once had they did not care they were hurting innocent people to further their cause. Marina did not believe she could ever do something that cold-hearted over something as ephemeral as power.

When they reached the village of Heatherwood, Fergus told his neighbors the story of Marina's miraculous immunity and purification of the pond. Marina tried to protest her involvement once again, but the denizens of Heatherwood were too excited to listen to her weak-hearted denials.

The townspeople prepared a huge lunch for the travelers, all while asking them for news of whatever was happening outside the village. They were not surprised to learn their guests were from Jamaria, citing their accents and dress as dead giveaways. Curtis was able to give them news of the newest plays and songs just coming in from Dura. Gerard, as a military advisor to the king, gave them some political news. Marina and Fahad stayed quiet.

Several people came up to Marina during her meal to thank her for cleansing the pond. After so many protests went unheard, she finally settled for mumbling 'you're welcome' and returning to her meal.

As they neared the end of the meal, the town's mayor stood at the head of the tables that were temporarily erected for the feast. He was a large, jovial man who acted as though he was the father of the entire village.

"My friends, in true Heatherwood fashion, we have put together a fine feast in no time a'tall." This elicited a round of huzzahs and raised cups of ale. "We have come together to celebrate a miracle bestowed upon us by this fine boy."

Marina blushed as more people cheered and lifted their cups to her honor. Several people shouted for her to stand so they could better see the mysterious youth.

Curtis choked in amusement at the idea that no one had seen past Marina's simple disguise. Marina glared at her brother as Fahad slapped him on the back. Fahad raised an eyebrow at Marina's expression and gave Curtis one last slap, a little harder than the others. Marina turned to Gerard to hide her smile at Fahad's small show of support.

Gerard stopped paying attention to the goings on around him and was frowning in concentration. Marina watched as he stood up and began to weave his way through the crowd toward the entrance to town.

She wanted to follow him but knew it would be impossible to slip away unnoticed like Gerard. Then, an idea occurred to her. She quickly quashed her sly smile as she stood up to another round of cheers from the villagers.

"Good people of Heatherwood. Though I am not sure how I have done this deed, I am happy to have helped your village. To show our appreciation for your hospitality, my brother, Curtis, would like to dance for you all," she placed a hand on Curtis' shoulder at the mention of his name and looked down to see how her little announcement went over with him.

She smiled mischievously when he glowered up at her through his thick eyelashes. Curtis, despite all his grace and dexterity, hated to perform in public. Now, however, Marina left him no choice whatsoever.

The excited populace helped to move him out of his chair and to a gazebo placed in the town square. Marina took this opportunity to follow Gerard. She hoped he had not gone too far, because she knew she would never be able to track him if he had.

The gods were apparently looking favorably upon her today, because she found him just at the edge of the woods, talking to another man. This man was wrapped in a horse blanket, leaving Marina to assume he was part of Gerard's pack. He had stringy brown hair that fell to his shoulders and a hint of wildness about him. This forced Marina to approach the men cautiously.

Wolves like this man were usually those who spent all their time in the Rejos. They either still did not fully trust humans after two hundred years of relative peace, or they were pups still within their first decade or two of being turned.

Gerard took the bag slung around the wolf's neck and dismissed him. The poor man looked so relieved, Marina felt sorry Gerard gave him a mission that brought him so close to humans.

"I'm glad you're here, princess," Gerard said before he turned around, "I've a package that just arrived from the palace for you."

Puzzled, Marina stepped forward to accept the pouch Gerard just received. She pulled out a leather-bound book with a letter tied to it with a piece of ribbon. The letter bore the royal seal and she recognized her mother's handwriting on it.

She tucked the book under one arm and held the letter to her chest.

"I want to be alone for a bit. As I am sure you will be able to track me easily, I ask that you refrain from such for a little while. If I am not back in two hours, I give you leave to come find me."

Gerard gave a jerky nod and Marina could feel his eyes upon her as she walked into the forest. She wanted to be alone, but she knew better than to be foolish about it. As she walked, she opened the book. Only the first three lines were legible. The rest of the book was filled with some unknown writing that made her head ache to look upon.

The first three lines read: "I beg of you, kind stranger, to protect my child from her father who hunts her—Nightshade. His deeds are terrible, but what he plans to do with my daughters will bring ruin upon two worlds. Marina will never know her sister, but so long as their father never finds them, a terrible fate might be avoided."

The words made the book seem heavier. She was not sure what she had been expecting, but something from her birth mother was not even in the realm of possibilities. Tears came sudden and hot, and she cursed her weakness. She sat down on a rock next to the pond she apparently purified.

This made her cry harder, and she cursed herself again, this time for making such a poor choice of isolated spots. She wanted to throw the book and letter into the still water, but she restrained herself. The tears were scrubbed away, and Marina looked at the letter with aching eyes.

She traced the delicate curves of her name penned on the front of the envelope. The thought of reading the words within brought Marina both a sense of dread as well as a wave of homesickness. Other than her sparring sessions with Curtis, she never traveled beyond the castle walls, let alone the borders of Jamaria. Any diplomatic journeys involved her parents, and only in recent years had her brothers participated as well. Her mother always insisted that Marina had no need to accompany them.

This usually left Marina feeling excluded and restless, but she always obediently stayed safe within the palace walls. Now, Marina had to wonder if Delia's actions were motivated by more than protective parenting.

Marina took a deep breath and slid a finger beneath the wax seal. The red impression of a griffin in flight cracked from the pressure and allowed her to read her mother's words.

* * *

My dearest Marina,

I have no idea how to write this letter. Curtis has told me of your reasons for leaving the palace, and my heart breaks to know that you have discovered the secret your father and I kept from you so long in that manner. Please believe that our intention was to reveal your true nature on your next birthday. We felt you were now old enough to know who you were, though we have only the vaguest idea ourselves.

Your mother revealed nothing of her nature in those brief lines of the journal I have sent with this letter, though the man who brought you to the castle claims she was a water creature of some sort. Of your father, however, we know much. The truth is, Nightshade is a powerful and evil sorcerer. He has been a terrible scourge to the Kingdoms for more than three decades and has gained more and more power in the last hundred years.

Your father and I fear that he will use you and your sister to gain ultimate power over the Kingdoms, and possibly the land of our forefathers. We do not know what Nightshade is seeking to do, only that whatever his intentions, they can only spell doom for the entire world.

Your sister is another mystery. We have done everything within our power to discover her whereabouts to ensure her safety as well but to no avail. Our greatest hope is that your mother sent her to another kingdom where she was raised by someone who loved her as much as we love you.

That is my most important message to you, my daughter. Know that while you may not be a child of my body, you are as much a child of my heart as any of your brothers. You came into our lives like a miracle, and you have been a joy to me and your father in every respect. We are so proud of the woman you have grown into and will always love you.

I had hoped Curtis, Fahad, and Gerard would bring you home to me, but the arrival of one of Gerard's wolves has forced me to consider that you will not be returning soon. So, I have sent your birth mother's journal along, hoping that it will reveal more to you than it ever did to me.

Stay safe on your journey and rely upon the men in your company to keep you safe. I know that Curtis has taught you some fighting techniques—for children never have as many secrets from their mother as they might think—but I still fear for your safety without them.

Come home soon, my darling. We will be waiting for you with arms and hearts open wide for your return.

With love and thoughts of protection,

Queen Delia de Griffin of Jamaria

Marina held the letter to her chest, not caring that the expensive vellum was crumpling. She was crying like a child, and she was glad no one was around to hear her behaving like one. She never meant to hurt the queen, and she knew without a doubt now the queen never meant to hurt her.

The book was lying on the rock beside her, and she picked it up to stroke the strange binding. It was not leather, but the material was familiar to her. As she contemplated the cover, she became aware of another presence. She frantically wiped away the last of her tears and turned to face the person invading her privacy.

"It has been nowhere near two hours, Gerard," she said peevishly. Whatever else she was about to say caught in her throat when she realized it was Fahad walking toward her.

He stopped at her annoyed tone and was looking unsure of himself now. "I'm sorry, Princess. I just noticed you were gone and wanted to be sure you were well. I can leave if you wish."

Marina turned back to the lake, "No, you may join me. I think I could use the company right now."

The sun was still high in the afternoon sky, but a nearby tree was casting a cool shadow over the rock. Fahad moved to sit next to her, and Marina moved the letter and journal to her lap to give him room.

Fahad sat quietly beside her, and Marina found comfort in the silence. He was not pushing for an explanation, but he was there for her all the same. Her stomach gave an unexpected dip at his nearness and she felt slightly warmer than before.

She surreptitiously put a hand to the cheek facing away from him to determine if her face was as hot as it felt. While she wanted to blame the midday sun, she knew that these feelings had more to do with the man sitting next to her than the weather.

Fahad turned to look at her and gave her a warm smile. Marina knew the heat that rose to her face was showing when Fahad looked at her curiously.

"Are you sure you are well, milady? You look as though the heat may be getting to you."

Marina scrambled hastily from the rock, gathering the items from her mothers. "I am quite well, but I believe we should return to the village before anyone else realizes I am missing."

Marina was not sure what was worse, all the sudden revelations, or the knowledge that Fahad was as dense as her brothers when it came to her feelings.

19

Kaia was bored out of her mind. She had been a guest at Marius' castle for three days now, and she was really missing her appliances. While she never pegged herself as someone obsessed with technology, she never realized just how much of her life revolved around it.

At the moment, she was especially missing toilets. It grossed her out to no end that Cossette was responsible for getting rid of her bodily fluids. Not to mention that she wasn't even sure where it was being disposed of. Considering the lack of plumbing, she was pretty sure it wasn't going in the ground.

Kaia shuddered and waved such thoughts away. She needed something else to occupy her mind. It both irked and saddened her that she hadn't seen her sister in any other visions. Now that she was safe and comfortable, she was really hoping that some meditation exercises would bring them together again. But not a yoga pose or deep breathing exercise she knew worked so far.

As she stared out the bedroom window at the daily activity below, Kaia's restlessness became too much to bear. She stormed over to the wardrobe and opened it with a vicious yank. The beautiful dresses that enchanted her on her first day were now tedious. She longed to return to good old pants and shirts.

She slammed the door shut and turned to the bag still sitting next to her bed. It hadn't been moved in all the time she was there. She dropped it on her bed and started to remove the contents one at a time.

Merry insisted on a few survivalist essentials, like the water bottle, the knife and lighter, some granola bars, a roll of duct tape, and some rope. Kaia wasn't really sure what the tape and rope were for, but she trusted that her mom knew what she was doing. Kaia also hid the amulet in a compartment in the bottom of the bag. It was a plastic container, so the amulet wouldn't get crushed, and no one could tell that there was anything in it by squeezing the bottom of the bag.

Kaia left the amulet alone, not quite trusting her surroundings enough to bring it out. She did, however, sort through the few pieces of clothing she brought with her. There were several extra pairs of underwear and socks. That was actually her idea because Merry couldn't give her a straight answer about the possibility of laundry facilities.

She quickly stripped off the dress and returned to her old clothing. It felt far nicer than it probably should have to wear her own clothing again. Cossette took away the shirt and capris Kaia entered with and they never returned. Given the look of disgust on Cossette's face when she took them away, Kaia had a feeling she would never see those clothes again.

"Alrighty then," she said to her reflection in the floor-length mirror, "let's see what kind of shenanigans we can get up to today. I'm thinking an unauthorized tour is in order."

She nodded at herself and laughed at the thought that her reflection concurred. Feeling very spy-like, she stuck her head carefully out the door, searching for any servants. Usually, they seemed to know when she was out of her room and set upon her within moments. Today, however, there was no one in sight.

"A little freaky," Kaia whispered to herself, "but since when do I question good luck?"

She snuck out of the room, closing the door behind her as quietly as possible. The castle was so well tended the hinges barely made any noise. Kaia looked around again, checking to be sure the coast was clear before setting off.

She wasn't headed in any particular direction, nor was she looking for anything. That didn't stop her from playing the Mission Impossible theme in her head as she slunk along. Nor did it keep her from hugging the walls and walking like she was trying to sneak past her sleeping mom.

Every time she thought she heard a servant, she would duck into an alcove or behind something to hide until they passed. She was only correct three out of the nine times she did this, but that didn't stop her heart from beating wildly or swiping the terrified—yet excited—grin away all nine times.

As she was hiding from a group of servants, she was suddenly struck by how quiet they were. Her only warning had been the sound of their footsteps as they approached. This was the same every time. As an American, she didn't know a lot about servants. But didn't they gripe and gossip like everyone else? These people just marched along and did their work like busy little ants.

Kaia was no longer singing in her head, and the excitement over being a fake spy was well over. Now she was considering her time at the castle. In the three days since arriving, she couldn't remember a time when she heard any unnecessary conversation or saw any teasing, laughter, or fun of any kind. The more she thought about it, the more this castle and its inhabitants reminded her of Stepford people.

The fun was now completely over, and Kaia felt real fear when she heard someone approaching from the opposite direction. She hid in the curtains of a nearby window. The fabric reached the floor and the curtains were completely closed like all the others leaving no sunlight in the hall. As the person passed, she looked out the window and saw something that took her breath away.

The window was facing the western courtyard. She never saw this side of the castle before because all the windows showing that side was blocked. Now, she knew why. The courtyard was bare of any vegetation and there was only one thing in the entire twenty-foot square space.

A wooden post, driven deep into the sand and given a stone base to keep it steady, stood in the middle of the barren square. Waitimu was tied to the post with no way to escape the midday sun beating down on him. Kaia couldn't see him very clearly but she could tell from the spots of black and red on the sand he had been severely beaten. He was lying on his side with his legs splayed out. She couldn't tell if he was alive, and she covered her mouth to keep her horrified sobs muffled.

After standing there for a few minutes, trying to compose herself, she almost fell with relief when she saw Waitimu move. He was trying to stand up, but he was too weak. Kaia rested a hand on the glass, silently imploring him to stay down. It took Kaia a second to figure out just why he was moving.

Robin was stalking toward him with a whip coiled in one hand. Kaia's eyes widened at the sight of his evil expression, unable to reconcile the kind and amusing man who entertained her at dinner for the last two nights with this man with the hard-set mouth and cruel eyes.

Kaia couldn't hear what Robin was saying, but she did hear the vicious crack of his whip. She turned away, but not fast enough to keep herself from seeing the leather bite into Waitimu's human back, flaying the skin open and flecking the sand with more red.

She stumbled away from the window, tripping on the curtains and landing on the floor with a thud. When she heard the sound of approaching footsteps, she quickly disentangled her foot from the curtain and ran in the opposite direction. If anyone pursued her, she couldn't hear them over her feet and thumping heart.

Once she was well away from the west side of the house, she stopped running. As she caught her breath, she heard footsteps approaching once again, this time in front of her. Kaia forced herself to keep her breathing even and kept walking. She didn't need to hide anymore. She was also afraid of what else she might discover if she took any more unexpected detours.

When she met the servant walking toward her, she tried not to flinch when he smiled at her.

"Do you need anything, Lady Kaia?"

"No."

She winced at how harsh she sounded. She cleared her throat and gave the man a tight smile. His returning smile was gorgeous. But, just like Cosette, it never reached his eyes. They weren't as cold and vicious as Robin's just were but they still unsettled her.

"Sorry, no" she tried again. "No, I'm good. I'm headed back to my room now. Thanks though."

"Very good, milady."

The servant bowed and walked past her. Kaia barely dared to move until he turned a corner. She finally breathed easier when she reached her door without meeting anyone else. When she returned to her room, Cosette was there waiting for her.

"Milady, I have set out a lovely gown for you. I am sorry the purple did not meet with your approval." Cossette curtsied gracefully and swept her hand toward the bed where the dress lay along with the undergarments that went with it.

"No thank you," Kaia said, trying to keep her voice steady, "I think I'll just stay with what I've got on."

Cossette clucked with disapproval at Kaia's choice, "Oh no, milady, his lordship would never approve of such unsightly garb. The master is a connoisseur of all things to do with beauty. To disobey him in this regard would be unaccountably rude." Cossette's warm smile was still in place, but Kaia saw a coldness in the servant's eyes that said there would be no further argument.

"Fine," Kaia was getting really angry now. Part of this was for allowing her fear to keep her from finding out what else Marius was up to. Marius was responsible for Waitimu's torture, and if she had to suffer through another stupid dress to figure out how to save Waitimu and get back at Marius, then she would do it.

Cossette's smile widened and she hurried to help Kaia out of her sturdier clothing and back into the loathsome dress. Kaia was at least able to stand her ground on the issue of undergarments. The novelty of those had quickly worn off, and she flatly refused to give up her bras and underwear. Cossette only relented when Kaia made the argument that Marius would never know, as he would never have the chance to see them. She was also able to convince Cossette the clothing she just took off was to stay with her this time.

"Oh, milady," Cossette sighed when they were finished, "you look absolutely beautiful. All the maids agree that you are, by far, the prettiest girl in the castle." Cossette giggled like they were the best of friends and left the room. She never saw the disbelieving look Kaia aimed at her back.

Kaia examined her reflection for the second time that day. She had enough self-esteem to recognize that she was rather pretty, especially when she really got herself dressed up, but the caliber of women at this castle completely blew her out of the water. The women in this place belonged on runways and fashion spreads, not emptying out chamber pots and polishing silver.

The more she thought about it, the more she began to wonder how Marius could convince that many beautiful people to be his servants. He must literally have money growing on trees for the amount it must have taken to keep everyone happy enough to stay on. Maybe it was shallow of her, but she assumed at least some of the servants could have found better ways of supporting themselves using their good looks.

Kaia forgot about this line of thought when she noticed that her bag was back on the floor. She knew she left everything out on the bed when she left earlier on her spying mission.

"That chick better not have taken anything," she muttered to herself. She would be royally ticked off if her clothes were gone.

She breathed a sigh of relief to see her clothes were still there. That relief was quickly replaced by anger when she saw her water bottle, knife, and rope were missing. The granola, lighter and tape were still there, and Kaia wondered if their oddness in the face of all the medieval technology kept Cossette from taking them as well.

"Son of a—" Kaia muttered, unable to believe the empty-headed servant stole her stuff. Then, she felt a moment of panic as she thought about the amulet. She turned the bag upside down, dumping her clothes on top of what Cossette hadn't taken. Finally, the bag was empty.

She felt along the bottom feeling for the lip. Sliding her fingernail beneath it, she released the Velcro with an audible rip. This revealed the space occupied by the black plastic box that lined the bottom of the bag. She opened it with her heart in her throat and almost sobbed in relief to see it was still there. She hesitated a moment before grabbing it to reassure herself that the amulet was still inside. Her luck was still holding because not only was the amulet still there, but it didn't send her into another vision. There was only a slight zing of electricity before it sat there quietly in her palm.

"I swear, if she took this, I would have ripped out every single one of her curls. And enjoyed the process, darn it."

Kaia wasn't usually this vindictive--or violent--but she felt slightly violated at the intrusion of Cossette's search and seizure. The amulet dropped to the bed when someone knocked on Kaia's door.

"Just a minute," she cried as she hastily stuffed everything back into her bag. The amulet went back into its box, with everything else shoved on top. When she was satisfied that nothing was left on the bed, she put the bag over her shoulder and answered the door.

"Milady," Cossette curtsied again, and Kaia harbored the unkind hope that the girl would fall over, "the master has requested your presence at luncheon. Would you like me to fix your hair before the meal?"

Kaia smiled stiffly before replying, "No, I like my hair the way it is; slightly mussed and still purple."

Cossette looked like she wanted to argue, but Kaia pushed past her to head toward the dining hall. Marius insisted on having every meal in the large space, despite the fact that Kaia and Robin were the only other people present. There was no Robin at the moment, and Kaia's stomach churned at the implication.

Marius was in his normal place at the head of the dark mahogany table. He looked just as handsome as ever, but this served to make Kaia feel angry rather than charmed. How dare he looked calm and unruffled when she knew he ordered Robin to brutally beat Waitimu?

"Kaia, my dear," Marius' voice was silky and saccharine. Kaia wondered how she hadn't noticed this before. "I'm so glad you were available to join me," he continued.

"No problem," she replied, seating herself at the only other place setting to his left. There was a sumptuous feast spread before them, but this failed to impress her today. Every meal had been elaborate and delicious. It turned out, even fine meats and desserts got old after a while. Kaia longed for a slice of pizza.

"Have you been finding everything to your liking?" Kaia noticed that Marius looked as though he already knew the answer to the question, and he was making the assumption that he had thoroughly impressed her. Kaia weighed the options of telling him the truth. In the spirit of keeping her host in the dark, she opted for a mix of truth and lie.

"I have never seen so many interesting things in all my life. Your castle is full of so many beautiful sights, I never get tired of looking around. I feel like I could stay here forever."

Kaia hoped he heard the truth in what she said and was too caught up in himself to notice the lies. She released a tense breath when Marius looked smug as he sat back and relaxed in his chair. Yet, Kaia found she couldn't stand that self-satisfied expression for more than a few seconds.

"However," Marius' look darkened at this, "I was a little upset when I found that some of my supplies have gone missing," Kaia stated. She figured a little honesty wouldn't hurt. Plus, she assumed Marius would be anticipating the subject coming up at some point. Kaia decided it would be better sooner rather than later.

"Ah, yes," Marius was relaxed again, and back to looking smug. Kaia gritted her teeth and forced herself to let him continue before she ended up like Waitimu. "Cossette was afraid you might hurt yourself with a few of those items, so she brought them to me for safekeeping."

"I don't see how a bottle or rope could possibly bring me any harm. I'd appreciate it if you returned everything to me. They wouldn't have been in my bag if I didn't know how to handle them properly."

This was another tiny lie. She really wasn't very good with a knife, and she had no idea what to use the rope for, but they were hers and she wanted them back. Marius pouted, and Kaia fought back the urge to tell him it wasn't an attractive look on a guy who looked like he was pushing forty.

"My dear Kaia," he sighed, "I have no wish to deprive you of your supplies, though I do not see why you have any need of them when you are so happily situated here."

"Yeah, sure, I'm happy to be here, but the fact remains I'd like to have my stuff back. They have sentimental value," she improvised. At Marius' dubious look, she added, "Well the knife and bottle do. The rope is just a helpful tool in a pinch. You never know when you'll need one." She smiled innocently and stared at him.

He stared back, and she tried not to shiver at the calculating glint in his cold green eyes. She relaxed slightly when he looked away and motioned to one of the servants standing to the side.

"Hamish, please bring the lady's items. We wish to please our guest after all," he added smoothly for Kaia's benefit.

As they waited for Hamish, Kaia decided to interrogate her host a little. She wasn't naturally subtle, but she was going to try. "So, I never did ask, what brought you to the Krax'mran desert? Didn't your family have a castle where you were from?"

Marius gave her a thin smile, "Actually, I'm the seventh son of a minor baron. I had to make my own way in this land, and the desert has served me well these many years."

"Aren't you worried about the Krax'mran? From what I could tell, they aren't big fans of humans."

"Ah, well I have my ways of deterring their kind. I am only glad our gentle Robin was able to wrest you away from the savages." Marius shivered dramatically, and Kaia once again had to force down a reaction. She wondered if she was going to acquire a twitch if she stayed with Marius much longer.

Kaia gave Marius her own thin smile and sipped her water. Marius offered her wine for every meal, but the exhilaration of drinking before she was legal paled before the bitter taste of the alcohol. She didn't get how anyone could prefer that nasty stuff to Coke or even just plain old water. This upset Marius at first, but Kaia claimed an allergy and he was forced to bow to her preference.

"You know, my dear, you never fully explained where you came from or who cursed you to die so far from home."

Kaia's mind raced to come up with a suitable lie. She didn't know how he would react to finding out she was from Earth, but she had a feeling it wouldn't be pleasant.

"Umm, well I come from a family of nomads. We ran into a witch in a village on the coast, and she got angry when we ate her...cabbages. So she told my mother that we could either be her servants for fifty years or she would kill the youngest member of our family. That got me pretty irate, so I took a swing at her. All of a sudden, I'm in the desert and I have no idea where the rest of my family is."

Marius assessed Kaia's animated face. She'd really gotten into her story there at the end, so she hoped her expression conveyed the right kind of enthusiasm for the story.

"What an unusual way to react to a witch. So, you are Sarosian?"

"Umm," Kaia wasn't sure how to answer. She didn't want to get caught in a lie, and she didn't know enough about this world to guess the right answer.

"Here you are, milady," a voice said beside her. Kaia jumped in surprise when she saw Hamish beside her with her supplies. She hadn't even heard the man walk in despite his nearly 6'6", 200-pound frame.

"Oh, thanks," she burst out, grabbing and shoving them into her bag. Marius leaned over to see what she was doing, and she saw his face cloud over in anger at the sight of her pack.

"My darling, Kaia," he bit out, "Are you planning to leave us so soon?"

"No, umm, I'm just a little leery of leaving my stuff in my room anymore. I'm not one of those twice fooled kinds of people."

"Twice what?" Marius shifted quickly from anger to confusion, and Kaia wondered if he had these kinds of mood swings often.

"You know: fool me once, shame on you; fool me twice, shame on me. Sure, Cossette took my stuff once and that was her bad. I'm not about to wait around and see if she'll do it again."

"Ah," Marius still seemed a little confused, but at the very least he wasn't angry any longer.

"Listen, I'm not feeling too hungry at the moment, so I'm just going to go back to my room if that's cool with you."

"Your manner of speech is most odd at times," Marius declared.

"Yeah, well, the life of a nomad will do that to you," Kaia quipped as she stood. Hamish stepped forward to carry her bag, but Kaia put the strap over her arm and gave him a look that made him back off.

"You are quite pale for a Sarosian," Marius was fishing now.

"I was adopted. Never knew who my real parents were."

She turned around before he could answer, so she never saw him sit up taller in his chair or the glint of speculation in his eyes.

20

Marina knew she was dreaming, but she did not feel like waking, despite the fear her dream self was feeling. She was skulking around dark corridors, searching for someone. That person was in danger, and she had a feeling her dream self might be as well. Her heart was beating frantically, and her breath sounded far too loud to her own ears.

Every movement was a potential enemy, and she was glad to be in a place with so many nooks and crannies. She was approaching a part of the castle she knew to be forbidden, but Marina could tell this was the right direction.

She did not know who she was, because she certainly did not feel like herself. Marina never had a dream like this before. It was so vivid and yet so surreal. Her head felt too full like she was sharing space with someone else.

Suddenly, there was a movement ahead of her, and panic overrode her thoughts. A shadow beside a cabinet provided a hiding spot, but she knew that if the person ahead walked past, she would be discovered.

A door opened and closed nearby, and she knew that whomever it had been was gone now. She crept forward but stopped when she heard voices behind a nearby door. A light seeped beneath the crack, beckoning her forward.

The voices were slightly muffled, but she was able to make out most of what was being said. "We must find out more about our little guest," she heard a man say. His voice made her shiver in dread but Marina did not know why.

"Master, do you wish to interrogate her yourself, or would you prefer to have me do so?" This voice made her feel both anger and betrayal.

"I believe we will save interrogation for when she proves unwilling to cooperate. First, I believe we should try to charm the information from her. After all, what is the point of the good looks and personality I have given you if they are put aside at this moment?"

"Very good, Master. What would you like me to discover?"

"Well, Robin, I would first like to know her exact age. Also, see if the people who raised her knew her mother or where she was from. If my suspicions prove correct, we may have need of the child."

"As you wish, my lord Nightshade."

Marina felt as though fireworks were going off in her mind at this revelation. The surprise catapulted her out of the dream and to full wakefulness. She sat up in the bed provided by the mayor of Heatherwood, breathing hard. Curtis, who was sharing the room with her, woke up beside her, rumpled and confused.

"Marina," he mumbled sleepily, "what's going on?"

Curtis blinked to clear his vision and searched the moonlit room for possible intruders. He doubted anyone would get past Gerard but he knew Marina didn't often have nightmares. Normally, he was also a light sleeper but the citizens of Heatherwood kept him dancing from afternoon well into the evening. He knew his Duran friends would laugh at his lack of stamina but he decided to blame Marina's hare-brained trip and the stress it cause the family for his current fatigue.

"I—I do not know," she stuttered. "I think I dreamt of my father. I was in a strange castle, searching for someone, and I was almost caught. There was a door and two men were conversing behind it about—someone. It might have been me, but it did not feel like me."

Curtis shook his head again, reminding Marina of a wet dog.

"I'm afraid I'm too tired to keep up with this," he admitted, "start again but slow down. You're speaking too fast, and I think you're hitting a pitch only Gerard can hear."

Marina glared at her brother and threw her down pillow into his face. As he spat out a couple of feathers, she worked to calm her breathing.

Once she composed herself, she told Curtis of her dream. The details were growing hazy the longer she was awake, but the last bit stayed with her.

"That Robin person called the other man Nightshade. My mother's diary said my father means me ill. Our parents say he is a powerful sorcerer bent upon some unknown evil. In my dream, I was afraid of him, but I am unsure why."

"Perhaps because he is, oh I don't know, a powerful sorcerer bent upon evil?" Curtis said acerbically.

"Oh do be quiet," Marina said without heat, "this felt different. It felt like I feared him because I did not wish to be caught, not because I felt he might use his power upon me. Besides, while his intentions did not sound pleasant, neither did they feel evil. He spoke of interrogation, not torture."

"Perhaps interrogation by an evil sorcerer is like torture," Curtis stroked his chin mockingly, and Marina wished for a second pillow to throw.

"I know it was only a dream, but it felt utterly real while I was in it. I only wish I could understand why it felt like I was someone other than me."

Marina's unease grew the more she thought of this. Something felt different about this dream. The longer it stewed within her mind, the more real it felt. The details may have begun to fade, but the fear was growing stronger. She put a hand to her chest and felt her heart hammering against her ribcage. Closing her eyes, she focused on that feeling and the way it pulled at her.

The room around her began to fade and slowly became the castle again. This time, it did not feel like a dream. She heard a sound and turned with her heart in her throat. Someone was nearby, but it was too dark to see who it was.

"Hello?" she whispered tentatively, almost afraid to hear a reply. The curtains to her right rustled slightly, and Marina reached for the knife at her belt. There was nothing there but her nightshirt and Marina cursed under her breath.

A sliver of moonlight appeared between the curtains, and she saw a face peeking out at her. She squeaked with alarm and prepared to defend herself. Footsteps down the hall made her turn to face a second assailant. The curtains rustled again, and the moonlight was gone, leaving Marina in darkness.

Someone turned a corner, and Marina was bathed in candlelight. She crouched into a defensive stance, but the man acted as though he could not see her.

"Who are you?" she demanded.

The man never faltered and walked past her without a word. He was handsome and vaguely familiar. Marina relaxed her stance and looked after him in confusion.

"Hello?" she ventured. She was not sure she really wanted an answer, but it was worth a try. The man never turned around and she wondered at the implications.

She spun when the curtains rustled again. This time, a figure stepped from between them, though the features were obscured by the play of shadows and moonlight. Marina was not as afraid as before, as it seemed she was only in another vision and was an observer as opposed to someone being observed.

"Hey, how'd you do that?" the figure whispered, making Marina squeak in alarm.

The person stepped closer, and Marina was finally able to recognize Kaia. She breathed a sigh of relief before answering.

"I am unsure. I thought this was only a vision, but then I would not be speaking to you if it was."

Kaia looked thoughtful at this. Marina's sight was spotty from the exposure to the moonlight before being cast into the deep darkness of the hall again. Kaia did not seem to be faring much better if the sound of flesh hitting furniture quickly followed by hushed cursing was any indication.

"Well, maybe it's like when I saw you in the forest," Kaia offered. "I wasn't quite there, but it felt real enough to me. Did you get transported—or whatever—there too?"

Marina shook her head, "No, I was traveling in that forest when you appeared before me. I did wonder how you were able to appear and disappear so quickly. I am still not precisely sure...but never mind that for now. Where are we?"

"We're in a castle in the middle of the Krax'mran desert," Kaia answered. "Right now, I'm trying to find this guy who's being tortured for God only knows what reason. I thought the people who lived here were pretty decent, but it turns out they're a bunch of jerks." Kaia sounded offended, as though their behavior was a disappointment to her.

"Well, by all means, let us find this person. Where do we begin?"

"Well, you could begin by telling me your name. Our conversation was a little too short last time."

"I am Marina DeGriffin, crown princess of Jamaria. Though, I have recently discovered I was not born of that house," she ended despondently.

"So you're adopted?" Kaia was able to make out Marina's face finally and could tell this line of questioning was upsetting her. But she needed to know if her suspicions that this was her sister standing in front of her were correct.

"It would appear so," Marina choked out, "I have only recently discovered this, and have also been told that I have a sister in the world."

Marina's eyes searched Kaia's, and Kaia could tell that Marina was beginning to have the same idea.

"Well that's funny, 'cause it turns out I have a sister too, and I'm pretty sure she's standing here."

Marina gave a broken sob, not sure if she was happy or upset by the revelation. Her emotions were running high, and it was clear from Kaia's face that she was feeling it as well. Marina was surprised when Kaia grabbed Marina's shoulders and brought her in for a fierce hug.

"I'm still not sure what the heck is going on, but it sure is nice to meet you," Kaia rasped. Marina nodded her agreement and tightened her hold on her newly discovered sibling.

A noise down the hall startled them and forced them to break apart. Kaia took Marina's hand in her own and pulled them both back behind the curtains. As they stood there, waiting for the person to pass, Marina wondered if she should tell Kaia about Nightshade. He was here somewhere in the castle, and Marina did not know if Kaia would be safer with or without the knowledge.

"Kaia," Marina started, "there is something you must know of our father."

Kaia didn't say anything, waiting for the footsteps to fade. She wasn't too sure that Marina should be talking, but given that Robin did not hear her a few moments before, perhaps it wouldn't be a big deal. She looked at Marina questioningly, all the while straining to hear if there was anyone coming for them.

"I think I was seeing through your eyes as you were sneaking through the castle," Kaia looked surprised, but Marina decided to save that conversation for later, "I heard two men speaking who called each other Robin and Nightshade."

Kaia nodded, still thinking it odd Robin called Marius by a different name.

"My—the queen of Jamaria gave me a journal that was written by our mother. It only has a few sentences that I can read, but they say that this Nightshade is our father."

Marina paused at Kaia's sharp breath and waited to see if Kaia would say anything about this. Kaia shook her head in denial and pushed back out into the hallway without a word. She grabbed a bag Marina did not notice before from one of the corners and let the fabric flutter in her wake. Marina followed her and waited for her eyes to adjust to the darkness again.

"Kaia, where are you?"

A hand grabbed hers in the darkness, and she was being pulled down the hall. Marina tried to pull away, afraid Kaia would run into something and alert someone to her presence.

"Slow down," Marina hissed, "or you will hurt yourself."

"Listen," Kaia spat back, "this little family reunion has been nice and all, but Waitimu needs rescuing, and I'm not in the mood for developing daddy issues. I'm no Luke Skywalker"

"Developing what? Luke who?"

"Never mind," Kaia huffed, pausing at the end of the corridor. It was T-shaped with a door in front of them. The hallways to the sides were only about five feet long, and those both ended indoors as well.

"Which way do we go?" Marina asked.

Kaia stood in front of the middle door and studied it. This was the only door with light spilling out from under it, but she wasn't sure if that was a good sign or bad. She gave Marina a speculative look and reached toward the knob.

"I'm going to start with this one. Since you apparently can't be seen by anyone but me, you scope it out and see if there's anyone in there. If there is, let's hope they don't come investigate the magically opening door. If there isn't, let's explore it for a bit."

Marina nodded, and Kaia turned the knob and opened the door. Marina was surprised by the lack of objects in the space. It was a long hallway that looked like it stretched at least one hundred feet. Doors lined the walls and torches were placed at regular intervals to light the way. This seemed to be the only hall like that, as every other hall she and Kaia went down was pitch-black.

"There is no one here," Marina announced. Kaia slipped in beside her and closed the door behind them.

"Well, looks like we've got a lot more exploring to do than I expected." Kaia sighed in frustration and marched forward.

Marina followed and stopped next to Kaia in front of the first door. It had a sliding panel at about eye level, making Marina think of the old dungeons back home. Kaia stepped forward and slid the panel open, peering inside.

Both girls jumped back when something large hit the door. Its snarls were deep and bone-chilling. The door held fast, and Kaia regained her courage long enough to give the room a second look. Two yellow eyes stared back at her through the panel, sending a shiver down her back.

The eyes disappeared, and Kaia could barely make out a large doglike form in the meager light from the hall. It began moving away from the door and pacing back and forth in the room. It still stared at her as if waiting for her to make a move. Kaia slid the panel closed again and looked at Marina with uncertainty.

"This may take a while. I think we're in the right place, but I have no idea which room Waitimu will be in."

"Well, we do not have all night. In fact, I am uncertain how long I can be here. We have not really tested this connection overmuch."

"No kidding," Kaia muttered. "Listen, I'll take this side of the hall, you take the other. We'll just open each panel until we find him. If we find him."

Kaia said the last with a large dose of worry in her voice, and Marina wondered if they would find Kaia's friend. She put a reassuring hand on her sister's shoulder and went to the adjacent door. Despite her apparently invisible nature, she was able to move the panel. There was someone in there, but she realized she had no idea whom she was looking for.

"Kaia, what does your friend look like? I can open the panels, but I cannot call out for him as you can."

"He's a Krax'mran. Half man, half spider. He shouldn't be too difficult to recognize." Kaia said distractedly as she opened the panel of an empty cell.

Marina looked at Kaia with disbelief.

"You have befriended a Krax'mran?" she shrilled. "But, they hate humans."

"I wouldn't necessarily call us friends," Kaia answered, running from one door to the next, opening and closing panels, "He and his dad captured me and carted me off to their village, where Robin rescued me. Now, they're torturing him, and I feel partially responsible."

Marina was frozen in shock. Kaia stopped in her search a few doors down. The people in the cells were calling out for release, and Kaia felt a vice of despair grip her heart as she tried to ignore them for the moment.

"Look, I'll explain it later, but like you said: we don't have all night. So, get your butt in gear and find him."

Marina raised an eyebrow at being spoken to in such a manner but decided to overlook it in light of Kaia's desperation. She turned back to the panel and peered inside. It was dark, but the person stirred when the light penetrated his cell.

"Who is there?" the man croaked hoarsely.

He moved with great difficulty, and Marina noticed that what she had assumed was bedding was actually his lower half. She had gotten lucky and her first door revealed a Krax'mran.

"Kaia," she cried, "I think I have found him."

Kaia was by her side in seconds, shoving her face against the panel to see inside. As she was solid, she blocked some of the light giving her even less to see than Marina.

"Waitimu, is that you?"

Marina watched as the Krax'mran tried to stand. He braced his hands on the wall and used it as a prop as his lifted his battered body. He was unsteady on his legs, but he made it to the door.

Kaia wasn't expecting the arm that shot through the panel to grab her by the front of her shirt. She yelped and struggled against the iron grip.

"What have you done with my family?" Waitimu roared.

"Nothing! I swear I didn't have anything to do with Robin and his men coming to the village. I didn't even know who they were. Please, I'm trying to help you. You've got to let me go!"

Marina tried to help Kaia pry Waitimu's fingers off of her shirt, but they were no match for his superior strength. She wanted to do something, but her only option would be to hurt this man who already endured so much torture.

"Kaia, what should I do?" Marina sobbed.

"There's a knife in my bag," Kaia ground out, still trying to wrest herself from Waitimu's grasp, "it's in the front compartment. Get that and I'll cut this stupid shirt off."

"Who do you speak to, woman?" Waitimu demanded.

"Dude," Kaia barked, "let me go and I'll explain everything, but if you don't shut your freaking mouth, someone's going to catch us." Kaia vaguely noticed that the other prisoners had stopped crying out for help. Apparently, they weren't impressed with her rescue attempt so far and preferred to take their chances in their cells.

Marina stared at the strange pack on Kaia's back, wondering how to get into the thing. There were strange fasteners with teeth holding the sides together, but she was unsure of how to open them. Finally, she decided to pull on the nearest tab and hope for the best. She was surprised when it began to move smoothly and release the two sides.

"Surely this is a powerful magic," she breathed in awe.

"What?" Kaia gasped, "Seriously, I need that knife. You've got to hurry it up." Waitimu twisted the fabric, making it a little difficult for Kaia to breathe.

Marina rummaged around and finally closed her hand around something metal. It did not look like any knife she ever saw before, so she held it up for Kaia's inspection.

"Is this it?"

She barely had enough time to get the words out before Kaia snatched it from her grasp. Kaia opened the blade with clumsy fingers and put the tip near the collar. She was careful not to hurt herself or

Waitimu as she slid the blade down, cutting through the thin cotton of her shirt with ease. Before she completely severed the fabric, she was spinning away from Waitimu's outstretched hand, tearing through the rest of the shirt.

Kaia was breathing hard from the excitement, and Waitimu was left clutching nothing but her thin blue T-shirt. Marina was looking at her with an odd look on her face, and Waitimu was staring through the opened panel with a look of mingled anger and shock.

Kaia looked down and was glad to see her bra survived the fray. She carefully grabbed the backpack that fell to the floor and began to rummage through it to find another shirt. The silence kept stretching out as she did and Kaia looked up to find Marina and Waitimu still staring at her.

"What?" she demanded peevishly, "Haven't you ever seen a girl in her underwear? Get a grip for Pete's sake!"

With that, she grabbed a shirt and pulled it over her head with unnecessary force.

21

Marina was torn between horror and amusement at Kaia's state of undress. Admittedly, the shirt Kaia donned did not offer much in the way of propriety, but Marina supposed it was better than going about in nothing but the flimsy undergarment her sister wore. She shook these foolish thoughts from her head and focused on the matter at hand.

Waitimu still looked furious, and Marina wished she could help Kaia convince him they were only trying to help. Kaia had her hands on her hips and was glaring at her ruined shirt on the floor.

"I hope you're happy. I didn't have a lot to wear in the first place, now I'm down another piece."

Waitimu looked confused for a moment, before reverting back to anger.

"What does this matter? Your master can surely replace such as this. I will not submit to this new form of interrogation. Your master will never discover the other Krax'mran villages, and my people will destroy this puny castle."

"Good, tear the whole freaking thing down. I don't live here, and Marius is most definitely not my master. Heck, I'm American. We're made to fight the power."

"Fight the power?" Marina raised an eyebrow at this odd phrase.

"Don't worry about it," Kaia muttered.

Waitimu looked to where Marina was standing, trying to follow Kaia's gaze.

"Whom do you speak to?" he demanded.

"Well, as it happens, I'm speaking to my sister. You just can't see her because she's not actually here."

Waitimu snorted in disbelief.

"Yeah," Kaia agreed, "it sounds crazy, but it's true all the same."

"This is another of Nightshade's tricks," Waitimu spat in disgust.

"What can I do to convince you this is not a trick? I mean, your mother seemed to believe me, but she's not here, so that's not going to do us much good."

Waitimu mulled this over for a moment before answering.

"Give me some of your blood," he decided, "I carry some of my mother's gift and can confer with Anansi."

Kaia looked at Marina for assurance but received only a worried shrug. Kaia weighed the options and decided to trust Waitimu like she wanted him to trust her. She unwrapped the bandage Cosette wrapped around the wound after Kaia's bath earlier and held the knife to her still-healing hand. With a deep breath and a grimace as she anticipated the pain, she reopened the wound Adebomi inflicted. As the blood flowed down her wrist, she wondered what she was supposed to do next.

Waitimu held out his hand once again and beckoned her forward. She approached him carefully, not wanting to repeat the events of a few moments ago.

"I will not hurt you," he assured her, "just place your hand in mine."

She did as he asked, and winced when he squeezed her injured hand for a moment before letting go. He licked the blood from his palm and closed his eyes. Kaia hoped it was to really get in touch with his god, and not to determine if she tasted good enough to eat.

Waitimu opened his eyes and looked at Kaia without any expression on his face. Kaia and Marina looked at each other nervously, both hoping he made up his mind in Kaia's favor. Waitimu looked in Marina's direction again, and his eyes widened in shock.

"Who is that girl?"

Marina gasped in surprise when their eyes met, and she realized he could see her. She decided Kaia's blood must have passed their bond to Waitimu, finally allowing him to see what he could not before. Kaia's gaze passed between Marina and Waitimu, her only response a startled, "huh." They looked at her after this hushed exclamation, as if expecting her to have all the answers.

"Waitimu, meet Marina. She's my sister, who I only found out about a few minutes ago. Now, do you believe that I'm not working for or with Marius?"

Waitimu's face had regained the lack of expression that seemed to be its natural state. Kaia would have rolled her eyes at his impassivity, but she was getting more nervous the longer they stood there in the unprotected hall.

"I have not been given a clear answer by Anansi, but he tells me you can be trusted—for now."

"Fine," Kaia sighed in exasperation, "then let's get you out of here."

"How do you propose we do that?" Marina hissed, "I do not see any keys in this hall, nor are there any locks or handles upon the doors. As far as I can tell, there is no way to open the cell door."

Kaia analyzed the door for a moment, trying to figure out how it was locked. She wasn't really thinking about it when she rested her bleeding hand on the door and was unprepared when the door swung inward.

"Son of a—" she mumbled.

Waitimu's hand gripped the edge of the door, pulling it open wide enough to let himself out. Kaia was a bit dazed, but even she heard the voices approaching them in the hall. Her horrified gaze caught a mirrored look in Marina's eyes. Kaia could hear the voices getting closer, and made a snap decision.

Scooping up the backpack and rag of a shirt, she quickly darted into Waitimu's cell, pushing him back as she did. With her good hand, she gently closed the door behind her. Marina stayed still during all of this, but when she heard the magical lock of Waitimu's door engage, she quickly closed the panel in the door.

Kaia and Waitimu were plunged into darkness, both barely daring to breathe lest they be caught. Outside, Marina turned and watched the door handle turn. It was only partially open when she felt herself pulling away again.

"No!" she shouted, "I cannot leave yet."

Marina sat straight up in her bed as sunlight began to stream through the window. She looked around frantically, both scared and angry to be back at the Heatherwood inn. Curtis was sitting in a chair beside her bed, snoring loudly. She thought about waking him, but he looked exhausted.

Using all the stealth at her disposal, she eased out of the bed and found some clothing. Curtis would have to be truly exhausted to remain asleep even with her silent movements. He was usually a light sleeper, citing his many early morning classes taught by strict professors in Dura.

Marina carried her boots to the door and carefully looked out to see if anyone else was awake at this early hour. Before she crept downstairs, she took care to secure her cap again and buttoned her vest to flatten her chest. Early morning sounds came from the kitchen, and an old couple was quietly breaking their fast in the dining room. They smiled at her as she snuck by, and Marina returned the smile, putting a finger to her lips to show that she did not want to disturb anyone.

The old man smiled and shook his head, saying to his wife, "Pretty young lad like that must have found an equally pretty girl with all of yesterday's goings ons."

Marina was glad she was already out the door when she heard that so the man could not see her blush. There were indeed a few girls trying to cozy up to her last night, and that was the only time she felt bad about keeping up her charade as a boy.

She sat down on the bench outside and put her boots on. There was a pleasant breeze rustling the trees to the northeast. The forest was beginning to thin out, signaling they were getting closer to the Krax'mran border. The Rejos stopped two miles from the border, and that was where the brushland began before melting into desert.

Marina was not looking forward to entering the desert at the hottest time of year, but there really was no choice. She had now seen Kaia's distress and felt her fear. Their father's castle was not safe, and Marina wanted to get Kaia out of there as soon as possible. She feared that the castle would be impossible to find without help from the Krax'mran.

Marina closed her eyes, soaking up the sun's early morning rays.

She felt that familiar pull and realized it was leading her to Kaia all along. The smile that spread across her face was radiant in its joy.

"It's good to see you enjoying the morning, Marcus."

Marina's eyes snapped open to find Fahad looking down at her. She heard nothing to suggest there was anyone around before he spoke. No scuffed dirt or squeaking boards beyond what she could hear from the kitchen. She did not respond right away, forgetting for a moment she supplied the men with a fake name to keep the villagers from guessing her true nature.

"Oh, yes," she finally stuttered, "I could not sleep any longer, so I thought I should at least enjoy the sunrise. I do not see many as it happens."

Fahad chuckled as he sat next to her. "I seem to recall a sunrise only a few days ago that you saw quite well."

Marina cursed her fair skin as she blushed. "Yes, well, it is not often one may see battle-hardened men make fools of themselves."

Fahad merely smiled at the gibe and stared straight ahead, enjoying the sunrise Marina mentioned. She turned as well and decided to make her quickly spoken lie a truth. The sun cast an almost peach glow over the village buildings, giving everything a dreamy quality. She turned to say something to Fahad, only to find him looking at her. His expression was softer than she had ever seen it, and she was unprepared for the feel of his hand against her forehead. Fahad smiled as he tucked a wayward lock of hair back into her hat.

"I remember once--when you were a little girl--your lady's maid brought you out to the garden to paint the sunrise. She left you alone for only a few moments, and you stretched out on the nearby bench, falling asleep instantly. The woman was furious at first, but I could tell even she couldn't find it within herself to disturb your sleep. I don't think I've ever seen someone so at peace as you were in that moment, with the early morning sun brushing across your face."

Marina was stunned. She remembered that morning. And Hilde's fury when she finally awoke. Marina always felt safe when close to the statue Fahad once was. Fahad's gray eyes held hers as they shared that memory.

Marina could feel something pulling her closer to Fahad, and could swear that it was pulling him closer as well. His hand came to rest on the back of her neck, and she relished the insistent pressure of it.

"Mari-Marcus!"

Curtis' bellow forced them to break apart. Marina watched in shock as Curtis burst through the inn door, wearing nothing but his nightshirt.

"What are you doing?" Marina shouted, standing up abruptly.

Curtis grabbed her by the shoulders, his breath ragged.

"Don't do that to me," he rasped out.

"Do what? I was only taking a walk. There is nothing to worry about."

Curtis' expression darkened and his grip tightened.

"Yes, by all means, tell me that after I watched you pass out in the middle of the night and could not wake you. If not for the fact that you kept breathing, I thought you dead. I stayed awake as long as I could, waiting for you to wake up again."

Marina felt shame wash over her. She should have suspected something like that happened. Only a terrible event could keep Curtis from his bed. They were very alike in that respect. Marina moved in closer and gripped her brother in an unconscious echo of the embrace she shared with Kaia in her vision.

"I am sorry," Marina finally whispered, "I forgot I woke you up before going into that latest vision. It was just so..."

Marina broke off when Curtis ended their embrace. He held her shoulders and looked her over. He was glad to see she wasn't as pale as she was last night. There was no way he would ever forget seeing her flop over like a downed enemy. Only seeing Marina do something similar kept him from calling Gerard or Fahad for help last night.

"Don't worry about it, Brat," Curtis bluffed, "I overreacted. You're just not usually that quiet."

Marina punched Curtis lightly in the shoulder before turning away to brush an errant tear from her eye. As she did this, she saw Gerard standing at the corner of the inn. His expression was unreadable, and Marina wondered why he looked so stoic this morning. She assumed he had arrived after Curtis came screaming down the stairs, so he probably saw that embarrassing show of emotion between them. He stepped forward to join the rest of the group.

"What is our plan today?" he asked.

"Oh, yes. I had a vision of Kaia. She is in Krax'mra."

The men exchanged significant glances at this.

"Yes, I know," Marina sighed, "I am unsure how she found herself in such a place, but she is in danger and we must go to her."

Curtis wiped a weary hand down his face. "Marina, we do not even know who this girl is, why should we risk our lives?"

"Because she is my sister," Marina admitted quietly.

Three jaws dropped at this revelation.

Surprisingly, Gerard was the first to protest.

"The last place you should go anywhere near is Krax'mra. Even if we don't encounter the Krax'mran themselves, the people who choose to live in that godsforsaken country are a few arrows short of a quiver."

"More like missing all their arrows," Curtis muttered as he ran through his hair in frustration. "You're basically asking us to get you killed, Brat."

Fahad could see immediately that was the wrong thing to say. Marinna's blue eyes narrowed dangerously on her brother. She stalked up to him and grabbed his collar. Fahad was surprised but Gerard was obviously amused. In all the time Fahad stood in the garden, he never saw this side of the princess. Within his sight she was always engaged in calming pursuits. She read, embroidered, sat thinking, or on rare occasions took a nap where no one but him could see.

She wasn't often joined by others in her family, but when she was they laughed and teased one another but never descended into violence. Even when their games got competitive the three brothers always treated Marina like glass and she never acted overly aggressive with them.

Though he knew now the two weren't related, she reminded him even more of her many times great-grandmother. He smiled ruefully at the sight of her shaking her taller and more muscular brother by the collar just like Brenda used to do to him.

"Isn't that right, Fahad?" Marina asked, turning to glare at him now.

Fahad blinked and looked from Gerard to Curtis for some hint of what he just missed. Marina was giving him a look full of expectant challenge. He didn't want to disappoint her.

"Of course."

Curtis groaned and Gerard chuckled darkly at his hasty agreement. Perhaps he should have said no. It was obvious from Marina's smug look he'd just agreed to go to Krax'mra. He wanted to groan too but chose to act as though he did not regret his words.

Curtis sighed in resignation.

"Okay, let's get some supplies and head for the border. We should be able to find a guide who can get us safely through Krax'mran territory in one of the border towns." Curtis ran his hand through his curls, a sure sign that he was worried.

"We will be fine, Curtis," Marina reassured him, placing a hand on his arm to stop him from messing with his hair again, "We are four capable fighters, only a fool would trifle with us."

"It only takes one lucky fool to harm even the most capable fighter," Gerard warned.

Marina scowled at him for ruining the calming effect her words achieved. She could not refute the truth of what he said, but that did not make her any more receptive to the sentiment.

"Well then," Fahad interjected, "let's all be doubly on guard and get moving. Talking about the dangers we may or may not face won't help us avoid them altogether, and the sooner we get on the road and rescue this new-found sister, the sooner we may return the princess to the castle."

Gerard nodded curtly at Fahad's words and turned back toward the woods. Marina chased after him and stopped him before he left the village.

"Gerard, where are you going?"

He stopped at the edge of the woods and turned to face her. Marina was surprised to find that his face was just as wooden as before. The wry amusement she usually found in his eyes was gone.

"I must tell my pack that I will be leaving and do not know when I might return. Rafe, my Beta, must know what is to be done if the worst happens."

Marina nodded her understanding, but Gerard never saw it. He turned abruptly after that explanation and quickly disappeared into the woods. She wanted to call him back and ask about his strange behavior but decided not to delay their departure any longer. With a heavy sigh, she turned back to the inn to make her own preparations for their journey.

22

The darkness in the cell was absolute. Their breathing seemed overly loud to Kaia, but it didn't stop her from hearing two people approaching the door. They weren't talking, and Kaia wasn't sure if that was a good or bad thing.

She pressed herself against the door to keep from being seen should someone open the panel. It was a good thing Marina thought about closing it before she was pulled out of her vision. She wondered if those visions felt as weird to Marina as they did to her. This was a fleeting thought because terror drove all thoughts from her mind when the panel was violently ripped open.

"Come for your breakfast, beast," Robin's cold voice echoed against the stone.

Waitimu shuffled forward, still hunched in pain from the lashes Robin laid across his back. If looks could kill, Robin would've been on the ground screaming. Kaia couldn't blame Waitimu for his anger, especially when she got a whiff of his foul-smelling breakfast. It made her want to gag, and only a great sense of self-preservation kept her from doing so.

Waitimu backed away from the door with a crude wooden bowl in his hand. Robin didn't wait for him to start eating before he closed the panel, once again casting them into utter darkness.

"Don't eat that," Kaia hissed.

"It is all I have," Waitimu ground out.

"No, seriously, don't. I've got something in my bag you can eat instead." Even though Kaia couldn't see him, she could imagine his look of distrust.

"Listen, Anansi said you could trust me, right?"

"Yes," Waitimu said grudgingly.

"Then trust me on this. Believe me, what I've got totally beats whatever slop Robin's been feeding you," Kaia assured him.

When she heard the wood clatter against the stone floor, she felt around until she found her bag. It was difficult finding the granola bars at first, but her hand eventually closed over the plastic wrapping. She unwrapped two of them, figuring a body like Waitimu's needed a little extra fueling.

"Here," she said, feeling her way toward him. When she encountered a hairy spider leg, her first inclination was to pull away in disgust. She repressed the urge and kept her hand there, waiting for Waitimu to take her hand. When he did, she pressed the granola bars into his warm palm.

Now that she kind of knew where he was, she reached a tentative hand toward him. The darkness made her want some contact, human or otherwise.

She pulled back quickly when she heard him hiss in pain.

"Oh crap, I'm sorry," she exclaimed.

"It is nothing," he brazened out around what she could only assume were gritted teeth.

"Bull," she countered, "I saw what Robin did to you in the courtyard, and that was most definitely something. I wish I would've stopped him." She said the last quietly, unable to hide the shame in her voice.

"There is nothing you could have done," Waitimu said in a comforting voice.

Kaia didn't reply, finding the conversation difficult. She headed back to her pack to grab her lighter. The cloying blackness was beginning to get to her. Her fingers barely brushed the backpack when she heard a surprised grunt from Waitimu.

"What!" she cried in panic.

"These food sticks are delicious," he said with wonder.

Kaia gave a strangled laugh and proceeded to dig through her bag once again. When she felt the cool metal of the lighter, she grinned in triumph. She was glad Merry insisted on the good kind that could be left burning without actually touching it. The flint struck and the tiny flame burst forth.

Waitimu's surprised cry almost made her drop the lighter, but she just barely kept her hold. She turned to him, bringing the flame closer.

He backed away, asking "What strange magic have you conjured?"

"Oh, this?" Kaia tried to think of something that would make sense. It didn't help that she had never really thought too much about what made a lighter work. "Umm, there's some kind of fluid in there that keeps the flame burning after it strikes. They're pretty common where I'm from." The explanation was lame, but it was all she had if she didn't want to lie to her frankly untrusting cellmate.

Waitimu held his hand out for the lighter, but Kaia demurred. "Hold on." She turned back to her bag, glad that the light made this search easier. The water bottle was filled this time. After being stranded in the desert without even a drop of water, Kaia kept it filled for emergencies. She dug a clean shirt out as well and placed the lighter in the middle of the cell to light the room.

"Let me look at your back," she ordered. Waitimu bristled at the command, so Kaia attempted to soothe his pride. "You're obviously in a lot of pain, and you can't do this yourself. Let me help you. Please."

Waitimu finally nodded and lowered himself so his spider's body completely rested on the floor. Kaia was still going to have to stretch to reach his shoulders, but that was better than the non-existent ladder she would've needed before.

She poured some of the water on her shirt and applied it to one of the worst-looking marks on his lower back. It was crusted with blood, and Kaia tried to be as careful as possible when cleaning the wound. Waitimu's harshly indrawn breath told her she wasn't doing a great job, and she wished she could do better.

A knot of tension was forming in her belly. Kaia passed it off as anxiety from hurting Waitimu. When the tension suddenly left and her hands started glowing with a pulsing white light, however, she knew anxiety wasn't currently a problem. Though she was shocked, that didn't stop her hands from moving almost of their own accord.

With her right hand, she tipped the remaining water over Waitimu's back. The bottle clattered to the floor, and she pressed both hands to his ruined flesh. The light grew brighter, and Kaia dimly heard Waitimu call her name in fear.

Her eyes were wide open in shock as she watched the wounds beneath her hands knit neatly together, leaving only dried blood in their stead. She moved her hands around wherever she saw a wound, and it was gone seconds later. Finally, there were no more wounds and the glowing slowly dimmed to nothing.

"Kaia," Waitimu ventured hoarsely, "was that something else that is common where you are from?"

"No, I can most definitely say that was a first."

Kaia peeked around the corner, still not thrilled with this plan. They'd been skulking around the castle for only ten minutes, but it felt like their escape was taking forever. She wanted to wait until night to take the risk, but Waitimu refused to sit idle in his prison cell and face another beating.

"Besides," he argued, "they will question my rapid healing and realize someone is helping me. It could only be you, as the servants of Nightshade are loyal even unto death."

Kaia huffed in displeasure over that fact and slapped her newly bleeding hand against the door. She was getting tired of cutting that hand, and she wasn't altogether thrilled that her newfound healing power apparently didn't work on her own cut.

They'd been lucky so far, and no one had discovered them with the rapidly brightening sunrise. She still thought this would've been far easier in the dark of night, but Waitimu was right that Marius would be suspicious. Then there was the matter of her stamina. Whatever newfound power Kaia used earlier had severely sapped her strength and still left her feeling a little shaky. She was worried about how that might affect their escape.

Knowing there was nothing she could do about it now, she brushed these thoughts aside and focused on their escape. They were on the ground floor, making their way to the back of the castle. Kaia hoped they would encounter fewer servants in that section, especially seeing as they were on the opposite side of where the kitchens were housed.

They crept down the hall, keeping an ear out for any servants who might decide to suddenly pop out. Kaia knew from her explorations yesterday this part of the castle wasn't used as much, and should therefore be easier to escape through. That didn't mean her heart wasn't in her throat. It did keep it from leaping out into the open though. She breathed a huge sigh of relief when they finally made it to the French doors leading out to a rarely used courtyard area. Waitimu was reaching for the handles when Kaia stopped him.

"Wait," she hissed, "I know it's not your idea of a good time, but I think we'd stand a better chance of both of us surviving this escape if I...um...ride you." Kaia blushed at Waitimu's glare. She wasn't necessarily thrilled with the idea either, but she really did believe it would work out better this way.

"Fine, but I will carry your bag. It will work better that way." Waitimu was still frowning over the idea of having a passenger, so Kaia tried not to show her reluctance over giving the bag to him. Her mother always told her it was a bad idea to tick off the driver, and Kaia decided this situation definitely called for adherence to that philosophy.

Waitimu had Kaia lengthen the strap before he slung it over his head, wearing it like a very tight messenger bag. He helped Kaia swing onto his back, and she was glad swimming made her legs muscular so she could hold on without too much effort. Once they were situated, Waitimu reached for the handle again. Kaia took a deep breath and sent up a quick prayer for safety to any god in this realm willing to listen. Waitimu threw the doors open and set off at a dead run. Kaia was again surprised at how his body barely moved from the movements of his legs.

Waitimu headed for the back entrance as they planned. This one didn't have the heavy portcullis like the front, though Kaia was still a little worried about the doors. They were both eight feet tall, looked like they were made of oak, and bound with iron.

Kaia could feel the adrenaline pumping through her veins as they reached the doors. Waitimu stopped suddenly in front of them and reached to lift an iron bar that blended in with the banding before. Kaia looked around to see if anyone noticed them streaking across the open yard.

She barely saw a red streak before something barreled into her middle, knocking her off Waitimu's back and to the ground, face first.

Sand filled her mouth and ground into her face. Fighting to turn over under the burden of another body, she tried to spit the gritty stuff out. By squirming, she was finally able to see who was sitting atop her.

It was Cossette, and the look on her face made Kaia's blood run cold. That same warm smile was spread across her lips, while her eyes glittered coldly. She then removed a knife from behind her back and held it across Kaia's neck. Grabbing a handful of purple hair, she forced Kaia's head back to better expose the throbbing vein in her throat. Kaia hardly dared to breathe as she felt the cold metal caress her skin.

Cossette's weight suddenly lifted away when Waitimu hit her with the iron bar he just removed from the door. Kaia gasped in surprise and clamped a hand to her neck, surprised Cossette hadn't sliced it open in reaction to the hit. Waitimu kicked the doors open with his front legs and held a hand out for Kaia. She scrambled to stand up, holding her hand out to catch Waitimu's.

Robin slid to a stop between their outstretched hands with his sword drawn. Waitimu scrambled back to avoid the deadly swipe of Robin's blade. Kaia saw a red line appear across his left bicep, and she knew he wouldn't be able to avoid getting seriously injured. She finally succeeded in getting to her feet and immediately leaped on Robin's back. He stumbled but did not fall over as she had hoped. The best she could do was pin his arms down by wrapping her arms and legs around his torso.

"Run!" she screamed.

Waitimu shook his head and scowled.

"Run, you idiot. You're unarmed. I'll hold him off for as long as I can."

She could see the uncertainty in his eyes and was almost glad when an arrow narrowly missed his head, forcing him to follow her instructions. Robin dropped his sword to try to pry her off him, but he hadn't counted on her legs being so strong. She watched as Waitimu ran at Superman speed, sending up a cloud of sand in his wake.

"Find Marina!" she screamed desperately, knowing he probably wouldn't be able to hear her.

She was finally wrenched away from Robin by several pairs of hands a few moments later. He was cursing violently, and she hid her fear behind a feral grin.

"Not so smooth now, are we, handsome?"

Kaia immediately regretted baiting him when his fist slammed into her face. The world went red, then black, as she passed out.

Kaia was incredibly uncomfortable. Her head felt like it was being squeezed with every beat of her heart. She also couldn't move her arms and legs. She opened her eyes but shut them again quickly when the light in the room seared her retina. Kaia cursed the headache besieging her and tried to open her eyes again, but slower this time. The light filtered through her pale eyelashes and barely open eyelids.

There was some movement around her, revealed only by the slight shift in light and shadow. She closed her eyes again and listened. There were two sets of footsteps. They moved quickly, but not loudly, and she could hear an occasional clink of glass, liquid being poured, and occasionally metal on metal.

The smell of the room reminded her of chemistry class, and that comparison didn't bring her any comfort. Not only did she suck at chemistry, but in her experience, most of the concoctions her classmates put together had the unfortunate propensity to blow up.

Her eyes flew open at that thought, not caring that it caused tiny explosions to go off inside her head. She turned her head to the right and saw Robin working with several vials and beakers filled with various colored liquids. A few were boiling, two looked like they were frozen and giving off steam like dry ice, and the rest didn't seem to be doing much at all.

This was proven untrue when one suddenly began swirling around of its own accord after Robin added a single drop from another solution. It was hypnotic but in an evil sort of way. Kaia was afraid to look away, but she forced herself to turn her head. What she saw on the table next to her made her heart rate spike.

There were dozens of knives and other sharp objects lying on a bed of red satin. The satin made it appear as if the blades were already edged with blood, causing Kaia to shiver at the idea her own might soon stain them.

That involuntary shudder made Kaia aware once again that she couldn't move the rest of her body. She panicked for a moment, thinking they already chopped her limbs off. The relief she felt when she discovered she was only bound by several leather belts subsided quickly when Marius stepped into her line of vision.

"I am so glad to see that you are awake, my dear," Marius crooned, gently caressing the side of her face Robin didn't hit.

Kaia jerked away saying, "Don't touch me."

Marius pretended to look hurt. Kaia rolled her eyes, but that sudden movement set her head to pounding again.

"Tsk tsk, is that any way to treat your honored host? Especially after you have caused so much havoc?" He hissed the last and grabbed a handful of her hair. She cried out in pain when he yanked her head closer to his so he could whisper, "You will pay for the plans you have ruined."

He let go, and Kaia felt tears running across her temples and into her hair. She cried quietly, not wanting to give Marius the satisfaction of knowing just how badly he hurt her.

She heard a door open behind her. Marius looked up to see who entered and a look of annoyance crossed his face.

"See what you have done to poor Cossette?" he held out a hand, and Kaia saw the newest arrival place her freckled hand in his. He pulled Cossette forward and Kaia gasped in shock at what she saw.

Cossette's beautiful face was caved in on one side, but there was no blood. She could see the bones of the maid's skull, but it was like the skin on it was crushed putty. Marius made soothing noises like he was comforting a small child, but Cossette wasn't even acting as though she was in any pain.

"Robin," he called, "please bring me the salve."

Robin placed one of the beakers in Marius' waiting hand and waited by his side patiently. It was the hypnotically evil-looking potion, and Kaia watched in horrified fascination as Marius dipped his hand into the mixture.

When he brought his hand out, it was glowing with a white light interspersed with black lightning. It was like a malevolent version of her own newfound healing ability. Marius pressed his hand to the ruined side of Cossette's face, muttering some kind of incantation as he did so.

The bones knit themselves back together while the putty-like skin slithered around to reform Cossette's beautiful features. When Marius pulled his hand away, it looked as though the maid never suffered a hideous blow to the head with an iron crossbeam. Even her creepy smile was back in place.

Marius chuckled at the stunned look on Kaia's face, "Yes, as you can see, I do not keep conventional servants. They are far too willful and given to free thought. My homunculi are significantly easier to control, and I am able to choose their features for myself. It is so very gratifying to be served by such beautiful creatures."

He caressed Cosette's face as he'd done with Kaia. Unlike her, Cosette leaned into the touch like an affectionate kitten. Kaia tried not to throw up at the sight.

Kaia looked at him in disgust and wondered if her father revealing what a jerk he could be was the beginning of her torture.

23

Gerard caught up to the other three the following day, but Marina was perturbed to notice he was still in a foul mood. She wanted to ask him what was wrong, but she knew it was not her place to meddle in his affairs. Being the princess of Jamaria did not give her the right to stick her nose where it did not belong.

She pounded on her makeshift pillow made from her extra clothes and shifted to find a better position to sleep. Her movement caused Curtis to snort and roll over, but she did not wake him. Gerard looked at her briefly from where he was keeping watch but otherwise ignored her. They were camped out on the Kentorian side of the border and were waiting until morning to cross into Krax'mra.

Sleep was not coming easily, as Marina had too much weighing on her mind. Not only was Gerard behaving oddly, but her near kiss with Fahad sent butterflies fluttering in her belly every time he so much as glanced at her. These problems of course paled in comparison with the danger Kaia was in, but they were moving as quickly as they could. The lack of conversation while riding gave Marina too much time to think.

She closed her eyes and tried to empty her mind of everything. Curtis taught her one of the meditative techniques used by the Ya'mäkazi. Normally she would have achieved serenity within seconds, but it took several minutes before her breathing regulated.

Marina's eyes opened, and she knew she wasn't in the camp any longer. A gentle breeze blew across her face while warm water lapped her toes to the rhythm of her heartbeat.

"Perhaps falling into a meditative state was not the best idea," she scolded herself.

The sand beneath her feet looked like warm caramel, and she slowly turned to see a tropical paradise. The sand ended after twenty feet, turning into scrub brush and then swaying palm trees. She walked toward the trees when movement caught her eye. There was something white fluttering around the base of one of the trees further inland.

A small but well-worn path wove into the foliage, and Marina hesitated for only a moment before following it. The white object drifted ahead of her, always staying out of sight just enough she could not really see what she was following, but close enough she would not lose track.

There was no real sense of time, so Marina was not sure how long she followed the path before she stopped at the edge of a clearing. A gorgeous manor house made of palm tree wood, seashells, animal bones, and grass stood before the base of a large volcano. Black smoke billowed out of the top, and Marina was glad this was only a vision.

"Don' worry, darlin'," a honeyed voice said from the darkened doorway.

A woman with nut-brown skin stepped forward. She was wearing a flowing white gown, and Marina knew this was the woman she had been following.

"Dat volcano is like me, always threatenin' but only blowin' up on rare occasions."

"You have not done much threatening so far, so I will hope this is not an occasion when you wish to blow up."

The woman laughed. A deep, throaty chuckle that sounded as though she inhaled far too much volcano smoke for far too long.

"I like you, child," she declared, swaying her hips as she walked toward Marina, "which is always gratifyin' when meetin' one's relatives."

Marina stared dumbly at the woman, who was stretching out a welcoming hand. "We are related?"

"Yes, child. I am your Aunt Calypso. It's been quite a while since I last seen you. Or has it been only a few moments?" Calypso's face screwed up in momentary confusion. She shook the thought away, her wide lips smoothing back into a warm smile. "Ah, no worries. Time moves differently on my island, but it don' matter. What does matter is dat you have grown into a beautiful woman, and we must catch up."

"But I—" Marina's protest was cut off when Calypso grabbed her hand and pulled her toward the manor.

It was as though Marina moved from the clearing to a porch facing the sea within the blink of her eyes. She was sitting down with a cup of tea in her hands, but no memory of how she got there.

"Now," Calypso began as though she was interrupting Marina, "we don' have much time, either here or in your world, so I'll be quick. Your mother hid on my island until she gave birth to you and your sister. I could not keep her here, for your father was able to follow her, despite even the wards of this island. I was able to delay him a month or two once he arrived, but it obviously wasn't enough time for your mother."

"But, who was she?"

Calypso clicked her tongue impatiently, not happy to be interrupted.

"She was a Nereid, like me. Her name was Yara, and I won' be able to tell you the really important t'ings if you don' hush. So stop interruptin' and listen to Auntie Calypso.

"Anyway, your mother kept a diary," Calypso nodded when excitement lit Marina's face but did not stop, "and it tells you more than I can. You must read it under a full moon, submerged in water." Marina gave Calypso a skeptical look but held her tongue.

"You and your sister are half Nereid, and dat will help you read what your mother left you."

"But won't that ruin the book?" Marina burst out, unable to stop herself.

Calypso clicked her tongue again and shot Marina an annoyed look, "Child, I may be older than the Kingdoms, but don' t'ink that means I've learned to be patient."

The whole island shook as the nearby volcano rumbled in a frightening counterpoint to Calypso's words.

"Now," Calypso said primly when the rumbling stopped, "we only have a few moments more, so there is no time for questions. I will, however, give you a gift that you can t'ank me later for."

With that, she produced a length of cloth. It was an opalescent pink, like the inside of a conch shell. Marina took it from her aunt and reveled in the silky quality.

"This cloth will hide whatever it covers from any spell or seer. It's large enough to cover one person, lying flat. Or, it could be wrapped about a smaller object. It's stronger than anything else made in the Kingdoms, and cannot be burned. Use it wisely, child."

Marina carefully tucked the fabric into her waistband. She blinked and was back on the ground next to a snoring Curtis. Gerard and Fahad had switched places, with Gerard now asleep on the other side of Curtis and Fahad at watch.

"Bad dream again, princess?" Fahad asked softly.

Marina blushed and laid back down saying, "No, I just thought I heard something."

"Nothing here but me and the stars," he said wryly, thinking Marina would not hear him. She smiled and closed her eyes, finally able to sleep.

The men did not let Marina go into the Krax'mran bar, leaving her to hold the reins. While she believed Gerard and Fahad were trying to downplay her importance with the rough crowd in this border town, she knew Curtis was just being annoying. She kicked a clod of dirt spitefully and scowled at the ground.

"Ah, and you even have a squire to see after our horses. Very smart, gentlemen, very smart."

She looked up to see who belonged to the patronizing voice and found herself looking into eyes as blue as her own. The man in front of her was lanky but dazzling. His aquiline nose, square jaw, and wide mouth gave him an almost aristocratic look. Shoulder-length brown hair tied back with twine and well-worn clothes made it look as though he had fallen on hard times.

Curtis was smirking at the man's assumption that Marina was a squire, and she really wanted to round-house kick the look off his face.

"Marcus," her brother said imperiously, "make sure you give Spitfire a double ration of oats tonight."

"Fine, but only because I feel sorry that he has to carry your sorry carcass around," she spat back. It did not matter to her she probably just blew what little cover the boys gave her. It was worth it to watch her brother grimace.

"Actually, Brian, Marcus is our traveling companion. He just drew the short straw when it came to watching the horses," Fahad explained.

Brian nodded, a thoughtful look on his face. "I see, well the agreed-upon price for safe passage through Krax'mran land is still two gold pieces per person."

"Could we not discuss a discount for children?" Curtis asked, shoving Marina slightly. Marina would have pushed back, but she did not want to draw any more attention to herself than necessary. Something about Brian unsettled her, and she just wanted to be on the way. The sooner they made it to Kaia, the sooner they could rid themselves of Brian's company.

Brian laughed at the jest, and shook his head. "Even a child costs two golds in this kind of business. Gather any supplies you need for the journey. We will meet back here in two hours, and then be on our way."

With that, he loped away. The town was small, so it was easy for Marina to follow him with her eyes as he disappeared into a dilapidated shack that doubled as an inn and apothecary.

"We will be back in a while, brat," Curtis said, forcing Marina to quell her suspicions about Brian. "Stay with the horses, and keep your head down." He tugged her hat a little further down her forehead before following Gerard and Fahad into a broken-down shed that passed for a dry-goods store.

Marina was ready to drop all her misgivings about Brian as she leaned against a tree, savoring her dinner. They stopped for the night at the edge of a scrubby forest and Brian insisted upon cooking. Given that no one in their party could cook even a passable meal, they all readily agreed.

Brian turned their meager supplies into a veritable feast. There was something in the way he threw the spices together in his beaten-up old pot that had turned simple rabbit stew into something Marina could see eating at court.

They, of course, waited until Gerard sniffed the food and gave the all-clear before tucking into the fare. Brian was not even upset by the show of distrust, saying, "Ah, how nice to finally be leading experienced travelers into the desert. As my da always said, never trust a stranger with your gut. Then again, we often wondered if he should have trusted mother. That woman couldn't cook to save her life, gods bless her."

He laughed robustly at his own joke, and Fahad and Curtis joined in. Marina and Gerard raised an eyebrow at the trio before turning their focus back to their delicious meal.

Marina set her plate to the side and sighed in contentment. She looked up and saw the stars twinkling through the thin canopy. The moon would not be full for another three days, and she feared she would not be able to find enough water in this desert to submerge the diary.

The cloth Calypso gave her was concealing the diary at the bottom of Marina's pack at the moment. She was not necessarily worried anyone was searching for it, she only wanted to be sure it was kept safe. This was her only tie to her birth mother, and it was too precious to lose.

A rustling noise drew her attention to Brian. He repacked all his spices and was currently cleaning his pot with some sand and grass. He rinsed it out once, throwing the water to the side somewhat close to Gerard's relaxed form. Marina was surprised Gerard did not move at least a little when the water streamed toward him but decided he knew it would not hit him.

When the next stream of rinse water flying directly in Gerard's face elicited absolutely no response, Marina was too stunned to move.

"Oh wonderful," Brian said with pleasure, "that worked even quicker than my master predicted."

Brian finished packing his supplies and crossed to Fahad and Curtis. Marina could barely breathe as he snapped his fingers in front of their faces. She did not know what Brian did to the men, but it apparently was not affecting her. The men were like statues, their breathing so slow that for a moment she thought they stopped.

Brian knelt in front of her and waved his hand in her face. He squawked in surprise when Marina grabbed his wrist and pulled him off balance. As he caught himself, Marina twisted around so she could kick him squarely in the jaw. The blow snapped his head back and left him gasping. He was laid flat, and Marina used his momentary weakness to pin him down.

She sat on his sternum, pinning his arms to his sides with her legs and feet. He turned a little red as she cut off his air supply. She let him suffer for a few moments before easing a little of her weight off of him.

"What did you do to my friends?" she demanded.

"They will be dead in an hour," he gasped, "my master demands your deaths."

"Why?" she screamed, rage and fear making her desperate. She put her arm across his throat and applied more pressure to restrict his breathing a little more. When she realized he could not answer that way, she eased back a bit.

Brian sputtered and drew in a deep, gasping breath. His face was beet red but he answered between breaths.

"I do not question my master, only do as commanded. The poison may not have worked on you, but mark me, you will die." Brian giggled insanely. Marina cut the hated sound off by resettling her weight back onto his chest.

"How do I save them?" she growled. Brian only gasped for air, and Marina gave him a considering look before allowing him to breathe again. She vaguely wondered how often she could cut off his breathing before he stopped altogether.

"There is no cure," he gloated between labored breaths.

Marina narrowed her eyes and reached for the knife strapped to her thigh. She allowed Brian to watch the ten-inch blade glitter in the firelight for a moment before holding it to his neck. No fear lit his eyes, and Marina tried not to let this disconcert her.

"You will tell me everything you know about your master, or the sand will drink your blood."

"Foolish child," he smirked, "I would never betray my master over something as paltry as my life. Nightshade gave me life, and I will give it back."

Brian said something in a language Marina did not know. She felt his body go rigid and watched in horrified amazement as his body began to melt before her eyes. Scrambling away from his quickly disintegrating flesh, Marina gulped air to calm herself.

Her only hope of finding a cure for whatever Brian gave the men was lost. Thoughts whirled through her mind as she checked on each of them. Their breathing was still shallow, and she could feel their heartbeats getting slower. Her eyes darted between the men, and she felt the panic threatening to overwhelm her.

"Think, Marina," she scolded herself, "why did the poison not work on you?"

She began to pace from one man to the other, trying to figure it out. Oasis snorted, drawing Marina's attention. They hobbled the horses next to a thin stream when they made camp. Marina stared at the water for a full minute before a memory hit her.

"I purified the poison at Heatherwood," she whispered. Excitement lit her eyes and she threw herself down next to the nearest man. She put her hands on Gerard's face and looked into his brown eyes. Nothing occurred to her, and she whimpered in fear as she felt his heartbeat slow a little more.

"Damn it," she ground out as tears threatened, "how did I purify it?"

She closed her eyes and focused on Gerard's heartbeat. The slow rhythm still worried her, but she pushed that thought aside for the moment. As she focused, she could feel the blood rushing through his veins.

It felt like she could see the thread-like network webbing through his body without opening her eyes. She looked harder and saw the vibrant red of his blood was streaked with a black ooze working its way through Gerard's body. Passing her hand over one of the dark spots made it instantly disappear.

The thrill of this discovery almost broke her out of her trance, so she tamped the emotion down and concentrated again. Starting at the top of Gerard's head, she passed both hands over his entire body. It only took a few seconds, but Marina felt as though she had run twice around the castle.

Opening her eyes to the real world took a moment, but she was finally able to see again. Gerard blinked and groaned, and Marina felt her heart soar. She quickly scrambled to Fahad's side and repeated the process. It went faster this time, now that she knew what she was doing. She crawled to Curtis and did the final purification.

Once she was done with Curtis, she felt as though her whole body had been wrung out as Hilde would do to a damp towel. Gerard was slowly sitting up now, still groggy from the effects of the poison.

"Princess?" he looked at her as though she was not quite there. Marina crawled over to him, unable to stand after healing all three of them.

"Yes, Gerard, I am here," she replied softly.

He blinked slowly, and she could see that his pupils were dilated. Moving in closer, she sought his pulse to determine if the poison was still affecting him. They were only inches apart when Gerard unexpectedly buried his nose in her neck.

At first, she thought he had passed out, but then she felt him deeply inhale her scent. He made a noise of contentment and Marina went rigid in shock.

"Excuse me, are you sniffing me?" she asked, outraged.

"You smell of the sea and something I need," he whispered huskily.

The words and his hot breath on her shoulder made her shiver. She scrambled away, unsure of what to do. When she met his eyes, they were no longer the deep brown they were before but the bright yellow of the wolf.

Marina opened her mouth to say something when Gerard's eyes rolled back in his head and he passed out. Her breath huffed out, and she was glad for the reprieve. She did not really know what to say.

After checking on Fahad and Curtis and finding them asleep but otherwise healthy, she checked on the pile of bones and melted flesh that remained of Brian. She kicked his grinning skull in futile rage. His words haunted her. As she stood watch over her friends, she tried to figure out how her father had known who she was and that she was coming for Kaia.

24

Kaia leaned her head against the cold, damp stone, and sighed in frustration. No matter how she worked it out in her mind, there was no way she would be able to escape without help. The math refused to math. If she and Waitimu were caught going faster than a speeding bullet, there was no way she would make it to the wall—or beyond—without him.

Getting out of her dungeon cell was the easy part. All she had to do was bleed on the stupid door and she was out. Obviously, Marius hadn't figured that out, or he wouldn't have put her in one of the cells.

"What an idiot," she muttered, imitating Emma Watson as Hermione. She smiled dryly at her ability to quote movies at the most idiotic times. The smile didn't last long, but Kaia appreciated the momentary lightheartedness.

"Okay, cinephile, how are all those movies gonna help you now? It's not like you really paid attention during *The Rock* or *The Great Escape*. So, other than waiting for a blue box that's bigger on the inside, what's your genius plan?"

Kaia rolled her eyes in the darkness and wished she could ignore herself. There were no plans, and she didn't want to give up her one advantage by leaving her cell without some idea of what she could do afterward.

There was no sense of time in the darkness, so she didn't know how long she'd been sitting on the freezing stone since Robin threw her in here. They didn't torture her like she thought they would. The knives were a scare tactic, but they only served to freak her out too much to say anything. The moment Marius slid the blunt edge of the blade down on the inside of her left arm still burned in her mind. The thought of that cool metal caressing her skin from armpit to wrist caused bile to rise in her throat. She choked it down and brought her knees up so she could rest her head.

The sudden light from the panel opening made her snap her head back up. She bumped it slightly but didn't even bother to rub the pain away. Instead, she scrambled to stand against the far wall as the door swung inward. Marius stood in the doorway as Robin reached for her. She struggled in his arms, but couldn't get away. No matter how much she kicked, bit, or scratched him, he never reacted. Some part of her supposed it made sense after seeing Cossette's caved-in skull, but it didn't mean she was going to give up without a fight.

"Let go of me," she demanded shrilly.

"Now, now, my dear," Marius soothed, setting her teeth on edge, "You must not fight Robin. He will not let go, and you will only end up harming yourself."

Kaia glared at this man whom Marina said was their father. She didn't want to believe they came from someone so black-hearted. Finding out she had a sister was amazing. Her father was proving far more disappointing.

Marius gestured to Robin, "Come, Robin, let us take our guest back to the laboratory."

Marius swept away, sure that Robin would easily follow with the struggling Kaia in tow.

"I don't know why you're interrogating me," she spat, "I don't know anything about Waitimu or where he's going. There's nothing I have that you need."

Marius paused to give her an assessing look. "I feel that you are not entirely correct in that assumption. You may be quite valuable to me indeed."

Despite her continued struggles, Kaia eventually found herself strapped to the same table as before. The leather straps were tight, not even allowing her to wiggle more than a few millimeters. Marius and Robin moved to the lab area and conferred for a few minutes behind her. Kaia twisted her head to try to see what they were doing, but could only catch glimpses.

Robin finally moved back into her line of sight, holding a small glass of some purple liquid. Kaia jerked her head away when he tried to hold her in place to get her to drink the stuff. Turning her head in the opposite direction she said, "There is no way I'm drinking that. I don't care if it does look like grape Kool-aid."

Kaia stopped moving when she felt the tip of a knife at the tender place beneath her jaw. Her head moved with the knife as it guided her head back toward Robin. His eyes were dead pieces of flinty grey as he slowly removed the knife, ready to use it again if Kaia made it necessary.

There was no struggling as Robin lifted her head just enough to help her drink the foul-tasting liquid. She wanted to throw it up but figured that would just get the knife stuck in another tender place if she did. That didn't stop her from gagging a little bit, but she kept the brew down.

"That tasted like rancid yogurt," she found herself saying. Her voice had sounded far away to her own ears and she realized the room was becoming fuzzy around the edges.

"You really shouldn't go out of focus like that," she chastised the men, "it's probably not good for you. Or for me for that matter." The words were flowing out of her without conscious thought, and she suddenly knew what happened.

"You guys just gave me some kind of truth serum. That's cheating. I'd say you should be ashamed of yourselves, but one of you is evil, and the other doesn't appear to have any emotions; so why waste my breath?"

Marius moved closer, "What a clever girl," he smirked, "now we will discover what you have been hiding."

"I'm not hiding anything," she slurred, her mouth feeling numb, "just hoping you don't figure certain things out."

"Where has the Krax'mran gone?"

"Dunno, we didn't really have a plan beyond 'get the hell out of here and find Waitimu's family.'"

Marius looked annoyed by that but pressed on.

"Who are you?"

"Oh, that's a complicated one," Kaia sighed regretfully, "turns out I'm not as sure as I once was."

"Fine," Marius snapped, "let us make it less complicated. Where are you from?"

"Upstate New York. I'd tell you the town, but let's face it, all anyone ever cares about is NYC. Seriously, like there's not an entire state there?"

Marius looked confused. "What Kingdom is this Enwhysee in?"

"The good 'ole US of A. Home of the grand old flag." With that, she broke into a sloppy rendition of You're a Grand Old Flag. Marius' frustrated command to stop finally penetrated the fog creeping into Kaia's brain. She looked at him with some hurt saying, "I've been told I'm a pretty good singer. Geez, now I really hope you're not my dad. You suck at parenting."

Marius went rigid at this and began to scrutinize Kaia's features. A growing numbness kept Kaia from feeling it when Marius viciously grabbed her hair. He bent closer, finally seeing the pale blonde roots growing out under the purple.

"You have her hair," he turned her face and looked into Kaia's eyes, "but my eyes."

Kaia yawned when he released her, the potion they forced on her was slowly making her lose consciousness. The last thing she heard before the fog closed in on her mind was Marius ordering Robin to release her and take her back to her room.

Sun shone through the lacy curtains, casting buttery spots of light across Kaia's face. She burrowed her head deeper into the downy pillow, pulling the silky covers over her head. The last remnants of her dream teased her with visions of a beautiful island house and a woman with honeyed skin. She knew the woman told her something important, but the warm sun was pulling the hazy memories away.

The sound of glass on metal made Kaia's eyes pop open, leaving only a sense that she was forgetting something hovering on the outskirts of her mind. She moved the sheet slowly, unsure of where she was, how she had gotten there, or who was in the room with her. The sight of Cossette's warm smile as she set out Kaia's breakfast caused Kaia to bolt upright with a frightened shriek.

"What do you want?" she demanded with a high-pitched squeak.

"I'm preparing the young lady's breakfast, as the master

commanded. Let me know when you are ready to dress." Cossette curtsied and left the room without a sound.

Kaia carefully extricated herself from the twisted bed sheets and moved toward the food. It was eggs, toast, milk, and something that looked like thickly cut bacon. Picking up a fork, she poked the food and sniffed it suspiciously. It smelled wonderful, and her stomach growled in appreciation.

Setting her mouth in a firm line, Kaia picked up the whole thing, crossed to the open window, and pitched it, tray and all, into the courtyard below. A few of the servants looked at her without expression, and Kaia treated them all to a rude hand gesture.

"Yeah, like I was gonna eat that," she growled to herself as she shut the window. Her stomach growled right back in protest, but Kaia ignored it.

Flinging the wardrobe doors open, she gazed balefully upon the dresses that occupied the space. She finally settled on a maroon number that looked fairly easy to get into. The laces at the back proved difficult, but not impossible. The final product was a little sloppy, but Kaia's goal was to be dressed, not to please anyone else.

Kaia stalked from the room, only to encounter a surprised Cossette on the other side of the door.

"Milady, please let me fix your dress." Cossette put a hand on Kaia's arm to stop her and tightened her grip when Kaia tried to pull away.

"Let go of me," Kaia warned through gritted teeth.

"The master will not allow such unpleasantness in his home," Cossette said with that permanent warm smile still affixed to her face.

The grip on her arm and Cossette's unwavering expression sent a spark of rage cascading throughout Kaia's body. Her stomach knotted as the anger welled up within her.

"Get your hand off me, or you'll regret it."

Kaia knew Cossette was aware this was an empty threat, which meant they were both surprised when the skin on Cossette's hand began to bubble and turn red.

Cossette pulled her hand away slowly as if fascinated by the sight of her skin almost melting away. Her palm was the red of a boiled lobster, and pieces of it began to drip onto the floor like melted wax.

Cossette looked at Kaia in confusion and watched silently as Kaia ran away.

Kaia finally stopped when she reached the foyer. Her breath came in short gasps, and she looked at the arm where Cossette grabbed her in horrified wonder. The velvet of the gown was slightly darker, and Kaia put her hand there. She jerked back in surprise when she found the spot hot and slightly damp. Now that she acknowledged it, she could feel the heat on her forearm.

Marius found her like this seconds later, a look of concern on his handsome face. "My dear, are you quite all right? Cossette told me something strange happened outside your room."

Kaia raised an eyebrow at his solicitous interest. The man who threatened to torture her and plied her with a truth potion had been replaced by the most caring of fathers. She wondered if he really thought she was that stupid, or if he believed a few kind words would make her forgive his actions.

Marius held out his hand and took a step forward. His worried look was replaced by a sad smile when Kaia recoiled.

"I am sorry for my behavior these last two days. My enemies have made me paranoid, and I am afraid you have suffered for it. There are no words for the depths of my regret that I gave you even a moment of disquiet"

Kaia crossed her arms over her chest and didn't even try to hide her ire. "Yeah, that's not even close to good enough. How about you let me leave, and I'll think about letting you off the hook for this one?"

She saw the corners of his mouth pinch in momentary annoyance before the mask of dejection fell back into place.

"My dear, Kaia," he sighed, "I could never let you face the harshness of Krax'mra on your own. Even if you could survive the desert, the Krax'mran, and the border bandits, I would be far too worried about your future to let you leave."

Kaia scoffed at this pretty speech. "Seriously? I think I'll be fine. And anyway, why should my future concern you? I've been doing pretty good these first seventeen years without you, the next seventy or so should go off without a hitch once I leave."

Marius gave her a pitying look and shook his head, "You do not know the dangers you face in the desert. A child of the Nereid would die in a matter of hours in that dry heat."

Kaia was thoroughly confused by this statement. That word teased her memory, and she knew it was important somehow. She almost never remembered her dreams but something told her if Marius hadn't given her that stupid drug she might remember more than a hint of sand and sun. Her thoughts were interrupted by Marius.

"I have only just discovered my daughter lives," he continued, "I do not wish to lose you so quickly." He placed a gentle hand on her shoulder, ignoring her flinch of fear.

Kaia let him guide her toward the breakfast room, knowing he would probably sic Robin on her if she tried to leave. Marius sat at the head of the table and gestured to the chair next to him.

"Please, join me for breakfast. I have heard that yours met a rather untimely end." He said this with a touch of amusement and an underlying sense of pride. Kaia sat reluctantly, glaring at Hamish when he tried to push her chair in for her.

"No thanks, I've got this."

She didn't trust these fake people, and she definitely didn't want them behind her. Hamish settled himself in a corner, and Kaia was satisfied she could see him. Marius ate a few bites before realizing Kaia wouldn't even touch her fork.

"You must eat, my dear. I promise that there will be nothing unsavory in your meal. The potion I gave you has worn off as you can see, and I have no wish to harm you."

Kaia's stomach growled at the mention of food, and she decided to take him up on his offer. At the very least, she thought to herself, it smells delicious, so I may as well enjoy myself before I croak. With that sardonic thought, she dug in.

Marius waited until she ate most of her food before starting a conversation.

"There is so much I wish to know about your life," he said with sincerity. Kaia didn't believe it for a minute, so she kept her mouth full to keep from talking. "Where have you been all these years? What do you know of your mother and me?"

He was looking at her earnestly, and Kaia realized there was no more food on her plate. The eggs were like glue in her throat, and she gulped some water to force it down.

"Everything I know about you, I've learned while staying here. I know absolutely nothing about my mother." Kaia paused and thought about Lisa. "No, wait, so much has happened, I forgot. My mother's name was Yara, and she was a Nereid. That's why I got so thirsty in the desert," she exclaimed, excited to finally remember her full encounter with the infernal kelpie.

"Yes, your mother was beautiful, but her head was as empty as your plate." His smile was rueful, as though he was embarrassed to have fallen for such a silly creature. Kaia wanted to be angry in her mother's defense, but she had no idea if he was telling her the truth or not.

They both turned when there was a knock on the door. Hamish answered, and allowed a gorgeous woman to walk into the room. Kaia's eyes widened when she saw the woman's curvy body and wavy brown hair. She undulated with every move, giving the appearance she could break into an exotic dance at any moment.

"Ah," Marius breathed with pleasure, "my dearest Snow, what have you brought me?"

Snow came closer, and revealed a man standing in the doorway. He was tall and thin with thick dark blonde hair. The look of ardor on his face as he looked at Snow made Kaia want to laugh with pity. It was obvious by the way Snow looked and acted she was just another of Marius' homunculi.

"Master Marius, may I present Lord Wently, of Jamaria," Snow swept a hand toward the man, who swaggered in as if he owned the place. Kaia wondered how Marius was taking this attitude and was surprised to see him smiling indulgently. The man's clothes seemed like they were quite nice at one point, but now they were wrinkled and stained with mud. His eyes, which Kaia thought were shining with admiration for Marius's homunculus, seemed glassy and unfocused as he got closer. He was also a little flushed from more than just the heat. Kaia wondered if he was suffering from some kind of fever.

"Lord Wently, how happy I am to see you have arrived safely. Please," he rose from his seat and gestured to the seat on his left, "join me and my daughter for breakfast."

Kaia thought about getting up in disgust at Marius' act that she was his loving daughter, but this man looked vaguely familiar, and she was curious.

"My thanks, Lord Marius," Wently bowed before making his way to the chair Marius offered.

When Hamish set out another plate of food, Kaia noticed something strange about Wently. He was using his left hand to eat but looked as though it was horribly awkward for him. There was no grace or ease of movement, and she could see he was getting frustrated as he chased his eggs around the platter.

When he finally succeeded in spearing some, they fell onto his coat halfway to his mouth. "Curse that jumped-up peasant," Wently exclaimed as he slammed the fork onto the table. He brought his right arm up from where it was resting on his lap and began to swipe at the eggs with a cloth-wrapped stump where his hand should've been.

Kaia recoiled at the sight of the bloodied rag at the end of his arm. The sight sparked her memory, and she finally realized where she saw Wently.

This was the man from that first vision at the pool. Her fists clenched her skirt, and she debated with herself about launching across the table to pop him in the nose for almost hitting Marina. She relaxed when she remembered how that statue sent Wently's hand flying and settled for turning a cold look at him and her father.

"I think I'll be going back to my room now," she declared, pushing her chair back to stand.

She didn't wait for permission or acknowledgment, only stopping when she was out of the door to hear her father saying, "My lord, I believe I can help you with that. Please, let us adjourn to my laboratory. We have much to discuss."

Kaia tamped down her curiosity and headed back to her room. She had an escape to plan after all.

Wently watched the purple-haired wench leave the room and tried to figure out why she looked vaguely familiar. When his host spoke to him, it took a moment for his clouded brain to make sense of the words.

He realized Lord Marius was looking at the bloody stump that once held his hand. Sighing mournfully, Wently replied to the man's invitation to assist Wently with his problem.

"I am afraid, my lord, there is nothing anyone can do for me. The best healer in Jamaria tried to staunch the bleeding, but even he could not speed the process. It mends slowly, and Healer Myles assured me magic could not touch the damnable thing."

Wently felt tears of frustration prick his eyes. His experience before the statue was that of immense privilege. There was nothing in Jamaria he could not possess with the right combination of money and manipulation. Yet now, here he was in this godsforsaken desert with a bloody stump and a fever that kept building day after day.

"I may surprise you, Lord Wently. Healer Myles has a widespread, and well-earned reputation, but he is far from an expert at magic. Come, I will show you."

Wently bristled at the command beneath Marius's invitation. However, he was not stupid enough to insult the magician before he could find out what benefits he could receive from the stranger. As they walked through the castle, Wently fought to cover his amusement at the ornate fixtures throughout Lord Marius's home. It was obvious to Wently Marius was not from old money like him. Wently's family held the Dukedom for centuries. At the moment, Wently was harboring the suspicion Marius added the "lord" to his name and hid in the middle of nowhere so no one could argue the point.

When they reached the laboratory, Wently felt the first niggling of fear. As a courtier of Jamaria, he saw his fair share of magicians and sorcerers. So he knew a practitioner of the dark arts when he saw one.

Marius had the obligatory potions and brews bubbling ominously, but there were also strange creatures suspended in cloudy liquids and the bloody remnants of some sacrifice or other with runes written in that creature's blood on the wall. The table in the center of the room had several leather straps, several of which carried mottled stains Wently could only assume were more blood.

"Please, sit," Marius ordered.

Wently chose to obey, sitting in a cushioned chair he assumed came from another room. This was mostly because the flowered brocade on the chair lacked any of the ominous stains almost everything else in the room bore.

Marius motioned for one of his servants to come forward. The man stood at the table without comment or expression. When Marius told him to place his arm on the table, he did so without question. Wently was impressed despite himself at how well-trained the servant was.

Admiration quickly turned to horror when Marius approached the unflinching servant with a wicked-looking saw and began to cut into the servant's right arm. He seemed to be disconnecting the man's entire lower arm from the elbow.

"What are you doing?" Wently exclaimed. He made to stand, but a wave of nausea forced him to stay seated.

"Do not concern yourself, Lord Wently. Bernard does not mind the sacrifice, and it is far easier to move pieces of him around. For you, however, I needed a base for your new appendage."

"You cannot think to attach that thing to me," Wently cried in disgust.

"That is precisely my plan," Marius declared calmly as he detached the last of the flesh from Bernard's elbow.

It was then Wently noticed the truly horrifying aspect of the procedure. Bernard not only never cried out in even the smallest amount of pain, but there was not one drop of blood anywhere to be seen. The arm Marius brought toward the earl looked like nothing more than hard-set wax with a bit of bone in the middle. Wently wondered if this whole experience was simply part of his raging fever from the last few days while he and Snow traveled. Perhaps he was finally dying and the gods sent him this final nightmare.

"Now, my lord, we must remove the poison from your blood and attach this new arm. I'm afraid you will not behave as agreeably as Bernard, so I will give you a potion to make you sleep," Marius explained calmly.

Wently felt his breaths becoming shorter as Bernard came forward and lifted the earl from the chair with only his left arm. Wently found himself lying on the wooden table before he knew what was happening.

"Why are you doing this?" he sobbed.

"Ah, well you see, I have need of your station and even your circumstances. There are some Kentorian rebels I need you to inspire to greater heights of insurrection. There is nothing more sympathetic to that rabble than a displaced nobleman. Even a foreign one. I will expect total anarchy in Kenter before two full moons have passed, or I will take back this gift I am about to bestow upon you. And there will be no potion to help you sleep through the procedure if that happens." Marius smiled coldly as he lifted Wently's head to administer that potion now.

As Wently succumbed to the liquid, he could not help the child-like fear as he was pulled down into the darkness. As his consciousness drifted away, he wondered if it would be best for him if he never awoke from this operation.

25

Marina wanted to go home. She missed her soft bed and Hilde's comforting ministrations. Most of all, she missed regular sleep. Fahad and Curtis were slow to recover from the poison. While Gerard was up and ready to fight the erstwhile melted Brian within a few hours. It took the others two more days before they were well enough to travel.

As they were recovering, Marina split the watch with Gerard despite his insistence he could do so himself. Other than that small argument--which Marina won--they didn't speak much. Marina was not sure if Gerard was just staying quiet to more fully recuperate, or if he was embarrassed about what he did the night he was poisoned.

Marina watched the sunrise as the four of them made the final preparations to leave camp and decided she'd had enough. She tied her bag to the saddle as Oasis stood patiently, and patted her friend on the shoulder.

"Just a minute, girl, then we will be on our way."

It took her a moment to find Gerard. With nothing to pack, he went for a final run in the woods. She came upon him just as he was walking back.

"Are we ready?" he asked guardedly.

"Almost." She hesitated, unsure how to proceed. She considered Gerard a friend since her coming out ball two years ago, and it was odd to confront him in this fashion. He looked at her expectantly when she did not say anything, so she plunged ahead.

"What did you mean the other night?"

Gerard lost all expression and moved to pass her. Marina halted him with a hand on his arm, unwilling to drop the subject now she had broached it.

"You should forget I said anything, princess," he said woodenly, refusing to look at her.

"Please, Gerard," she tried to get him to look at her, "I am confused and I need to know what you meant."

He finally looked at her and sighed in defeat. "I am also confused, princess." Gerard sat on a nearby rock, looking lost. Marina sat next to him and returned his half-hearted smile.

"How much do you know of wolves?" he asked after a moment.

Marina was surprised by the question. "Probably more than most girls," she replied after a short pause, "because my tutor found the werewolf treaty to be most fascinating. I found out later that he worked as an aide for the last ambassador with your pack."

Gerard grimaced, "Yes, Bernard was a far better ambassador than I. I curse that damnable shipping accident every time I'm forced to don my good suit."

Marina nodded and asked gently, "What does that have to do with the other night?"

Gerard sighed again and searched her face. Marina did not know what he was looking for and blushed at the inspection.

"Nothing," he finally said, "but also everything. Did you know that wolves mate for life?"

"Yes," Marina stammered, growing more embarrassed by the direction the conversation was taking.

"I have never been mated, not in all my many years. When I met you, I felt something...new."

He looked at her and cursed when she looked a little frightened by that revelation.

"No, I am sorry," she blurted out. "I just...what happens if..." She looked at the ground, sorry she ever brought this subject up.

"Go on," he urged, "you can ask anything."

"What happens if you feel a mate bond, but it is not returned?" The words were quiet, and Marina wondered if he would have heard her if he was not a wolf.

His harsh laughter surprised her, and she looked up from the ground to see the frustration on his face.

"That's just it, princess," his eyes bored into hers, "I don't feel a mate bond. But there is something in your scent that feels...I don't know." He jumped up at the last and began to pace.

Marina watched him for a moment, feeling a little better she was not the only person who was confused by what was happening between them.

"So, you do not love me?" she ventured.

Gerard looked pained as he stopped pacing. "I'm sorry, princess. I think you're funny and beautiful and wonderful, but there is something missing."

Marina regarded him evenly and smiled. "That is perfectly all right," she assured him, "I think the same of you."

Gerard looked relieved and sat down again. Marina thought about his behavior in Heatherwood and looked at him again.

"Did you..." she trailed off, feeling the blood rushing to her cheeks again. Gerard cocked his head to the side, waiting for her to finish.

Clearing her throat, she worked up her nerve and finished in a rush, "did you see Fahad try to kiss me?"

Gerard's mouth tightened in annoyance. "Yes."

Marina opened her mouth, but Gerard stopped her. "I am only a confused old wolf dealing with emotions of which I began to think I was incapable. Despite my reaction, Fahad is a fine warrior and an upstanding young man. He always was." Gerard's gaze lost focus as he remembered something from long ago. He shook the memory away and gave Marina a stern look. "However, I believe your parents would have my head, as well as your brother's if we were to allow you to become involved."

Marina narrowed her eyes and was prepared to set Gerard straight on who could choose whom she loved when Curtis interrupted them.

"Marina, Gerard, come on. We want to be on our way before it gets too hot. The next oasis is almost two days away."

Gerard nodded and quickly left to join Fahad.

"What was that about?" Curtis asked. Marina only glared at him and stalked back to Oasis. "Wait, why are you mad at me?" he called after her.

They rode for several hours before Marina begged to stop. She was feeling dizzy and unfocused. Fahad rode up next to her and held her shoulder when it looked as though she was going to fall.

"I'm fine," she protested weakly, "I just need to stop for a moment."

She reached for her water, hoping to quench her seared throat. There was nothing there. Marina could not hold back a whimper of distress. Fahad's fingers tightened, and she looked at him. His eyes were pinched with worry, and she wanted to reassure him again she was well. That thought was forgotten when she saw the water skin he was holding out to her. The queen would be horrified by Marina's lack of manners as she grabbed for the skin and drained it.

After it was gone, she lowered the skin to find all three men looking at her with concern. She sheepishly handed the skin back to Fahad and made to push on.

"Come," she said with renewed vigor, "let us proceed."

Oasis barely took two steps when Fahad and Curtis grabbed the reins on either side of the horse's head.

"Marina," Curtis protested, "you cannot keep going like this. We have only been traveling for four hours and you have already drained three skins."

"No, I have only used Fahad's and my own," she insisted.

Curtis held up his own empty skin and dangled it in her face.

"No, brat, you borrowed a little too liberally from me as well."

Marina was shocked. She did not remember taking Curtis' water, but the proof was before her eyes. Momentary panic set in when she thought about continuing their journey without more water.

"I'll go back to our former camp and refill the skins," Gerard offered. "Take my water and wait here. You might want to pitch the tent so you can stay out of the sun. She drank more as it got hotter." Fahad nodded and made to dismount. Marina was annoyed by their high-handedness and dissented.

"I will be fine. We should keep going until noon at least, then we can stop for some luncheon. Pitch the tent then if you've a mind to, but

I will be well enough in the sun."

Curtis dismounted as well, coming toward Marina with anger in his eyes.

"You are too stubborn by half," he scolded, "Gerard is right and you know it. Now get down from Oasis before I pull you down."

Marina kicked Curtis' hand away when he tried to grab her boot. Using her knees, she spun Oasis around and began to trot in a wide circle. As Fahad and Curtis scrambled back into their saddles, she found their heading again and let Oasis break into a canter for a few seconds before slowing her to a walk.

While she wanted to make her point, she did not want to overtax Oasis to do so. She pulled up short when Gerard ran in front, causing Oasis to rear in panic. Not even unicorns liked being confronted by a werewolf, and Oasis was still mostly horse.

"I will not be coddled," Marina argued as soon as she had Oasis under control. She glared at each man in his turn, ending with her brother. "Now that I know to be mindful, I will not be as greedy as before."

Curtis ran a hand through his hair, blowing out his breath in frustration. "Marina," he began, but he did not finish. Instead, something behind her caught his attention.

They all looked and tried to spot what Curtis saw. Gerard saw it next and cursed under his breath.

"We must go, Highness," he urged the prince.

Curtis shook his head in denial, his mouth set in a grim line. "They will catch us. Krax'mran move three times faster than horses. They might even catch you." No one was amused by his bleak attempt at humor.

Marina watched the cloud of sand on the horizon growing ever closer. They were surrounded in a matter of minutes, and Marina saw Curtis was correct. Ten Krax'mran warriors trained their bows upon them, ready to loose them at the least provocation.

"What are you doing on Krax'mran land?" one of them demanded. He looked young, though it was difficult to tell in creatures with a life span of five hundred years.

"We are searching for a girl," Curtis said calmly, keeping his hands on his pommel to show he had no weapons.

"Why have you come to our desert to search for this girl? If she is human or fae, she is surely dead. If she is Krax'mran, then she is not yours to trifle with."

"She is my sister," Marina spoke up timidly. These warriors frightened her, but she would not let that stop her from finding Kaia.

The Krax'mran leader gave her a speculative look. "Then your sister is dead, boy. Leave our desert or face death."

He motioned to his group and they began to back away, forming a line to keep her and her companions from going further.

"No," she protested, "she is alive. She is being held by Nightshade."

Her declaration caused an angry buzzing amongst the warriors, and she saw three of them tighten their holds on their bows. Their young leader was next to Marina in a flash, and she had to stop Oasis from bucking again. He searched her face, and his eyes widened in surprise. Before she could stop him, he snatched the cap from her head, sending her black curls tumbling down her back.

"You lie," he snarled, unsheathing the dagger at his waist, "you are a spy of that evil sorcerer. I will take you to my village and you will tell me how I can kill your master. Then you will also die."

Holding his dagger to Marina's throat, he called out orders to his men in Krax'mranan. They quickly tied everyone's hands, leaving Marina, Fahad, and Curtis on their horses. Gerard was put on a longer rope to be pulled by one of the Krax'mran.

"Please, you do not understand," Marina sobbed, "we must save my sister." As they started forward, Marina added desperately, "We are also going to rescue a Krax'mran man."

The leader stopped short and returned to her side. "Who is this man your master has taken?"

"He is not my master," she insisted, "he is my enemy as well as yours."

"Who is this Krax'mran?"

"His name is Waitimu. He is being held with my sister, and we must help them both."

Her captor called to one of the men and spoke with him quietly for a moment. The man nodded and was soon running off into the desert.

"Waitimu escaped this sorcerer only three days ago. His journey has been the talk of many tribes. He will tell the truth, and we will see what he knows of your master."

Marina swallowed her angry retort and allowed Oasis to be pulled forward. This man was bringing her to Waitimu. She clung to the hope Kaia would be with him.

The Krax'mran village was five hours away by horseback. Their captors complained at the slow pace, but their leader, Abrafo, told them to cease whining. Abrafo only called a halt once, when Marina fell from her saddle two hours into their journey.

The heat and dryness got to her again. It took two full skins of water to fully revive her. After that, Abrafo allowed her to ride with Curtis, who kept her hydrated and upright. Spitfire did not appreciate the added weight, but there was no other option. The Krax'mran refused to allow a human on their backs and did not trust them not to escape on a horse with unicorn blood. Marina could not blame them for their pride, but she resented their slow pace just as much as the warriors. The afternoon sun was forcing her to drink almost constantly.

"We are here," Abrafo finally said. Marina would have cried from relief, but she did not want to waste the moisture.

Abrafo barked out orders, and Marina and her companions soon found themselves in a crude cell. It was constructed from wood and web, the web being far stronger than any of the wood. There were holes throughout the design, and they could see the villagers going about their business. Marina collapsed against one of the walls on the shaded side of their prison.

"Princess, are you okay?" Fahad asked urgently, placing a gentle hand on her face.

Marina smiled ruefully at him, "After all we have been through these last few days, can you not call me Marina?"

"Marina then," he murmured, "are you okay?"

"I will be as soon as Waitimu gets here," she sighed. "Perhaps Kaia will be with him and we will not need to go any further into this blasted desert."

"How do you know this Krax'mran?" Fahad asked.

Marina caught a movement behind Fahad and looked up to see Curtis standing over them. His arms were crossed and a cold look she never saw before entered his eyes.

"Why don't you move away from the princess, and then she may answer."

Fahad stood slowly, his jaw clenched in suppressed anger. Marina stood quickly and placed a hand on Fahad's arm. This was both to stop him from moving toward Curtis and to keep herself from swaying at the sudden movement. She was a little angry herself, but she did not want Fahad and Curtis to fight.

"Oh do shut up, Curtis," she spat. Curtis looked offended by her rebuke, but she pretended not to notice. "I saw Waitimu in my vision of Kaia when we were in Heatherwood," she explained matter-of-factly.

Curtis forgot about Fahad for the moment and asked, "I thought your visions were strictly one-way. How will Waitimu know you?"

"He seems to know some magic that allowed him to see me when he tasted Kaia's blood. We met only briefly, but I think that night will stay with him just as much as it has with me."

Curtis started to ask her another question when a commotion at the edge of the village stopped him. The four captives went over to the far side of their cell to see what was happening.

Marina saw Waitimu entering the village with five of his people accompanying him. She realized then Waitimu and Abrafo's people looked slightly different. The human halves of Abrafo's people were varying shades of ochre and terra cotta, reminding her somewhat of Calypso. Their spider halves were also half the size of Waitimu's and his warriors'.

Waitimu and Abrafo spoke solemnly, each showing the other due deference. Their conversation was short, and Abrafo was soon leading Waitimu to Marina and her friends. Waitimu regarded her without expression for a moment, and her heart sank.

He did not recognize her and she and her friends would suffer for it. She swallowed her fear and gave Waitimu an equally expressionless look. He turned to one of his companions and gave him some orders. Marina was surprised to see the man returning with Kaia's strange knapsack.

"Where is she?" Marina rasped. She knew Kaia wasn't dead. There would have been some signal through their bond.

Waitimu held himself rigidly, and she began to realize it was with shame and not a lack of emotion as she thought earlier. "Nightshade still has her. She saved me, and I will repay the debt."

"Release them," Abrafo ordered.

Marina reached for her sister's bag as soon as she stepped out of the webbed door. She distantly heard Gerard speaking to Waitimu about Nightshade's defenses, but was too focused on the bag to really understand what was being said. Sitting on the ground, she searched through Kaia's things. She did not know why she was doing it, only that it felt like there was something important there. Finally, her hand touched the bottom.

Frustration almost made her throw the bag away, but she searched around the edges and found what felt like a tear in the bottom. She lifted and heard a strange ripping noise. Peering inside, she saw a black box made of a foreign material hidden beneath the flap.

It took her a minute to figure out how to open it, and she was surprised when it popped open, tossing its contents on the ground. The setting sun made the gold on the necklace shine like it was smeared with blood. Marina picked it up by the chain, and let it dangle in front of her for a moment so she could admire the way it made the stones sparkle. When she grabbed it, the world went dark.

The world slowly came back, but Marina was no longer in the desert. Light seemed to expand around her, revealing her surroundings as it spread. There was solid rock under her feet, and she began to see the walls and ceiling were also rock. There were columns throughout the cavern and in the very center a stone pedestal.

Then, figures began to appear. To her left, Marina was surprised to find she was looking at herself. It was not a mirror image. In fact, she looked quite different. Her hair was shorter, there was blood on the right side of her face, and dirt everywhere. Her vision self was looking at two figures, and Marina turned to look as well.

One figure was standing, while the other knelt. The person kneeling finally came into focus, and Marina recognized Kaia. Her vision self looked terrified as she stared at Kaia, confusing Marina.

The other person was a man. She had never seen him before, but malevolence emanated from him in an almost palpable form. Kaia held out an object to this man, and Marina recognized the amulet that sent her into this vision.

"No," she heard the vision of herself say. It was like listening to an echo, and she could only barely hear the words. "Nightshade must not possess the amulet."

Marina gasped and studied the man in front of Kaia. She recognized some of her own features in him and shuddered at the cruelty on a face not too dissimilar from her own. Marina watched as Kaia turned to face her in surprise. That surprise turned to hate-filled fear, and both versions of Marina gasped in shock this time.

Then, Kaia was picking up a decorative spear that was lying nearby and hurling it with all her strength toward the vision-Marina. The real version of Marina did not want to watch herself get impaled, so she closed her eyes in terror. Suddenly, there were hands gripping her shoulders, and she could feel the sand beneath her legs once more.

The sun was gone now, and Marina could barely see Fahad's worried features in the torchlight. "Marina, what happened?"

It was only when his fingers brushed her cheeks she realized she was crying. The tears poured down her face, but she made no sound. Fahad helped her stand as she futilely tried to brush the tears away with her other hand. The solid weight of his arm around her shoulder steadied her but could not completely erase her horror.

"We have to get Kaia away from Nightshade," she said, near hysterics. "He is corrupting her, and we must save her now."

Marina turned and found everyone looking at her.

"Come," Abrafo commanded, "we must have a war council."

He led the way to one of the few structures on the ground. Marina saw many curious faces in the trees, and was glad when she could escape into the lodge.

26

Kaia wanted to punch a wall but knew it wouldn't do her any good. The sun was rising on yet another day of captivity, and the frustration was becoming too much to bear.

After she left Marius and Wently yesterday, she wasn't able to come up with a single viable escape plan. She partly blamed this on Cossette. The servant wouldn't leave her side since the last escape attempt and Kaia was starting to wonder if she would ever be free of her creepy shadow.

As if summoned by the thought, Cossette stepped into the room.

"Speak of the devil," Kaia muttered, glaring at Cossette. "Ever hear of knocking?" Kaia asked coldly.

"Forgive the intrusion, milady. Your father instructed me to bring you to his chambers."

Cossette held the door open and signaled to Kaia to lead the way. Kaia shrugged to hide her trepidation and left the room. Cossette moved to Kaia's side, pulling just far enough ahead to show her where to turn until they were standing in front of the door Robin told her was not her concern that first day.

Cossette rapped on the door, and they waited in silence for Marius. When he answered, Cossette curtsied and made herself scarce. Though she knew Cossette wouldn't be much help if Marius decided to hurt her, the idea of being alone with him frightened her.

Not wanting to show that fear, Kaia swept into the room as if she owned the place. She took in the elaborate sitting room and chose the most comfortable-looking chair to flounce into. The frilly skirt Cossette practically forced her into that morning made the gesture slightly silly but Kaia pretended not to notice.

"So, what's on the agenda today?" Kaia gave him a bored look and began to look around as if he couldn't hold her attention. She knew it was juvenile, but she did want to get a peek at his rooms as well. There was a small glimmer of hope that every foray out of her room could become an opportunity for escape.

There were four doors in the room, including the one she just walked through. Each door was placed in a different wall, which explained why there were no windows in the room. Several lamps set in brackets at eye level gave the room a bright, cheery look.

"I see that you are still upset with me," Marius sighed dramatically. "Perhaps we can talk and clear the air."

He sat in the chair opposite her, calmly folded his hands, and crossed his ankle over his knee. He looked utterly relaxed, and Kaia decided to play along.

"What would you like to talk about?" she asked, sitting up straighter and mimicking his casual posture. Minus the crossed leg, as she didn't want to embarrass herself.

"I feel I have questioned you enough. It is now my turn to answer your questions. Please, ask anything you wish; I will not lie to you." His expression reeked of sincerity, and Kaia shifted uncomfortably.

"Okay," she said slowly, "Why is Cossette constantly tailing me?"

"I do not want you to leave until I can gain your trust. She will not try to harm you," he assured her.

Kaia didn't try to hide her annoyance. "I don't need a babysitter. It's pretty obvious from the other day that I don't stand much of a chance of leaving if you don't want me to."

"Then I will instruct Cossette to relax her guard somewhat. For how I can I ask for your trust if I am unwilling to give you mine?"

Kaia was struck by the reasonableness of this. Perhaps there was more to Marius than she thought. She wasn't any closer to trusting him, but at least he was being honest with her so far.

"Cool," she agreed. It was clear he wasn't sure what that meant, but she asked another question before he could ask.

"What do you have planned once you gain my trust; assuming you can."

Marius' lips thinned at her addendum, but he regained his composure and answered. "Frankly, my dear, I seek to revolutionize the way the Kingdoms are governed. War has plagued our world for many centuries. I believe with your help--as well as your sister's--I can bring harmony to our realm."

Kaia tensed when he mentioned Marina. "What do you mean, 'sister?'" she inquired. She decided to play dumb, and see what he could reveal about Marina.

"I am sorry," he said with earnest regret, "I did not think when I said that. You see, you have a twin sister somewhere in the world," he rose from his seat and knelt before Kaia, taking her limp hand.

"You mean, you don't know where she is?"

Marius gazed at her with a calculating gleam in his eyes. Kaia tried to look as confused as possible. Not the best actress, she was relieved when Marius lost some of his intensity and looked disappointed.

"No," he answered flatly, "I have had my servants searching the Kingdoms for you both ever since your mother hid you from me. I believed you were in Jamaria for a time, but if you were picked up by nomads, then she must have also been moved before I could discover where she was hidden."

Kaia didn't disabuse him of the notion that she was raised in the Kingdoms. The less he knew about her, the better. She hoped that by concealing her past, it might also help conceal Marina's.

"Then we'll have to find her now," Kaia said. Marius looked pleased when she included him in searching for Marina, and Kaia worked to hide her derision. Luckily, he moved away from her and resumed his position across from her.

Kaia continued questioning him. "So how are we supposed to help you bring harmony? I'm not the most harmonious person."

Marius laughed, and Kaia was surprised at how pleasant the sound was. "You and your sister were born under a blood moon," he explained, "They occur once every eighteen years, and with your mother's blood, it is when you and your sister are at your most powerful.

"Your mother possessed an amulet that has the ability to tap into power from another world. She grew frightened of me and hid both the amulet and our daughters from me. I do not blame her," he admitted woefully, "she did not understand why I needed to increase my powers, or even why I wanted to bring peace to our world. Your mother was not the most intelligent of Nereid, but she was so very beautiful."

Marius got a dreamy look on his face, and Kaia tried not to feel too weirded out. She could understand him finding her mother attractive, otherwise—given how much importance Marius placed on beauty—she probably wouldn't be Kaia's mother. But Kaia didn't think Marius was thinking of Yara. Some other memory was causing that wistful look. Kaia had a feeling she didn't really want to know what it was.

"So what is this other world you're looking to get power from?" Kaia interjected, breaking Marius out of his thoughts.

"What do you know of the land of our ancestors—Earth?" Marius answered with his own question. Kaia knew by the tone of his voice that she needed to tread carefully with her answer.

"Not a whole lot. Maybe a few myths and legends, but not much."

"Do you know the story of the Great Shift?"

"I can't say that I've heard that one," Kaia said honestly.

"Then your adoptive parents have sorely neglected your education," Marius sneered.

Kaia felt anger rise at this insult to Merry. "My mom gave me a great education. Not to mention a lot of love and kindness, so how about you leave her out of this."

"My apologies, my dear. I see you are fiercely loyal to the woman who raised you. However, since she did not tell you of the Shift, please allow me to do so."

Kaia swallowed her ire and nodded.

"Many years ago, there were but three worlds. Earth was the world of men, Underhill the world of the fae, and the heavens the world of the gods. Humans were always full of fear and awe with respect to Underhill and the heavens. It was their fear that drove humans to hunt the children of the fae and the gods. For a long time, the gods and fae were able to protect themselves and their children, because most men still prayed to the gods and held the fae in fearful respect.

"But then, more and more people forgot their gods. Without the belief of humans, the gods began to lose their ability to protect the magical creatures they created. The fae were able to escape Underhill, but the gods could not bring their children to the heavens. So, they created the Kingdoms.

"All the creatures humans thought of as supernatural were brought to the lands we live in today. As for the humans, those who were chosen by the gods were given the choice. Stay in the land of their ancestors, or come to the new world and continue to keep their gods. But, once the choice was made, there could be no going back. The eight gods who separated the worlds did it in such a way that no one could cross from one world to the other."

The room was silent for a moment while Kaia digested Marius's story. She thought back to the vision she had while visiting with Sister Mary—when she first touched the amulet. There were eight people at that stone pedestal, and she knew that at least three of them were gods.

Apparently, she saw the Great Shift happen and didn't even know it. She looked at Marius who was patiently waiting for her reaction and knew he could never find out that part of his story was wrong. People could pass between Earth and the Kingdoms, and she knew Marius should never be one of them.

"If all the magical creatures and gods and stuff are here, what kind of power could Earth possibly have?"

"Ah, but you see, with all the magical creatures and people here, there is much in the way of untapped potential magic on Earth. The amulet your mother had would have allowed me to draw upon that potential."

"I suppose that makes sense. So you need Yara's amulet and that blood moon thing? When is the next blood moon?"

"Several months away, I am afraid. But that gives us plenty of time to get to know each other and find your sister." He smiled, and Kaia nervously returned the gesture.

"And that's it?"

"Well," he seemed reluctant to share the next piece of information, "there are some other elements to the ritual that I recently discovered, but they are mere trinkets and I think I will find them easily."

Kaia smiled thinly and decided not to press further for now. She made to stand up and leave but stopped when the door behind Marius caught her eye. Deciding to keep up the bravado, she settled back into the comfy chair and regarded Marius thoughtfully.

"What's behind those doors?" she asked, indicating the three that didn't lead to the main hall.

Marius rose and offered his hand to Kaia. She took it carefully and tried not to shudder when he tucked it into the crook of his elbow to lead her around the room. He started with the door behind her.

"This is my bedroom," he informed her, opening it to show a darkly masculine chamber. Everything was made of heavy, dark wood, and all the fabric was either black or a deep crimson. Meager amounts of light spilled through the dense brocade curtains, so Kaia couldn't see much in the room.

Closing that door, Marius led her to the opposite side of the room, skipping the door directly across from the one she entered. This door opened into Marius' lab, and Kaia shuddered in remembered horror at her time in this room.

"I regret that you are familiar with my laboratory," he said silkily. She was grateful when he closed that door and led her to the final one. There was some pride in his voice when he announced, "This is my treasure room. It is where I house my most precious possessions."

He opened this door with a flourish, and Kaia couldn't stop a gasp of amazement. Even though Marius' castle was filled with breathtaking artwork, everything in this room was a feast for the eyes. She could tell he saved his most elaborate prizes for this room.

However, there were a couple of items that didn't quite fit in. A harp made of an intricately chiseled dark wood, and a large broadsword that looked like it was beginning to rust. While both sported some rather elaborate jewelry and looked as though they were once well-tended, they did not stand up to the majesty of the other prizes.

At Kaia's curious look, Marius moved to place the objects in an ornate glass case. "Those are merely part of a unique set I am collecting. I've only six pieces left to find."

"Wow," Kaia breathed, deciding to drop the issue for the moment, "you could fund a small nation with this room. Actually, you might be able to fund a medium-sized nation here."

Marius looked pleased by her assessment. "Yes, I am quite proud of my collection. It has taken decades to accumulate."

Marius closed the door and led Kaia back to the hallway. Cossette was still waiting, and Kaia looked at Marius to see what he would do.

"Kaia, please allow Cossette to escort you to your room. I do not wish for you to become lost. Cossette, you will attend Kaia only when summoned, or when Kaia wishes to leave the castle."

Kaia was surprised she might be allowed outside the castle. "Does that mean I can go outside the walls?" she ventured.

Marius gave her a look full of regret, and Kaia tried not to show her disbelief or disgust at his performance. "I am afraid that you must stay within the protection of the outer walls. The Krax'mran are a constant danger, and I still worry for your safety."

Kaia shrugged as if this didn't matter, and slipped her hand from Marius' arm. She walked away without another word and allowed Cossette to lead her back to her plush prison. She dismissed the servant as soon as they got close to the door.

"Are you sure you do not need anything, miss?" Cossette asked.

Kaia narrowed her eyes and answered, "No, I think I've taken about all I can from you."

Cossette either ignored the insult or didn't understand it, because she just gave Kaia that warm smile, curtsied, and walked away.

Kaia leaned against the closed door once she was back in her room, and thought about her conversation with Marius. As she stepped forward, she tripped on a piece of lace fringe that had come loose from the bottom of the poufy dress Cossette forced on her. Seething, she began to tear the dress away until she was left in her medieval undergarments, with the remnants of the flounces and furbelows of the hated dress at her feet.

Kaia eyed the wardrobe balefully, knowing there were only more dresses like that inside. Stalking forward she asked, "Can't you come up with some pants and shirts? I'm sick to death of dresses. They were fine for a day or so, but I want some freaking pants!"

With that, she threw the doors open. What she found inside made her mouth drop open in amazement. All the dresses were replaced by dozens of pants, shirts, waistcoats, and jackets. Kaia carefully plucked a fine blue jacket from the wardrobe and put it on over her chemise.

It fit her perfectly. She admired the cut of the fabric in the nearby mirror. Taking it off and replacing it on its hanger, she eyed the rest of the clothing. She spied a few pieces of lace and some bows and closed the doors again.

"Maybe something a little simpler," she instructed, "I'm not a fan of lace and stuff like that. Oh," she stopped herself from opening the doors, "but don't be afraid to use soft fabrics. I'm not big into wool either."

Hoping this would work, she opened the doors. She gave a whoop of excitement, but quickly covered her mouth and darted a glance at her door. The one thing that would ruin this discovery would be Cossette walking in, wondering what was up. When no one came knocking, Kaia turned back to her magical wardrobe.

"I take back all the mean things I thought about you," she apologized, grabbing for the clothes. "This is so more like it."

When she finished dressing, she hurried to admire herself in the mirror. The wardrobe provided a soft linen shirt, which she covered with a waistcoat. It was hunter green and quilted, and it fit so snugly she got some much-needed support upstairs even without the bra Cosette stole from her. The pants were a honey brown and felt like incredibly soft leather.

As she stood there, she realized she needed shoes to go with this ensemble. The wardrobe revealed nothing suitable, still full of feminine shoes more fitted to the former dresses. She closed the doors and considered them.

"Man," she chastised, "you really won't let that fashion go. But, listen, I need something a bit sturdier. I'm thinking some dark brown boots." She thought about it for a moment, and an eager smile covered her face when she decided what she wanted. "Definitely knee-high. I'm going to look so B.A. when I'm done."

The wardrobe provided the perfect pair of boots. They had a slight heel, only raising her an inch. She didn't need extra height, but it made her butt look good, so she commended the wardrobe for its efforts. The leather was deep mahogany and the leather hugged her calves like they never wanted to leave her feet.

"Oh yeah," she nodded at her reflection, "this will definitely work for me."

The best part of her wardrobe was that she needed absolutely no help in getting it on or off. That meant Cossette was out of a job, and Kaia couldn't be happier. She was too agitated to stay cooped up in her room and decided to venture out to show off her new outfit.

Cossette met her at the door leading outside, and Kaia felt some of her good mood souring. She'd forgotten Marius' order she was to be escorted when going out. Fighting down the urge to kick someone, she chose to ignore Cossette's presence and continue.

The sun felt welcoming at first, though Kaia soon began to feel the effects of its drying heat. She decided to ignore this as well for the moment and kept exploring the keep. There were no buildings in front of the castle and only two buildings in the back. One looked like a blacksmith's, with several horseshoes and weapons hanging about. Nearby, but slightly further away was a large stable. There was a well between the two, and Kaia felt somewhat parched.

She led the way to the well and felt a bit of gratitude when Cossette pulled the bucket up so Kaia could drink. As she sipped the water from a cup Cossette produced from nowhere, she assessed the castle. It still felt strange to see something so European in a desert. Looking at Cossette, Kaia decided to try getting some answers.

"Why did Marius build this castle here?"

"He moved this structure from his homeland to be alone. He needed time to prepare for the revolution and did not wish to be disturbed."

"What do you mean he moved it? Where did it come from?"

"The master removed his home from its native soil and placed it here. This was originally the home of the Baron DeWinter of Brookland, the master's father."

"What happened to the baron? Did Marius inherit this place?"

"The baron died, as did his six eldest sons. The master took this castle as his birthright."

Cossette's words made Kaia feel uneasy. "How did Marius' father and brothers die?"

Cossette looked at Kaia with those dead eyes, and Kaia felt chilled despite the burning sun. "All is as the master wishes," Cossette stated calmly.

Kaia put her cup down, shaken to the core. Her father murdered his own father, as well as his six brothers. She felt sick and stood to get away from Cossette. The smithy was right in front of her, and she hurried into its open door.

The heat from the forge hit her like a wall, and Kaia cursed her stupidity for choosing such a place to run to. This much heat made her dizzy and she turned to leave. Cossette blocked the doorway, causing a sudden, burning anger to well up in Kaia's heart. The forge fire felt like nothing compared to the rage within her. This creature Marius created spoke of murder with no emotion, and would keep Kaia with that murderer at any cost.

"I'm leaving," Kaia uttered evenly, "if you try to stop me I'll—" she broke off, uncertain of how to end that threat. Then, she saw one of the swords. Choosing one that looked easy to manage, she held it up and leveled it at Cossette's chest. "I'll slice you like a turkey," she finished.

Cossette surveyed the cold iron at her breast before giving Kaia a significant look.

"I cannot allow you to leave," she asserted, "and I do not believe you will harm me."

"Of course I will," Kaia protested. "You're not even a proper person. You're just something Marius cooked up in his lab. I have no problem stabbing you."

Kaia lunged forward to prove her point and was amazed when Cossette stepped forward as well, instead of away. The sword was buried to the hilt in Cossette's stomach, and the girl acted as though nothing happened. Kaia backed away, watching as Cossette pulled the sword from her flesh and tossed it away like a toothpick. Kaia turned to find another way out and heard Cossette move forward quickly. She soon had Kaia wrapped in her arms. Kaia struggled, but couldn't break free. She felt her anger rising again and felt that same knot in her stomach from yesterday.

A smell like broiled chicken reached Kaia's nose, and she felt Cossette's grip loosen for a moment before gripping her harder. The tightening hold fueled Kaia's rage, and the knot grew. Kaia looked down and saw with detached amazement that Cossette's arms looked thinner than before. The skin upon them was also red and bubbly.

Cossette let go abruptly, and Kaia stumbled back. She slipped on something and was falling back, unable to catch herself. Something warm and slightly sharp broke her fall, and she scrambled to get away from it. Standing quickly, she prepared herself for another fray with Cossette. She was most assuredly not prepared for what she saw. Cossette was the thing that broke Kaia's fall. But the lump of flesh, bone, and fabric on the ground didn't look much like Cossette anymore.

"What the..." Kaia said in horrified wonder. "C-Cossette?"

She poked the thing on the ground with the toe of her boot and jumped when it began to melt further. The skin sloughed through and off of the bones, leaving a pile of goo surrounding Cossette's well-dressed skeleton.

"Did I...was that me?"

Tears spilled from Kaia's eyes and she covered her mouth to hold back the sobs. Robin found her like that mere minutes later. Kaia didn't fight when he placed an iron grip on her arm and dragged her back to the castle.

27

The lodge was long and made almost entirely of wood. This was a rarity for Krax'mran structures. Marina paused to admire the workmanship before joining Curtis and Fahad along one wall. Gerard left the village so no one could watch him change as the full moon demanded. He told Marina he would return once the council was over. Abrafo settled himself at the far end, directly opposite the door. He was flanked on each side by three older Krax'mran. The three to his right were all men, while the three to his left were women.

Marina looked at the woman next to Abrafo, dazzled by her costume. She was covered in feathers and webbing, and Marina recognized this woman as the tribe's spiritual leader. The traditions of the Krax'mran fascinated Marina. They had very strict rules about who could be warriors, leaders, and Anansini—their shaman.

Leaders were always the oldest child of the former leader, no matter that child's gender. However, their younger siblings could challenge for leadership through battle. Warriors were predominantly men but women could also join the ranks. This usually only happened in wartime, according to the books Marina read.

The Anansini, however, was always a woman. Often, she was the wife of the leader. It was said the Anansini represented the mother of all Krax'mran, Kraximmra. The texts Marina read stated the Krax'mran were children solely of the Kingdoms and never saw the first world.

Their god, Anansi, mated with Kraximmra, one of his human worshipers. She gave birth to an entire nation, half human and half spider. Kraximmra's tribe left the desert in fear of her children, who named the land Krax'mra in her honor.

"We will have silence as Dalili confers with the Father."

A hush fell over the small crowd as Dalili raised herself until all eight legs were fully extended. Her hands reached to the ceiling, and she began to sway and chant. The feathers of her costume fluttered in the slight breeze caused by her movements, and Marina felt slightly hypnotized.

Dalili began to move around the room, her large body moving gracefully. She said something, and Marina jumped when the crowd of twenty replied. This happened a few more times. Marina realized this must be a call-and-response moment in the chant. She wished she knew what was being said, but she did not understand Krax'mranan.

Finally, Dalili returned to her place at Abrafo's side. She said something to the crowd, and Abrafo translated.

"The blood of the council must be mixed. Step forward if you wish to have your voice heard by the people and the Father."

Marina walked forward to stand in front of Dalili. The woman's mask concealed her face, but Marina could see the suspicion in her amber eyes.

"You have traveled far, young one," Dalili whispered as she removed her ceremonial knife from its sheath, "humans are not much trusted in this desert, and none live after breaking our trust."

Marina was chilled by the words, but she held Dalili's gaze and offered her hand. Because she was prepared for the pain, she did not flinch when the Anansini sliced her palm. The small stream of blood was captured in a stone bowl, and one of Dalili's attendants gave Marina a cloth to bind the wound.

As Marina stepped back, she saw her companions step up for the sacrifice as well as Waitimu and one of his warriors. The rest all belonged to Abrafo's tribe. Dalili was the last to mix her blood, after which she handed the sloshing bowl to her attendant. That girl took it outside, and Marina didn't see her come back inside.

"Our blood has been mixed, and now so shall our words." Abrafo's voice rang with solemnity, and Marina wondered at the ritual.

"The council may begin," Dalili intoned, motioning for Abrafo to start.

"Waitimu, our brother from the south, has vouched for this girl. He has been a captive of our enemy, Nightshade," Abrafo paused when this caused an angry buzzing, and held up his hands for quiet. "He was Nightshade's prisoner, and this girl's sister healed him, and helped him escape. This, despite resulting in her own capture.

"Now this girl," he motioned to Marina.

"Marina," she stated quietly, made nervous by the suspicious and curious gazes pointed at her.

"This Marina asks for our help to rescue her sister. Let us hear arguments."

An elderly man at Abrafo's far-right rose slowly, his thin legs creaking with age. "The humans have never been trustworthy," he said, his voice deep and melodious. "Waitimu, son of the chieftain, Reth, has told us this girl's sister helped him. I do not doubt his words, but we cannot know why she has done this. Maybe she is aligned with Nightshade and sought to ingratiate herself with our honored guest."

The man bowed his head, apparently done making his case.

"Waitimu, what say you to this?" Abrafo asked.

"I tasted the girl, Kaia's, blood. Anansi does not speak to me as he would an Anansini, but even my weak skill told me she could be trusted. She fought bravely in our escape, and I believe she is against Nightshade, as are we all."

The crowd muttered amongst themselves at Waitimu's reply. Abrafo raised his hands again for silence.

"Are there any other voices?"

A young woman to Abrafo's left stood tall to speak next.

"Waitimu speaks well for this Marina, and her sister Kaia. However, we must weigh the price of Krax'mran blood against that of this Kaia's. If we seek to rescue this one human, how many Krax'mran might die in the attempt? Nightshade's minions defy death, while a Krax'mran is all too mortal."

Marina heard several people agreeing, and she worried they would get no help. Then, Fahad stepped forward.

"What if no Krax'mran fights Nightshade's minions?"

Abrafo and his council looked confused. "If you do not want us to fight, why do you ask our help?"

"I suggest a distraction. Your people obviously worry Nightshade greatly, as well he should be worried. I ask that the Krax'mran allow themselves to be seen by Nightshade's minions, allowing my group the opportunity to rescue Kaia."

The council discussed this idea for a moment. Dalili made a noise of protest, and Abrafo let her speak.

"A distraction does not mean we will not fight the deathless ones. What do you say to this?"

Curtis spoke up this time. "You are wrong in thinking his servants are deathless. If you go to our camp from this morning, you will see for yourself a pile of clothing and bones. It was once one of Nightshade's creatures."

"And how did this creature die? We have hacked pieces from their flesh, but they do not bleed nor feel pain."

Curtis looked at Marina, who said, "He simply melted." She shrank back a bit when the entire crowd focused on her but tamped down her timidity to continue. "He said a spell and began to melt. I know that does not sound helpful, but the sight of his melted flesh, but intact bones, made me think that there must be a spell holding that flesh together. If the flesh is molded to a real skeleton, then I imagine that removing the head will result in killing these creatures."

"We have crushed many of the enemy's skulls, and pierced many more than that. They always returned to the fray," Dalili argued.

"But were their heads still intact in those cases? I believe that not even these creatures can survive without their heads, and even if their bodies keep going, how would they know where to aim?" Marina countered.

Dalili looked stunned by this question.

"Besides," Curtis interjected, "if the Krax'mran need to fight, what good are tiny humans and their swords against the might of the Krax'mran?"

This brought a lot of nodding heads and arrogant smiles from the crowd. Marina smiled at her brother, amazed once again at the way he could so easily charm anyone. Even the wary Krax'mran were patting him on the back like he was one of them.

Raising his hands, and hiding a smile, Abrafo called for order. "A truth indeed, small one," he said, eliciting a round of laughter at Curtis' expense. Curtis smiled good-naturedly and gave Abrafo a courtly bow.

"Does anyone else wish to give voice?" Abrafo looked around, but no one else stepped forward. "Let us then decide. Who would leave the human, Kaia, in the hands of Nightshade?"

Only three scowling Krax'mran raised their hands. Among them the elder who first objected, and also Dalili. The third Krax'mran never spoke the entire time, but he looked so much like Abrafo, Marina concluded he must be a brother or otherwise related.

"And who," Abrafo continued, "would test their might against the followers of Nightshade?"

The cheering Krax'mran almost shook the lodge. Marina grinned and hugged her brother in joy. Not even Dalili's spiteful glare could thwart her happiness.

"We are decided. Let all those who wish to join meet at first light at the edge of the village."

After one more cheer, the council broke up and people began to exit the lodge. Abrafo spoke to Waitimu in hushed tones for a few moments before they both came to speak with Marina and her group.

"I will be leaving now," Waitimu said.

Marina felt her heart sink. "Why?"

"I must speak to my father and get permission to bring our warriors to the fight."

Marina grinned, and Waitimu answered with a small smile of his own.

"Thank you, Waitimu," she said around a lump in her throat, "Your help is invaluable. I do not know how I will ever repay your kindness."

"This is repayment of my debt to your sister. No thanks are needed."

"Yes, you did say she helped you. What did Abrafo mean when he said she healed you though?"

Waitimu hesitated a second before answering. "Your sister has the power to heal. Even she did not know of it until she healed me. Do you have such a power?"

Marina looked at her companions, only among the living still because she was able to purify the poison in their blood. "I think I have something like it."

"This will be good in the coming battle. If a Krax'mran is harmed, you and Kaia will heal our ranks."

Marina nodded, "I am sure Kaia would agree that healing whatever wounds you receive in her rescue is the least we can do."

Waitimu nodded, then turned to leave the lodge. Marina was about to follow him when Abrafo stopped her.

"You and your group will sleep in my web this night."

Marina, Fahad, and Curtis all voiced their appreciation for the honor Abrafo was giving them. He led the way to his home and the humans followed. Marina exited the lodge to find the moon staring back at her. She had forgotten about its importance to her journey during the council but felt an anxious thrill as the silvery glow caressed her face.

"Abrafo," she blurted out, causing their small party to stop, "I have another request. Is there perhaps a small pool of water or a well in the village?"

"We have no well," he replied, and Marina felt her excitement wane. "But, there is a lagoon in the middle of this oasis. It is in the meeting of two cave entrances."

Marina grinned and grabbed Abrafo's hand to squeeze it in happiness. When he looked startled by the affectionate gesture, she quickly let go. She knew her face was red from embarrassment and hoped the pale moonlight would obscure the color.

"Forgive me," she apologized, "I was overcome with emotion."

Abrafo just grunted and motioned for her to follow him as he led them in the opposite direction.

Curtis came closer, whispering, "Why can this not wait until morning, brat? I'm bloody tired and we need to be ready by first light. Unless, of course, you don't feel like rescuing this new sister of yours."

Marina smacked Curtis in the arm and fought a smile as he behaved as though it were broken. He ceased making noise when he had to concentrate on getting down to the water safely. The lagoon was surrounded by rock and dirt, with only a steep path leading down to it.

"If you must know, I need the light of the full moon. The lagoon is also imperative, as I am sure you were about to ask. Now, watch my things while I do this." Once they arrived at the lagoon, she removed her bag and Kaia's from her shoulder. After taking the diary from her pack, she sat down to remove her boots and roll her pant legs up.

Gerard appeared beside her on silent paws and eyed the water with mistrust. The other men watched with the wolf as she waded into the shallow water. Holding the book under, she tried to read her mother's writing as Calypso instructed. The moon's rays shimmered and danced across the surface of the water whenever she moved, making reading impossible. Marina gritted her teeth in frustration and tried to hold perfectly still. When her back began to ache, and the water kept moving with an almost imperceptible current as it passed from one cave to the other, she decided to try a different tack.

The water only came up to her knees where she was standing, so she ventured out a bit further until it lapped her upper thighs. She knelt, sitting on her heels until her head was beneath the surface. Perhaps holding my breath in the bath was preparing me for this moment, she thought as she became able to decipher the words on the first page.

My sisters think me foolish to write about my day, but I think them jealous they did not think of it first. We Nereid should remember the fun we have playing amongst the kelp and coral. Perhaps by writing this down, we could share our love of the sea as well as mischief with others. I suppose I should write, first, my name. I am Yara, daughter of Neptune, and therefore the sea. I think I am the prettiest of the Nereid, though my sisters often disagree. Today I am wearing a most becoming string of pearls tied by only the choicest pieces of kelp. My father insists we wear human clothing when upon the land so we will not be caught by smelly land-dwellers. I shall not tell him of the many times I defied this order. Clothing is so very cumbersome, and I delight in the feel of the sun upon my skin when I am above water.

Marina frowned slightly as the diary continued like this. It was full of fanciful nonsense and descriptions of jewelry. Yara sounded as naïve and foolish as her sisters believed. Marina was about to turn the page to read on, when the sound of someone jumping into the water startled her. She turned just as Fahad grabbed her under her arms and pulled her up.

"What are you doing?" Marina sputtered.

"We thought you drowned," Fahad gasped.

"What? Why would you think that?"

"You were under there for four minutes. We were worried you had gone into one of your trances and were drowning."

Marina looked around to see Curtis and Gerard. Both had looks of relief on their faces, and Marina felt her heart sink with guilt. Even Abrafo looked relieved to see her breathing.

"I am sorry," she whispered. "I did not think."

"No kidding," Curtis muttered petulantly from the bank.

Marina still felt too guilty to take offense. Curtis sighed when he saw tears form in her eyes and sat down on the rocky bank.

"Well, if you are done scaring us, pray continue. We will take turns making sure you are not dead." He turned to Abrafo, saying, "You may as well seek your bed. Knowing her, this could take all night."

Abrafo surveyed their odd group and satisfied himself with an indifferent shrug before turning away. "Humans," Marina heard him say in exasperation.

"How long can you hold your breath?" Fahad asked when Abrafo was gone.

"Umm, I am not exactly sure," Marina admitted. "I think around twelve minutes." She may have only attempted up to ten but she always felt she could go longer. Not to mention she had a feeling that Fahad would pull her out a minute or two earlier than whatever she told him.

"I'll be pulling you up in ten minutes then," he said stubbornly. Marina bit her lip to hide her amusement at being so right about him.

Now that she knew they were not going to let her stay in the water forever, she tried to skim through to find important information. After flipping through a quarter of the diary, she found a mention of her father.

I never found humans all that attractive until I met Marius. He is a gorgeous specimen, and he tells me often that I am beautiful. It is no wonder I feel as though I am falling in love with this mortal. Who indeed could not love someone so sweetly attentive? He brings me wondrous gifts that sparkle and shine like stars. Marius is all that a suitor should be, and I feel my father would not disapprove of him so if only he were immortal like me.

Marina skipped ahead, as the next few pages were filled with more praise for Marius. It was saccharine to the point of making Marina's headache. After several pages, she stopped on an interesting passage.

Marius has asked to see the Spark. Father would be furious to know, and I admit I feel uneasy at Marius' interest. The Spark is most beautiful, and I know Marius would appreciate this, but it is far too powerful to trust to a human. Even my dear, sweet, attentive Marius might be tempted by all the Spark can offer. I am decided then: I will not give in to his charming requests to compare my beauty to that of the Spark.

Marina turned to the next page and saw there was an angry slant to the words.

Oh, how I hate to be teased, even by my love. He has called me a coward and implied I am too afraid of Neptune's guards to attempt retrieving the Spark. How dare he! No merman is a match for a Nereid, and I shall prove that this is so!!

Marina pitied her simple mother for falling for such a silly ploy. She started when she felt Fahad's hand on her shoulder. Apparently, her ten minutes were up. Standing, she looked into Fahad's eyes. The worry was still there, and she sighed knowing he would not let her keep going for much longer. Gerard was watching her as well, pacing back and forth and emitting a low whine of frustration. Only Curtis was relaxed, reclining on his ledge, letting the water lap his newly bare toes. Marina's eyes widened in shock when she heard a soft snore escape his slightly parted lips.

"Well, it is good to know my brother is so concerned for my safety," she said indignantly.

Curtis cracked one eye open, apparently deciding not to move anything else. "There's no point in all three of us staying so alert," he replied with a yawn, "If there was any real danger these lads would wake me with their squawking."

Marina opened her mouth to give him a set down but clapped her hand over the ready retort when Gerard suddenly pushed Curtis into the water. Curtis came up spluttering while Fahad and Marina laughed and Gerard only gave the prince an arch look.

"Why you—" Curtis began, stalking toward the wolf. Gerard only sat there with a smug smile, something Marina was not aware he could do as a wolf. "Well I hope you broke your paw," Curtis spat, reminding Marina of a wet cat. Gerard let his tongue hang out in a lupine laugh at Curtis' grumblings

Dismissing the quarreling pair from her mind, Marina turned to Fahad. He was grinning widely at the spectacle Curtis and Gerard were providing. Marina put a hand on his arm and was dazzled when that smile was turned her way. His look gentled, and Marina admired his features in the moonlight for a moment before she remembered why she got his attention.

"I am going to read a bit more," she stated. His smile turned into a worried and slightly disapproving frown, and Marina mourned the loss for a moment before continuing. "I will only stay under for three minutes this time, and then we can seek our beds."

She did not wait for Fahad's agreement and resumed her position in the water. There was not enough time to keep going as she was before. The diary was only half-read, and there was still no truly helpful information. Flipping to the last page, she felt her heart go cold as she read her mother's words.

I can feel them coming. My wonderful, innocent daughters. Yet Marius is breaking through as well. Calypso cannot hold the barriers against his onslaught for much longer. We have hours at the most, even with the way time flows on her island. Surely Marius has only been working minutes to breach her defenses, and in his mind, I have only been gone mere days. I have blessed these many months away from the horror of what I have done, and the betrayals I have committed. Only Calypso has given me refuge, concealing me only because it is in her nature to do so. I do not blame my family for hating me and can only hope my daughters can undo what I have done.

I must flee back to the Kingdoms for their birth, for Calypso has just warned me Marius is almost through. There will be no time to write more in this diary once I cross, so I must be quick. Calypso has consulted a seer and told me what must be done if I am to right my wrongs.

My dearest Marina, she has told me this diary will be yours, and you must learn from it as best you can. I beg only that you do not judge me too harshly for my brash stupidity. Though I am older than this world, and much of the last, my life was always sheltered and, I suppose, so very silly. How can one learn about humans if one has only had other Nereid, merpeople, and the creatures of the sea to swim and play with? It is a paltry excuse, but the only one I know. Calypso has said you will be safe in your early life, but I have included a note in this diary that can be read even by humans.

For your sister, I have penned a short note. I will send the Spark with her, for I hope it will be safer where I am to send her. I shudder to think of her alone in a world full of danger for our kind, but Calypso tells me she will find a kindred spirit there.

Be brave my darling, and know that your sister will join you someday. Calypso has said nothing of me, and I fear I will not live past this night. So know that this foolish daughter of the sea loves you and Kaia with all her heart.

Marina was glad she was underwater. No one would notice the tears flowing from her eyes. She turned the page back to read one last passage before Fahad tapped her shoulder to signal her time was up.

28

The moonlight shone through the open curtains, casting everything in an eerie light. Even though it had been a couple of days, Kaia still couldn't close her eyes without seeing the pile of distorted flesh and bones that was once Cosette. Rubbing her aching eyes, she tossed back the sheets and paced around the room. She finally stopped in front of her window to stare at the moon.

There was something strange about it. The longer she stared, the more she was disturbed by the pale sphere. Finally, she realized the man in the moon was backwards. The craters and streaks were completely different.

"Well that's just dumb," she sulked. "I can't even count on the moon in this place. What's next, gravity makes you fall up?"

Kaia turned away from the unfamiliar moon and began pacing again. Her stomach churned with anxiety as she thought about what she did to Cosette. The sight of red bubbling flesh was seared into her brain.

While she wanted to deny any part in it, she knew she did something to cause Cosette's death. There was something about this world that seemed to be mutating her. Kaia fell back on the bed and glared at the canopy, knowing it probably wasn't a mutation.

"I wish it were," she muttered to herself, "then I could at least hope for a visit from Wolverine and Professor X. But no, I've just got a psycho magician for a father. Even Magneto would be preferable."

Dashing away the tears of self-pity that found their way out of her eyes, she sat up again and scowled at the moon. "You know, I depend upon the man in my moon. He's a sympathetic listener. You're just his creepy doppelganger, and the icing on a real cake of a day."

Kaia felt weary to her bones and just wanted to sleep. It didn't seem likely with Cosette's death weighing on her mind. Kaia cursed the unfairness of mourning the death of someone who wasn't even a real person. Especially when that non-real person tried to kill her only a few days before. That didn't seem to matter, however, because Kaia was the one to cause Cosette's death.

As her thoughts turned maudlin, Kaia decided to focus on something else. She realized she hadn't been in contact with Marina for a couple of days. Closing her eyes, she reached out along their bond to see if they could talk again. The bond seemed stronger than before, almost like a piece of wire where there was once only a tenuous thread.

There was a sense Marina was closer than before. Kaia briefly lost the connection in her excitement, so she calmed her breathing and reached out again. This time, she got a tiny hint of Marina's emotions. She was sad, but Kaia couldn't figure out why. Her sister was also worried, and Kaia got a vague feeling this worry centered around her. She wanted to reassure Marina, so she pushed herself a little further along the connection.

Suddenly, she was standing in a strange place, surrounded by oddly fuzzy scenery. Kaia felt like she was in a large forest, and that thought snapped the scenery into focus. It was a little wild and it looked different than the forest she saw Marina in. The trees were sparse and contained mostly evergreens as opposed to the broad-leaf trees Marina stood under when they first met.

Kaia began walking and came upon a large clearing. The landscape around her was hilly, and she could see larger peaks in the distance. Turning slowly, she saw someone else on the hill with her. As she got nearer, she realized it was Marina.

"Marina," she cried joyfully. Marina turned in surprise, and Kaia was confused to see a wary look on Marina's face.

"Where are you?" Kaia asked. Marina looked confused.

"What do you mean? Is this not a vision of your surroundings?"

Kaia stopped and surveyed the scene in consternation. "Well, I'm still in Marius' castle trying to escape, so I assumed I was coming to you."

Marina sat down on a nearby rock and contemplated their situation. "We do not really know how this works. I was having a perfectly normal dream when the scene changed and I was here. Are you asleep as well?"

Kaia thought for a moment before replying. "Not officially I suppose, but my eyes were closed and I was trying to contact you. Maybe, if neither of us is awake, we'll come here. This is all too freaking confusing."

Kaia sat next to Marina and put her head in her hands. There was so much about this world she didn't understand, and more about herself that was becoming unfamiliar. I've only been here a week or so and I'm already killing people, she thought to herself.

Marina stiffened at her side. Kaia looked at her and saw Marina was expressionless. She had the uncomfortable feeling Marina somehow heard her last thought. Marina spoke first, unintentionally cutting off Kaia's explanation.

"We have enlisted the aid of the Krax'mran. Waitimu has helped us gain the trust of the other tribes, but my group will try to keep the killing to a minimum."

"So Waitimu's okay?" Kaia asked in relief.

Marina nodded and kept her silence as she regarded Kaia. This dream world they were in amplified their bond. She could feel Kaia's emotions if she concentrated and caught the tail end of her last thought. Marina worried about her last vision of Kaia but tried to push that aside lest Kaia read her thoughts as well.

"How much longer will you be?" Kaia asked desperately. "I need to get out of that castle. It's driving me crazy being cooped up."

"I am not sure," Marina replied carefully. Kaia looked at her sister sharply as a sense Marina didn't trust her brushed the edge of her awareness.

"Well hopefully it's sooner rather than later," Kaia said testily, "Marius is planning something, and I have a feeling it's not good. He's saying he wants to improve the government in the Kingdoms, but I paid just enough attention in history to know that doesn't usually work out well for the other people involved. I think Marius' idea of utopia would involve a lot of suffering for the people he doesn't like."

"What do you mean?" Marina asked sharply.

"Listen, I don't know anything about this world, but people are pretty much the same wherever you go. Our dad wants power, and something tells me that spells disaster for everyone else. He said something about our mom having an amulet, and I think it's the one I brought with me from Earth."

Marina stood suddenly, a feeling of unease spreading through her. Kaia's words made no sense. "Why do you speak such nonsense? Earth is the land of our ancestors, but no person of this land may cross over to that realm and vice versa. That would spell destruction for both worlds."

"Well, that's obviously not true, because I'm here and so are the Kingdoms." Kaia shifted uneasily as she thought about Marina's words. "And I'm assuming Earth is fine. That would suck if I caused the end of the world."

"But—" Marina sat down again to accommodate her suddenly weak knees, "but that is impossible. Legend says that crossing the boundaries would rain death upon both worlds."

"Legends can be wrong. There are apparently dozens of people from the Kingdoms living on Earth. My mom—the woman who raised me—came from here." Kaia stopped as the memory of what Merry told her came back. Meeting Marina was so surprising her name and title didn't even register. "Actually, her name was Merylyn DeGriffin. She was a crown princess of Jamaria at one point as well."

Marina was shocked. She heard of Merylyn many times, mostly because of what her transformation meant for relations between the Jamarians and the Rejos pack. There were so many questions running through her mind she opened her mouth to voice one only to stop and think of another.

"I'm sorry, that was a little out of the blue. I've had other things on my mind, and that one just seemed unimportant in the face of all the others. But, I don't think there's time to dwell on that one. I need to know if you have the amulet. Waitimu had my bag when he escaped, and it was in the bottom. If Marius needs it, we need to make sure he never gets it."

Marina closed her mouth and studied Kaia's earnest face. The amulet showed her Kaia's possible betrayal and Marina did not know what might cause it. If she lied and said Waitimu lost Kaia's bag, that could stop the events of her vision from coming to pass. Then again, Kaia might sense Marina's lie, which could cause Kaia to turn away and join Nightshade.

"I—Waitimu brought me your bag. The amulet is safe."

Marina was never very good at lying and she wanted to trust her sister. She hoped her vision was wrong. Or perhaps her actions in this dream world would stop it from happening.

"Thank God," Kaia sighed in relief, some of her tension draining away. "This has been a very stressful trip," Kaia stated dryly, "First I find out my mom not only comes from another world but is also a werewolf. Then, I go on the worst trip through space, which lands me in a desert. And, to top it all off, I find out my new-found father wants to use us in some weird way to gain power."

"What did he say he needed us for?"

"He was pretty vague. All I know is that he wants to use us—on what I can only assume will be our eighteenth birthday—to tap into power from another world using that amulet. I have a bad feeling the other world he's talking about is Earth. That bad feeling is also telling me he's not too concerned with how whatever he's planning will affect our health—or anyone else's for that matter."

Marina nodded in worried agreement and thought about their mother's journal. She hesitated briefly before deciding to continue trusting Kaia.

"Do you remember the journal our mother wrote?" Kaia nodded, and Marina took a deep breath to continue. "I have read part of it. I had a vision of an aunt of ours, who told me how to read the words. Our mother's name was Yara, and she stole the amulet from her father. It is called the Spark.

"I was not given much time to read her diary, so I have only gotten pieces of the story. The last entry I read said Marius means to drain the Earth of life and use the power to control the Kingdoms. According to Yara, he needs the amulet, the help of a water creature, and something she called the eight artifacts. I will need to wait until next month before I can find out what those are. Tomorrow we will not be near any water, and only the gods know what the day after that will bring."

Kaia didn't really know what Marina meant by that last part, but she was too distracted to worry about it. Something about the eight artifacts sparked a memory from that morning. Marina interrupted her thoughts by putting a hand on her shoulder.

"Do not worry, Kaia," she said, misinterpreting the faraway look on Kaia's face, "We will come for you soon, and we will stop Nightshade together."

Kaia smiled, shaking off the uneasy feeling from earlier Marina didn't trust her. They sat in silence for a moment, neither knowing what else to say. Marina heard her name being called and looked off into the distance. There was no one there and Kaia did not react.

"I think it is time for me to wake," Marina said, finally recognizing Curtis' voice. "Just think, soon we will be able to have a conversation in the real world." The girls smiled at one another in excitement. While their time together seemed real enough, they both wanted to have more time than their visions seemed to allow.

"Do you think I'll stay here when you go?" Kaia mused, looking around at the rolling hills. She didn't really want to go back. It was probably childish but she really wanted this adventure to stop. Why couldn't she have landed in a pretty place like this dreamscape? Or maybe a beach somewhere warm and tropical?

Marina shrugged and turned to admire the view as well. It looked like it was spring, and they were somewhere near mountains unknown to her. Marina felt a pang of regret her parents never allowed her to travel at all, so she did not know if they were in Brookland, Ya'mäk, or Dura.

Kaia stiffened beside her, and Marina glanced at her. A look of terrified awe covered her face. Marina scanned the area where Kaia was looking, seeing only the trees at the edge of the forest. She heard Curtis call her name again and watched as the scenery began to fade around her.

"Marina," she heard Kaia say in a strangled voice, "is that a freaking dragon?"

Kaia turned just in time to see Marina fade from view. She snapped her head back to the tree line to find the reptilian face that was staring at her moments before. There was nothing there but Kaia kept her eyes trained on the spot where she last saw it as the world faded around her too.

Kaia kept her eyes closed against the pale light of the slowly rising sun. While she appreciated the fact the traitorous moon was likely gone, she didn't want to face another day in Marius' castle. Her eyes snapped open as she remembered Marina's assurance she would be at the castle soon.

"I've got to get some stuff ready," Kaia yawned.

She dragged herself out of her soft, warm bed and shuffled to her wardrobe. Thinking about what she wanted, she opened the doors to reveal some additions to her apparel. There were more things made of leather this time, and she approved of the wardrobe's idea of traveling clothes. The magical closet also provided a nice bag to replace the one she lost. After stuffing the bag full, Kaia contemplated it ruefully.

"I can't very well carry this around everywhere, but I don't want to run the risk Cossette..." she trailed off when she remembered Cossette wouldn't be snooping through her things ever again. Pushing down a sudden wave of nausea, Kaia put the bag back in the wardrobe.

"Just don't let that disappear," she begged.

The doors to the wardrobe were barely closed when Kaia heard a knock at her door. Her unwanted visitor didn't give her time to grant or deny entrance before it flew open. Robin leveled a blank look at her, and Kaia shivered.

"Your father wishes to see you," Robin intoned.

"Give me a few minutes to get ready, and I'll be right there."

Robin nodded curtly and closed the door. Kaia didn't have to check to be sure he was waiting outside her door. She also knew if she took too long, he wouldn't hesitate to drag her out, so she hurried to get washed up and dressed.

As they made their way to Marius' rooms, Kaia suddenly remembered what struck her about the artifacts Marina mentioned. She needed to get into Marius' treasure room again. Robin was ignoring her, so she began to plan.

29

Marina came awake slowly as Curtis shook her shoulder and called her name. His voice was edged with impatience, and Marina felt like turning over and going back to sleep just to spite him. The sight of Fahad leaving their webbed room made her remember just what today would bring.

"Why did you not wake me sooner?" Marina grumbled, wiping the sleep from her eyes. A weak light filtered through the webbing. As she stumbled from her makeshift bed on the floor to the door, she saw the sun was not yet risen.

"It is difficult to wake someone sleeping like the dead," Curtis snapped. Marina smiled as she remembered Curtis hated waking up early almost as much as she did.

Marina hid a yawn behind her hand as she walked back to her bedroll. She noticed then all her supplies were packed and ready to go. Curtis was gone, so she was not able to ask him if she should thank him or Fahad for the kindness.

Abrafo provided some water for his guests and Marina used a piece of cloth to wipe some of the sand from her face. It wasn't completely gone, but the lukewarm water helped to wake her up. When she swiped the water from her eyes, she noticed the quarterstaff propped against the wall near her bag. At that point, she realized it was more likely Curtis himself who saw to her comfort. It was crudely made, but the wood was smooth, and when she tested its height and weight she was surprised to find it perfectly suited to her size.

Taking up her pack in her other hand, she left Abrafo's web and climbed down the webbing that served as a ladder. There were dozens of warriors from Abrafo's village as well as Waitimu's crowded around her friends. Marina was relieved to see Waitimu return with more warriors so quickly.

"Pardon me," Marina pushed her way through the crowd to stand near Waitimu and her brother. Curtis looked worried about something, a feeling apparently shared by Fahad and Gerard.

"You ask too much, Waitimu," Abrafo said with a voice like thunder.

Waitimu's face did not betray any emotion, and Marina wondered what was going on. She turned to Curtis and whispered, "What is Waitimu asking?"

Curtis shushed her and focused on the conversation between the two leaders.

"I know this is an insulting request, but it is one we must bear. Consider how long it took to travel with the humans yesterday. We can travel in hours what takes these humans and their horses days."

Waitimu waited until the crowd around them ceased to grumble before continuing. "We need only three more volunteers, for I will carry the girl myself."

Gerard stepped forward to speak. "You only need two more, Waitimu. I may not be as fast as the Krax'mran, but I can keep up well enough."

Marina realized they were talking about the travel arrangements to Nightshade's castle. She never heard of Krax'mran acting as glorified horses, and knew that was why Abrafo and his men were so offended.

Marina stood before Abrafo and said, "I am sorry that this troubles you and your men, but I must ask: would it not be faster to travel as Waitimu suggests? My sister is at Nightshade's mercy, and I believe we can all agree that does not bode well for her. Please, let us make haste and not waste time with horses."

Abrafo scowled at her, and Marina felt a tremor of fear run through her body. She refused to let Abrafo see she was intimidated however and stood before him without expression.

"Very well," Abrafo acceded resentfully, "but I will carry you. Waitimu will have to make do with one of your menfolk."

Marina fought to keep any expression from her face when she saw Waitimu regarding Fahad and her brother with obvious dismay. "Take Fahad," Marina suggested mischievously, "he is less likely to cause problems."

Waitimu gave a jerky nod and allowed Fahad to sit on his back. The rest of the Krax'mran drew straws to see who would be forced to carry Curtis. Marina turned away so no one would see her stifling a grin. Abrafo lowered himself so Marina could sit, adjusting her so they would both be comfortable. She was sitting with her legs on either side of his waist, allowing her to wrap her arms around his chest. He passed her quarterstaff to one of his men, who fashioned a sling for it from his webbing.

Looking over at Fahad and Curtis, she smiled again to see Waitimu and the other Krax'mran were not allowing them to sit the same way as her. The men were all trying to touch each other as little as possible. Abrafo turned his head to look at her and gave her a flirtatious wink.

"If I must allow such an insult, I will at least get the pretty human," Abrafo teased. Marina felt herself blush and tried to hide her embarrassed smile as she made herself comfortable for the long journey.

Kaia sat in the same chair as last time and tried not to look at the treasure room door. Instead, she trained her eyes on her father, who was pacing back and forth in front of her. She tried to think of more questions to ask that wouldn't raise his suspicions. Nothing sprang to mind, but she was saved from sitting there awkwardly when Marius spoke first.

"I am afraid, my dear, that something dangerous is coming." He waited for Kaia to respond, but she wasn't really sure of what to say. When the silence stretched on, he continued.

"The Krax'mran are on their way, and I believe they mean to kill us all this time." Kaia tried to stifle her gasp, but Marius heard the small intake of breath. She didn't know how Marius figured out Marina and Waitimu's plan but she did know it didn't bode well for anyone. He stopped in his pacing to crouch in front of her and hold her hands in his. While it looked like he was concerned for her, she noticed the gleam of speculation in his eyes.

"Are you—," her voice sounded high-pitched, so she cleared her throat, hoping he attributed the break to fear of the Krax'mran, and continued in a more normal voice, "Are you sure?"

"Yes, I have received word from one of my spies that the Krax'mran left a village far to the north only twenty minutes ago. That gives us until this evening to prepare. Can you tell me anything about Waitimu's people? I do not know how long they held you in their village, but any information could be helpful."

"I'm sorry," Kaia apologized with fake solemnity, "they were all pretty tight-lipped. I get the feeling they don't trust humans much. Wonder why that is?"

Marius stood abruptly, dropping Kaia's hands as if they were poisonous. "In that case, I think it would be best if you returned to the dungeon until the attack is over. We would not want you to be carried off by the Krax'mran."

Marius motioned to Robin, and Kaia couldn't help a furtive glance toward the treasure room. Marius' eyes narrowed in suspicion and Kaia cast her eyes to the floor to avoid his gaze. Robin took her by the arm and led her out of the room. Kaia inwardly cursed her luck before remembering she had an advantage Marius apparently still knew nothing about.

Robin marched her to the cells and Kaia looked around furtively to mark the passage. She thanked her lucky stars Marius had so much crap it was easy to mark the way using his unique art pieces.

Turn left at the waterfall painting; left at the goat boy playing the pipes; right at the half-naked couple getting busy; left at the tapestry that looks like it's covered in blood spatters; right at the massive clock; his door is across from the claw-footed table.

"Get your hands off of me," Kaia demanded when she and Robin were standing in front of her cell door. He didn't resist when she jerked her arm away. It turned out he needed the use of both hands to release the key ring on his belt, making Kaia feel stupid for demanding a release that was already coming.

The key ring had only one object on it and it didn't look like any key Kaia ever saw before. Instead, it held a metal tube with something that looked like a red sponge at one end.

Robin touched the sponge to the door, leaving a small red spot on the heavy oak. Kaia tried to lean in closer, but Robin pulled her away from the mark and cruelly pushed her into the windowless room. When the door shut, Kaia reached her hands out to find the door again. She put her back to it and slid into a seated position. It was time for a new plan.

According to Abrafo, their party was making excellent time. Marina exhausted her supply of water in the hours they spent traveling. She was thankful to Abrafo, Fahad, and Gerard for sharing theirs. Even though she was trying to pace her drinking more than before, she was still using far too much water.

"How much longer do you think it will be?" Marina asked, raising her voice to be heard over the wind their passage was creating.

"We will stop in the village coming up to enlist help from our allies. It will take only two hours more to get there. We will get you more water while there also. I have never seen a human drink so much."

Marina heard the laughter in his voice and was grateful he couldn't see her blushing in embarrassment. "I am sorry. My mother was a Nereid, so the desert climate seems to affect me far sooner than anyone else."

"Ah, this explains much," Abrafo said.

"How much longer after the village?" Marina asked.

"If it does not take too much time to organize the warriors of the Kag'mro clan, we should be at Nightshade's castle many hours before sunset."

Marina thanked Abrafo and stayed silent while they traveled to the Kag'mro village. Her thoughts were with Kaia. There was so much about her sister that confused Marina. It seemed as though Kaia wanted to escape their father, but the look of hate on Kaia's face in that vision still plagued Marina's thoughts.

There was not much talking as they traveled, especially by those toward the back of the group. Waitimu and Fahad were running abreast of Abrafo and Marina, but Curtis was behind them and covered in a fine dusting of white sand. He almost sparkled in the sunlight and Marina hid a smile at how ridiculous he looked. He covered his mouth and nose with a handkerchief, making him look like a pixie bandit.

After two hours, the heat was beginning to get to Marina again. She depleted Waitimu's supply of water almost half an hour before. The dry air seemed to pull the moisture from her body faster than she could replenish it. A giddy relief swelled in her chest when she saw the treetops of an oasis ahead.

"Is that the Kag'mro village?" she asked hopefully.

"Yes," Abrafo confirmed, putting on more speed.

They were the first to cross into the village, and Abrafo immediately called for water. He swung her down to the ground with a powerful arm and kept a hand beneath her arm to keep her from falling. Marina was an experienced rider, but a horse and a Krax'mran were different in too many ways to count. Her legs and backside were numb, and she wished for privacy to rub the sting away.

"I've got her, Abrafo," Fahad said, putting an arm around her shoulders. Abrafo nodded and handed Fahad the water skin just delivered by one of the villagers.

"Waitimu, we will speak to Saburi together," Abrafo said.

The pair set off together to go deeper into the village. Marina noticed a sudden silence among the villagers. She turned to see the whole village regarding her party with mingled hostility and curiosity.

Waitimu and Abrafo's warriors were speaking to some of the young men of the village, but Marina could not understand Krax'mran. The men looked at the humans frequently during the conversation, so Marina felt safe in assuming she and her group was their topic.

"Come, Marina, drink as much as you can now so you won't need as much while we travel." Fahad offered her the skin, and Marina suddenly remembered her thirst. The water revived her, and she was ready to continue their journey.

Unfortunately, the meeting with Saburi lasted almost an hour. Marina and her group were still waiting by the edge of the village when Waitimu, Abrafo, and another Krax'mran approached them. Marina already assumed this was Saburi when Abrafo introduced him.

"Waitimu has told me of your sister," Saburi said. Marina tried not to react to Saburi's blank gaze. She was learning the Krax'mran were not much for emotional displays with strangers. "My village owes a debt to the N'tiru, and Waitimu says this will be the payment. But, more than that, all Krax'mran are aligned against Nightshade."

Saburi was no longer addressing Marina. He faced the men of his clan, a fierce look on his face. "The sorcerer lied to us, taking our winter hunting grounds for his own. The land once shared by all clans now shares an infestation that must be exterminated."

The Kag'mro raised their fists in the air with a mighty cheer at their chieftain's words. Marina bit her lip to hide her excited grin. Waitimu worked miracles and she knew she would have to find a way to repay him someday. It did not matter he would deny she owed him anything, she knew better.

"Thank you, Saburi," Marina said with a slight bow of her head.

"Your thanks are not wanted, human," Saburi replied impatiently.

"That may be, but I will continue to be grateful."

Saburi huffed irritably and turned to Waitimu and Abrafo. "We will follow you shortly. My warriors need only arm themselves and we will be ready. You need not wait for us."

Abrafo nodded and turned to Marina. "You are ready," he said. It did not sound like a question, so she did not bother replying. She simply held her hand out for his, the refilled water skin already slung over one shoulder.

It was easier to arrange herself this time, so they were off running soon after she hit his back. As they journeyed further toward her sister, Marina began to pray to the gods Kaia would be unharmed—and unchanged.

30

It took Kaia a few hours to be sure Robin or another of Marius' servants wouldn't be back to bother her. She didn't want to venture out too soon for fear he would do hourly checks. But when the only interruption in the darkness came in the form of lunch two hours ago, Kaia knew it would be okay to try her luck.

The binding around her wound took some time to get off in the dark, but she was given hours to work around that problem. It was all too easy to reopen the cut on her palm, and she wondered if that was going to leave a nasty scar. She smiled at the petty vanity of that thought when her life was hanging in the balance.

"So long as it doesn't mess with my fine motor skills, why should I really care?" she asked herself with wry amusement.

She pressed her palm to the thick oak, pushing the door open with extreme caution. It would be particularly unfair to find out someone was guarding her door after all that waiting.

A sigh of relief blew across her lips, and she left the door open a crack before risking the open hallway. The plan was to dart back into her cell if she heard anyone coming. As she surveyed the long corridor, her heart sank to realize she couldn't look in every door like she planned and keep close to her door. She would just have to hope no one came.

Robin put her in Waitimu's old cell, so she was the first on the left.

She remembered the cell across from hers contained some kind of animal. Her first instinct was to pass it by but something drew her to it.

Her new plan was to find some people who could help her fight off the servants and get through the castle. Those hours of darkness helped her memory and that teasing thought finally resettled. The artifacts Marina spoke about reminded her of the two objects in Marius' treasure room.

Among all of the glitter and finery, those two pieces stood out the most to Kaia. Even though each possessed shiny gems, they looked older and less shiny than everything else. They also seemed almost practical when compared to everything else Marius owned. Plus, he'd mentioned a set of eight just like Marina.

She shook the thought away and put her non-bleeding hand on the panel. That small touch brought the beast crashing into the door again, causing her to jump back in surprise. There was no fear though. That surprised her too, but she didn't have the time to analyze that revelation.

Sliding the panel open, she looked inside carefully. Her encounter with Waitimu taught her not to get too close but she knew how dark it could be in there. The snarls coming from the room didn't frighten her like they did before. They seemed more afraid than angry and her heart ached to hear the sound.

"Stop that," she commanded harshly. To her utter surprise, the animal did. "Hmm, something tells me there's more to you than just canine." She thought of Merry, and knew at that moment she was talking to a werewolf. "If you could just change back to human, I think you and I could help each other out."

It took the person inside a few minutes to change, and Kaia could barely stand to hear the sounds. Not only were there pained whimpers and cries, but she could also hear the sounds of bones shifting, sinews popping, and flesh tearing. This brought back memories of the vision of Merry's first change, and she choked back tears of sympathy.

"Who are you?" a harsh voice finally rasped.

"My name is Kaia. What's yours?"

"Rafe," he said shortly. He moved to the panel and stuck his nose out to take a mighty sniff. "What are you?" he asked. Kaia heard anguish amidst the confusion and hurried to explain herself.

"I'm a prisoner here, like you. If I let you out, will you promise not to hurt me?"

Rafe's eyes appeared, and Kaia marveled at their amber color. "Yes," he answered, "let me out."

"Who's afraid of the Big Bad Wolf?" Kaia muttered under her breath. She put her bloody palm on the door before she could second guess herself further.

It swung open quickly, revealing a medium-sized man with only a thin, dirty rag wrapped around his waist. Kaia covered her mouth and nose at the stench emanating from his cell. She cursed her father for his cruelty. At that moment she decided she would never think of him as anything but Nightshade. Only an evil person could do something like this, and she refused to call such a person father even if only in her head.

"You smell of pack, but not pack; enemy, but not enemy," Rafe accused her.

It took Kaia a few seconds to work that one out. Rafe paced in front of his open door almost as if he was still afraid to trust her. She couldn't blame her after the way Nightshade treated him. Thinking of that jerk helped her sort through the last of her confusion.

"I think I smell of pack because I was raised by a werewolf. I smell of enemy because, as much as I wish I weren't, I am Nightshade's daughter."

Rafe backed away at that revelation and Kaia held up her hands to reassure him.

"I'm not like him," she insisted. "I only found out I was his daughter a few days ago, and believe me, I'd change that fact if I could. But, that's not important right now. What is important is the fact that I have a rescue party coming, and I think I'll need a little help getting out of here. What do you say? Can you help me?"

Rafe was thinking this over when a voice surprised them both.

"I'll help you, milady."

Kaia looked at the hall door in fear, and then confusion when she saw no one was there.

"And how are you supposed to help me? I can't even see you."

A hand waved out of the panel in the door three doors down from

Rafe's. She approached cautiously to see a pair of smiling blue eyes peering out at her.

"Hello," she said cautiously, "I'm Kaia. What's your name?"

"Jack Reynolds, at your service, Lady Kaia." His eyes disappeared for a moment, and Kaia had a sneaking suspicion he just bowed to her.

"How did you get that panel open? Mine's as smooth as glass with no edges—at least none I could find."

"Ah, that would be giving away the tricks of the trade," Jack said in amusement. "But if it's help you need, old Jack has never turned down a beautiful person. Or the chance to escape."

The scouts brought back word the castle was locked up tight. There was no movement outside the wall and very little on top. Marina gripped her new quarterstaff in nervous fingers. She and Curtis knew this was beyond strange. Their castle walls were always crawling with helmeted guards and archers. Even the off-duty soldiers walked the top if only to get a view of the city below.

"There has always been very little movement outside the wall," Waitimu said, "but it is as you say, Curtis. The top of the wall is always guarded. It is as if they are baiting the web."

Abrafo nodded, "It is almost as if Nightshade knew we were coming. It could not be his people; one of our scouts would have noticed a human gathering information. Our own people would not dare betray us, so how could he have known?"

Marina felt a sinking feeling in the pit of her stomach. She prayed to the gods she was wrong in her suspicion, but if Abrafo was correct there was only one logical explanation.

Kaia told Nightshade.

Taking a deep breath, Marina began to voice her fears but a stray thought stopped her. Nightshade was a powerful sorcerer. There was every chance he had a way to spy upon his enemies that had nothing to do with Kaia. Marina kept her mouth shut and listened to the clan leaders as they adapted their original plan.

"Nightshade knows archery is our best skill," Saburi said, "so he has taken away that advantage. He thinks to draw us out, but now that we know this, it will not be to his advantage. There is much Nightshade does not know of the Krax'mran."

"We should not give away too much, Saburi," Waitimu

interjected, "Nightshade might not know our every strength or weakness, but he is clever."

"We all know this, Waitimu," Saburi answered impatiently, "If we are to fulfill our bargain with the humans, we must provide a distraction. We will use the mwako web. Even if it does not kill Nightshade's monsters, it will keep them distracted while they try to kill the flames."

The other Krax'mran nodded, while the humans looked at each other in confusion.

"The mwako web is flammable," Gerard explained to his friends, "the webbing sticks to any surface, including skin. It has been known to burn for hours."

Marina was amazed. The books she read about the Krax'mran alluded to fire weapons but the author apparently never knew what that weapon was called or how it worked. He also never made any allusion to it being made of webbing.

"So, the Krax'mran produce this from their own webs?" she asked Gerard.

"It is something only the warriors can do," Waitimu answered her. "This is a great secret of our people. How do you know of it, wolf?"

Gerard met Waitimu's furious gaze with a cool one of his own. "I have been alive longer than any of your warriors here," he answered calmly, "You are not the first Krax'mran I have met, though you are the first I have fought beside."

Marina could tell the Krax'mran were not comforted by Gerard's words. The younger warriors looked mutinous, while their elders merely looked wary.

"We do not have time for this," Marina said forcefully, "Kaia's life could be in danger the longer we wait. Saburi, I believe you should concentrate your forces on the western wall. My friends and I will try to find a way in through the east. We can hopefully use the setting sun to keep Nightshade's forces from seeing us."

Saburi looked surprised and a little offended at Marina's authoritative tone. She regretted losing her temper, but she knew this was their best bet. All that mattered to her was getting Kaia out of Nightshade's clutches. There was still hope that Kaia had not been corrupted, but Marina did not wish to tempt Fate by leaving her sister there any longer.

"It will be as you say," Saburi finally conceded. Marina released the breath she did not even realize she was holding. "Come, warriors," he called, "prepare the mwako web, and let us give Nightshade nightmares."

The Krax'mran roared their approval and set off to the west. Marina turned to her companions and smiled ruefully.

"I am sorry to have volunteered your efforts without your input."

"Oh come off it, brat," Curtis sighed dramatically, "you've always been pushy. I'm just surprised it took you this long to push the Krax'mran around as well."

Marina started to defend her actions, but Gerard cut her off.

"Marina, it is as you said before, we do not have time for this. The Krax'mran are putting themselves in danger for our sake. We must finish this quickly so we may keep our bargain and keep any of them from being killed."

Marina nodded and followed Gerard's lead toward the eastern wall. Fahad ran by her side and flashed her a confident grin. "Don't worry, Marina," he said so only she could hear him, "your sister will be free soon."

Marina smiled gratefully. Fahad's words helped calm her somewhat, but the sight of the wall set her heart to racing wildly. Gerard crouched down, and the others followed his lead. They were slightly hidden by a sand dune, and the lack of guards on the wall worked in their favor.

The four companions lowered themselves to their bellies at Gerard's signal. They crawled forward so only their heads topped the temporary hill. Marina's breath seemed harsh to her own ears as they waited for a sign the Krax'mran had begun their attack.

It seemed as though they were waiting for hours when the alarm was sounded in Nightshade's keep a few minutes later. Marina wanted to make a run for the wall right away, but Curtis and Fahad both put a hand on her shoulders to keep her waiting.

"Not yet, Marina," Fahad warned, "Nightshade's minions will look for attacks on the other three sides at first. We must wait until Gerard gives us the signal to move."

Marina looked at Gerard and saw his eyes had turned their wolfish yellow. He was staring at the tops of the wall, following some movement her human eyes could not perceive.

"Is there to be no end to this waiting?" Marina asked through gritted teeth.

"They are gone," Gerard answered moments later. He crawled forward carefully, his eyes still trained upon the keep's wall. "We must move quickly lest they come back."

Fahad, Curtis, and Marina got up quickly and ran with Gerard to the castle. Marina wondered at the castle's design. It looked like something from the north that was transplanted into these harsh environs. Gerard found a door near the middle of the wall, and Marina set aside any thoughts not concerning their mission. The door was locked and Marina felt a frustrated fear rise within her. Gerard was also frustrated if the way he slammed himself against the door was any indication.

"Stop," Fahad commanded in a harsh whisper, "You'll alert the whole castle that we're here if you keep on like that. Let me have a go."

Gerard stepped away angrily, and they all watched as Fahad pulled a few slim pieces of metal from the pouch at his waist. He knelt in front of the door and assessed the lock. Giving Marina another confident smile, he set about picking the lock.

When it sprang loose a few seconds later, Marina could not stop herself from throwing her arms around Fahad's neck in joy. Fahad caught her in his arms, and Marina suddenly realized what she had done. She pulled back a little and looked into his eyes, ready to apologize. Something she saw there stopped the apology in her throat.

"Do you mind if we continued with our mission?" Curtis asked in a mockingly sweet voice.

Marina and Fahad sprang apart guiltily. Each stammered out an apology to the other but broke off when Curtis forced himself between them--making sure to slam into Fahad's shoulder--to look through the now open door. He peered around it, seeing a large, open garden in front of them. Frowning, he relayed what he saw to the group.

"I don't like it," he said darkly, "that's too much open ground to get to the castle without being seen. I think we need to split up to make this work."

"What do you suggest?" Gerard asked.

"There seems to be a smithy and stables to the south, if two of us make a break for those, it could cause enough of a distraction for the other two to make it into the castle."

"That sounds practical, but who goes with whom?"

"I will be going into the castle," Marina declared. "I am the only one who knows what Kaia looks like. Not to mention I have some experience within the walls, though it may look different in the daylight."

"Okay, then I'll go with you," Fahad volunteered.

Marina could tell Gerard and Curtis were not pleased with his quick response. She, however, was quite happy with the turn of events.

"Then let's get moving," she said. She knew the others heard the excitement in her voice and she tried to meet their curious stares with an innocent smile.

"On my count then," Curtis said, easing the door open, "Gerard and I will break right and you two will go straight on." Gerard moved to stand behind him while Marina and Fahad stayed back. "One, two, go!"

Marina watched as Gerard and her brother disappeared through the door. Fahad held her back for a few seconds before leading the way through. She saw the castle looming large before them and sent a brief prayer to the gods that her friends, family, and new allies would all stay safe in the battle ahead.

31

Kaia could hear the sounds of fighting outside and knew it was time to make her move. Jack suggested returning to their cells earlier on the off chance Nightshade sent someone to check on them when the Krax'mran appeared. She heard Jack whistle a few minutes after the attack began and no one came running.

She couldn't see her hand in the darkness, but it was easy to find the scab that had already begun to form since she last opened the wound. She picked at it until she felt it grow slippery with blood. It only took the barest touch and the door was swinging open.

She released Jack first because they all agreed Rafe might need some help maintaining his human form. Jack gave her a debonair smile, and Kaia couldn't help but be amused by his flirtatious attitude despite the danger.

"Stop it," she demanded without any heat.

"Never," Jack quipped. He slid Rafe's panel open, stopping her before she opened the door.

"How are things in there, friend?" Jack called, "We're hoping to find you on two feet instead of four."

"Just open the door," Rafe growled, "We need to get out of here before things go wrong."

"Ever the pessimists, wolves," Jack sighed. He got out of Kaia's way and let her place her bloody hand on the door. Rafe stepped out slowly, blinking in the bright torchlight.

"Let's hurry," Kaia said. She held out her hand, letting Jack and Rafe smear the blood on their own hands. Together, the three applied Kaia's blood to every door along the corridor. Some were empty, but many held grateful humans and other creatures. Soon, they were all running through the hall, escaping their prison. There were a few who were openly hostile, but one growl from Rafe had them running away with the others. Jack assured her trolls and ogres were like that with everyone. Kaia filed that information away for later and hoped they would all find their way out. She then forced thoughts of others from her mind for the moment.

"I remember the way to Nightshade's rooms. Follow me, and don't be afraid to take out anyone else in the hall. Nightshade's minions won't hesitate to take us down." Kaia barely saw Jack and Rafe nod before she was running through the door to Nightshade's private rooms.

All extraneous thoughts were pushed from her mind as she watched for the markers she memorized. They had to retrace their steps once when she turned left when she should have gone right. That was her only mistake, however, and they were soon in the parlor.

"It would appear everyone else is occupied," Jack observed.

"Wait here, I've got to retrieve something from the treasure room, then we can leave."

Kaia noticed a gleam of speculation in Jack's eyes at the mention of treasure.

"Rafe can watch the door," Jack said smoothly, "I'll just take a look at that treasure room. You know, to make sure none of the servants have hidden in there."

"Whatever," Kaia snapped, not believing him for a second. "Just don't take more than you can carry, this needs to be a quick escape, and I'm not waiting for you if you get too loaded down with stuff."

"You would leave me?" Jack asked, hurt.

"In a heartbeat, Casanova. Now get a move on!"

Kaia ran to the treasure room but opened the door cautiously. Jack's warning may not have been sincere, but it didn't mean he didn't have a good point. No one attacked her, so she peeked around the corner. Jack poked his head around too, putting his head above hers to see.

"Not too bad," Jack said. He pushed her forward to make room for himself. "You get your treasures, I'll see what else the bad magician has to offer."

Kaia ignored him and ran to the glass case. The harp and sword were still there, and Kaia breathed a sigh of relief. She was afraid Marius would move them after she showed interest in them. The door was unlocked and she reached for the harp.

Jack found a chest filled with gold and gems and wasn't paying any attention to her. Instead, he focused on shoveling jewelry and small items into his pockets. So he never saw his newfound friend and savior touch the old harp and immediately stiffen as her green eyes turned a foggy white.

Kaia felt herself being thrown into a vision without warning. It was like the drop on a fifty-foot rollercoaster but she couldn't scream. Finally, her stomach settled but her head was spinning. Images and scenes flashed across her vision like a series of videos at warp speed.

She saw a Black girl in a tower topped by a glass bubble. The girl was pacing and tossing a braid that fell to her calves over her shoulder.

Next, Kaia saw a mermaid with a tail that reminded her of a beta fish. Her honey-blonde hair flowed back as she swam and her blue eyes crinkled with her mischievous smile.

The final, longest vision showed the moon. It was her old moon but a second moon was emerging from it. The second moon was the mirror image of Earth's. It was also the moon she chastised the night before. Both moons turned red and began to meld together again.

The vision shifted and Kaia could see the moons merging above constantly shifting landscapes. No matter what location was flashing before her eyes, there were people screaming and fleeing earthquakes. The carnage flipped from locations and people Kaia found familiar to completely foreign ones.

The Eiffel Tower crashed to the ground in a mass of twisted metal was followed by what looked like dwarves straight out of Lord of the Rings running from the gaping mouth of a collapsing cave. The whole of Los Angeles fell into the Pacific like a scene out of 2012 or San Andreas or a dozen other disaster movies. A castle that looked like the Acropolis but was on the edge of a cliff instead of a mountain crumbled into an unknown sea while ships and boats tried to sail away from the chaos. Over and over again, faster and faster, Kaia was subjected to visions of death and overwhelming tragedy until the two moons became one again and everything went dark.

With a mental wrench she felt in her whole body, Kaia forced her way out of the vision. She stood in front of the harp, breathing hard while tears ran down her face. She looked over at Jack and realized what felt like hours passing in the vision was barely a minute in the real world.

Jack spared her no more than a single glance as he kept on looking. "Did you say something?" he asked.

She opened her mouth to say she was fine when she heard Marina's voice in the next room.

"What have you done with my sister? I know she is here, I can sense her presence."

Kaia ran to the next room to find Marina threatening Rafe with a big stick that was almost as tall as he was. Rafe was growling low in his throat at Marina, and Kaia put a hand on his shoulder to reassure him. He immediately calmed, letting Kaia pass him to stand in front of her sister.

Marina relaxed her stance, though Kaia could tell she was keeping an eye on Rafe. Kaia felt awkward, finally meeting Marina in the flesh. She felt solid enough the other times they were together but somehow this was different.

"Umm—what's up?"

Marina smiled ruefully, "What does that mean? I cannot imagine you are asking for a description of the ceiling."

"How—How are you doing today?"

"Well, I am in the midst of a battle trying to free my sister from an evil sorcerer who happens to be our father. While I am grateful you saved me another trip to the prison cells, I think it would be best if we saved our reunion until after we are all safe."

"That sounds pretty reasonable to me," Jack interjected from the door. Kaia turned to see he was covered in jewelry. The diamond tiara perched on his brown curls and the emerald earrings dangling from his ears made him look like a child playing dress-up. A sight that helped Kaia calm down a bit more after her harrowing vision.

"Wow, Jack, you look ridiculous," Kaia snorted. She turned back to her stunned sister. "Never mind him, help me carry a couple of things and we can get out of here."

Kaia grabbed Marina's hand and pulled her past the bejeweled Jack to the room beyond. Kaia ripped a curtain from the wall and led Marina to the harp and sword.

"Wrap the harp with this," Kaia said, handing the curtain over. "Believe me, you don't want to touch that with your bare hands."

Marina nodded and carefully picked the harp up. She accidentally jostled it enough to cause a few notes to sing from the ancient instrument. Marina stumbled slightly as a wave of dizziness came over her. Suddenly, Fahad was there, holding her steady.

"Are you well, Marina?"

Marina nodded and wrapped the harp more tightly with the curtain. The last thing any of them needed was to become dizzy or disoriented in the middle of a fight. Fahad kept a close eye on her while also keeping a mistrustful eye on Kaia as Marina left the room.

Fahad knew Marina believed the girl to be her sister but the way they communicated through visions before now made him wary. He watched as the purple-haired girl contemplated the sword before her like a snake about to strike and wondered at her behavior. She finally grabbed a piece of brocaded cloth from under some priceless treasure that went crashing to the floor and used it to grab the sword's hilt.

Fahad was completely confused by her behavior. She was wincing and bracing herself like she was preparing for the sword to strike her on its own. The girl's eyes were squeezed tightly shut and he wanted to scoff at how differently she behaved compared to Marina. There was none of the princess's bravery in this girl who was supposedly related.

Kaia was pretty sure the guy Marina brought was judging her hard for acting like a coward with the sword. But, much like period pain, she refused to accept judgment from someone who never experienced the same situation. When she was sure no vision was waiting to hit her between the eyes, she straightened up and went to take the sword out of the case.

She grunted in surprise when the darn thing barely shifted. Using the cloth and both hands, she tried again. It moved on the hooks displaying it but she couldn't lift and pull at the same time. With a low curse, she tried a third time. She only succeeded in somehow putting her boot through the glass at the bottom of the cabinet door.

Marina poked her head back through the door. "Kaia, we must make haste. The Krax'mran will not be able to hold their defenses for much longer."

The man beside her sighed and gently pushed her out of the way. She was about to tell him off when she decided not to mess with him. Especially when he grabbed the hilt and lifted the sword as easily as she might pick up a book. He was being a jerk but she was impressed despite herself.

"Thanks," she said to his back as he followed the princess out of the room.

Kaia rejoined the rest, which seemed to be the signal to leave. Rafe and Fahad took the lead. Marina did not want anything to happen to the harp, so she relinquished her quarterstaff to Rafe. She offered it to Jack first but he refused saying, "No, that will only mess up my form."

"But the jewelry will not?" she asked incredulously.

"Jewelry can only ever enhance my performance," he replied, giving her a rakish wink.

Marina was about to follow Rafe out of the room when Kaia stopped her. "Listen, I'm going to do one last thing. Go on ahead, I'll catch up with you."

"No," Marina protested, "I will not leave you now that we are together. Especially with nothing to protect you."

"No offense, Marina, but what kind of help would you be? It's not like you can bash people over the head with the harp there. It would kind of defeat the purpose of this whole mission."

"Perhaps you should take it then."

Marina put the harp in Kaia's hands before she could protest. Her whole body tensed for another hit of visions. Marina gave her a curious look while she retrieved her quarterstaff from Rafe. "You can carry the harp and I will watch your back."

"I'll be right behind you," Kaia protested as she readjusted the harp. She didn't want Marina to see the vindictive side of her plan.

"Kaia, be reasonable." Marina was worried. She did not know Kaia's capabilities. But, worse, she was still unsure of Kaia's loyalties. There was a possibility Kaia was sending them away to rejoin their father.

Jack stepped in to stop the disagreement. "Don't worry, milady. I'll look after her. We'll be by your side again in a flash."

Marina gave Jack a long look, not sure if she could trust the greedy rogue. He matched her stare, and she thought she saw a flicker of something deeper than his attitude portrayed.

"Fine," she acceded, "but if you are not out of this room in three minutes, I will be coming back for you. We will meet you at the door leading to the stables." Once again, Marina chose to trust Kaia despite all evidence she should be wary.

Kaia nodded and watched her sister go racing after Rafe and Fahad. As soon as Marina cleared the door, Kaia turned to one of the sconces in the room. The torch didn't want to leave the iron ring, but Jack helped her wiggle it free.

"Ah, planning to burn the place down, eh?" Jack smiled in approval.

"I plan to hit Nightshade where it hurts, and nothing will hurt him more than losing his precious treasure."

Kaia ran back to the treasure room and touched the flame to as many of the tapestries as possible. It was disheartening to be responsible for destroying all that beauty, but Kaia meant what she said. There was also the matter of covering up her theft. Perhaps if Nightshade didn't know what she took, he wouldn't know she was on to him.

Kaia ran from the room, prepared to do the same damage to Nightshade's bedroom. She grinned wildly to see Jack already beat her to it. They reached the lab door at the same time and gave each other a conspiratorial grin.

Neither expected the door to fly open at that moment. Kaia dropped the torch from suddenly numb fingers as she stared into Robin's cold eyes. Jack pulled her back and brandished his own torch in Robin's face. Robin backed away slightly from the heat but did not appear otherwise fazed by the display.

Jack forced Kaia backward as the rug at their feet caught fire from her torch. Kaia could see the flames quickly eat at the fabric from the corner of her eye. She couldn't look away from Robin, more afraid of what he would do than the fire.

"The master will be most displeased by this," Robin declared, "He will be forced to punish you, milady. I am afraid there is no escape from a painful death at your father's hands."

"Bite me," Kaia snapped. Jack gave her a startled glance before turning back to Robin. "Nightshade can go to hell, and I hope you burn with him you jackass," she finished.

Robin didn't answer, only watched them as they slowly backed away. Jack kept his torch up, despite the fact Robin couldn't possibly get past the wall of flame building up between them. Kaia clutched the wooden harp to her chest, afraid of what the heat might do to it.

"Let's go, Jack," Kaia pleaded, clutching his arm. Jack nodded without looking at her and threw his torch at Robin's head to distract him as they ran from the burning room. Kaia's last glimpse of Robin was of him catching the torch in midair and watching them with no expression.

They sprinted down the hall, Kaia in the lead. She made Jack stop once to retrieve the bag the wardrobe provided. "Thank you," she murmured, patting it like a dog. She hoped the fire would stop before it reached her inanimate friend, but she had neither the time nor the ability to do anything.

Jack grabbed her free hand and they were off and running again. They turned corners quickly, not having the time to look for danger. If not for Jack pulling her back in time, she would have run headlong into a man running toward them.

The servant regarded them without expression for a moment before launching into an attack. Kaia ducked to avoid his first blow and fell to the floor on her back. Jack quickly prepared to defend them both. As she sat up, she saw Jack's demeanor completely change. His pleasant expression disappeared behind a deadly serious mask of concentration.

He was all fluid grace. Kaia watched in fascination as he did a lethal dance. The jewelry flashed and danced along with him, making his movements look like elegant fireworks. The servant matched every one of Jack's moves, and none of the blows Jack landed had any effect on the homunculus at all. Jack moved quickly enough that the servant could not land a single blow of his own, but Kaia could see he was tiring. She also knew Nightshade's creatures couldn't be defeated so easily.

Standing, Kaia placed the harp against the wall and tried to call up the power she knew was somewhere within her. Her encounter with Cossette proved Kaia had the ability to destroy these monsters. Yet, the thought of Cossette's melted flesh distracted her every time she thought she called that power forth.

Jack's cry of pain broke Kaia's concentration, and she looked up in time to see him move his head just in time to miss the servant's fist from going through his head. Instead, the creature's fist sunk into the stone wall beside Jack's head. Kaia saw Jack gaping at the creature hovering over him, and watched helplessly as it pulled back its other fist to try again.

Marina's battle cry shocked Kaia almost as much as the homunculus. Marina struck the homunculus's arm and Kaia could hear the bone snap. Despite his arm now hanging at an unnatural angle, the creature reached for Marina while also trying to extract his other fist from the wall.

Jack slid to the floor and rolled beneath the servant's arm to come up on the opposite side from Marina. Marina, seeing Jack was clear, swung her staff vertically to come down hard on the homunculus's head. Her blow caved in a section of his skull, but he kept moving. Kaia saw an ornate sword on the wall beside her and made a snap decision.

Pulling the sword from the wall took all her strength. Finally, she had the heavy thing in both hands.

"Marina, move!" she cried as she swung the blade as hard as she could at the servant's neck. He turned just in time to see the blade coming at him before it cut threw him like a hot knife through butter. The distant thought that these homunculi apparently didn't have any muscle or sinew passed through Kaia's mind as his head rolled away and his body fell limply to the floor. Kaia felt a wave of nausea overwhelm her.

"I think I'm gonna hurl," she moaned as she let the sword drop from her limp fingers and collapsed against the wall.

32

Nightshade watched from the ramparts as the Krax'mran hit his castle with wave after wave of fiery torpedoes. He laughed inwardly at their pathetic attempts to set his castle afire. Fire was his element, and he could put out the flames with only a wave of his hand. The first wave surprised him with how much of his power it took to make that wave look effortless, but he would never admit so to anyone else.

The Krax'mran were struggling against his forces, and Nightshade grinned to see some of the warriors fall beneath the weapons he gave his minions. They were enchanted with different spells. Some would poison whomever the blade cut, others would heat to extreme levels, cutting through tissue, bone, and armor like paper.

Nightshade was slightly less pleased when he noticed the Krax'mran discovered the one weakness of his homunculi and began to aim for their necks to sever heads from bodies. The spell that powered his creations could only work if the head stayed intact. It was a simple thing to reattach the heads and reenact the spell, but that took time the sorcerer would not be given to do so during the battle.

He then noticed that some of his troops were pulling back to the portcullis, and some of the flames around him were coming from behind him.

"What is the meaning of this," he demanded.

"My lord," one of his servants bowed and Nightshade motioned for him to speak. "All the prisoners in the eastern cells have escaped. Our troops have been divided between the Krax'mra and recapturing the escapees."

"Get them back in their cells," Nightshade roared. Kaia was in that bloc, and he knew it was no coincidence. He cursed her for ruining his plans. "And get more servants to the battle. The Krax'mran are cutting through them faster than before, and they show no sign of pulling back."

Minutes later, he felt a tremor run through him as the wards he placed on his rooms announced something was terribly wrong. With a snap he was in his receiving room, surrounded by flames. Roaring in rage, Nightshade quelled the blazing fire. He was shocked to see Robin's blackened and slightly melted features staring at him from the lab. He was holding a heavy cloth that looked as though it was once a beautiful tapestry. The ends were black and smoking where the homunculus tried to beat back the flames from his master's laboratory.

"Who has done this?" Nightshade hissed, seeing some flames still licking through his bedroom door that he choked out with a squeeze of his fist.

"It was your daughter, my lord," Robin revealed with a bow.

"That little bitch will pay," the sorcerer growled as he looked at the ruins of his treasures.

"This is as I warned her, my lord. She and her accomplices went to the right, I assume to escape."

"We will see about that," Nightshade said, smoothing his black jacket and removing the ash where his hands passed. He closed his eyes for a moment and felt throughout his castle to find the intruders. Some were waiting by the doors leading to the stables, and he sent some of his homunculi to that location to attack. When he finally found Kaia and her accomplices, he moved himself to her location to find one of his homunculi on the floor. The eyes of its severed head looked as lifeless as always but without the admiration for him in its gaze he spelled into all his creations.

Kaia was crouched against the wall, another girl trying to make her stand again, and a man in front of them, looking for danger. He did not expect Nightshade however and he froze at the sight of the sorcerer.

"I see you have been at my treasure, Captain Reynolds," Marius said with a sneer.

"Well, you seemed to have enough to spare. I didn't think you'd miss a few baubles," Jack replied, his normal bantering tone strained by fear.

"And you seem to have fingers to spare. When this is over, I will be happy to relieve you of some to pay for those 'baubles' as you call them."

Jack swallowed back whatever retort he was about to make when Kaia placed a hand on his shoulder.

"You're not going to touch him. You have no right to keep prisoners, and no right to keep me. We're leaving, and you can just deal with it."

Nightshade waved his hand at Jack and sent the Death Dancer slamming against the wall. He watched as the man slid down to rest beside the slightly battered harp. The anger that was always close to the surface burned forward and he knew his normally beautiful face was distorted and twisted with anger.

Kaia and Marina both pulled back at the evil look on Nightshade's face. Marina gripped her staff so tightly that her whole hand turned white.

"You little bitch," he hissed, "leaving my dungeon is bad enough, but stealing my artifact is unacceptable. My spell can work beautifully without you. I truly only need one twin to make the spell work, and now that I have your blood, finding your sister will be child's play."

With that, Nightshade flung Kaia against the wall with the same careless wave of his hand. Kaia screamed as she felt herself being propelled toward the hard surface, and barely had time to cover her head with her arms. She both heard and felt the sharp crack as her forearm snapped. Her shriek of pain seemed to wake Jack from the daze his own flight against the wall caused.

"Kaia," he gasped as he saw what Nightshade had done. Unlike the homunculus she beheaded, Kaia barely wanted to wiggle her fingers, the pain was so severe.

Marina screamed in rage as she brought her staff swinging toward Nightshade's head. The sorcerer caught the swinging wood with his hand, not seeming at all affected by the hit.

"Foolish child," he sneered. Sending a spark deep into the staff, he set the weapon on fire. Marina was forced to drop her grip. Nightshade merely readjusted his own grip and swung the weapon in a few experimental sweeps. Marina backed away, as much from the fierce look upon his face as the heat of the flames.

"Why is it," Nightshade wondered with quiet menace, "that every plan I make seems to come slightly undone whenever a woman is involved?"

"Because we're smarter than you, you jackass," Kaia growled through gritted teeth as she made to stand. Jack quickly made a binding for her arm from one of the pants from Kaia's bag and even used one of his stolen necklaces to create a stunning makeshift sling.

Both Marina and Nightshade looked surprised to see her standing, and Kaia took that advantage to throw whatever she had at Nightshade. She felt that familiar knot in her chest that preceded melting Cossette, and she knew she had to use it now to protect them all.

She stood in front of Marina and tried to direct the knot toward the sorcerer threatening them. Aiming her uninjured arm at him like she was in a Stranger Things episode, she willed her power to leave through her right hand. Yet even she wasn't expecting the jet of steam that poured forth from her palm in a direct line toward Nightshade. The wetness of the steam extinguished the flames on the quarterstaff, leaving it black and smoking.

Nightshade didn't even put up an arm to protect himself from the scalding cloud directed at him. He merely closed his eyes and received the heat and moisture like a refreshing bath. Shaking the wet strands of hair from his eyes, Nightshade laughed. Kaia felt her heart freeze at the cold sound, and she wondered how they would possibly get out of this situation.

Nightshade walked right up to Kaia before she could move to escape, and lifted her by the throat with one arm. Kaia struggled against his iron grip, trying to pry his hand open with her own.

"You may have delayed my plans, but this little rebellion is only that. A delay. I will find your sister, and she will help me whether she wishes to or not."

Kaia gasped for air that would not come through the grip

Nightshade had on her. As darkness edged her vision, she felt Marina behind her.

"Not bloody likely," Marina rasped.

Marina felt helpless for a moment watching Kaia dangle from their father's grip. She no longer had a weapon and Jack was too woozy to do more than lean on the sword Kaia used to protect them. But she knew there was power within her as well as Kaia, and she only needed to concentrate to find a way to stop Nightshade.

Closing her eyes, she focused on the magician and searched inside him as she did with the boys when they were poisoned. She quickly found the blood in his veins and tracked the rushing liquid to its source. Nightshade's heartbeat was slower than expected given the anger she saw on his face and the effort of lifting Kaia with one arm. It was difficult to concentrate with the sound of Kaia's struggles, but Marina tried to shut the sounds out. Focusing on his heart, Marina willed the blood to stop flowing in and out.

For a moment, nothing happened. Then, Marina heard the distinct thud of Kaia hitting the floor followed quickly by the wonderful sound of Kaia gasping for air with greedy, starving lungs.

Marina opened her eyes to see Nightshade clutching at his chest, his eyes open wide in surprise. He fell to one knee and Marina concentrated harder on keeping his heart from moving. Without the blood moving in and out, the muscles of his heart quivered, but could not perform a full pump with the pressure on the openings. She was concentrating on his heart so much she barely recognized the fact Nightshade was lifting his arm.

Though she did not get thrown against the wall like Jack, the push she felt from Nightshade's power was enough to break her concentration. She tried to get the feeling back, but she felt completely drained. There was barely enough energy within her to keep her upright.

"Kaia, get up," Marina commanded, pulling at Kaia's right shoulder.

Kaia raised herself from her knees and stood on shaky legs. Her throat burned from the pressure of Nightshade's fingers. Seeing whatever Marina did was wearing off, Kaia began to back away toward Jack.

"Jack, can you run?" Marina asked. She spared a quick look to see

Jack standing with one hand braced against the wall, the other holding onto the harp.

"I think so," he answered with a slight slur, "the question is, can he?" Marina turned to see Nightshade standing once again and uttered a word that would have greatly angered the queen.

Jack clutched the harp with both hands and absently began to strum the strings. It was a bad habit of his to play whatever instrument was at hand, no matter the circumstances. He was raised in Dura, and while his particular talents leaned toward athleticism, every Duran knew how to play at least three instruments. With the first strum of his fingers, Jack knew there was something different about this harp.

First of all, he generally played the harp horribly. But the sound coming from the instrument was nothing short of gorgeous. Then there was the matter of all three of the people in front of him instantly relaxing and standing motionless.

Jack stopped and watched as all three people shook their heads as if shaking away a long night of sleep. While Jack wouldn't have minded this with the girls, having Nightshade aware and able to throw people against walls was not Jack's idea of fun. Jack moved his fingers, not caring what tune he was picking out. All three began to slightly sway back and forth to the rhythm of the harp and Jack was struck by an idea.

"Ladies fair, O ladies light,
Move away, to thine right,"
He was thrilled when Marina and Kaia moved as he sang.
"From that man you must turn away,
and run to safety from this fray,"

Jack barely sang the last phrase before the girls sprinted away. He hoped they were headed in the same direction Rafe and the other man went. He waited until they turned the corner before he focused on the sorcerer. Keeping his fingers moving, he tried to decide how to deal with the evil man. Seeing the sword lying at his feet, Jack decided to end the threat Nightshade posed once and for all.

"Take this sword lying on the floor,
and end your reign forever more.
Hold the blade to thy evil heart;

Pull it forward, and from this life part."

Jack held his breath as Nightshade followed the commands of his first three lines. But at the last, the sorcerer stopped and looked at the sword in his hands with equal parts confusion and surprise. He dropped the weapon, moving slowly with the effects of the harp still upon him. Jack's breath caught in his throat as he plied the strings at a faster pace, trying to put Nightshade back under the harp's spell.

The force of the music hit Nightshade like a physical blow, causing him to hit his head against the wall. Jack smirked at the sight of Nightshade suffering the same action he threw at Jack only moments before.

The magic threw Nightshade far enough away Jack couldn't readily tell if he was still breathing. He was bending to pick up the sword and make sure the job was done when three of Nightshade's unnatural servants appeared from one side of the hall. While he was still a little woozy from his own abrupt meeting with the wall, he was more than able to take three of these creatures now that Kaia showed him how to manage them. However, he was stopped short when he heard Kaia scream his name in pain and fear.

"We shall dance another day, my friends," Jack promised as he brushed his hand hard against the strings, throwing a wall of sound at the servants that threw them even harder than it did Nightshade. Leaving the sword where it lay, Jack sprinted to where he last saw the girls.

Kaia had no idea how she and Marina ended up at the back door with Rafe and Fahad but she was glad they escaped Nightshade without further harm. But they weren't out of the woods yet. Fahad and Rafe were on the losing side of a fight with six homunculi. While Marina was quickly able to join the fight, pulling a curtain down and using the iron rod as a weapon, Kaia was forced to stay behind. With her arm, she'd be all hindrance and no help.

"Jack," she screamed as one of the homunculi fell into her after a particularly hard hit from Fahad. They needed reinforcements, fast. Rafe was imprisoned so long that Kaia knew his werewolf strength wasn't serving him as it should.

"Take off their heads," Kaia shouted as Fahad swung the rusted sword she made him take.

She thought he was going to ignore her, but saw he was actually planning his move to come up under one of the homunculi's guard and part his head from his shoulders. Fahad turned and swept another head from the homunculus fighting Marina.

By the time Jack arrived moments later, there was only one homunculus left. Rafe and Marina harried the servant to keep her from keeping her guard up against Fahad's deadly blade. It was over in seconds, and Kaia tried not to feel completely useless. She knew her arm was the biggest deterrent from fighting but she was really feeling her lack of any fighting ability.

"Now that we've all had our fun, I believe it's time to leave this party," Jack said, keeping an eye on the hallway he exited.

Fahad grimaced at the choice of words but followed Jack's meaning. He opened the door leading out slightly and surveyed the grounds. He frowned harder when he saw Curtis and Gerard near the stables, fighting more of Nightshade's servants.

"They're in trouble," he told Marina. She pushed past him to look out and unwittingly mimicked his grave expression.

"Then we should go help them." Marina turned to the others and explained that her friends needed their help.

"Perfect," Jack said with a fierce grin, "that little scrap in the hall made me realize just how much fun I've been missing these last two years. Not to mention I didn't get to finish as I wanted."

Marina could not help returning that grin. Her experience with Nightshade and her own powers left her spoiling for more of a fight as well. Fahad grunted in annoyance and scowled at Jack when the other man winked at him.

"Yeah, I'm sorry, but there's no way I'll be helpful in a fight," Kaia stated, "Plus, someone needs to take care of the harp during all this."

Marina lost her smile and realized Kaia was right. She did not know her sister well, but it was obvious the girl had more fight in her attitude than her physicality. Not to mention Kaia's face was taut with pain and exhaustion. This realization sparked another.

"Then someone needs to go with you. If any of Nightshade's servants pursue you, you will need someone to defend you. It will do us no good to stage this rescue just to have you recaptured so near the end."

"I'll go," Rafe volunteered. "I've been locked up too long to do any good in another fight. At least if I'm with Kaia we stand a chance of getting out of here without fighting. If not, I can keep Nightshade's servants busy with me so I won't have to worry about hurting her or any of you."

Marina didn't seem reassured by this, but Kaia caught a glimpse of the fighting outside and made the decision for her. "Sounds like a plan, now get out there. Your friends are getting their butts handed to them, and they don't have time for us to argue about this."

Kaia carefully took the harp from Jack. Gently placing a foot on her sister's rear, she pushed her toward the fight. "Now go. I'll be fine."

Marina cursed under her breath at having to be separated again. The logic behind Kaia's words did not soothe her worried mind, but she knew there was no time. She gripped her makeshift quarterstaff tighter and led Fahad and Jack outside to aid their friends.

33

Gerard was no stranger to fighting but even he was getting worn out by these undying creatures. His wolf-enhanced strength helped him pull limbs from bodies, land vicious punches, and even extend his stamina. Yet the fiends kept coming.

Curtis surprised him with how well he was able to keep up in the battle. He knew the prince was a good fighter but it wasn't until now he realized the boy must be a Death Dancer. His movements were lissome but fatal.

Gerard stumbled under a blow from behind and felt a moment's fear his long life might finally come to an end as he saw a sword coming toward him. That blade was stopped by another, mere inches from his face. He quickly moved out of the way to find Fahad at the end of the sword that saved him.

"About time you got here," he growled.

Fahad flashed him a grim smile and proceeded to confront his opponent. Gerard turned to face another and saw Marina and another man join the fight. It was now five against fifteen.

Gerard liked those odds. In his periphery, he saw Fahad behead his foe. The man didn't get up again, and Gerard decided to learn from Fahad's example.

Within minutes, they defeated Nightshade's servants. Those who weren't missing their heads were incapacitated enough they no longer posed a threat. All five combatants looked around for more challengers. When they found none, they began to run for the eastern gate by unspoken accord.

"Jack, what are you doing here?" Curtis asked incredulously when he caught sight of the bejeweled former prisoner.

"The same could be asked of you, Prince," Jack replied coldly, refusing to look anywhere but ahead. "I've been gone two years, didn't any of you try to find me?"

"What?" Curtis exclaimed, stopping suddenly. Jack stopped as well, confusion, hurt, and anger flashing in his eyes.

Marina looked back and saw them staring at each other. "There's no time for this," she screamed at them.

They both looked at her in surprise and began sprinting toward the gate again. Curtis gave Jack a side-long glance. Something was terribly wrong, and he needed to talk to Jack alone to find out what was happening.

Gerard was first through the gate. He saw a party of Krax'mran heading toward them with a human in the lead.

"We should go straight out to the desert and try to make those hills again," Gerard said.

The others nodded their agreement. They began to run in the direction he pointed and he let loose a shrill whistle to get the Krax'mran's attention.

He waited until he saw them change directions slightly to intersect with their course before he followed the others. It was surprising to see the strange man with them didn't seem to have much trouble keeping up with the Krax'mran. He was still trailing behind but not as much as most humans would.

The group reached the hill a little after the first Krax'mran and Marina smiled when she recognized Abrafo and Waitimu. Her smile dimmed a little when she realized Kaia was not with them.

"Where is she?" Marina demanded frantically.

"Calm yourself," Abrafo soothed. "She is with Saburi. Many of Nightshade's prisoners were recaptured but those that made it out were taken by our men. Kaia stayed with them to keep the humans calm. Saburi is taking them to his village, but she sent us along with the wolf to make sure you were all safe."

Marina closed her eyes in relief, only to snap them open again when she heard an angry growl from behind the Krax'mran. Kaia never mentioned the other man's name and Marina did not take the time to ask. But Gerard knew him immediately.

"Rafe?" He was stunned to find his Beta so far from the pack. His orders to stay behind were explicit.

"You," Rafe's voice was low, and Gerard knew the other man's ears would have been pinned back in anger if he were in wolf form. He could tell Rafe was fighting the change, and he wondered at the Beta's lack of discipline. Even this close to moonrise, Rafe usually had better control of his wolf. Gerard couldn't remember a time he ever saw Rafe so angry.

"You left me to rot for twenty years, and I find you here to help a human escape?" Rafe's hands and feet began to change. His muscles began to bulge and twist.

"Hey, calm down, friend," Jack cried, "That shirt was a loan."

"I saw you only a few days ago," Gerard protested, "you will control yourself, so we can discuss this."

"No," Rafe slurred around suddenly sharp teeth, "I chall—"

"Silence," Gerard commanded harshly. Rafe fought against his Alpha's command, but the bond was stronger than he remembered.

"You are too weak to challenge me," Gerard continued, "and we must find out what Nightshade has done. You will help me with that. For now, we must get away from this castle before Nightshade decides to give chase."

"Don't worry about that," Jack interjected, "I see you Krax'mran have been busy up front, but Kaia and I did some damage to the interior as well." He indicated the plume of smoke coming from the rear of the castle. "I believe Nightshade will be busy for a bit longer yet. However, I wouldn't say no to getting out of here and finding a proper meal."

Gerard's words and use of his powers as Alpha calmed Rafe for the moment. The Krax'mran did not waste time deciding who would be forced to carry the humans, and each plucked a person from the sand before anyone had time to protest. Even the wolves were given no choice in the matter.

"You bipeds are most amusing," Abrafo said to Marina. She merely smiled thinly and settled in for the journey.

Gerard and Rafe barely took the time to get water in Saburi's village before they were off and running for the border. They changed during the trip, much to the discomfort of the Krax'mran carrying them. Marina heard them both warning the Krax'mran but the warriors failed to listen until the men began to accidentally claw their backs.

Marina waved goodbye, receiving an answering yip from Gerard. They soon disappeared into the darkness, and Marina rushed to find her sister. One of Saburi's men pointed her in the direction of the tribe's council lodge.

It looked similar to the lodge in Abrafo's village. She found Kaia awkwardly helping the women prepare beds for Nightshade's former prisoners. There were five men and three women, and all appeared to be human. The Krax'mran healers tried to get Kaia to stop to tend to her arm but she refused to stop. That was until Marina arrived.

"Kaia," Marina cried, relieved to see her sister safe. She believed Abrafo but it still felt good to see the truth for herself. Kaia handed some blankets to one of the former captives and walked over to Marina.

They embraced tightly but carefully, neither wanting to let go. Someone cleared his throat beside them, finally forcing them to release one another. Curtis, Fahad, and Jack stood nearby watching the sisters. Curtis stepped forward and bowed to Kaia.

"It is good to finally meet the woman my sister was searching for."

Kaia took a step back in surprise. "Wait," she stammered, "I have a brother now, too?"

"No," the siblings denied together. Marina raised an eyebrow at Curtis' vehement tone. It was then she noticed a look in his eyes she had seen before. Glaring at him, she continued. "No, Curtis and I are not related by blood. The king and queen of Jamaria raised me as their own. I have two other brothers, Antonio and Benedict."

"Ah, well, okay," Kaia muttered. She wondered to herself if the other two brothers were as handsome as Curtis. There was no problem imagining this guy as a prince. He looked like he was engineered by Disney.

"I do not believe you were properly introduced to Fahad," Marina indicated the man standing between Jack and Curtis.

"Hi, Fahad," Kaia said with a little wave, "I've finally figured out where I've seen you before."

"We have never met," Fahad replied, his words stilted.

"No, but I have seen you before. You used to be made of gold. Stood around in a garden? Chopped a guy's hand off when you turned human? Any of this sound familiar?"

"These all sound like things the princess could have told you," he answered.

"I never mentioned anything about you to Kaia," Marina admitted. Fahad looked slightly hurt by that confession, and Marina rushed to explain. "I am sorry, but we were busy finding out about each other, and trying to figure out how to get Kaia away from our father."

Fahad jerked his head in a nod, and Marina knew he wanted to drop the conversation. She turned back to Kaia and took her hand. "We need to talk," she said, "but let us go somewhere more private."

Kaia looked around and saw their little group was indeed garnering attention, both from the Krax'mran and the humans.

"Yeah, no prob," she agreed, allowing Marina to lead them from the lodge. Then, she remembered something and pulled her hand away. "Hold on for a sec, I want to grab the harp."

Marina watched her run to the far corner of the room and pick up the instrument. Kaia looked at Fahad for a few seconds as she weighed her options. She finally decided it was best to drag him along so he could bring the sword. Of course, as soon as she asked him to join, Curtis and Jack felt like they had to follow as well.

"Why do you need those?" Marina asked as she led the way out of the lodge.

"I'll explain in a sec."

Marina nodded and led the way to the edge of the village. Most of the Krax'mran were in their webs, making supper. She noticed two of the women in the lodge preparing food as well and held a hand to her suddenly protesting belly. Ignoring it for now, she led the group to a clearing at the edge of the village.

"We are away from prying eyes and ears. What do you need to tell me?" Fahad demanded of Kaia.

He was still looking at her with suspicion. In fact, he was even standing between her and Marina as if Marina wasn't out there a few hours before kicking some major butt. And that wasn't even counting Kaia's broken arm.

"Rude," she muttered under her breath before launching into her theory. "I think the sword Fahad is holding and this harp are the artifacts Marius is looking for. There's definitely something weird about them."

Fahad pulled the sword from the scabbard he tied haphazardly around his waist. They all analyzed the worn steel of the blade and jewels on the cross-guard and pommel.

"This is a Kentorian design," Fahad said finally, "but it is an ancient one."

Jack pulled the hilt nearer to him and examined the jewels a little closer.

"You can't have the sparkly rocks," Kaia chided. Jack winked at her before turning back to the jewels.

"That is a Kentorian ruby if I'm not much mistaken. And believe me, when it comes to treasure, I'm never mistaken." Jack pointed to the largest jewel set into the pommel. "Let me see the harp."

Kaia handed him the delicate instrument, careful not to jar the strings. Jack turned the harp in his hands, studying the carvings as well as the jewels. He held it out for Curtis to inspect as well. When Curtis was finished, Jack asked, "Duran?"

Curtis nodded and explained to the others. "This is a Duran design, though it's a Celtic version that hasn't been used in a few centuries. The gem at the top of the column is a Duran garnet." He turned the harp so the others could see the glittering jewel.

"So these are artifacts from two of the kingdoms," Fahad said, more of a statement than a question. "They each have gems from their prospective countries, and are both ancient designs."

"That about sums it up," Jack confirmed.

"What makes these artifacts so important to Nightshade?" Fahad inquired, looking at Kaia and Marina.

"He is planning to use them in a ritual of some kind," Marina responded absently. She was fixated on the jewels. Something about them made her think of the amulet.

Marina reached for the purse tucked into her waist. The amulet felt warm in her hands, and she paused, afraid it would send her into another vision. When it did not, she began to scrutinize the jewels set at intervals along the edge.

"That's it!" she cried. The others looked at her expectantly, so she hurried to explain. "The eight gems set around the opal are the eight jewels of the Kingdoms. Here are the garnet and ruby on opposite sides," she pointed to the stones before naming the others one by one. "This is Jamarian yellow topaz, Ya'mäk jade, Sarosian onyx, Brookland amber, a Krax'mran emerald, and the pearl for Banor's Bile. If the ruby and garnet in this amulet correspond with the two artifacts we have, then that must mean the other six correspond to the other gems."

"Wait, I'm lost," Kaia admitted, "are you saying there is an artifact for each of the kingdoms?"

"Exactly," Marina confirmed, excitement burning in her eyes, "That means we have a general idea of where to find the other six artifacts."

"Then what are we waiting for?" Kaia asked, catching Marina's enthusiasm. "Looks like we're going on a treasure hunt."

34

The salty air and the press of the crowds were making it difficult to discern between scents. Merry inhaled deeply but only got a sneeze out of the action. She pulled her hood up, trying to conceal her face. The guards were suspicious of her because she had been loitering around the palace for the last five days.

There was no guarantee the scent that brought her this far was Kaia's. Something was interfering with her daughter's scent, but the trail had an edge to it that was distinctly Kaia.

Merry moved away from the wall and blended in with the crowd jostling her along the marketplace. She forgot how pungent Tern could be on market day. The capital was the largest city in Jamaria and that was never driven home more clearly than on a day like this.

As she worked her way through the mass of humans, fae, and others, she caught a stronger whiff of Kaia. She tried not to let the excitement overwhelm her, and attempted to keep her pace steady. It would not do to alert the guards. The trail led her further and further out of the city and Merry began to worry her nose was leading her astray. She cursed Lisa for the millionth time for doing this to her and Kaia. The cursing also pertained to whoever blocked up the only secret entrance to the palace grounds she knew.

A twig snapped, and Merry realized she was at the edge of the Rejos Forest. A shiver of remembered pain and sorrow traveled up and down her spine. She wondered if he was still out there, but pushed that thought aside to focus on the path her nose was leading her on.

The scent forked at one point, with a weaker trail leading deeper into the forest, and a stronger one leading toward the castle. Merry debated with herself for a moment before deciding to follow the stronger trail. This led her to another wall, but without any guards at the moment. She could hear them further along and paused to hear if they were getting closer or not.

When their voices did not move, she decided to risk going out into the open. Someone cut a swath around the wall to leave ten feet of open ground, but the precaution was not worth much when no one seemed to guard it. Merry darted across the short distance, reveling in her increased strength. She had not felt this good since the last time she was in the Kingdoms.

The wall seemed unbroken by a hidden door, but Merry trusted her nose. Using her enhanced vision, she was able to find a seam in the wall. It took her a few minutes to find the release. She was just about to press it when she heard the guards moving toward her. Praying the stones would not grind together too much, she pressed the stone that activated the levers inside the hidden passage and stepped through.

Shutting the door gently, she immediately moved in the direction her nose led her. She was confused by how strong the scent was, and wondered if Kaia had been in the Kingdoms much longer than Merry.

"It would be just like Lisa to delay my arrival by a couple of months," Merry muttered angrily.

The trail branched off several times, and Merry decided to stay with her first instinct and follow the strongest trace. Eventually, she was led up and found herself in a bedroom. Merry moved through the room carefully. There was something about the scent that was beginning to make her uneasy. The longer she stood in that room, the less it smelled of Kaia. The nuances Merry knew so well were radically different, and only that underlying edge remained the same.

Someone rattled the door handle, and Merry moved behind the tapestry that hid the secret passage. She peeked out just enough to see a rotund gnome passing through the room, dusting everything and muttering tearfully to herself the entire time. The gnome gasped in terror when a flinty-eyed Merry stepped out into the room.

"Who are you?" the maid demanded shrilly, holding her feather duster like a sword, "and what are you doing in my mistress' room?"

"I am Merlyn DeGriffin, and I demand to know what you have done with my daughter."

www.ingramcontent.com/pod-product-compliance
Lightning Source LLC
LaVergne TN
LVHW010051170826
845678LV00012B/2112